Praise for *Six Days in Marapore*:

"To Marapore, in India, came Joe MacKendrick, an American, to solve the mystery of his dead brother's rejection of a married woman who had deeply loved him. . . . Paul Scott weaves a deeply absorbing story of individual, racial and national conflict in a tiny corner of India: Excellently, he portrays the ferment and confusion of the changing scene. . . . It is a time of transition when the hitherto governing English must give place to the native rulers of a free India. . . . The story moves with pace and color toward an ending which is never foreseen but which is exactly right."

New York Herald Tribune Book Review

"The atmosphere is thick with the feel of intense, dry heat, stealth and impending disaster. . . ." *Savannah Morning News*

"The most clearly observed figures are those Anglo-Indian types painted over life-size by Kipling, benevolently satirized by Mr. Forster, and caricatured by Orwell. . . . For Mr. Scott's purposes these people . . . are confronted with problems undreamed of by Kipling and only vaguely understood by Orwell. . . . Uncommonly well told and interesting."

Times Literary Supplement

Praise for Paul Scott:

"Paul Scott is a novelist who understands how to employ image and scene to convey reality . . . Climate and feeling thus compliment each other in *The Jewel in the Crown*, to delineate with dazzling brilliance the turbulence of India in 1942. . . . Scott sees with an artist's eye and a humanist's understanding."

New York Times Book Review

"Mr. Scott uses his remarkable techniques to portray a place and a time, a society and its social arrangements, that are now history." *New Yorker*

Novels by Paul Scott:

Johnnie Sahib
Six Days in Marapore
A Male Child
The Mark of the Warrior
The Love Pavilion
The Birds of Paradise
The Bender
The Corrida at San Feliu

The Raj Quartet:
The Jewel in the Crown
The Day of the Scorpion
The Towers of Silence
A Division of the Spoils

Staying On

Six Days in Marapore

PAUL SCOTT

Six Days in Marapore

THE UNIVERSITY OF CHICAGO PRESS

The University of Chicago Press, Chicago, 60637
Copyright 1953 by Paul Scott
All rights reserved.
First published in 1953
University of Chicago Press edition 2005

Printed in the United States of America
10 09 08 07 06 05   1 2 3 4 5
ISBN 0-226-74319-5 (paperback)

Library of Congress Cataloging-in-Publication Data

Scott, Paul, 1920–
     Six days in Marapore / Paul Scott.
          p.   cm.
     ISBN 0-226-74319-5 (pbk. : alk. paper)
     1. Women—India—Fiction.   2. Secrecy—Fiction.   3. India—
Fiction.   I. Title.
     PR6069.C596S59 2005
     823'.914—dc22

                                        2004030075

For
RENE & ALFRED
affectionately

The characters, the cantonment of Marapore, the village of Ooni and the princely state of Kalipur are all imaginary.

Part One

1

The rains had not yet reached Marapore and the dry heat was almost more than MacKendrick could bear. He lay on his back, staring up at the high rafters of the bedroom, and thought of Calcutta where the hotel floors were tiled and where the bathroom was more than a prison-cell with a zinc tub, more than a dim place haunted by grotesque spiders which raced across the duckboards from beneath the wooden doors.

In Calcutta he had sweated: here, the sweat dried as soon as it broke through the pores of his skin. A tumbler of water and a bottle of salt-tablets were within reach, and he turned his head so that he could see them and be reassured. Behind the tumbler, visually distorted by the stale water, was his wrist-watch, but he could not see the position of its hands. He guessed it was nearly three o'clock. The window, set high up in the wall so that it could only be opened and shut by cords, let in a shaft of sunlight directly on to the shabby leather couch, to which the manager had pointed with pride, for its presence put an extra three rupees a day on the bill. Room Three was the most expensive in Smith's Hotel, as the manager had been at pains to explain to MacKendrick when he arrived the night before. It had not occurred to Mac-Kendrick to ask for a cheaper room. Bombay and Calcutta had cured him of working out the cost of things in dollars.

The shouting which had disturbed his after-lunch sleep began all over again, this time right outside the door of his bedroom. The door opened a few inches only to be shut hastily: then someone knocked. MacKendrick groaned.

"Come!"

The door opened again. "Please excuse me, Mr. MacKendrick, but there is a matter of importance." The manager spoke scarcely above a whisper as though he had been oblivious to the row he and his staff had made, was now considerate of his guest's privacy, apologetic for disturbing him.

"What is it?"

"You were sleeping, Mr. MacKendrick?"

"Not for some time now, Mr. Desai."

"All this I find distressing. Please, may I come in?"

"Please do." Quickly schooled to the modesty of Indians he adjusted the towel which lay loosely over his loins and leaned up on one elbow. Desai shut the door with what MacKendrick could only call a conspiratorial air. Indeed, with the door closed, the manager glanced swiftly round the room as if to assure himself the two of them were alone. He put his head on one side and smiled.

"You will be forgiving me, Mr. MacKendrick, no doubt. But I must ask you if you would be so kind as to allow me to move you and your belongings into another room. Room Twelve you will find very comfortable, although it is lacking a couch unfortunately. Your bearer I have already sent for, so if . . ."

"No."

"But, Mr. MacKendrick . . ."

"I said no. No dice. I like Room Three."

Desai was gratified yet troubled. "Please, Mr. MacKendrick. All is most embarrassing for me as no doubt you will appreciate."

"Why should I move my room?"

"Mr. Smith *always* has Room Three."

"Who's Mr. Smith? The owner?"

"No, sir. Mr. Smith is the gentleman who is coming this evening. So said his telegram."

"Mr. Smith must be a very important person."

"Ah!" Desai lowered his eyelids and peeped at MacKendrick coyly. "You are understanding?"

"I'm sorry. I'm tired. I'm hot. I can't get any sleep. And I'm not moving into another room. The hotel's almost empty."

"But . . ."

"If Mr. Smith is such an important man you shouldn't have given me his room yesterday."

"But I did not know he would be coming."

"Okay. Tell him that."

"But this is not a thing . . ."

"Look. *I'm* the guest who's renting Room Three. If Mr. Smith doesn't like any of the other rooms he'll have to camp out on the verandah." MacKendrick lay back and closed his eyes. For a while there was silence. When Desai spoke again, diffidently, his voice gave warning of tears.

"I am in a very difficult position, you will understand."

"Sure."

"Mr. MacKendrick. Excuse me. But last night you could not say how long you would stay with us. Is it possible you can be telling me now so that in turn I can report the facts to Mr. Smith? If in a few days you propose . . ."

"I can't tell you, Mr. Desai. I know no more than I did last night."

When Desai had gone the shouting began again and Mac-Kendrick opened his eyes and thought: Why shouldn't I give up the room? He stared at the pale, distempered walls, at the mosquito net, bunched above his head. This was the room. Its bareness fascinated him. Its simplicity both puzzled and refreshed him. But beyond the door at the far end lay the dreadful bath-house. In India the emotions were always subject to shock. Behind beauty was ugliness. Even as the phrase came to him he knew it to be trite.

Here on his bed, alone, he could twist the knife in his wound. His discomfort was contained within these walls which were already familiar and had seemed, last night, to close round him and say: So far you have come. Stay now. Outside there is nothing for you. Not even disappointment. Not even regret. Nothing. Stay and be at peace.

Then, it had been night-time. This morning, after a breakfast eaten in solitude in the empty dining-room, he had ventured into the road outside, ventured to the fringe of the cantonment shops, gazed across the railway tracks at the town, and returned to the

13

hotel, passing on his way the lumbering ox-carts which the drivers guided through the sand-like dust by twisting the tails of the white, humped oxen harnessed on either side of the single shafts.

The heat had oppressed him for he had not accepted it. The old Indian, asleep on a charpoy in the shade of the peepul trees, the single files of women, dressed in unlovely, magenta coloured sarees, walking purposefully from nothing towards nothing, the naked children, the bitch on heat dragging its hind-quarters through the dust and followed dazedly by panting dogs; all these had accepted it, seemed content to be exhausted by it. But Mac-Kendrick could not accept it and dare not let it exhaust him. He had stood for a few moments before turning in at the driveway and the road had become deserted. The tinkling of the bells around the necks of the oxen had faded away; there had been utter silence. He had not known silence before, in India. Bombay and Calcutta never slept, and now, standing there outside the white-painted hotel, a bungalow hiding behind trees, he had become instinctively alert. A thousand eyes were watching him and a thousand voices whispering – Why are you here? What do you want?

He had returned to Room Three, and lunch had been served to him there on a tray. He clung to the room and let the room cling to him, and he knew that this was folly. The room gave him no clues. It was static. Confined in it he was static too, and he had not come to Marapore to lie on his back and stare at four walls like a prisoner. He had come for quite a different reason, and when he thought about that reason he was both appalled and excited by it.

He jerked himself upright and swung his legs to the floor, stood up, letting the towel fall so that he was naked, and thus, powerful, extrovert. For an instant he imagined himself poised, toes curled round the edge of a pool, then diving into the intimate world of water. He yelled for Bholu and outside someone echoed his call as he reached for his clothes and began to dress. Bholu came in.

"Look. Swimming. *Malum?*"

14

"I know swimming."

MacKendrick glanced at him, abruptly moved from momentary arrogance by the familiar sulkiness of the servant's speech. Bholu was small, at first glance shiftless like a man who is at home on the fringe of holiday crowds whose pockets his fingers lightly explore: but MacKendrick prided himself he saw purpose in the shape of the mouth and chin, the lights of passion in eyes which set him above men of his kind. He had hired Bholu in Bombay, selecting him from a dozen other itinerant bearers who had offered their services having heard the Sahib was American, and gullible.

"Where? Where can I swim?"

"There is club."

"Right. Get tonga. *Malum?*"

"Yes, Sahib."

Bholu went, using the back way through the bathroom, and as he walked through the dusty gravel to the front of the hotel he wondered whether he should make sure that there was, in fact, a swimming pool at the club. But there was no-one in sight whom he cared to ask. It was hot. If MacKendrick Sahib went to the club for nothing, it couldn't be helped. He disliked MacKendrick more than any man he had ever worked for.

He wandered down the driveway and, at the roadside, squatted down on his haunches, thinking of MacKendrick, and of how soon he could make his get-away. At the rate MacKendrick paid him he could go back to Lahore in a month. In Lahore was his family. There were arrangements to be made for them, and he cursed the American for making this sudden, unexpected trip to Marapore which had put pause to a promising connection in Calcutta.

He looked up. Now, it was June. In August the British were going and in Lahore the long knives would be out. Each day spent fruitlessly in Marapore was like a thrust of the knife into his own flesh. He hated Marapore. He had hated Calcutta too. Only his need of money, his family's need, kept him at MacKendrick's side. In Calcutta he had collected his few belongings together against the moment that would be ripe for absconding. But he had seen the stuffed wallet of the American, seen it crammed full under his own eyes as MacKendrick told him to make ready for this trip.

Suddenly a pistol cracked in the distance and following the crack Bholu heard the sharp cries of an excited crowd. A string of crows wheeled into the air and flew westward. For ten seconds the shouting continued, exploding finally into the fainter sound of hand-clapping. The end of a race. The college sports. Bholu remembered, and remembering, he realised he was supposed to be finding a tonga. He rose. Perhaps there would be no need to steal. The American might be induced to part with the money in other ways. He began walking towards the cantonment shops, thinking of the wallet.

Last night, as MacKendrick bathed, Bholu had had the wallet in his hands, counting the notes. MacKendrick's sudden call had startled him so much that he had nearly forgotten to replace the photograph of the girl that MacKendrick was always taking out, always staring at. To have forgotten to replace it this time would have been disastrous, for when he rejoined MacKendrick after making a pretence of removing the spiders from the bathroom, he had found the American sealing the photograph in an envelope. The envelope had been placed in his inner pocket, separately: as though, in Marapore, there were suddenly a reason for secrecy about it.

Bholu stood still and stared ahead. Was it, he wondered, because of the girl in the photograph that they had come at such short notice all the way from Calcutta? If that were so then it was more than likely that the girl had been the reason for MacKendrick Sahib's uncertain behaviour in the past, in Bombay, in Calcutta; the inexplicable departures, the unexpected returns, all of which had made life so difficult to bear. He had been a fool not to consider the problem of the girl in the photograph before.

He did not notice the tonga until it was level with him. He would have stepped into the road to hail the driver but he saw that an English army officer already travelled in it. Thoughtfully he began walking more quickly towards the station where there were

16

sure to be plenty of tongas to be had. MacKendrick could wait. For the first time for days Bholu was content to let time pass. Deep inside him, unformed as yet, a scheme quickened. He knew from long experience that it was the scheme conceived in the belly of a man, rather than in his brain, which came fruitfully into the world and, in the end, proved worth the pain of waiting.

2

Major Milner was drunk. During the past fifteen years it could truthfully be said that he was sober only on those occasions when his movements from one job to another, either as a civilian or as a soldier, involved him personally in the checking of stores and equipment; a duty he fulfilled aggressively, in determined possession of his faculties. Drunk, little escaped him; sober, nothing. Yet his career had been so far undistinguished. This surprised him: but whether failure led to his drunkenness or stemmed from it, no-one in India could recall and he himself had never thought to connect the two phenomena.

He sat sprawled in the cushioned seat of the tonga, staring over the tonga-wallah's shoulder at the raised tail of the horse and broke wind in sympathy. He was at home with horses, had mastered many in his time, was ignorant of their sensitivity, alive to their strength which he observed as a challenge to his own. He was forty-five. His soft spot was, perhaps, the pride he took in not having one.

He saw Bholu and beyond Bholu the gateway of Smith's Hotel. He spoke to the tonga-wallah. "*Idder.*" The tonga-wallah urgently slashed the ribs of the horse with his beribboned whip as though afraid the hotel would miraculously vanish before they came abreast of it. With bells jingling on the harness they bowled through the open gates and came to a halt opposite the porch. Milner, alighting, turned to the driver. "*Thairo,*" he said. "*Ham maidan ki taraf jana chahie, thori der ke bad.*"

As he went up the steps he glowed. His knowledge of Urdu was not exact, but it was a language he admired and enjoyed speaking. As a young man in 1932 he had learned the essential words and phrases and had been impressed over the years by the seemingly infinite variety of ways in which those words and phrases could be used. "Urdu's a man's language," he had said once, during the war, to a very young officer fresh from home. "For Christ's sake don't ponce it up with that bastard higher standard muck." He had doubled his fist expressively. "That's your bloody conjugation and" (raising his highly polished boot) "here's your bloody syntax." Yet Milner himself seldom threatened with either boot or fist. His voice and manner made sure of obedience, even of admiration. As a war-time instructor at an Officers' Training School he had been, comparatively, a success. The rooms in which he lectured had echoed to laughter only slightly sycophantic. Under him, field training had been tough, relentless; but the obscene curses of men who laboured for breath in the merciless sun were directed not at Milner so much as at the authority he stood for. The test completed, beer slaking their long thirsts, they were not unaware that he had helped them to the masculine quality of endurance.

When he came into the hotel he yelled for the manager, whom he knew by name, and as Desai came out from his glass-topped cage of an office, Milner noticed that a white man whom he did not know and whose arrival in Marapore he had not heard about was standing close by him; an extremely well-dressed, well-built, dark haired young man who held a rolled towel in his left hand. Milner nodded in MacKendrick's direction, half raised a hand to detain him, and turned to Desai.

"Look, Desai. There's a Miss Anderson coming tomorrow. She'll want a room. Single. Cheap. Clean. Arriving 1500 hours. Staying one week. Right?"

"Yes, Major Milner. Miss Anderson. Will she come alone from the station?"

"I'll bring her myself. Just have the room ready. And none of your extras for flowers and fal-lals."

"Room Number Nine it will be, Major Milner."

"Number Nine. Appropriate."

"Sir?"

"Nothing." Milner winked at MacKendrick and came towards him. "Name's Milner," he said.

"MacKendrick."

They shook hands. Himself exerting pressure MacKendrick was surprised to find Milner's hand limp, whereas he had expected otherwise. Milner jerked his head up, a trick of emphasis. "Been here long? Haven't seen you before."

"I got in yesterday."

"Staying?"

Desai hovered. MacKendrick hesitated before replying, "I don't know."

"Know anybody here?"

"I guess not."

"What you in? Journalism?"

MacKendrick licked his lips, but he managed to say fairly steadily, "I'm just on vacation."

"Vacation? Marapore? Odd place for a vacation. Still, your business. If you don't know anyone you'd better come up to the club tonight. I'll speak to the secretary."

"That's very nice of you."

"Anything I can do now?"

"I don't think so. My boy's just gone for a tonga."

"Tonga? Won't get a tonga this afternoon. All up at the *maidan*."

MacKendrick did not understand the word. "*Maidan?*"

"Playing fields. Sports day. Races. Bloody hot but I've got to make an appearance. We're putting in a tug-o'-war team. Where were you going?"

"My boy said I could swim at the club." He raised his towel as evidence.

"Right, I'll drive you round. Probably got the only free tonga in Marapore waiting outside if the bastard hasn't sneaked off."

They walked to the porch. Milner went on, "Don't like swimming myself, but it's Saturday so you're lucky because they change the water. Or should." He helped the American mount, and as MacKendrick put his foot on the plate another pistol cracked. "After your bathe," Milner said, "come round to the *maidan*. Soon see me. They put all the talent on the dais like a lot of pregnant monkeys. Up you get. I'll send the tonga back for you if you'd like to come. Everyone there. Meet 'em all. Cigarette?" As he thrust the gun-metal case under MacKendrick's nose he shifted in his seat and gave the driver directions.

"Thanks."

"Young Vidyasagar's worth watching. Bloody fine athlete. But then on the whole Indians are. Poor boxers though. Not enough stamina. No bulk. But Vidyasagar's high jump's in a class by itself. Goes straight for the rope, you think he's going to dive under it, then at the last moment he seems to soar up into the air with his heels glued together. Odd. Style though."

"How old is he?"

"Sixteen. Thereabouts. Go far. Laxminarayan College here. Riddled with politics of course but it's our fault. We lost the Indian Empire when we introduced Matriculation or whatever bloody thing it is they fail every year. We've taught 'em to read and write a la bloody Whitehall so's they can write us our marching orders. Evolution. Matriculation. Same thing."

"I see."

"I planted tea before I went into the army in '39. That and being a soldier are the only two occupations for an Englishman in India that leave him with a sense of proportion. You a soldier?"

Milner paused and MacKendrick thought: This is where the questions begin.

"No," he said, "I was during the war though."

"What outfit? That's the Yankee expression isn't it? What outfit? Sounds like a fancy dress ball. Still, the war was."

"I'm afraid I was on duty stateside. Never went abroad."

"Same here. Shoved from one bloody depot to another."

"You're a regular aren't you?"

"I am now." He broke off to shout at the driver, "*Ai! Club ki taraf mera hukm tha!* Where d'you bloody think you're bloody going? *Maidan abhi nai.* Christ!"

The whip cracked in response and the tonga gyrated upon its axis, straining to the right course, as if intoxicated by the smell of liquor on Milner's breath.

"I wish I could speak the language."

"Time. That's all you need."

"You've lived here long?"

"Fifteen years."

"You'll be going home soon, I suppose. August, isn't it?"

Milner stared at him. "Home? No, I'm staying in the army."

"But can you do that?"

"Why not? If the British don't want me the Indians do. They'll go on their knees for any of us that'll stay on."

"But aren't they dividing the army up though? What'd you be, India or Pakistan?"

"What odds? I get on with Hindus and Muslims alike. No communal problem in the army. Never has been. No matriculation. No politics. India, I expect though. I'm acting commandant of the M.T. N.C.O.s' school here. We've been Indianising for some time you know. Matter of fact I'm the only European officer left in the School. Suits me. Most of 'em were toffee-nosed."

Milner mopped his forehead. "Marapore suits my book. Only a matter of time before I'm appointed Commandant proper. Waiting for the official posting now. Lieutenant-Colonelcy. Not bad. Otherwise I can always go back to tea. Here's the club."

They had turned into a tree lined driveway and Milner stopped the tonga at a point where a narrower path led off, skirting a parched lawn. Water glimmered beyond.

"There's your pool. Nobody there, so don't drown. You'll find the boy though. I'll send the tonga back for you. Anyone asks why you're in the club tell 'em Major Milner brought you. They know me."

MacKendrick, getting down, said, "You've been very kind."

"*Acchcha. Maidan ki taraf* bloody *jeldi jao*." Milner raised a hand and stared until MacKendrick was out of sight. Pleasant boy. Weakish. But no side. No swank. Do well in the East. Swank and snobbery had done for the whites in India. He shut his eyes. Swank and snobbery. If you weren't out of the ·top bloody drawer you'd had it. Now it was a new era. The era of men with a bit of common sense. He opened his eyes again and the greenness and the sunlight and the heat embraced him with arms within whose circle he was infinitely content.

3

The doors of the row of bathing cubicles were open, but not with any particular air of welcome. The pool lay behind a screen of trellis-work, and the whole place was deserted. There was no sign of the 'boy' to whom Milner had referred.

MacKendrick entered the first cubicle and shut the door. Now he had time to think. He stared round at the three concrete walls. A little mirror was plugged on to one of them. Automatically he began to undress. When it was time for him to take off his shoes he sat down on the narrow wooden bench. Somewhere in the past there had been a moment such as this. He paused, trying to remember, trying to break through the confining boundaries of this present place, this present time. As he removed his right shoe a picture returned with startling clarity.

Aged seven he ran away from home, hysterical from unjust punishment that his elder brother Dwight had brought upon him. He could not now remember the crime, perhaps even then he had not comprehended: but there was the locked room, the high ornate ceiling, the heavy and unfriendly furniture which had terrified him as a child, but which in later years he had guessed to be pretentious. Still sobbing he had called for his mother whose silence he could not, dare not understand. The room in which he was caged was on the ground floor and looked on to the side of

22

the house where shrubs grew thickly. There was an irony in locking him in a room from which it was so easy to escape, although he did not see it then. Had Dwight been punished so, even the attic would not have been thought safe to keep him prisoner. Perhaps it surprised his father that he, Joe, had had the initiative to unlock the window and jump, unthinkingly, the few feet to the ground below. Perhaps it surprised them all that he had even formulated a plan, had fixed an objective in his mind. But the MacKendricks, with the obvious and displeasing exception of Joe – whose lack of what they called moral stamina never ceased to dismay them – were a family it was impossible to hold at bay for long.

Three miles away in the tiny house the MacKendricks, with charitable grace, had rented to Aunt Dora (who had married badly and suffered near-penury in her widowhood), three miles away and three hours later Joe's father had tracked him down, coming upon Aunt Dora in the act of telephoning to the big house to say that the boy was with her; an act which had cost her an hour and a half of heart searching, an hour and a half during which she had passed from a nervous determination to say nothing until morning to frantic fear that she had delayed too long. And father had brought Dwight. Together, with Aunt Dora behind them, weeping, they had mounted the stairs and flung open the door of the little bedroom where Joe, in the act of undressing, held his right shoe in his hand.

The three of them had stared at him and he had stared back, tears of hopelessness springing into his eyes. His father's face had been expressionless and Dwight, already forming himself in his father's image, looked graver than was suitable to his years. This new, suddenly adult Dwight, terrified him more than the look on his father's face. Aunt Dora, strung up with pity for Joe and fear for her allowance, stood in the background, her tightly clutched handkerchief held just below her chin; and fleetingly Joe had seen her problem with the eyes of a man.

"Your Aunt Dora hasn't the means to entertain guests, I'm

23

afraid. We're leaving in ten minutes. Be dressed and down in nine."

And they had gone to wait for him downstairs.

Now, as then, with the shoe (how much larger, grosser by comparison) suspended limply in his hand, he sat in emptiness of heart and spirit, the victim of his own impetuousness; the journey over, its reasons questionable, absurdly foolish by any ordinary standard of behaviour. The business trip to India and the journey from Bombay to Calcutta (Calcutta, where Dwight had been), these gave no cause for cross-examination, sealed as they had been with his father's authority. But the journey to Marapore was an escapade, like that of childhood. And had not even the trip to India itself, in spite of his father's approval, a taste, a smell of truancy? His father might have ordered it, but he had willed him to do so.

He stood up, reassured. He was again the man he had been, climbing down from the taxi at the porchway of the house in Calcutta whose address had been etched in his memory these past two years. The fact that the house had proved empty had not deterred him. This momentary sense of being a child again with no life of his own to live must not deter him either.

Undressed, he drew on his trunks; then, from the inside pocket of his jacket he took the envelope in which the photograph was sealed. Beneath the blank whiteness of the paper lay the memorised features of the girl. In Calcutta they had told him she lived now in Marapore; or rather, that her husband did. It would be so easy, so easy, to ask the first person he met exactly where he could find her. Tell me, he could say, where can I find Dorothy Gower? Or better still: Mrs. Tom Gower lives hereabouts, I believe?

He put the envelope back. How brash, how exactly like him that would be. Surely there were other, subtler means? By choosing them he would be in control. It was all very well to ask those questions of a stranger, but such questions could only call forth that other: Why? Do you know her? And, unless he were to lie, he could only answer – No.

24

The surface of the water was oily and far from inviting. A few blown leaves bobbed up and down at one end where the pool was shaded by the overhanging branches of a tree; they floated in tight little masses, as though congealing there.

He stood, toes curled over the edge of the pool, arms folded over his chest. In the brief satin trunks which he had bought in Miami he felt a little foolish, conspicuously alone, like a peacock with no hen to preen before. He glanced at the club-house which stood, its white, flaking plaster embroidered by creeper, beyond the parched square of lawn. On the edge of the deeply shadowed verandah a servant, in white uniform, stood watching him and wondering, no doubt, just who he was.

Was she there, he thought, behind the white pillars? Or at the *maidan*? He looked at the pool. Had these waters closed over her body, broken again to admit her head to the sun, the air?

He breathed deeply and plunged in. Here was the familiar, opaque world, a world of his own making which in the past had seemed sometimes the only world with which he had come to terms.

Cynthia Mapleton was still talking. She had been talking almost without pause ever since tiffin, but Miss Haig had long since ceased to listen.

From the darkest and coolest part of the verandah she had an excellent view across the lawn, and for the past few minutes she had been watching the young man who had just dived so gracefully into the pool.

She knew Cynthia talked mainly to save herself screaming with boredom, a trait of younger people whose natural exuberance, as yet unstilled by age, was caged up in a life prematurely, emotionally cut short by unfulfillment. But it was odd, she felt, that today some of Cynthia's restiveness should have communicated itself. Her own life was so placid; yet ever since tiffin she had felt disturbed, had been aware of a desire struggling to form itself in the deep recesses of her mind. Somehow the young man's appearance at the pool had been symbolic and she had concentrated her thoughts upon him. She had even prayed: Don't let Cynthia see him. It seemed important that she should keep his presence secret, at least until the desire had become clear and the day, begun so ordinarily, fallen again into normality.

But Cynthia had heard the splash. She twisted her head like a predatory bird and said, "Who's that?"

"Who's what, dear?" Miss Haig resumed her knitting; for a time it had lain neglected on her lap.

"There's someone in the pool. Is it a man? I can't see from here. I thought everyone was on the *maidan*."

"Apparently not."

"But who is it? It is a man, isn't it? Yes."

MacKendrick was climbing out of the pool preparatory to another dive. Miss Haig took a glance at her stitches. "It must be Mr. MacKendrick," she said.

Cynthia looked at her, suspiciously. "MacKendrick? Never heard of him. Is he new?"

"He's staying at Smith's, I'm told."

"Since when?"

"Since last night."

"Who told you?"

"Hussein."

"That bearer of yours knows things before they happen almost. Have you met him?"

"Not yet."

"What does he do?"

"I've no idea. He's an American."

Cynthia turned to watch the pool, but all she could see of MacKendrick was the churning water. "American, eh? Here already. They might let us get out of India first –" She broke off; then, her tone changing, some of her assurance going, she said, "Ronnie says he's going to Kenya. I may go too. For good."

"Can you afford it?"

26

"No, I can't afford it. I can't afford a bloody thing, which reminds me I haven't paid you for five weeks unless you want to call the last two weeks quits while I was in Murree."

"Yes, we'll call that quits."

"That makes it only three then. You're a brick. If I go to Kenya, Harriet, is there a chance you'd come too, share expenses again?"

"No."

"I thought not, but God knows why you want to stay *now*. All this 'd 've killed Robbie. I'm glad the Japs did it decently first. He'd turn in his grave if he knew what they were doing to the army. The whole thing's an utter disgrace. And if we have to go why they choose the hot weather God alone knows. It's ruined everyone's last year. They were livid, but livid in Murree all streaming back into the bloody heat to pack bags and sort out all kinds of bloody mess. I'm *really* going to Kenya, Harriet, that's why I came back. If there isn't a chance of you coming and giving me a leg up so to speak, is there a chance of tapping you for a loan?"

Harriet looked up. Cynthia was staring at her, smiling slightly, and now that the real point had been made, her protective armour was renewed and shining.

"I don't know, Cynthia. I'm afraid that won't be possible."

"Fair enough. You've been a brick and without your taking me in I'd 've gone to the dogs months ago. May as well go to 'em now with Ronnie in Kenya. He can't afford it either, but you know Ronnie. He'll always take a chance." Her eyes strayed to the rings on Harriet's fingers. "After all," she went on, "you've only got your pension too, though it's a bit more impressive than mine." She narrowed her eyes. "I must say you didn't do badly for yourself, considering you never got married."

"You can stay in the bungalow as long as you want. But I can't lend you any money, and I can't go to Kenya just to help you set up house."

"Why? I know you won't, but why?"

27

"Because I'm going to die. Quite soon. I'm sixty-six."

"Nonsense. We're all going to die."

"I'm going to die in India. Not Kenya."

They fell silent and Cynthia looked out across the lawn, towards the pool where MacKendrick floated on his back, at peace, in the sunshine.

She said, "I've *had* India."

"Why not go home? There's still the family isn't there?"

Cynthia laughed. "Home? What for? My dear, I've no illusions about the sort of background I'd go back to. Ten years as a Memsahib's given me different ideas about life. Let's face it." She fumbled with her handbag, searching for her cigarette case. When she had found it and lighted a scent-impregnated cigarette she said suddenly, "Ask him over."

"What?"

"Ask him over."

"Who?"

"The athletic young man in the pool." She spun the match to the ground. Her face was coiled about with the smoke, her eyelids screwed down against it. "I'm bored to tears and I'm damned if I'm going up to the *maidan* until it's time for the party. Here's some paper and here's a pencil. Ask him over for tea."

"Wouldn't that be better coming from you?"

"Well, I'm not going to stand the racket. I haven't a bean until Monday."

It was pleasant to float, face to the sun, borne gently on the water, to feel the sun burn, and then to go down into the embracing, sun-flecked world below; to be alone there, as in a dream, where sound was muted.

Surfacing, he swam lazily to the end where the pool was shadowed and then, on his back, into the sunlight again. For a time he amused himself by performing what friends back home called Joe MacKendrick's Sealion: (The Aqua Special. Try it. Look at Joe. Hey, get Joe will ya?): and then the agile leap from the water on to the side, the straightening up, vigorous, admired.

28

And then, so soon, the return to *gaucherie*. This was the pattern of his life.

Brushing water from his limbs, combing his hands through his hair, he saw the club servant, the one who had watched him, coming towards the pool. When the servant drew near Mac-Kendrick smiled and said, "*Thik hai?*" The agent in Bombay had taught him that. It meant 'Okay'. '*Malum*' meant 'understand'. '*Kitne*' meant 'how much', (not that it mattered), and '*jao*' meant 'go away'. On that vocabulary he had travelled three thousand miles.

The servant put his head on one side, a gesture MacKendrick never really understood, and offered a note. He took it and read it while the man waited.

> *When you have had your bathe, won't you take tea with us? You look so lonely.*
>
> Harriet Haig.

Who was Harriet Haig? He looked at the bearer, trying to formulate the right question, but none of the words he knew, except '*malum*', had any possible connection. He stammered the word out and the man inclined his head once more.

"Sahib?"

"*Malum* Miss Haig?"

"*Han, Sahib.*" They stared at one another hopelessly.

"*Thik hai.* Tell Miss Haig, *thik hai.*"

"*Han, Sahib.*"

The servant went back along the way he had come. Mac-Kendrick stared at the distant verandah, hoping for some sign – but what? A waved handkerchief, perhaps? There was only the seemingly deserted verandah, the deep shadows, the trailing creeper.

He turned, and made his way to the cubicle. He dressed carefully. "Look elegant," his father had said. "You'll be representing the firm, and representing the family. Look elegant. Whatever else the limeys did they set standards out East."

He stared at his reflection in the mirror, knotting his green silk tie, buttoning down the collar wings of his cellular shirt. Harriet Haig? Take tea with us? *Us?* Harriet Haig and another; a man? No, if it had been a man the invitation would have come from him, he imagined. A woman then; or a gauky child, awkward, shy as himself. Already his mouth was impossibly dry, his face flushed with premature embarrassment.

Towel in hand, bare-headed, he walked across the deserted lawn, conscious each step he took was watched, conscious that this was the beginning of the test he had set himself. He cleared his throat several times, and moistened his lips with his tongue. Now, only the short flight of steps up to the verandah confronted him.

"Hello – I've ordered tea."

The voice came from his left and, turning, he saw the two women seated in basket chairs around a wicker-work table. The elder faced him. The younger was twisted round, looking at him over her shoulder. It was not the girl. For this moment he was reprieved and relief gave him some confidence, enough to walk steadily to the table and bow slightly.

"It was kind of you to invite me." He looked from one to the other.

"Not at all. We're delighted you've come over. I'm Harriet Haig and this is Mrs. Mapleton."

The younger woman nodded. She was the sort of woman who frightened him; taut, skinny, calculating. She looked him swiftly up and down and smiled brassily. She had no breasts to speak of and the hand which after some unfriendly hesitation she put into his own was bony.

He turned to Miss Haig again and the first thing he noticed about her was that her left hand was heavy with glittering rings which shone, self-radiant, in the half light of the shaded verandah as she smoothed her grey, cropped hair. She was bulky, her bones were large; but in spite of this, the boyish hair and the severe grey linen suit, he sensed her frailty.

30

"You're Mr. MacKendrick, of course." She smiled, her dentures were fierce, at odds with the soft, fallen contours of her face.

"Why yes. How did you know my name?"

Mrs. Mapleton laughed. "In Marapore we know everyone. You're staying at Smith's. Please sit down." He did so, and because she went on speaking he had to turn slightly in her direction.

"Everyone's on the *maidan*. Everyone except us. And I wouldn't be here only I had to come back from Murree. Why aren't you at the sports, anyway? I'd have thought they'd 've been in your line. You have an impressive physique, and I do like a man to be big, it gives me a sense of security." She paused, drawing on her cigarette. "Or is that an old-fashioned idea? I'm afraid you'll find us all fearful backnumbers and of course we're all dying to talk to somebody *new*."

He was feeling in his pocket for his own cigarettes, but Mrs. Mapleton had her case out before he succeeded.

"Have one of mine. Unless you don't like them fouled up with scent. I'm afraid these are, but try one all the same. Harriet doesn't smoke which is frightfully wise of her considering how much everything costs these days, although of course with the dollar exchange rate you come off pretty well anywhere don't you? Or have the markets fallen over-night? I never keep track of these things."

"I'm afraid I don't either, Mrs. Mapleton."

"No? You're not a business man, then?"

He realised her cunning. Cautiously he said, "I – I don't keep a general track. But things are pretty stable." He turned to Miss Haig, but her eyes were downcast. He got the feeling she was ashamed of her companion's manner. Mrs. Mapleton was talking again. "I wish they were for us. Stability's just about the last thing *we* have. We're all clearing out and I must say now that it's come to it it's a relief. We know what we're in for and I've a good idea what the Indians are in for. They don't see it, they can't see anything in my opinion. The British are going and now it's *your*

31

turn. Whether you like it or not, all they're doing here is exchanging the Union Jack for the dollar sign."

The bearer brought tea but Cynthia ignored the diversion, her flow of conversation continuing as though the bearer were not leaning over the table with the tray, cutting her off from MacKendrick's view. When the boy had gone MacKendrick realised she was waiting for an answer to a question he had not heard.

"I'm sorry, I didn't quite hear that –"

"I said I thought if you weren't a business man you might be a journalist or something."

"Why no."

"Well it's all terribly mysterious. I'll begin to think you're an official observer from Uno or one of those dreary organisations come to watch the British skedaddle with their tails between their legs. Though why choose a God-forsaken cantonment like Marapore to watch that in I can't think. Anyway, what do you think of our tails, or is that indelicate?"

He detected the note of hysteria. She was perspiring. There was an angry flush on her cheeks. Had she suddenly laid about her and swept the china from the table he would not have been surprised. It was the sort of vicious, controlled anger he was familiar with in his own family.

"I can't say I've noticed any particular consternation, Mrs. Mapleton. I think that's a tribute to all you people."

"Oh, we're not crying our bloody eyes out if that's what you mean. But all that smarmy talk in Delhi doesn't mean a bloody thing. Our occupation's gone and our lives are bloody well messed up. Or perhaps being married to an army officer gave me the wrong sort of outlook."

He failed to notice her use of the past tense. Conversationally he said, "Will you both be going home?" He added, remembering Miss Haig's presence. "I mean you and your husband?"

Her mouth was opened to speak. For a few seconds it remained so. It was months since someone had made that easy mistake of

32

referring to Robbie. Oneself grew used to death. Oneself accepted the end. And then a chance remark broke down the barrier so carefully built against the past.

"My husband's dead."

She drank the scalding tea which made her blink her eyes. She looked, then, across the rim of her cup and caught the swift glance that passed between the other two. So she said, "He was killed in the war. He got it in Burma. Almost right at the end, too, when we took back Mandalay. But as I was saying to Harriet a little while ago, in a way I'm glad he did. All this would have been the end for Robbie."

"I'm sorry." Genuinely, he was. She had become stridently pathetic. "You'll go home yourself, though?"

"I'm going to Kenya." She banged down her cup. "It should be fun. My dear," her voice rose, "everyone's going to turn up in Nairobi, it'll be just like Simla or Srinagar in the season. At least I say I'm going to Kenya, but that all depends on whether I can raise the wind."

Her eyes glittered. "You see, Mr. MacKendrick, this particular Memsahib is bloody broke. You don't get the sort of pension that makes you sit up and cheer as the widow of a mere Captain. Harriet took me into her jolly little bungalow as a P.G. although for her there must be something ironic about the paying part of it."

Her candour embarrassed him.

"And you, Miss Haig," he said. "Do you go to Kenya, too?"

"No, I'm not going to Kenya. Are you ready for more tea?"

"This is fine." He raised his nearly full cup. "Then it's England, Home and Beauty?" He grinned, reddening at his triviality.

"What a nice thing for an American to say," Miss Haig replied. "But it's not true in my case. England's not home and I'm afraid its beauty is only memory for me. I've got rather used to India and so I'm staying."

"You're a fool."

They both looked at Cynthia. She clattered her cup again on

her saucer, and put both on the chromium tray. "You're a fool, Harriet. You'll find yourself staying along with all the cranks and the gone-natives. Like your precious Tom Gower."

Just like that, casually, the girl's husband could be mentioned.

He cleared his throat and asked Miss Haig, "Gower? I seem to know that name?"

She looked at him with new interest. "Do you? Oh, Tom's a great friend of mine."

Cynthia broke in, "Well, he's a crank, all the same. He'll end up wearing a *dhoti* and eating with his fingers. What he and his kind never see is how much the Indians really despise them."

"Tom's not despised. He's made his home here and they know he's a friend."

"Oh, all right, but from what I heard at tiffin he'd better watch his step. One thing Indians won't stand for is Europeans interfering with their politics and religion."

"Tom doesn't interfere."

"Oh, let's drop him. I know he's your pet. But if you ask me he's for the high jump. And the same goes for that no-good Frank Milner."

"I wouldn't call Frank a no-good, whatever that is."

"I would. How any officer can stick about in a depot with no-one else in the mess except a lot of Indian types beats me."

"Is Frank Milner Major Milner?" MacKendrick asked. He had to talk. Only by doing so could he steer the conversation round again to Gower – and to Gower's wife.

Miss Haig nodded. Cynthia smiled. "Why, do you know him?"

"He brought me to the club. Actually he's sending a tonga back to take me up to the sports. Rather short and thick. Reddish hair?"

"Squat, fat and ginger, my dear. Don't be so delicate. Frank doesn't appreciate delicacy. He doesn't appreciate anything except one thing. No decent officer is staying on."

"How can they, anyway?"

"Oh, they'll do it on contract with India or Pakistan. Which-

34

ever pays highest. Soldier adventurers without the guts of a louse. But if Frank Milner's your friend I'd better dry up, hadn't I?"

"He was friendly, but he isn't my friend. He called at the hotel just as I was looking for a tonga to come up to the pool."

"Called to see you?" It was half question, half statement.

"Why no – to engage a room."

"Is he moving in there?"

"No, he was engaging a room for –"

He stopped. She had trapped him again. He felt the first tightening grip of anger and because he did there was also between them suddenly a challenge; a sexual challenge.

Only she knew how clever she had been.

"Booking a room for who?" She was now sufficiently armed to smooth her face with an innocence which would otherwise have looked out of place and made him cautious.

"I – I don't know. I didn't catch the name."

She laughed, but it seemed as though she laughed with him, rather than at him. "What a shame. And how trying. I'm dying to know who Frankie's latest is. A bit of chi-chi as usual, I expect." She grinned, in good fellowship. On this sort of level, her eyes were saying, we're equals, you and I.

He found himself smiling. "Chi-chi? What's that?"

"Half-caste. Of the country. Half-breed. Anglo-Indian. Eurasian. Different names, same gravy, as Robbie used to say. The results of mis-directed passion. My dear! They're quite laughable. I've known some, black as your hat, who try and pull your leg they were born and raised in some respectable London suburb. You want to be careful. They look it all up – details of places, I mean – so's they can talk as if they've been there."

"You mean they pretend they're English?"

"If they can get away with it. Some do, for ages. But there are ways of telling." She spread her hands. "Their hands are usually small-boned, like Indians'. Most of them talk a sort of sing-song. Like Welsh. They're the end."

"But doesn't the colour of their skin give them away?"

35

"Not always. If it does then it turns out their mother was Spanish or something swarthy. They'll tell you anything."

Miss Haig coughed, the cough of the shy who prepare themselves to speak in company. "They're only like that because both we and the Indians treat them so abominably. They're made to feel like social pariahs." A deep flush spread over her neck and face, and the ringed hand came up to pat the neck line of her blouse.

"My dear, Mr. MacKendrick'll think you're Eurasian yourself if you speak up for them like that."

"Will he? Oh well, somebody ought to speak up for them. They could be the backbone of the country. Half-breeds have an exceptionally strong sense of self-preservation, and India needs people like that now."

She saw his eyes on her hands, interpreted his thoughts. "No, I'm really not an Anglo-Indian. My parents were good, honest Yorkshire folk. Father was in the Church."

He nodded. A missionary. That seemed to place her. He wanted to place her. He wanted to talk to her, for she was a friend of Tom Gower. A retired missionary, then. Or did missionaries retire? And then he looked again at her hands, saw again the rings. Rubies, diamonds, sapphires. Fabulous adornment of the ordinary, they gave those broad, capable hands an air of foreign extravagance.

"Is this your first visit to India?"

Reluctantly he faced Cynthia again and answered her question. "Yes."

"Is it business or pleasure?"

"A little of each."

"And what is the business?"

"My father manufactures agricultural machinery. We have agents here in Bombay and Calcutta."

"And you've been sent to check up on them?"

He nodded.

"You poor man. And you don't like seeing them a bit. You far prefer to swim madly up and down that bitch of a little pool. They didn't change the water this morning. I asked. So I didn't bathe." She added, suddenly, "But it intrigues me why you came to Marapore just to get away from those awful agents."

"Sort of a vacation. Pleasure trip."

"Pleasure trip! To Marapore! My dear man, we're miles away from anything remotely civilised. Think what you might have let yourself in for. There mightn't even have been an hotel. Not that Smith's is what you'd call a proper hotel."

"I knew about Smith's."

"You made enquiries then?"

His temper was roused again. "Yes, I made enquiries in Calcutta. They told me Marapore was the right place for me to come."

She hesitated. She wanted to say, 'For what?' But had she overdone it, she wondered? One worked to such a narrow margin with men like this. "Well," she said, earnestly, "I hope they're treating you well at Smith's. We're pretty off-hand with guests in this sort of place."

He thought: She means well. She hasn't spoken to anyone new in months, maybe. "Sure. Except they make an awful lot of noise when you want to get some sleep."

"Noise? At Smith's? Oh dear, things *have* changed. I always whisper when I go into that awful lounge."

"I guess I know what you mean." He looked closely at her, as she leaned to stub her cigarette. Yes, she would whisper. But her eyes would be laughing. They were turned on him now. They did have that quality. However taut, however ravaged by heat, by sun, by ill luck she was, her eyes were at least alive. "I guess I know what you mean," he said again. "But I wish Desai and his boys felt that way. There was such a mêlée outside my room after tiffin – " proudly he presented the word: a Roman in Rome: ". . . such a mêlée I couldn't get any sleep so I decided to take a swim."

"A mêlée! It must be you. You've done something to them

37

down there. Harriet, imagine. One night at Smith's and he causes a mêlée. Did you find out what it was?"

"Yes. Desai tried to make me move to another room because some big shot was coming."

"Of all the bloody cheek. What did you tell him?"

He reached for his cigarettes. "I told him no dice. I like Room Three."

"Room Three?"

He turned to Miss Haig who had spoken, almost sharply.

"Yes. Room Three. Last night Desai practically threw me into it because it had a couch and rated the highest rent."

"He would." Cynthia bent towards the light he cupped in his hands.

Miss Haig said, "Did Mr. Desai say who it was? I mean who was coming to Smith's?"

He lighted his own cigarette before answering. She had stopped knitting and was sitting forward.

"Somebody called Smith. I thought it was the owner, maybe."

"Mr. Smith? Are you *sure*?"

"Yes. I'm sure. Because of the co-incidence of name –"

"Jimmy Smith?" Miss Haig stressed each word.

"I wouldn't know his first name. Desai just said Mr. Smith and the way they were all running around you'd have thought this Mr. Smith whoever he is was a Maharajah at least."

Miss Haig sat back.

"But, Mr. MacKendrick, Mr. Smith *is* a Maharajah."

4

As soon as the tonga carrying MacKendrick and Milner had been driven down the path and disappeared in the direction of the club, Mr. Desai gave orders for the American Sahib's luggage to be taken to Room Twelve. This, he decided, was the moment for a display of initiative, although as he watched his boys running backwards and forwards between the two rooms he could not help feeling that fate had dealt him an unwarranted blow in sending, within twenty-four hours, a guest who would pay highly, and in cash, and the ubiquitous 'Mr. Smith', who turned up at such irregular intervals at such short notice, and was likely to leave his bill outstanding for months.

But Mr. Smith was royalty and, indeed, the bungalow now known as Smith's Hotel had been built by Mr. Smith's grandfather in the days when Marapore had been part of the neighbouring, Princely State of Kalipur, a state which had tended to absorb itself bit by bit into British India as its ruler's fortunes wavered and cash was needed to replenish the private exchequer. Under the present Maharajah stability had returned and the state's boundaries had remained intact, some twenty miles south of Marapore; a phenomenon which his enemies attributed to his being 'in with the Raj'. But the phenomenon was, in fact, no phenomenon but a clear indication of the young Maharajah's good sense. The exchequer was replenished now by increased productivity within the state, itself due, perhaps, to his awareness that there was a world outside Kalipur which needed no encouragement to encroach upon his territory; a world not only outside Kalipur, which when all was said and done was but one of over five hundred Princely States over which the British Crown held paramountcy, but a world outside India as well – one which was not necessarily a playground but on which, with the rest of India, one ultimately depended.

And so, both as Prince and Maharajah, a title succeeded to at the age of twenty when his father died in 1923, he travelled the length and breadth of India, to Europe, to Malaya and once as far as Japan. It had pleased him on these travels to adopt an incognito and because by then the old hunting lodge in Marapore was known as Smith's Hotel he could think of no more suitable surname. Harriet Haig had suggested the 'Jimmy'. The pseudonym deceived nobody but, oddly, he had discovered that rather more deference was shown to 'Mr. Smith' than to the Maharajah of Kalipur should he happen to discard the incognito, as he once did.

Unwittingly he had spoiled the pleasure people get from being 'in the know'. To speak affectionately, however deeply they disliked or feared him, of 'Jimmy', helped them to assume an air of being on intimate terms with Royalty.

As soon as Room Three was cleared a couple of sweepers were summoned. For ten minutes they happily raised the dust with their short brooms and then a further ten minutes was allowed to pass so that the dust could settle. When it had done so additional furniture was dragged in and extra effects introduced under Mr. Desai's appraising eyes, eyes which at this instant gazed sadly out above wrinkling nostrils as he stood in the open doorway.

Mr. Desai was not happy. Now that Mr. MacKendrick's belongings had gone, now that the bed was stripped, the room looked like a prison-cell; and prodding a suspicious bulge he discovered the presence of a broken spring in the leather couch. He hesitated. It would, perhaps, be simpler to put things back exactly as they had been and explain to Mr. Smith, when he arrived at six o'clock as his telegram had said, that Room Three was, this time, occupied. The telegram had panicked him. Now the panic was subsiding, giving way to memory of the disagreeable rumours he had heard about the Maharajah. Should he, he wondered, suggest to Mr. Smith that some other, more suitable lodging be found? How long did he intend to stay? Where, indeed, was he going? The political climate was changing, and Desai's close association with European ways and European thought had schooled him to regard such things with respect.

He stood over the couch, exploring the raised knob of leather where the recalcitrant spring revealed itself. The couch had been beautiful. The couch, like life, had been dependable. Now its symmetry was disturbed. There would be people in Marapore, influential people, who might hold it against him that he had entertained beneath his roof a man who had recently stated views that could only be looked upon as pro-British propaganda.

Mr. Desai took his politics seriously. But he wavered, for he also took his hotel-keeping seriously. A guest was a guest, whatever his nationality, whatever his politics. He called his staff and the couch was seized and dragged into the adjoining lounge where it was exchanged for a larger one covered in faded cretonne. In the midst of familiar activity the last of his doubts were gone and he was possessed once more with the pride of his calling. The substitute couch was proving difficult to move and difficult to push through the door into Room Three. He hopped up and down shouting, "Pull it, you see! This way! His Highness is just coming! His Highness is here already!"

As this was obviously untrue the boys took no notice, but relaxed in order to discuss ways of dealing with the situation. The deadlock inevitably reached was broken at last by a decision to let brawn have its way, and the new couch was pushed victoriously through the doorway with only the sharp complaint of tearing cretonne to reproach them.

Flowers were sent for, and the lounge and other bedrooms were cannibalised for rugs, bowls, cushions and magazines. A search in Mr. Desai's office brought to light some hotel stationery, rather yellow round the edges and with no envelopes to match; and this, together with wafer-thin pink blotting paper and blue-black ink in a tarnished chromium well, thickly encrusted round the rim with a silver-green chemical deposit, were set neatly on a table which had to be supported under one leg by a folded copy of the *Marapore Gazette*.

As Desai folded the *Gazette* and handed it to one of the boys he was aware that the act was symbolic, for Gower Sahib, the *Gazette's* editor, and the Maharajah of Kalipur had been linked in people's minds since the last issue had appeared as usual last Thursday. "This is amusing," he thought. "Here one still supports the other." He tapped the table – slight doubts returning. But then he shrugged. The room would be rented and the table propped. He gave a last look round and smiled, pleased if vaguely troubled with the thought that faults could be found. Then he closed the door, gave a cursory glance inside the room being prepared for His Highness's personal assistant, a rather critical one into Room Twelve where Bholu was restoring some sort of order – bad-tempered after the row with the tonga wallah whom he had at last and unnecessarily brought back. Desai retreated, hesitated outside Room Nine where Milner Sahib's young lady was to be installed, and decided that no work need be done there until morning. Then he passed through the lounge and took up a position of observation on the porch.

Smith's Hotel was situated at the northern end of the cantonment, close to the station and the bazaar. Beyond the station was the town where the European air of exhausted respectability, drifting across the railway, was befouled and soured and inextricably mixed with the smell which rose from the cluttered streets; a smell compounded of the individual scents of burning joss-sticks, cow dung, hot spiced food, urine and rotting piles of refuse. The tongas which jingled along the quiet, suburban roads of the cantonment brought the smell with them, as Charon's boat, ferrying the dead, must have retained about its timbers the pungent breath of the farther bank.

When evening came the smell rose high and drifted, as though reclaiming the departing warmth of the sun which gave it being. It drifted now—past Smith's Hotel, wrinkling the nose of Mr. Desai who noticed such things; blowing warmly down the broad Cannon Road which ran parallel with a branch line of the railway until the abrupt pimple of Cannon Hill separated them and sent Cannon Road in a broad sweep left, past the bronze and corroded statue of Queen Victoria whose blank, imperious eyes gazed forever towards the high trees gathered protectively around the Marapore Club.

Beyond the club, Cannon Road divided itself into two smaller roads, the Kalipur Road which, on its way to the state border, went past the squat, geometrically laid-out buildings of the M.T. N.C.O.'s School, and Victoria Avenue which curved south-east and round to north to form, with Cannon Road, a pear-shaped area suspended from the railway and cut by narrower, unmetalled roads where the *Sahib-log* lived in whitewashed bungalows which

42

peeped from the profuse screenings of bush and tree with a smug air of being, like their tenants, on hand when wanted.

Victoria Avenue linked up with the Station road. On the right of the Avenue, set far back in open ground (the *maidan*), was the ugly, red-brick Laxminarayan Memorial College whose playing fields were, at this hour, on this day, ajostle with crowds making their way to a canvas-protected dais from which prizes were to be distributed (mostly to Vidyasagar); fields which gave on to the flat, cultivated plain and eventually on to the low foothills of Ooni, which rose, tree-studded, brooding, into the distance. Here, in the past, men and women had trekked, pith-helmeted, to the hunt, but the last tiger (a poor specimen) had been seen and shot in 1926.

It was for the game that Jimmy Smith's grandfather had built the lodge, now known as Smith's Hotel, and he had built it with both eyes on Europe, although turned occasionally, perhaps, to the future, foreseeing a time when it would have to be sold, and to someone who would have none of this 'damned native nonsense', even in a thing like architecture. It was, then, only a slightly larger edition of the run-of-the-mill civil bungalows, most of which had been built towards the end of the nineteenth century.

There was a ground floor only, and this was divided into a lounge and a dining-room from both of which doors led into the bedrooms. The roof was steeply sloping against the heavy rains of summer, and from inside it seemed, at its highest point, remote, a safe harbour for winged creatures. No amount of change in time and ownership (of the latter there had been many and few could now recall the Smith who had given his name to the hotel) had altered the gloomy and Victorian interior, although both had introduced anachronisms such as the oil lamp on the oval table in the lounge set directly beneath the electric ceiling-fan; the table itself covered by a green, bobble-fringed cloth and stared at, as it were, down the chromium noses of ultra-modern wall lights purchased in the Thirties by a new proprietor who had ended, like so

43

many new brooms, by metaphorically sweeping the dust of the Hotel under the carpets.

Lined up round the walls of the lounge were imitation-leather arm-chairs, their dark stain paled in shapeless patches on the arms and across the backs by the toll taken year after year by clenched fists and squared shoulders. Other chairs stood round like poor relations on the verge of giggling at a funeral; the dumpy cretonned, the cane-bottomed, the plebeian rocker upholstered in orange plush, its woodwork threatened by white ant.

There were pictures on the wall, Royal portraits and reproductions of photographs taken in the Swiss Alps, violently and unbelievably blue and white, framed in passe-partout. Over the fireplace there was an old print of a very complicated battle scene, its detail partly obscured by vicious puffs of smoke from cannon which were surrounded by bewhiskered and tattered soldiers whose flashing eyes challenged comrades in the rear, whose arms were thrust forward in the direction of swirling banners; a picture to invoke nostalgia in disillusioned hearts which had once beat wildly to Kipling's music in front of nursery fires in quiet Pimlico houses.

From the lounge the visitor could pass unhindered by any dividing wall – for it failed inexplicably to meet in the middle – through a hazard of bead curtains and draught screens – into the dining-room, whose solemn, white-clothed tables were hidden from public view by a token screen which stood athwart the exit on to the porticoed verandah. Just inside the porch there was a glass-windowed cage where Mr. Desai conducted his administrative business in a flurry of papers littered upon a roll-topped desk. From this paper sea, like a periscope, a telephone rose as though at once inviting and forbidding contact with the outside world.

It began to ring at exactly the same moment Mr. Desai heard the unmistakable sound of the klaxon horn on His Highness's Cadillac. With a sure grasp of the situation he shrieked indiscriminately so that, as he had intended, the entire staff came at the double. Despatching one boy to answer the telephone and lining the rest up along the verandah, he took his place in front of them just as the car drew to a stop, pleased with himself for not having lost his head, but aware from the corner of his all-seeing eye that one of the boys, caught off-balance by the peremptory summons, was rather foolishly holding a vase of flowers.

"A Maharajah!" MacKendrick stared at Miss Haig in consternation.

"Don't worry," said Cynthia. "You've struck a blow for the rights of man. Your Maharajah'll have to get used to a change of climate, won't he, Harriet?"

Miss Haig flushed. She said, "Poor Jimmy. Yes, I suppose so."

"Do you know him? Personally I mean?" MacKendrick asked. Cynthia laughed and the flush on Miss Haig's face deepened.

"Actually I'm one of his pensioners." She looked up and saw his eyes dart to the rings on her fingers. She stopped mentally in her tracks. Then she grew a little angry at his presumption, but almost at once she was amused. Thinking *that* about herself and Jimmy! But it was romantic; and flattering. The fact that she had blushed, was still blushing, had helped of course, helped him to interpret 'pensioner' in the way he undoubtedly was interpreting it; and yet she had only blushed because it was embarrassing to admit one was dependent on another for one's means.

The others were talking again, or rather Cynthia was, and she was able to settle back and think more clearly about the news the young man had passed on in such an off-hand way. She turned this news over in her mind, thinking: That's why I feel on edge. But now that I know what's different about today, I'll be calm again.

She contemplated the quality of calmness. But the restlessness was still there in her mind, aching in her bones. It was unusual for Jimmy to come to Marapore without warning her beforehand. She was a little hurt. She enjoyed anticipating his visits, enjoyed the sense of being back in harness that ringing Smith's herself and

45

making a few little arrangements for him brought to her. And for days now she had been thinking about him. Why had he come? How soon would she know? Surely he would send for her tonight?

It was odd to think that life had been lived, not bleakly in Yorkshire, in growing heavy and bearing a good man's children, but in waiting to be sent for by a Maharajah. How odd that sounded. A little risqué even. But even as a boy, a Prince, he had always by Royal Prerogative sent for her rather than she for him when it was time for lessons. Memories came – she tried at first to side-track them but, growing older, she found that thoughts evolved their own pattern without regard to the mind's instruction – and now, in spite of her wish to think of other things, there was a sudden vision of the high, bare room in the Palace, a gold-fringed punkah fluttering the thin pages of Hall and Knight's *Algebra*, or *David Copperfield* (Dickens, remote but reassuring in Kalipur), and then in later years the same books, the same room, with Jimmy's children, oneself older, aware rather that one had become an institution and did not quite like what one had become; aware that one's work was possibly outmoded, an occupation for oneself rather than an exercise for one's pupils; but there it was still – is still? Would one ever go back to see it? – the same place, the same echoing room, but with an electric fan working from the Palace generator . . .

. . . and Jimmy sending for her: yes, at those moments, and they had been frequent, one knew that wisdom glimpsed by the boy was respected by the man. Is this right, Miss Haig? – but this now in a voice lower, more penetrating, had become, What shall I do, Harriet? What would you do? Thus and thus and thus – (was that a quotation? How troublesome a thing a declining memory was) – thus another pattern had emerged. Jimmy was a good boy. One had seen how good, one had seen the goodness expressed in the changing lives of the people he ruled; for there had been so many things which had made one's heart ache in his father's day: poverty and squalor and wretchedness contrasting so strongly with Royal luxury. Had one been *too* militant? Had one influenced the boy too much to see the barrier which separated the ruled and the ruler, influenced him too strongly – (was that the reason for so much Dickens?) – to try to break it, to lead his people into a new life of self-respect? "Was that well done, Harriet?" Oh yes, it was! It had been, and one rejoiced to know one could work creatively through others.

Miss Haig stopped knitting, and looked down at the rings. Some frozen assets, Harriet my dear, something for the little pension to fall back on. And suddenly she saw herself as an old woman sitting foolishly on the verandah of an almost deserted club. She could hear its silence and across its silence the echo of someone saying: Our lives are bloody well messed up and our occupation's gone. Around her in the emptiness were voices, voices which betrayed the anguish there was in being forced to hang on to what was already moving away, because there seemed to be no other support. What was she becoming? An aged power behind a tottering throne? No doubt that she was old. No doubt that Jimmy's throne was tottering, for the States had been deserted and left as vulnerable islands to be eaten away by hungry seas. Surely he had come to see *her*? But what use was she, now?

MacKendrick had watched her, had seen her eyes go to the jewels on her hands, had seen them look away, veiled, sad. What visions of the past was she conjuring, he wondered? His only knowledge of Indian palaces came from photographs of the Taj Mahal and he couldn't be sure whether that were a palace or a temple. But it would do. He set her, in his imagination, outside it: Harriet Haig, incongruous in her grey linen, with her close-cropped hair, a tourist, wafted suddenly into a Hollywoodesque interior by a fat man wearing a turban.

He felt slightly shocked.

No good, he was sure, could come of that sort of union. He looked at the rings. No good had come of it for Harriet Haig if you discounted the sparklers. Had he kept her in purdah? Or did only Muslims do that?

47

Their eyes met.

"What is the time, Mr. MacKendrick?"

"Why – a quarter to five." A glance at the familiar watch on his wrist brought him back to a knowledge of time, of time passing. He realised he had made no headway. For all their gossiping, neither of these two women had mentioned the girl.

Miss Haig nodded. "A quarter to five. That means they'll be giving the prizes, and afterwards there's going to be a cocktail party at the Principal's bungalow." She hesitated. She wanted to be alone to think, to plan. Yet she did not wholly like the idea of surrendering the young man to Cynthia. She said, "We're both going to the party and you must come too. I'm rather a slow creature though, so perhaps you'd like to go with Mrs. Mapleton and leave me to follow up?"

The last thing he wanted was to go with Cynthia. Alone with the older woman he could get her to talk. "I haven't been invited," he said.

Cynthia shrugged irritably and broke in, "The colour of your skin automatically invites you, not but that you'll find plenty of niggers there. Schoolmasters and suchlike. What about a tonga?"

"Frank Milner's sending one."

She rose, and MacKendrick rising with her found her shorter than he had imagined she would be. She said, "Wait for me a moment. I've got to clean up a bit. You're quite ready, I suppose?" She looked him up and down. "You can't take the towel with you. Leave it here, they'll look after it."

Cynthia went, he felt possessed by her, a little boy, waiting to be taken out. He lit a cigarette to hide his confusion.

"I should sit down again if I were you. Cynthia will be ages."

He did so, gratefully.

"How long are you staying with us?"

The question found him off guard. "A few days, I guess. It depends."

She did not ask: On what?: but he knew she would have liked

48

to, and he liked her for not saying it, and for a moment he considered the possibility of taking her into his confidence. But almost at once she began to speak again.

"Well, even if it's for only a few days it'll be useful for you to go to the party. Everyone will be there, though I'm afraid you won't find many young people. Marapore's what I call a middle-aged cantonment. It used to be quite different, we had lots of parties then. I used to come up from Kalipur to see people like the Mapletons. Cynthia and Robbie were terribly popular. He had a brilliant future, poor boy, anyway as much as a career in the army can be brilliant. I've been middle-aged for centuries of course, but I've always liked to have young people round me." She paused. "I was governess, you know, at the Palace in Kalipur. I'm sixty-six now and I came out when I was thirty and Jimmy just eight." She hesitated. She had lost the thread of what she was saying, or had set out to say. Now she was back again to Jimmy, wondering what she should do, wondering whether his silence meant he did not want, this time, to see her. Should she go round to Smith's? Or ring? To ring would be better. When Cynthia and Mr. MacKendrick had gone she would ring.

"What was it like?" he asked.

She stared at him, blankly.

He added, "In the old days, I mean. Here in Marapore?"

"Oh –" She looked beyond his shoulder, out towards the pool, across the scorched grass that needed the beat of rain upon its cheeks. She said, "It's odd, and can't possibly be true, but then it was so green. We had parties in the gardens and it always seemed so wonderfully green and alive, and full of things. One used to be here in the cooler weather only of course. In the hot seasons one went up to the hills. Perhaps I'm mixing the two. But now it seems always so hot and parched and of course none of us is looking forward any longer." She smiled at him. "I've put that awfully badly but then I can't talk intelligently about India. Tom Gower can. Did you say you knew him?"

"No. No, I don't. I – the name's familiar, that's all."

49

She jerked a length of wool free. "Well, you must meet him. Oh, you must, because you sell farm equipment, don't you?"

"Why, yes."

"Then you'll have to sell some to Tom. He runs a model farm up at Ooni, that's a place about thirty miles away, and he gets wonderful results using proper equipment and fertilisers and things."

"Thirty miles away?" His heart sank.

"Oh, but you won't have to go out there. He works in Marapore too. Tom's an awfully busy man because as well as running the farm he edits the *Marapore Gazette*, that's our weekly paper, and quite influential too, though you won't believe it."

"I don't suppose he'll want farm equipment now?"

"Why? Oh, you mean because of what's happening? No, it won't affect Tom. Tom won't go home, he's like me, his roots are in India. I can't see anything dragging him away. Besides, the Indians are very fond of him, he's done so much for them always. He's been out here for years. Why, he's almost an institution." Like herself, in Kalipur. She looked down, counting stitches.

"Does he live here, or up at Ooni?"

His tone perplexed her. Really, he seemed quite urgent. "Both," she replied. "He has a nice bungalow in Cannon Avenue and a lovely place at Ooni. At least *I* think it's lovely. It's not much more than a few huts huddled on a hillside, his and John Steele's – that's his assistant up there. But it's delightful after this place."

"What's delightful after this place?" Cynthia had come back, her face made up, a white felt hat hiding her hair.

"Ooni."

"Oh, God. That hole!" She smiled at MacKendrick. "Harriet has a taste for the primitive. And for lame ducks like Tom Gower."

"Tom's not a lame duck."

"Well, I think he's wet. You can't live in the pockets of Indians like he does without getting like them. Unreliable. It won't be long before they tell him where he gets off. That'll shake him.

I'm ready when you are, and by the way, don't give the tonga-wallah more than two or three chips. You Americans always spoil them by overpaying wildly."

He nodded, but he had not been listening. He looked at Miss Haig who said, "I'll be along later. You might send the tonga back for me?"

"Sure." He hesitated. Then he said, without thinking, "Will Mr. and Mrs. Gower be at the party?"

"Tom's sure to be because he's giving the prizes at the sports. But I'm not sure about Dorothy."

They stared at each other.

She opened her mouth to say: Did I mention he had a wife?

But the astonished look on his deeply flushed face told her that she had not.

5

He felt that Marapore had subtly changed. Before he had given himself away to Miss Haig it had oppressed him, it had been inscrutable. Now, driving through its streets in the tonga with Cynthia Mapleton, he felt it had turned its back on him mockingly. No longer was he the stranger, the man of mystery. He was a fool, and the story he had to tell would seem like the old story. It was even obvious he would not tell it well, so *gauche*, so immature he was. He fixed his eyes upon the tail of dust the tonga's passage raised, on the deep ditches at the sides of the road, on the stone walls with their flaking plaster, the trees whose leaves were grey with summer pallor. Thus it had been before he came, thus it would be after he had gone; thus, he was nothing.

The feeling was not, to him, unfamiliar, but this time he found himself angry, not passively as usual but militantly. He looked at Mrs. Mapleton and longed to show her in some way that he was to be reckoned with, that he was not to be used casually, callously, by a dried-up, frustrated Englishwoman. It was as though something inside him rose up, long-suffering, patient, its fund of passivity exhausted at last; as though this thing forced its way through the pores of his skin and formed itself into a thin, hard shell upon his body, a resilient shell of unfriendliness.

So far, he knew, a man could travel a certain road: so far, no farther. There came always the moment when a burden had to be tossed away as when, for instance, the eyes were open to the non-existence of the road beyond. That moment, he told himself, had come now to him. He had seen the blankness, the improbability. He had travelled thousands of miles to find a woman called Dorothy Gower, a woman he had never seen before, a woman whose only link with him was his brother Dwight. And Dwight was dead. And he had come to her, he had done this unreasonable thing, this extraordinary thing, reasonably, ordinarily, armed only with his own foolish impulsiveness. He needed the hardness he had always lacked. There was still time, he felt, to learn to acquire it.

They had turned on to the open, heat-plastered *maidan*, taking the cinder track which skirted it. On their right they could see the crowds gathered round the dais, could hear the regular bursts of clapping.

"They're giving the prizes," she said, "so we're just in time to go straight in to cocktails without looking indecently early."

"I'd prefer to watch for a moment."

She raised her eyebrows. What was up with him now, she wondered. Those few minutes alone at the Principal's bungalow before all this riff-raff got there would have been useful. She began to think he was not going to be worth the trouble she was taking. He was acting like a spoilt child. "It'll be an awful bore," she said, "and anyway we shan't get near the dais, so we shan't see anything."

"We could draw up as close as possible and stop a moment."

"Very well." She hesitated. "Tell the driver."

"I don't speak the language well enough."

She smiled, maliciously, leaned back and gave the man directions. The tonga slowed. On the dais he could see a score or so of people, Indian and European. In the centre, on the edge of the dais, a solitary European stood by a table on which silver glinted. He was leaning forward, shaking hands with a young Indian boy. As the boy stepped back the cheers broke out and then the European straightened up and turned to the table where one large silver cup remained.

Although MacKendrick guessed, he said, "Who's the man giving the prizes?"

"Tom Gower, I think, yes it is. Harriet's pet."

He searched the dais for signs of someone who could be Gower's wife, without success. They were too far away. The cheering died down. "We're right at the end," Cynthia said, "that's the Victor Ludorum by the look of it."

Gower was speaking. MacKendrick could not see what sort of man he was. Standing alone he seemed tall, but he stooped a little, and he was thin. The voice was pitched high, and sometimes words came across, meaningless outside their context; then right at the end MacKendrick caught the name Vidyasagar, for Gower pronounced it clearly, almost with pride. As soon as he had done so everyone clapped enthusiastically; the heads of the crowd swayed as though a breeze rippled through it and arms were raised to clap the young athlete on his shoulders as he went towards the dais. MacKendrick watched intently, and afterwards he told himself he had sensed that something untoward was about to happen. At the back of the crowd some boys were laying hold of long poles; groups of boys were detaching themselves one by one, standing a little apart as if awaiting a signal.

When Vidyasagar stood in front of Gower both of them waited for the cheers to die down. The crowd quietened and in the following silence Gower picked up the large silver cup and held it out for Vidyasagar to take.

But instead of taking it the boy suddenly turned on his heel and marched back along the way he had come. The crowd became motionless and at the back someone shouted. Immediately the boys lifted the poles up into the air and MacKendrick saw that between the poles was stretched a long white banner. Other banners rose up and the crowd broke loose as voices were raised, singing.

"My God! It's a demonstration!" Cynthia clutched his arm. Her lips were parted; excitement shone in her eyes. "The bloody cheek! Of all the bloody cheek! Did you *see*? That black bastard insulted Tom."

MacKendrick nodded. Gower was still standing in front of the dais, holding the Victor Ludorum which Vidyasagar had refused to accept. Behind him the others had come to their feet and now he was lost to sight as they thronged round him.

"What do the banners say? What's that writing?"

"It's not in English. It's Hindi. I don't read Hindi. My God. The bloody little bastards."

"Are those people on the dais in any danger?"

"No, but we are. They're coming this way and they'll scare the horse." Already the tonga-wallah was jabbering and stretching his arm heavenwards, urging the horse round. Cynthia shouted at him and talked to MacKendrick at the same time. "*Dusre taraf!* He's a fool. He's going the wrong way. *Nai, nai,* Sanderson Sahib *ki bungalow, jeldi!* He'll panic the bloody horse. I know these damned drivers. *Dusre taraf!* We'll end our days in a bloody monsoon ditch. *Harn, harn,* Sanderson Sahib *ki bungalow.*"

The tonga jerked forward. Dust swirled, and dust swirled round the crowd on the *maidan*. As they swept away down the cinder track MacKendrick thought he saw young Vidyasagar chaired on comrades' shoulders, and then the ugly brick walls of the Laxminarayan College cut off all further view of the prizegiving.

But out of the tumult a procession was forming. It uncoiled itself slowly from the *maidan* like a serpent: Vidyasagar, borne by two youths, behind them the banner with the inscription *India for Indians*, behind that another banner, *Back Up Fair Play* (this, in English); then youths with Gandhi caps perched jauntily, whitely on black-haired heads, all manner of youths, laughing, gesticulating, engaged uproariously in private jokes in the midst of public endeavour. The procession threaded down the dust road which joined the road to Ooni, turned left towards the station, the barking of dogs marking its advance, great clouds of dust its retreat.

At the station the rear carriage of a waiting passenger train was uncoupled; a fruit-seller's wares were upset in a tumble of red oranges from the portable basket counter with its twisted stem, while a score of brown and black hands beat on the closed grille of the ticket office and chanting voices demanded free rides to Ooni. The grille remained shut and, finding his forces scattered in various and unco-ordinated mischiefs, Vidyasagar made an attempt to rally them and reform them for a march through the town. At this moment the police stepped in, because a harmless, high-spirited prank on the outer fringe of the cantonment, in the no-man's land of the railway station, was one thing, a procession with banners through the town, another. Already word had it that Muslims were barring doors and shuttering windows.

The students were scattered but Vidyasagar and a few chosen stalwarts returned to the cantonment and went gleefully into the Chinese Restaurant in Cannon Road. Upstairs they sat by the open window and looked across the road to the offices of the *Marapore Gazette*. Beneath their table a brush and tin of white paint were hidden. When it grew dark the boys clattered down the wooden stairs and surged across the road to stand clustered around the building while Vidyasagar, screened by his companions from watchful eyes, painted letters with bold strokes on the wall. Then, laughing, arm in arm they went singing into the darkness.

The proprietor of the Chinese Restaurant waddled across the road from his doorway to see what the boys had been up to. Plain, for all to see, the newly painted words shone luminously:
Go Home Gower.

The room in Sanderson's bungalow had been empty when he and Mrs. Mapleton arrived, empty except for the whispering bearers who waited beneath the arched doorways which led into adjacent rooms. At one end of the main room, a long trestle table, laid with a white cloth, held glasses, bottles and a silver punch bowl. It was dark inside. Chicks, dampened throughout the day, screened the verandah. A ceiling fan swirled the parched air around the room. She had called for drinks. She had talked. She had talked the sunlight outside away, for now it was dusk. She had talked the emptiness away for now the room was full. It was full of people he did not know and to whom she did not bother to introduce him. He knew it was her way of paying him out for not rising to her bait. He guessed the little man who kept looking furtively at him through myopic eyes was his host. Sometimes he heard Sanderson's voice, high-pitched and effeminate. He swallowed his third glass of punch. The punch was warm and sticky. He stared round the room. Unreal it was, unexpected like the end of all journeys. He knew he was going to get drunk.

"Enjoy your swim?" Milner, planting himself in front of Mac-Kendrick, suppressed a belch.

"Sure. It was great. Skol."

"Cheers. Glad to see you've found your way around. Who d'you know?"

"You. Mrs. Mapleton. She brought me here."

Milner grinned and winked. "Quick work, even for Cynth. Don't call her Cynth by the way. Hates it. I always call her Cynth. Hates me. Know Sanderson?"

"That little guy?"

"That's him. Hey, Sandy!"

The little man came over, cautiously, peering. His hand, in MacKendrick's, was cold and smooth. MacKendrick, smiling, thought: He's a fairy.

Milner was saying, "Sandy, you ought to meet one of your guests. Yankee type. Name of MacKendrick."

MacKendrick nodded and said, "*Joe* MacKendrick. Hi." He realised that he was drunker than he had thought; consciously adopting the mannerisms limeys expected. Sanderson held on to his hand and said something he did not catch. He leaned closer.

"I only said 'Hello, Joe'." Sanderson, blushing and nodding, backed away a little. Then he said, "I'm sorry I didn't say hello before, only I couldn't quite think who you were, and of course we're all frightfully *distrait* about the *prize*-giving episode." Sanderson retreated into the crowd and, looking round, Mac-Kendrick found that Milner had gone too. He caught a glimpse of him standing in a corner, talking to one of the Indian women, whose sarees splashed colour into the room. The Indian men, dressed with one exception in European clothes, were teachers at the College, he supposed; the women their wives and daughters. They all seemed to be drinking orange squash.

"These are known as fraternisation parties."

MacKendrick looked down. A short, middle-aged Indian in a brown lounge suit and striped shirt stood by his side. He was darker skinned than most of the others, and the skin beneath his finger nails was pink. He raised his glass and drank. Then he said, "You are an American, I believe?"

"That's so. Name's MacKendrick. Joe G. MacKendrick."

"My name is Gupta. You are a journalist?"

"No. Are you?" He looked over Gupta's head and manoeuvred so that he could watch the entrance.

"Yes, I am a journalist," Gupta replied. "I was thinking perhaps you came to be in at the kill?"

"I don't get you."

Gupta sipped delicately. He was drinking punch.

He said, "To see, in a manner of speaking, the last days of the British Raj."

"I'm here for a vacation."

"Nevertheless, you will be seeing it. Here already you are seeing. Let me tell you something. I have known there to be such parties – such fraternisation parties – held you will understand in most cases in the out-of-doors. At one end of the lawn there will be gathered the representatives of the Raj, and at the other those of us who have passed some test of whose nature we are not aware but the reward for which is the invitation to the party."

"Well?"

"Then, at a signal, perhaps that of a raised eyebrow from the Sahib to his Memsahib, the Raj will cross the lawn *en bloc* and they will then – I am thinking the expression is *mingle*."

"Well?"

"After the mingling has been going on for, say, half-an-hour, all will politely bid farewell, the Raj will return across the lawn, and we, we will heave sighs of relief and find our way back to where we came from."

"Is that so?"

"Here you will see there is, unfortunately, no lawn. It is difficult. But you will be observing soon that the middle of the floor serves the same purpose. Already there are, shall I say, embryo groups."

"You speak English well."

"I learned to speak it in England. There would be no career you will understand without sufficient knowledge of this foreign tongue."

"You don't like this party?"

Gupta put his head on one side, in the now familiar Indian gesture. Then he said, "I do not care much at all for parties, but I would not insult Mr. Sanderson by refusing his invitation when I had no previous engagement."

MacKendrick turned round and held out his glass to the sullen servant behind the punch bowl. It was refilled. He carried it, spilling a little, to his mouth and drank deeply. Then he turned again to Gupta who was watching him with some amusement. There was no doubt, MacKendrick thought, that the Indians had a distinctive smell.

"Talking of insults, Mr. Gupta – what are they going to do to that little bastard?"

"Who is the little bastard?"

"That Vidyasagar."

Gupta laughed, gently. "He is only a boy. It is a gesture he has made."

"He needs someone to make a gesture on his ass."

"So?" Then, "You are not in India before?"

"No. But my brother – " He cut himself short. This was no place to conjure visions to himself of Dwight.

"Your brother you were saying?"

"He's dead." Abruptly, like that, you could dismiss a man. MacKendrick moved, as if to dismiss Gupta too, but Gupta clung.

"In the war? He is dead in the war?"

"Yes. In the war."

"He died in India? In Burma? And you make a pilgrimage?"

"No. I make business. I sell." He drank again. The glass was empty. He said, "But Vidyasagar now. Pity he doesn't feel like you about insulting people. Mr. Gower was insulted today."

Why, he thought, should he champion Gower?

Gupta's eyes brightened. The smile on his lips remained. "Mr. Gower is knowing India many years, Mr. MacKandrick. There is a tradition of insults. Perhaps Vidyasagar is remembering those?"

"Y' mean it's all right for Vidyasagar to insult Tom Gower because Gower's British?"

Gupta shrugged, disclaiming responsibility. "In the past were many insults, you will understand. Not involving persons, Mr. MacKandrick . . ."

"MacKendrick."

". . . but involving the soul."

"The soul?"

"There is no insult between Vidyasagar and Mr. Gower as men. . . ."

"Men? Why, you call that little bastard . . ."

". . . as men." Gupta paused. "But in the souls who shall decide who insults and who is insulted?"

"What's all that add up to? That Gower's soul insulted Vidyasagar's?"

59

"I am saying – Who shall decide that?"

"You, apparently."

"Excuse me. You are a friend of Mr. Gower?"

"I've never met him. I've heard his name. And I saw him insulted today on the *maidan*."

"Tom Gower is a name not unknown, you see. He is in India many years and takes our problems to his heart."

"Well, then . . ."

"But, Mr. MacKandrick, they are *our* problems, but his heart is not our heart. A solution to the problems of one is not found in the heart of another but in one's own. We cannot accept *his* solutions to *our* problems."

"What solutions? What'you talking about, Gupta? I don't understand all this high-flown stuff."

Gupta's eyes dulled. MacKendrick thought: He's a fanatic. About what though? Instinctively he shrank from him and Gupta noticed it. He came closer. "Mr. Gower is a very kind-hearted gentleman. In the war, you will understand, he did admirable work trying to pass on some of the lessons he had learned to others of his race more – impulsive, more imperialistic, shall I say? They came, these young impulsive ones, to lead our own young men in battle. But Mr. Gower helped to make them see that our young men were also men, with thoughts and feelings much as theirs. He went to the schools where they trained and told them of India and of we who live in it. All this is good. All this is admirable. When he tells people of his own race how they should comport themselves in our country, we applaud him. But when, for some reason, he begins to tell us how *we* should comport ourselves, what *we* should do, what we should think, what solutions to our problems we should find – "

"You insult him?"

Gupta sighed. "Our modern young men are less restrained than we who have been schooled to listen quietly to well-meant advice."

"Listen to it but not take it?"

60

"Perhaps that is so. Lord Mountbatten, you will understand, thinks perhaps he is giving us advice and that we are taking it. But he is merely formalising with impressive documents those plans which we ourselves have made."

"For Pakistan and India?"

"Precisely."

"Don't tell me that as a Hindu – I guess you are a Hindu with a name like Gupta?" Gupta nodded, smilingly. "Don't tell me you planned Pakistan. I thought Hindus hated Pakistan."

"I was not speaking of religions, but of the people of India. The people of India have planned Pakistan and they have planned India. If we Hindus regret Pakistan then equally the Muslims regret its size and lack of any corridor between its two isolated areas. This is of no importance to the argument I am making."

"And where does Tom Gower fit into all this?"

"He tells us we should accept Pakistan with warm hearts."

Gupta sipped his drink and waited for MacKendrick's reaction. MacKendrick stared at him.

"I don't get your particular line of double-talk, Mr. Gupta. You said just now – "

"I know. I said just now that we had planned Pakistan as a people. And you think that therefore we should accept it. Who though is 'we'? Now I am speaking as a Hindu. When Mr. Gower speaks to us through the columns of the little paper he edits he should be speaking to us as Hindus. Although I must add I regret that Mr. Gower, as an Englishman, should speak to us through the columns of the *Marapore Gazette* at all. It is an appointment given to him by Mr. Gopi Nair, who is a gentleman of some standing and wealth. It is Mr. Nair's paper. He has another in Travanapatam. That is in Southern India where he also has a cotton mill. He has a considerable quantity of land in and around Marapore. He is present owner of Smith's Hotel where you are staying. He is standing over there, by himself, watching us."

MacKendrick looked round. It was the man in the odd costume: a long-skirted coat with a high neckband. He was sipping an orangeade and gazing thoughtfully, not now as Gupta had said at them, but into space; a thin, ascetic-looking man with a light skin, a hooked, aquisitive nose; a lonely man, MacKendrick guessed.

He said, "Let's forget Mr. Nair. I want to know why Tom Gower should adopt an all-Hindu policy for the *Marapore Gazette*. Apart from the fact he's British, and liberal-minded I guess, there must be some Muslims in Marapore."

"Oh, there are. But then, Mr. MacKandrick, is it not so that these same Muslims should not now be in Marapore?"

"Hell, where else should they be?"

"But in Pakistan. If they are insisting on tearing asunder our mother-country, then they should go to their own part of it. As no doubt many of them will." Gupta finished his drink and placed it carefully on the table, brushing lightly against MacKendrick as he did so. He said, "I am thinking you find Indian politics a little complicated, Mr. MacKandrick."

"That's an understatement."

"No doubt. But it is for this reason people who are not Indians should not interfere with them." Suddenly Gupta paused. The smile vanished. MacKendrick thought, when Gupta spoke again, that his voice faltered occasionally. He said, "There are those here, Mr. MacKandrick, who will tell you never have the British been so popular. You will see Indians and British alike fraternising as never before. The reactionaries among the Europeans will say, Ha! Already they regret we are going. And the reactionaries among ourselves will perhaps feel such regret. But all the time, you will understand, there will be much laughter and pleasantries. I do not myself ignore the fact that the British are leaving with some good grace. But I will not disguise, even from myself, that I am glad they are taking heed of us at last. And that it is a good grace thrust upon them, like greatness. Now we are on the brink of our freedom. To forget what we have suffered for it would be infamous. Now we wish to be alone with our problem. We do not wish for interference in matters which I have said already

62

concern the soul. Buy our goods from us. Sell your goods to us. Accept us as a nation among nations. Be extending the hand of friendship – we will place our own in yours. But do not let that hand hold also a dissecting knife to probe our ills. We have our own knife. Sharper than yours. When you go home, be telling your countrymen this thing and you will be doing better service for us than if you were living here twenty years 'understanding' us. Twenty years interfering with us."

Gupta bowed and turned away to join one of the tutors' wives, who smiled and flung her slim brown arm up to him from where she sat, regally upon a sofa. Gold bangles fell from wrist to elbow, an accompaniment to bell-like laughter as Gupta took her hand; as though they were comrades.

MacKendrick glanced round the room. Gupta had been right. The centre of the floor had become empty. Groups had settled intimately around the walls, the Indians on one side, the Europeans on the other. He was aware, for the first time, of intrigue. It was like a ghost in the room, a ghost acknowledged by eyes, by the movements of hands, by turned shoulders; denied only in speech. Nair, alone, stared at him.

The Gowers had not come. The party had passed its peak. Now there were only the minutes moving towards the moment of first farewells. Cynthia was talking to Milner, with animation and, he guessed, with false flattery. It was the hour for masks, the hour of lies. It was just then that he saw Miss Haig. As he crossed the room to the chair in which she sat he saw the two thick walking sticks with their rubber ferrules which were propped against it.

"I've been waiting to catch your eye," she said as he came to her, then added when she saw he was looking at the sticks, "Yes, they're mine. I'm rather a lame old thing. I came in while you and Mr. Gupta were having your talk. Have you had a nice time?"

He sat, without permission, on the arm of her chair. Her hand sought his and clasped it with a timid offer of friendship. "No," he replied, "and I'm glad you've come."

"You didn't send the tonga back, you know."

"Hell! Oh hell, I'm sorry." Seated, liquor haze caressed his mind, smoothed out his speech. "It was all – all rather a mêlée – "

"Another?"

"A mêlée. Crowds of people on the *maidan*. We had to run away from 'em. Cynth said the hoss'd be scared." He pulled himself together, seeing her rueful smile. He said seriously, "They insulted Tom Gower."

Her eyes clouded as she nodded. "Yes, I heard. But I want you to tell me about it. The story's got a bit confused by now." She indicated the nearest group of Europeans.

"It was the prizes," he said. "He was handing 'em out. Then Vidyasagar comes up for the Victor Ludorum. It's the big moment. We're all ready to cheer like hell and wham! the little bastard turns on his heel and leaves Tom Gower standing there like –"; his voice petered out. Miss Haig said, "Then there was a demonstration I hear, with banners and everything. What did the banners say?"

"I couldn't read 'em. They were all in that funny sort of script. Hindi, I guess."

"Was the demonstration *really* against Tom, or just us in general, or the staff or what? Indian students demonstrate on the slightest provocation you know. I hear they're coming out on strike."

"Why?"

"In sympathy with half-a-dozen of them who were suspended for cheating in the exams."

"Hell."

"So the demonstration might have been against anything. Perhaps Vidyasagar would have refused the cup whoever was handing it to him?" She seemed eager for him to agree.

"Maybe. But I don't think so." He searched for a cigarette.

"Why not?"

"I've been talking to Mr. Gupta."

"Mr. Gupta is not a gentleman I trust."

64

"He's certainly anti-Tom Gower."

"He has quite an ordinary reason. He used to edit the *Gazette* before Mr. Nair offered the post to Tom." She hesitated. "I've heard he's also a member of the Rashtriya Swayam Sewak Sangh."

"The which?"

"R.S.S. is easier to say. It's a militant Hindu organisation. Fascist I'm told. Like a Ku Klux Klan." She looked up at him. "Perhaps not quite like that, but I like to draw easy comparisons."

He turned away from her and said, "D'you know if Tom Gower's coming to the party?"

"Sandy says he is."

"Where'd he go from the *maidan*?"

"Sandy says he went home in the jeep. They have a lovely little jeep, all painted yellow. Not shiny yellow. Flat yellow."

He lighted his cigarette.

She said, "He had to take his wife home. She wasn't well." She hesitated. "So Sandy says." She had been twisting the rings round her fingers. Suddenly she looked up at him again. Dorothy's unspoken name lay between them. He thought she was going to say: How did you know Tom was married? And perhaps she had intended to. He had an odd feeling that she was prepared to be his ally.

But when she spoke all she said was, "You've met Sandy of course?"

"Yeh. Major Milner introduced us."

She was looking round the room from one group to another. "Poor Sandy," she said; then, "Poor Sandy, poor Tom, poor Frank. And me. It's going to be as Cynthia said. All the pukka people are going home or to Kenya and places like that. There'll just be the cranks, the Eurasians, the gone-natives and the no-goods."

"Perhaps –" he began.

"Perhaps what?"

"Perhaps it'll be quite nice like that."

She said nothing for a moment, but he saw her smile, and then her hand patted his and she replied, "That's nice of you to say that. And I think I'll ask you to fetch me another drink. I've just time for one."

He stood up, dismayed. "You're not going?"

She nodded. "Very soon now."

He wanted to say: Are you going to Tom Gower's place? But with the words on the tip of his tongue he found he dare not say them. "But you've only just got here."

"That's not my fault. It's yours. It took ages to find a tonga for me, and ages to get me into it. And I'd arranged to be called for here, otherwise I wouldn't have come at all."

He licked his lips, they were so dry. "Where are you going?"

"I'm going to see Jimmy at Smith's."

For a moment he did not understand.

"The Maharajah of Kalipur," she explained. He remembered. As he went over to the table to fetch her drink he found he had left the European section. Here were the Indians. He was isolated. Suddenly he was angry; angry at not having the guts to ask Miss Haig straight out exactly where in Cannon Avenue the Gowers lived; angry at the people who pressed round him, hemming him in; as his own gutlessness hemmed him in.

A room full of niggers. A room full of goddam niggers. As he returned with a drink for Miss Haig and a drink for himself he found himself wondering how any white person could stay in a place where a sawn-off little runt of a schoolboy was allowed to insult a European and get away with it; how Miss Haig, herself, could stay. But as he handed her the glass she took it in her left hand, the hand with the rings. Governess! She'd been laid by a nigger. In her time she must've been laid by a nigger. It was obscene, the thought of it, for she was old and lame, and the flesh of her neck was withered.

There were other people gathered round her chair now. He stood to one side, avoiding their eyes, ignoring their smiles. He drank. He found he could not focus properly. Was this tall woman with the dry skin talking to him? He watched her mouth, fascinated. Her lipstick had become gummy with perspiration. Her thin, English voice nauseated him, so sexless it was, so hard, penetrating. And the man by her side, nodding, staring at him and through him; he too, by his immobility, his peculiarly English complacency, helped him to feel again the strength of the shell with which, earlier, he had tried to arm himself. He stood outside them all, beyond them, and saw them with their heads in the sands, their rears ripe and ready for the boot. They were stubborn, these Britishers on the point of departure, stubborn like the aged and the dying. About them was the smell of decay, the smell of the sickroom. They were clearing out of India and leaving the smell behind them. If you sniffed, now, it smarted in your nostrils. Decay. Death. An end to ambition. A burial of pride.

He turned away, tired of the eyes and the lips, aghast in his drunkenness at the reflection of himself he saw in these people who hemmed him tightly into his corner, for was he not the same, at heart, as they? Self-absorbed, afraid? Kids, he thought: kids playing with all the bitter resourcefulness of children, as he and Dwight had played, himself bound, his feet, his legs, his body blackened and scorched by burning twigs which Dwight, big and tough and mocking, thrust at him. Which of these people here was a Dwight, and which a victim of someone like Dwight? Dwight throwing him into the cold pond one Autumn morning when an early frost rimed the brittle, yellowing leaves: Swim, you yellow belly! Swim, you bastard! and then Dwight's fist pounding; his arms held tightly behind him by another boy whose fear of Dwight matched his own fear.

He felt sick.

And he was glad *she* had not come and would not, if Miss Haig were right, be coming after all. Perhaps she had known there would be ghosts to face in this haunted room. What woman could watch her husband move amongst enemies? Unless she did not love him. And he remembered there must have been a time

67

when she had not loved him, had been unfaithful to him. If Gower came now, she would be alone: but where?

There had been a sound outside and suddenly everyone stopped talking and listened. It came again, close, quite close, and then again; a klaxon horn and the noise of a car braking, its wheels biting into the gravel of the drive.

Miss Haig was already struggling to her feet and everyone was looking at her. It was MacKendrick who remembered she needed help and came to her side to hand her the heavy sticks.

Sanderson called, "You're not going, Harriet?"

"Yes, I'm afraid so. The car's for me –"; already a servant hovered in the doorway.

"But, Harriet, I didn't know you had a car!"

"I have tonight, Sandy."

She said to MacKendrick, "See me to the door."

She said goodbye, and now the room came to life again. She whispered to him, "They all know whose car it is, do you?"

"The Maharajah's?"

"Yes." She walked very slowly. Tiny beads of sweat pricked out upon her upper lip. "Yes," she repeated, "it's Jimmy's. And do you know? I think it's thought to be rather *fast* of me." She stopped, as though for breath, but now MacKendrick saw that coming up the steps towards them was a handsome young Indian dressed in chauffeur's uniform. He saluted and came, grinning, to take her other arm. A reunion. Somewhere in the world, then, there was gentleness.

" Hello, Shafi. That's kind of you."

Slowly they went down the steps. The door of the Cadillac was already open for her, and sitting next to the driver's seat there was another man.

"You've got an escort, Miss Haig," MacKendrick pointed out.

She peered, and waved a hand to the other man, saying, in a low voice, "Jimmy's doing me proud. That's his bodyguard." Her fingers tightened on his arm. "He can take over from you

68

now, Mr. MacKendrick, and *he* won't get drunk. Or should I have said just tiddly?"

To help her in, Shafi had to go round and open the other door so that he could receive her in his arms as she painfully stepped inside. When at last she was settled, the door shut, the window turned down so that she could speak to him, she said, "Now go back and enjoy the party."

"I couldn't hitch a ride with you?"

She seemed surprised. "But why?"

"You're going to Smith's, aren't you? Isn't that where you're meeting this Maharajah?"

"Yes, I'm going to Smith's. But you *must* stay at the party." She paused. "Aren't you going to wait so that you can meet Tom Gower?"

A voice behind him said, "Who wants to meet Tom Gower?"

MacKendrick swung round, startled, and Miss Haig, leaning closer to the open window, called, "Why, Tom? Is that you?"

MacKendrick stepped back, nodding in answer to Gower's nod, then Gower bent over the window and said, "Hello, Harriet."

"Hello, Tom."

"Are you just leaving?"

"What d'you think I'm doing? Tom, dear. How awful that was about this afternoon."

"You mean about Vidyasagar?"

"What else should I mean? I think it was dreadful for you. You were asked all the way down from Ooni especially to give the prizes, weren't you?"

"Yes, we came from Ooni."

"How's Dorothy?"

"She has a head."

"I'm sorry." She cleared her throat. "Tom," she said at last, "this is Mr. MacKendrick. He's an American and he's come to Marapore because someone said he could have a nice vacation here. But he sells farm equipment and you and he must go and have a drink. Actually it's all rather depressing and ghosty in there tonight and if it gets too bad take the poor boy home and entertain him."

Gower straightened up. The lights from the bungalow shone on one side of his face. The cheeks looked quite sunken and the hand MacKendrick grasped was skeletal.

"Tom?"

Gower turned back, "Yes, Harriet?"

MacKendrick, his brain cleared, studied the thin line of Gower's back, the narrow shoulders. He was wearing a soiled and crumpled bush shirt and khaki drill trousers.

"You *are* the most unobservant man."

"What d'you mean?"

"Here I am sitting up like a Duchess in a limousine and you don't even say, 'What a nice car'!"

"It is a nice car. Is it yours?"

"Hopeless! Absolutely hopeless! Bend closer." She whispered to him, then leaning back she waved a hand. "Now go and give Mr. MacKendrick a good time. He wants to know all about India and he's a beautiful swimmer. That should be enough to start the ball rolling." She called out, "Look me up some time, Mr. MacKendrick."

"I surely will."

They stood back, waved, and watched the car slide away, the klaxon sounding as it turned out of the driveway on to the road. Then, together, awkward in each other's company, they turned and mounted the steps.

It was odd, MacKendrick thought, to find himself walking with the man he had, in his heart, already cuckolded.

6

There was no moon but the car's headlamps created their own tunnel of light through the tree-lined road. The car slowed; a column of ox-carts lumbered towards them, the animals' large eyes touched to flame. Where were they going, she wondered? She closed her eyes and tried to assemble her thoughts into coherence. The day, which had begun like any other day with only heat and tiredness to combat, had become confused and shapeless. She should, she knew, be thinking of Jimmy, and of all the things she had to tell him; small, unimportant things which always seemed to interest him, so eager was he for news, so kind.

Pain came. Perhaps he only pretended. Perhaps she was a 'duty', his letters duty letters, his visits duty visits. Oh, no! Not that! Her mother's firm, northern voice had given such duties their callous place in life: now, if she listened, that voice was still there, like a warning; it came clearly, so that the years seemed but so many pebbles dropped one by one into a well, a well of echoes and ripples. She pressed her lips together. Soon the ripples would quieten, the echoes die away. But, as yet, they stirred, danced intricate measures of sound and light: and here they came capering, her thoughts, motley and undisciplined; thoughts of Jimmy, of Mr. MacKendrick, of Cynthia, Sandy and Tom – above all of Tom – and Tom's wife. Had she and Mr. MacKendrick been lovers? There was something, something unexplained.

She came to with a start. The car had stopped and Shafi had opened the door. She saw they were already at Smith's, and this, she felt, was wrong. For a moment she sat where she was. A voice, clear, unmistakably her mother's, said: Your life is ending. She leaned forward into Shafi's sturdy arms with a fluttering heart.

"I must phone," she whispered to him.

Desai helped her to the office. She heard voices, Shafi's and her own, and knew that someone had gone in to Jimmy to say that she was here. Her focus was wrong, her surroundings distorted. She asked for a number and, having done so, could not understand why she was ringing. The action had been dictated. Tom's gaunt, weary face swam in front of her eyes. He had looked so hurt.

"This is Miss Haig. I want to speak to Mrs. Gower, please, Abdul." She was speaking to Tom's servant. The Cadillac was driven round to the back of the hotel. She waited a long time.

71

"Hello?"

"Harriet Haig speaking. Are you all right?"

"I had a head, but it's nearly gone."

"Dorothy –" She knew her voice sounded unnatural.

"Yes?"

"How awful for Tom."

"Yes."

"Were you on the dais?"

"Yes."

"What will Tom do?"

A pause.

"Nothing, I expect."

Miss Haig said, "I've just come from the party at Sandy's and I saw Tom for a few moments. It's all rather dreary there."

"I expect it is."

Without thinking, "Try and help him, Dorothy."

Another pause. She felt it was not herself holding the telephone; not herself, but a new, perhaps despicable woman.

Dorothy said, "I'm not sure I know what you mean."

"He looked ghastly tonight, I thought. Try and understand what I'm saying."

"Then why don't you say it?"

"Because I haven't really the right."

"Then why did you ring?"

"Because I'm fond of Tom. You must have seen what's been happening recently."

"Nothing's happening."

Miss Haig detected the other woman's bitterness. Her own bitterness flowed. "There's a campaign against him," she said.

"Tom's never been popular."

"He was with the Indians."

"Isn't he still?"

"How can you say that after what happened today? They were all in it. Mr. Gupta and Mr. Nair as well."

"He's only got himself to blame."

"And only himself to depend on?"

No answer. Miss Haig went on, "Tom's dedicated his whole life to India, you must have known that when you married him."

"I did."

"Then help him now. He's blind to the fact he's losing touch with them. No, that's wrong. He sees that, but he's not understanding why. He doesn't see that *they* don't see any more what he stands for."

"Do you?"

Did she? She said, "I think so."

"Then you help him."

"You're his wife."

"Haven't we talked long enough to no purpose? Why've you rung like this?"

"Tom's in danger of losing his job on the *Gazette*."

"There's always Ooni."

"Nair finances that too. And you hate Ooni."

"Do I?"

"You hate Ooni and you hate Marapore. But, Dorothy, there's nothing at home in England for a man like Tom. If things fall apart here he's a broken man."

"Why do you say there's nothing at home?"

"Only as a warning. That's what you'd like, isn't it? You want to take Tom back to England. You can't bear the thought of staying now that everyone's going. You want him to lose his job and see no prospect for another." She paused for breath. She thought for a moment that Dorothy had rung off. She called, "Hello? Dorothy?"

And Dorothy said, then, "You don't begin to understand."

"You should have gone to Sandy's with him."

"What's that got to do with it?"

"You should stand by him."

"I'm going to ring off –"

"Dorothy!"

73

"Well?"

"Forgive me. I'm –"

"What?"

"It doesn't matter." But it does, she thought. It matters that something should be saved for the future, for when we can breathe again, something which will help to fashion the new in the comfortable image of the old.

"Are you unwell?"

Her surroundings were pulled back into focus by the unkindness in the girl's voice. She felt spiritless. She said, "I'm all right. Why not ring Tom and tell him to come home. He can't be enjoying that party. They're all against him."

"He'll be home for dinner."

"He wants company, Dorothy. Ring him at Sandy's and tell him to bring back that young American."

"What young American?"

"A nice boy. He doesn't seem to know anyone. He's here – here on a vacation and only got into Smith's last night." She hesitated. Then she said, "His name's Mr. MacKendrick." And now her courage failed her. Despising herself she put the receiver back on the hook. She sat still for a moment – praying; indiscriminate prayers for grace, for safety, for those she loved and for those she feared, and for those whose motives she did not understand.

And the first words Jimmy said to her as he came out of Room Three, with arms extended in welcome, were – "Harriet! Harriet! Tell me something I want to know. Who is Tom Gower?"

They embraced. She was taller than he. He was so very much like a bright-eyed, mischievous, well-fed bird, she thought, as with exaggerated care he helped her through the hazard of draught screens into the empty lounge. The ultra-modern wall lights glowed behind their pink glass.

"Oh, let me get my breath first." She sank gratefully into a leather armchair. He stood in front of her, compact, alive, a boy

74

still; a boy whose mind and manners she had shaped. He was her one creation, and only now did she realise how much she had feared he would have no time for her. Tears of relief came into her eyes, but he pretended not to have seen them. He strutted round the room on his short, stocky legs, waving his arms. "Good old Smith's! Look! At that very window my great-uncle bled to death from a hunting wound. So they say. And they say he deserved it for he was such a very rotten shot. Freddie!" He shouted. "I've brought Freddie with me. He's my new personal assistant – you see how civilised I've become? But he's no good." His voice dropped to a whisper. The corners of his mouth turned down in mock dismay. And then laughter electrified his whole face. "There's a lovely rude story about Freddie, but I'm not going to tell it to you until –"

"Stop misbehaving, Jimmy."

He came and sat at her feet on a leather pouffe. "Do you know why I'm here, Harriet? Apart from coming to see you? Shall I tell you or do you want to guess? No, that would lead you into indiscretions. Guessing always does. Who's Tom Gower?"

But Freddie came in: a tall, bony Hindu whose real name Harriet never discovered. He seemed intimidated by the informality with which the Maharajah was surrounding himself. He had been given strict instructions to call him 'Mr. Smith' and the name came with difficulty to his tongue and to his sense of propriety. "Your High –"

"Ah!"

"Mr. Smith was calling?"

"Bring the paper I was reading. And tell the Manager we'll drink gin and lemon squash. You see, I've remembered your favourite drink. Tell him too that I've changed my mind and that we'll dine in my room. Suggest to him that we have both reached the age of discretion. My dear . . . ." He turned to her, and Freddie went away like an outraged gazelle. "I came all the way from Romantic Kalipur – remind me to tell you of a plan I have to issue highly coloured travel brochures with a photo of myself on an

75

elephant – all the way to see and talk to my Harriet. The children send their love of course and Boo told me I mustn't bore you with a lot of twaddle."

She was laughing, a handkerchief held ready to dry her eyes when next he looked away. Boo was his wife. How they had laughed when first Boo had said, "Don't talk twaddle." She had said the word, picked up from Harriet, so beautifully, and when they laughed she had half covered her face with the edge of her saree in the traditional gesture of modesty.

"So I mustn't talk twaddle if Boo tells me not to. I came to see you and to ask you about this admirable Mr. Gower."

"Oh, he is. He *is* admirable."

"Tell me about him."

"He edits the *Marapore Gazette*."

"I know that. That much I have discovered." He grimaced. She felt herself borne up on the familiar waves of the past. He went on, "I know all that. Tell me what I don't know."

Freddie appeared. This time, to Harriet, he looked like a heron, tricked into wearing a dark blue lounge suit. He gave Jimmy a creased and folded copy of the *Gazette* and retired once more, disconsolate, hand in hand with the ghost of his own ineffectualness.

"Here in this paper I find a man of my own heart. And it was fate, Harriet." He looked round the room and leaned forward. "The table in my room was shorter in one leg than in the others. But Mr. Desai introduced this paper into the scheme of things and put the matter to rights. If there's one thing I do not like it's rickety tables. And if there's anything I like less than rickety tables it's rickety tables with paper crutches." He shook the paper. Pages dropped out on to the floor. He ignored them. "With my own hands I removed the paper, and having removed it what normal man could resist opening and reading it? Remember how you used to find me reading in all sorts of odd places?"

"Indeed I do."

"Well, reading the paper, the latest issue believe it or not, I find this Mr. Gower publicly supporting my recent decision to

76

become an independent state and cede neither to India or to Pakistan. What do you think of that?"

She smiled. She said, "I think you're a fraud."

His eyes widened. "Why?"

"You told me you came to see me and find out about Tom Gower. It's quite obvious that the first you ever heard of Tom Gower was when you spread that dirty paper out on the floor in this hotel."

"How do you know I spread it on the floor?"

"You always did. Anyway, I've caught you out. I'm still spry enough to spot *that* sort of inconsistency."

He was crestfallen. Then, with a bound, he was on his feet. "Mere play with words, Harriet. I said I came to see you. That is true. There you are in front of me. I said I came to find out about Tom Gower. Well, I'm finding out, if slowly. Tell me more."

The drinks arrived. She took advantage of the interruption to say, "No, you tell me more about you."

"What do you want to know? Is this enough gin, by the way?"

"Too much."

"I'll have this one, then."

"I want to know two things."

"Ask away."

"First and foremost, where are you going?"

"Delhi."

"When?"

"When I can find the energy." He handed her a glass. "I always go to Delhi in easy stages, whenever possible."

"What are you going to do there?"

"Confer. My dear Harriet! What a question! In Delhi at this moment, history is being made. Don't deny me the right to participate, and try to suppress your surprise at my doing so." He drank.

"Very well. I take it you felt Smith's Hotel would be a pleasant place to rest and get your courage up." He smiled, but she saw the faint shadow of hurt upon his face. "Now the other thing," she said.

"What's that?"

"This so-called declaration of independence of yours. It's created quite a fuss and bother."

"Has it? Oh, only in Kalipur and surrounding districts, dear Harriet."

"And in Marapore."

"Well, we're close neighbours. But our little volley of small-arms fire is a mere trickle of sound punctuating the brief silences of a larger artillery barrage. So to speak."

"You talk as if it's not seriously meant. A sort of private joke. Is it?"

He shrugged. Then he raised his glass and they drank in silence. When he spoke again, although he kept up the light, bantering tone, she saw a Jimmy she had not seen before: one who had gone beyond her into the incomprehensible world of affairs; as Tom, in his way, had gone.

Jimmy was saying, "The Mountbatten plan leaves the Princely States in the lurch, my dear. He hadn't any other choice, of course, but the lurch is the lurch. Half my subjects are Muslims and half are Hindus. I am a Hindu. I have three alternatives. I can become a part of Pakistan and then from the religious point of view half my subjects will be aliens with the right to become refugees. I can cede to India. The same applies in reverse. The third alternative is for me to declare my independence. I can become a sovereign state. It is an interesting thought, don't you agree?"

"From what we hear it's more than a thought. You've said quite clearly you were going to do that. That's why Tom mentioned it in his article."

He looked at her, smiling. "I see you don't approve."

She flushed. "I wouldn't admit it to anyone but you."

"Why don't you approve?"

"It's – capricious. It's irresponsible. It couldn't work. You couldn't exist economically. You've always seen yourself how much we depend on each other."

"Capricious? The world is a caprice. Wouldn't work? The world's works are always seized up. Harriet, my dear, there's something you don't see. I see it. Your Tom Gower sees it. I can state it quite simply. Freedom is a starting point, not a goal. We're always fooling ourselves we can work towards it."

He poured himself more gin and lemon. She half raised a hand to stop him.

He was talking again. "Pakistan and India are not ends achieved. They are beginnings created by an effort of –" he paused, his chubby, small-boned hands waving in circles as though a word could be shaped by their play – " by an effort of will. I quote our Mr. Gower of course. That is what there must be in the beginning. An effort of will. Tom Gower sees that. I'm not joking, Harriet, when I say this thing he writes in his paper impresses me. He writes words I've only felt and haven't been able to express. But it's because I've felt them that I understand them when they're written. When he applauds Pakistan he is applauding this evidence of a will exerted, not a political achievement." He smiled. "I suspect our Hindu friends here fail to see that."

She nodded.

"And also," he said, moving away, returning, "I suspect they fail completely to comprehend that he praises *them* equally, praises me and praises his compatriots for precisely the same virtues. They don't understand a man who hasn't any familiar colours to show. To them that represents a subtle enemy in their midst. They want to see the colour of Tom Gower's flag, I expect. But Tom Gower hasn't got a flag, and neither have I for that matter. A flag begins as a symbol and ends as an idol. We have too many idols already." He stood in front of her. "I like your Tom Gower, but I suspect he is an unhappy man."

She felt he meant, as well: Because he is like me and I am an unhappy man. But he left the words unsaid.

79

"He was insulted today."

He raised his eyebrows. "By whom?"

She told him, and then she told him all she knew about Gower. When she had finished he drained his glass and said, "I know of this Nair. He is intimidated by the R.S.S., I'm told. He is a rich man who would have done well in Fascist Italy or Nazi Germany before the war." He grinned. "He'll – what's the expression? – put the skids under Mr. Gower if pressure is brought to bear on him. He toys with the R.S.S. and consequently toys with Gower."

"I think Tom's job *is* in the balance."

"Then he will go home to England with a broken heart."

She shook her head. "It'd be like uprooting a tree."

"Ah." Then: "Has he a wife?"

"Yes. They don't get on."

"What's she like, this wife of my idealistic friend Tom Gower?"

Harriet thought. But a vision of Dorothy would not come. "I don't know, Jimmy. I know I don't like her. She seems so shallow. Theatrical, too, if someone as cold as she is could ever be called theatrical. And I know she's an unhappy woman, but then Tom's never been in the mainstream of British Indian life. The pukka people rather despise him, although he's never actually been charged with going native, as we say. So perhaps Dorothy feels cut off." She shook her head. "I just don't know. She'd be glad if his career out here ended, I think, and they could go home to England. She's not the sort who's always talking about home, like some of them, home this and home that, but you can see she loathes it out here." She flushed. "It's so unfair," she said, angrily; "when she married Tom she was living in Calcutta with an aunt of some sort. Her parents were dead – planters, I think – and I believe she was actually born out here, so it isn't as if she was fresh out from England and married Tom in a sort of great romantic moment. They both *knew* India and she knew very well India was his life. She must have done. The right woman would have been a blessing to him."

"And she's the wrong one?"

She paused. "What have you in mind, Jimmy?"

"I have in mind to offer your Mr. Gower a job in Kalipur."
He watched her quietly. Then he said, "What's wrong, dear
Harriet?"

"It would be – so wonderful for him."

He knelt on the pouffe. He took her hand. "Why such a champion of this Tom Gower?"

"I don't know that either. Oh, don't ask so many questions.
You're being wretched to me." She squeezed his hand. "Tom's so
vulnerable. He's far too charitable, too."

"Like you?"

"Not like me. I'm old and stupid and self-absorbed. I'm
inquisitive, as well."

"Then like someone you knew?"

She stared at him.

"Someone you knew," he added, "a long time ago?"

"What do you mean?"

"Someone you came out to India to marry, my dear Harriet?"

"What do you know about that? It's not –"

"I know a little. When you first came to Kalipur father said
I wasn't to be unkind to you because of what he called your sad
history." He smiled, slightly.

Her hand twitched in his. She said, "No, no. It's all years ago."

"This man, he died, didn't he?"

"Typhus."

"I often wanted to ask you about him but I never dared. Was
he like Tom Gower?"

"Not to look at. Why, Tom's not at all good-looking."

"What was he?"

"A missionary."

"Will you come to Kalipur to live again if I keep on asking?"

"No, Jimmy."

"Why?"

"In Marapore I'm a person in my own right. In Kalipur I'm
an ancient monument."

81

"A revered one."

He rose. "Will Mrs. Gower try and stand in her husband's way if I get him to come to Kalipur?"

"She might. Yes, I'm sure she would."

"Then we'll have to count her out in a manner of speaking. Perhaps we can arrange for her a diversion?" He looked at her and then he added, "Ah well, in this new world we're shaping a lot of us'll be left out in the cold."

"Jimmy?"

"Yes?"

"Are you serious about this job?"

He seemed surprised. "Why shouldn't I be?"

He helped her up and led her towards his room. Supporting her he seemed to her wise, dependable. So easily she could believe in him and in what, when he was a boy, she had called his destiny. As they walked he said, "How does Tom Gower feel towards this wife of his?"

"That's the tragedy," she replied. "In his own undemonstrative way, I think he adores her."

7

When Gower returned from the telephone, the conversation in the room at Sanderson's died again, as it had when he had been called to answer it. He stood uncertainly and MacKendrick saw how his eyes flicked obliquely from face to face, how his thin lips twitched a little at the corners. His hands hung limply at his sides, so that the slope of his narrow shoulders was accentuated. Mac-Kendrick felt uncomfortable. Until now there had been a dignity about the man which MacKendrick could not but admire. He had not seemed oppressed by the atmosphere of reproof, even of enmity; rather he seemed to have stood away from it and observed it. Now, quite suddenly, he seemed to shrink as though the nerves of his courage had been exposed.

Abruptly people began talking again and Gower said, "That

was my wife. I'm rather absent-minded about a lot of things and she rang to remind me about dinner." Gower still held a glass half-full of punch. He raised it to his mouth and as he drank he thought: I needed her here.

He put the glass down on a nearby table and pulled up the cuff of his bush-shirt to see how much longer there was to dinner time. Staring at his naked wrist he remembered where the watch was. He could see it, its broad straps curled upwards from the trinket tray on the dressing-table in Dorothy's bedroom at Ooni, the dressing-table at which she had sat this morning staring at him through the mirror; the dressing-table at which she had said, "I hate you more than any man I know."

Stricken, he looked at the young man who had hardly left his side all evening. Gower could not even remember the man's name, and he found some comfort in this anonymity in a place where the familiar had become grotesque. Or was it he himself who had undergone a repulsive metamorphosis?

He said to MacKendrick, "Would you like to come back and have dinner with us?" He was pleased, inordinately pleased, when the young American thanked him and said he would be glad to, although he had seen the momentary hesitation, that look of – what? Guile? But he forgave MacKendrick the hesitation, conscious that tonight no man would treat with him impulsively. "Good. Then we'll pay our respects to Sanderson and be on our way." But Sanderson had disappeared and no one knew where. Gower was disinclined to seek him out and so they left without thanking their host; and this, in itself, added to Gower's sense of being, tonight, a social outcast. "They'll think I've cleared off with my tail between my legs." He did not voice the thought. They were walking down the drive. He half turned to go back.

"Have you forgotten something, Mr. Gower?"

Gower stared at his companion. As he did so he was filled with gratitude. He wasn't alone. This stranger had come with him, had accepted his hospitality. But then he *was* a stranger. Before he could stop himself he had said, "I see you're not afraid of leprosy."

"I don't understand."

"Never mind."

Gower, in turning again towards the gate, touched the young man's arm, to guide him. In the road outside a group of tongas loomed, the horses listless between the shafts.

"Sahib! Tonga, Sahib!"

Gower waved them away and he and MacKendrick walked on through the feathery dust at the side of the road. There was no air, no breeze. A single lamp standard shed its feeble light a hundred yards ahead. They walked through the darkness towards it, bearing the heat and the silence on their shoulders. "Tell me," MacKendrick said at last, "you run a sort of farm up at a place called Ooni, don't you? As well as this paper?"

Glad to talk of everyday things Gower clutched at the straw of conversation. And as he talked he told himself, "Ooni is safety. Nothing that goes wrong here can touch me in Ooni." Ooni, with its gently sloping hills, its slow, sure pulse of seedtime and harvest, its fundamental hold on himself as a man, spread itself before him with the words he spoke. He told MacKendrick of his work, his experiments, with crops, with seed, with grass; of his failures and of his successes. "There's a model village, too. That's where our pupils come to live. They bring their wives and families. Apart from farming we go in for cottage crafts as well. Hygiene and sanitation."

"It sounds great. Just what's needed."

"Yes. I wonder though how much they take back with them? Knowledge I mean, and the keenness to put it into practice."

MacKendrick wondered too. "Who finances it?" he asked.

"Chap called Nair. You saw him tonight, I expect."

And then Ooni faded away. Gower saw only Nair's eyes on him. He said, "But I hope the Government 'll take over. They've lots of plans for that sort of thing."

"You'd stay on, though?"

84

"I'd like to. I don't know." Gower cleared his throat. "You've been in Marapore long enough, I think, to know that my future's rather uncertain. In fact you probably see that more clearly than I do myself. You've got a couple of hour or so's clear evidence. I've got fifteen years' self-deception standing between myself and reality."

"That sounds awfully bitter, Mr. Gower."

"Don't let's be formal."

"Okay, then. Tom."

Gower smiled to himself. Should there be a halt upon the road? A Roman handclasp? He looked across his shoulder at the tall young man who walked beside him.

"Not bitter," he went on. "Disappointed perhaps. Tonight, for instance, back there. I don't mean the European section. As far as they're concerned I've just got what's been coming to me. But my Indian friends. Yes, disappointed. That's natural when you're faced with the fact you've spent a long time learning to understand something only to find it's changed as quickly as you've understood it."

"What?"

"India."

"Tell me about it."

"I can't I'm afraid. There are too many. There's mine, and then there's yours."

"My India? Why no, I haven't had time."

"You don't particularly need time. I thought you did once."

"What do you need?"

"Love first, I suppose. Then divine inspiration. Then forgiveness."

He felt the younger man's embarrassment. He fell silent. MacKendrick said, "Can you love something without knowing it properly? Without ever having seen it? Something or – somebody?"

Gower wanted to answer: Yes, God. He shook his head. "I don't know."

85

"Tell me about your India, Tom."

Ahead of them the lights from the town were creating an artificial bowl of light in the sky. He said, "Over there you'll see a light in the sky. Go towards it, into it, it becomes a town with noise and people and smells. Beautiful and squalid. Sometimes I forget what is under the light." But it was not a light, nor what was beneath the light. It was the darkness surrounding the light, the space beyond it that no light could penetrate, no sound disturb. As you grew older the area of light diminished. You could watch it growing smaller, smaller. In the end there would be nothing.

They turned left, past the station, the one eye of its ticket office awake. From the town beyond they could hear drums and bells. And now they followed the road through the cantonment bazaar, its shop fronts shuttered, papers scattered in front of them, the wrack of the sun's tide. A shaft of light from the open Chinese Restaurant drew them forward. Beyond that lay darkness again, the silhouette of Cannon Hill against the open sky of the night marking where the plain swept westward for mile after dark mile, a kingdom, now, of jackals who hunted in packs on the outskirts of sleeping villages.

But this is my world, Gower told himself: and a man and his world are inseparable.

They stopped outside the restaurant, for Gower laid a hand on MacKendrick's arm. "Here's where I work," he said, and they turned to look at the shuttered building where the *Gazette* offices were.

It was MacKendrick who first noticed the high, white-painted words. "Look."

Gower hesitated. Then he went towards the wall and put out an exploratory finger, touching the H in Home. His voice, when he spoke, was expressionless. "It must have been done tonight. It's still wet."

"Bastards."

"Where are you going?"

86

"Someone in here might have seen who did it." MacKendrick was crossing the road to the restaurant.

"Don't bother. Good of you, but don't bother."

MacKendrick returned to Gower's side. They stood staring at the words. *Go Home Gower.*

As they came away, leaving the cantonment shops behind, Gower said, "Young Vidyasagar and his friends, I expect," and MacKendrick found himself laid hold of, as it were, by the restraining arm of his companion's frailty, and what seemed innocence. It was as though something weak and crushable had turned its face to his. The thought came to him: You aren't dealing with images but with people who exist outside you and in spite of you. You may know the image backwards but you don't know what's behind it or within it. You don't know *her* in the way you knew Dwight. You've set an image against a man and you've judged.

He longed for Gower to talk, or to find the power of speech himself, but Gower had become part of the night, as though he wished to return to the void wherein MacKendrick had always placed him. But he was within that void now in a different way, as a man who had been, for a moment, alive, to be reckoned with.

Gower had guided him to the left; they had entered an even quieter, darker street. "I live just here," he said, and MacKendrick had to fight an almost irresistible desire to turn and run.

It was only the memory of the words she had written to Dwight, 'For God's sake don't desert me now', only the knowledge that she had never had Dwight's reply, that enabled him to follow Gower down the gravel driveway and up the short flight of steps on to the verandah.

A bearer in white uniform met them as they passed through the entrance porch into the sitting-room. Before Gower could himself speak the bearer began talking to him. Gower kept nodding, and asking questions; but their conversation was in Urdu. MacKendrick waited patiently.

Gower said, "Sit down and make yourself at home. I've got to

87

make a phone call. This is Abdul, he'll get you a drink. And Abdul, tell Memsahib that Mr. – that Mr. –"

"MacKendrick."

"Of course. I'm terrible on names. Tell Memsahib that Mr. MacKendrick is dining with us."

Abdul was watching MacKendrick, his mouth a little open. Instinctively MacKendrick thought: He knew Dwight. He sees the resemblance, such as it is.

Gower, with a nod, went into an adjoining room and closed the communicating door. Abdul crossed to a table in the corner of the sitting-room and returned with a circular tray on which was a glass, a bottle of gin, a bottle of lemon squash. He set the tray on a low table by an easy chair, and by it he set down a jug of water.

"Sahib?"

"Thanks."

"Gin and is-squash, Sahib?"

"Sure. I'll fix it. Don't you bother." He grinned, but there was no answering friendliness. He sat down on the chair, watching Abdul's bare feet moving on the polished floorboards. He watched them as silently they went out of sight.

He was alone.

Looking up he took in the shape, the feel of the room. He was struck by its emptiness. The walls were bare, the chairs shabby in their faded cretonne covers. There were no flowers, no photographs. He looked from side to side, expecting to see somewhere a duplicate of the photograph which lay in his coat pocket. He stood up. Now, he listened for sounds. There was silence. In a moment she would come in. It was a dream. He would not recognise her. She would be a stranger.

He started, suddenly. But it was only Gower's muffled voice, heard from the room adjoining, as he got his telephone connection. MacKendrick moved towards the door of the room in which Gower had shut himself up. He felt it was Dwight talking. Dwight still in possession. His back chilled. He had never thought of Dwight as an invisible force. He had never –

88

Then he knew she had come into the room.

He turned slowly. As they looked at one another he wanted to say: Don't look like that. It's Joe. Not Dwight. You don't know me. You've never seen me. Don't look like that. Don't be afraid. I'm here to help.

He wanted to say the words, to wrap them round her so that he should not see the trembling which possessed her, nor the sudden curbing of it against the shock of disappointment. But he could not say the words. He stood before her without purpose.

He said, "My name's MacKendrick. Joe MacKendrick. I guess you're Mrs. Gower."

Without moving she said, "Yes."

"Tom brought me home. We – we met at the cocktail party. I hope it's all right?"

Her voice was surer. "Of course. Miss Haig mentioned your name when she phoned me. I meant to ask Tom to bring you home." She waited. Then, "But I forgot," she ended.

She had become, at once, quite calm. She came over to him and they shook hands. Her own hand, in his, was cold.

"You'll have a drink, won't you? Abdul should have given you one." She bent over the tray. She was wearing a dinner gown, dark green in colour. He watched the cloth stretch and fold across her back and shoulders as she moved her arms to mix the drinks. When she straightened up and handed him a glass he saw what he had often wondered about – the colour of her eyes. They were brown –

"Thank you."

– but she was different. More beautiful than the photograph suggested. Her hair was lighter than he had imagined. In the photograph it had looked almost black. But it was coppery, with bleached highlights almost like corn. And she had cut it short. It no longer framed her face, falling to her shoulders. It was bobbed, curled. Her face looked more pointed, its features sharper. Far younger than Gower – a fact he had taken for granted – she had yet assumed some of her husband's lack of

89

warmth, his dryness, his appearance of living within himself and exposing to the world only what could not be hurt.

He raised his glass.

"Skol."

She made no move beyond the slightest of nods. She stood in front of him, now utterly composed as far as he could see. He drank, self-consciously. It was wrong. All wrong. He felt so cut off from her, as though he saw her only through a thick barrier of unbreakable glass. Hands, it seemed, pressed him away from her, and voices seemed to be whispering in his ear: This is the girl, but you can't touch her. Like this she still belongs to Dwight. Or Tom Gower. Not to you.

His glass was empty. She took it and made to fill it again.

He said, "I oughtn't to. I –"

"As you wish." She left the glass on the table and, turning to him, she said, "How long are you staying in Marapore?"

"Not long, I guess. I ought – I ought to head back to Bombay in a day or two."

"Only a short visit then?"

He nodded. He wished she would sit down, but she remained obstinately against the fireplace. He had never seen anyone so – contained.

"Has Marapore proved a fruitful place?" she asked, suddenly.

"Fruitful?"

"I'm sorry. I keep thinking you're here on business, but of course Miss Haig told me you were on holiday."

Again he nodded and wondered what else Miss Haig had said.

She asked, "Do you know Marapore well?"

"No. I just happened on it."

She gazed at him steadily. "Tom and I happened on it too. We used to live in Calcutta."

She turned away and Tom, returning, said – "I had to ring Steele."

"What about? There's some gin on the table."

"I'll tell you. Got yours, MacKendrick? Oh – you've met. Are you drinking, Dor?"

She said, "No."

"MacKendrick?"

"Thanks, I –"

"Mr. MacKendrick's glass is just by your hand."

Gower found it, and said, "There's trouble at Ooni." He got the glasses mixed up. "No, no this is yours, MacKendrick. I think. Yes – there's trouble at Ooni."

"What sort of trouble?"

"The staff's out on strike. Steele's holding the fort. Steele's assistant manager of the estate," he explained. "Quite a young chap. Stayed on here after the war. He had an awfully good record in Burma."

MacKendrick nodded again. Then he said, "Why are they on strike?"

"Some talk of conditions. Usual thing. Dor –" he turned to her, "– they've been writing on the wall." He drank. Mac-Kendrick noticed that his hand was unsteady. Some of the liquid spilled on to the collar of his bush-shirt. "What d'you think of that?"

"Think of what?"

"They've been writing on the wall."

"Who?" Her tone of voice was level, stripped even of exasperation.

"Vidyasagar and his friends, I think."

"Which wall? At Ooni?"

"No. Ours."

"Ours?"

"Yes."

"Outside here?"

"No. The *Gazette*."

"I see."

"They get some pleasure out of it, I suppose. I'll have to go up to Ooni."

"What did they write?"

" 'Go Home Gower'."

Tom went to his wife's side. She looked steadily at him. He looked away from her, into his glass. He said, "I'll have to make arrangements."

"What arrangements?"

"Have it painted over."

"Yes."

"I brought Mr. MacKendrick round that way."

"You were longer than usual, I thought, getting here."

"Sorry. Is supper spoiled?"

"It's not ready." She turned to MacKendrick. "We dine at half-past eight. Do you like Indian food?"

"I suspect I've not eaten any, yet, Mrs. Gower. Real Indian food."

"Tom likes it."

"What's that, Dor?"

"I was telling Mr. MacKendrick you like Indian food."

"Yes, yes. Our version of it anyway. Actually it's better up at Ooni because we usually have the same as the staff. I've a little Madrassi cook there who does a first-class curry. You'll have to come –"; he faltered, then sipped his drink, the elbow exaggeratedly high, to steady the wrist.

They stood, uncomfortably. From over Gower's shoulder MacKendrick saw Dorothy staring at him. For an instant, before MacKendrick dropped his eyes, he felt her question: Well?

Gower, mixing new drinks, was saying, "I'll have to attend to several things in the morning but we might take a trip somewhere in the jeep. Why not come up to Ooni, MacKendrick? Pity to come to this part without seeing some of the country. There used to be some first-class shooting but at least there's still some scenery worth looking at. What d'you say, Dor?"

"It's rather hot for sight-seeing, isn't it?"

"Yes. Yes, perhaps it is. Anyway –"

"Thanks a lot, Tom – but I shan't be staying."

"Won't you? You should have seen Ooni."

"I'd like to have."

"Some other time then." Gower drank. His unspoken words: But there'll be no other time, for any of us, left their mark of dismay on his brow, their echo in the room.

They had supper formally.

There was jasmine in the silver bowl which appeared to float in its own reflection on the polished table. MacKendrick sat between the other two, who faced each other across the length of the table. He drank copiously from the glass of water which Abdul refilled punctiliously at each slight gesture of Dorothy's hand. He noticed that she never spoke to the servant. The man performed his duties like an automaton. But Gower spoke to him, and Gower alone seemed able to break down his reserve, to bring by some muttered word a smile to his lips, a suggestion of loyalty to his bearing.

Above them a ceiling fan turned lethargically: insects fluttered round the harsh electric lights, and found their way into the soup. They ate in silence, and MacKendrick felt sick with apprehension, with disappointment, and from too much to drink. He reached out and took a chilli from a small bowl in front of him, bit it, and found his mouth and tongue on fire. Tears flooded into his eyes.

"Holy Smoke!"

"What's that, old chap?"

"These green things."

"Chillies."

"They've burned my tongue off."

"Give him some water, Dor."

He was already drinking it. He turned to the girl.

"How c'n you eat those things?"

"I never eat them."

"Never?"

"I never eat curry."

He stared at her, then down at her plate which held the

93

remains of a fresh green salad. "But Tom said a while ago –" He stopped. "Tom said that up at Ooni . . ."

"I never eat Indian food."

Abdul removed her plate, and then MacKendrick's. Leaning back to give the servant more room MacKendrick looked at Gower and saw that he was staring into space, munching a piece of one of the chappatties which were piled on the small plate at his elbow. He wasn't listening. He ate mechanically and it was not difficult to believe that in this way he ate all his meals, presuming she ate the things he ate himself; never really noticing her, or what she was doing.

Fruit came, and then coffee, and suddenly Dorothy said, "I knew someone called MacKendrick who was an American, too."

His mouth was dry. He said, "You did?"

"Yes. During the war when we were in Calcutta."

"My brother – my brother was in Calcutta."

"Really? What was his name?"

"Dwight."

They were looking at each other warily.

"Really? But that's who I mean."

She called over to Gower, and at once MacKendrick knew what was wrong. Gower, in his thoughts, had never been present at this meeting. She was saying, "Mr. MacKendrick is Dwight MacKendrick's brother."

"Who, dear?"

"You remember Dwight MacKendrick?"

"Who?"

"Dwight MacKendrick. In Calcutta." She paused. "You ought to remember Dwight. You introduced me to him."

Without conviction Gower said, "Of course." He turned to MacKendrick. "How is he?" It was obvious he neither remembered nor cared. It was Dorothy who should have asked this question and Dorothy to whom the answer should have been given. But now MacKendrick had not even the courage to watch her face. He twisted round in his chair towards Gower.

94

"I'm afraid he's dead."

Gower glanced up from his chappattie. But he looked at MacKendrick and not at his wife as MacKendrick had half expected. "Dead? Oh, I'm sorry."

Afraid to stop talking, MacKendrick went on, "He was killed in the Pacific. Right at the end of the war, in May of 1945."

"I'm so sorry. Was he older than you?"

"Yes."

"I'm afraid I can't remember him really. One – one met so many people then. I met him in something to do with the army, didn't I, Dor?"

She must have nodded. Gower looked back at MacKendrick. "I'm sorry," he said again. "Did he like India?"

"I don't know, Tom. I didn't see him when he got back home from here. I was away in the army myself and he was only home a few weeks. Then he was sent to the Pacific."

"Was he married?"

"He – he got engaged to a girl his last week at home."

Gower nodded. "What was so tragic about the war," he said, "well, about any war, was the young people whose lives got messed up like that. Like the Mapletons, for instance. You've met her, haven't you?"

"Yes."

"Young Robbie Mapleton was an awfully nice chap. They say he had a very promising future in the army. Now of course poor Cynthia Mapleton's almost without means."

"She says she's going to Kenya."

"Kenya? Ah, yes. There'll be a lot of us in places like that."

"Are you thinking of going?"

Gower smiled. "I don't think I'm cut out for a place like Kenya."

"Only India?"

"You might say that."

"Don't you ever feel you want to go back home?"

Gower looked down at his plate. "I haven't been home for

95

something like twelve years now. And, Dor – how long for you? About the same?"

MacKendrick turned his head now, and looked at Dorothy. With his eyes he wanted to apologise for the cruelty that had been forced on him. He expected to see her on the verge of tears; tears for Dwight. But what he saw shocked him immeasurably. Her expression was utterly blank.

"You see, MacKendrick," Gower was explaining, "Dor hasn't been home since she came out again after leaving school. We've never been home together either. This is our place. So it isn't a question of feeling we want to go to England. We haven't really faced the probability yet – Oh, I'm sorry, Dor." He rose, for she had risen. "I mustn't start rambling. We can have more coffee next door."

MacKendrick, on his feet, felt fresh waves of sickness spread through his body. He caught his foot on the leg of his chair and had to swallow quickly to stop himself vomiting. He knew that Dorothy had gone ahead into the sitting-room. Tom was at his elbow.

"Feeling under the weather? It's this heat. And perhaps the curry wasn't the ideal thing for you to have."

"I'm sorry, Tom. I guess I've drunk too much. Beginning about half-past five –"

He knew vaguely that Gower led him from the room, steadying him as they went. In the dim cell through which they passed he could feel giant spiders lying in wait. A door opened. He vomited.

When it was all over he was abjectly ashamed.

"I'll be all right. Jus' leave me here, Tom. Don't tell y'r wife – hell, don' tell y'r wife –"

He was alone. He realised he was standing outside at the rear of the bungalow. His forehead was cold and damp, the taste of vomit thick in his mouth. Gower returned and gave him a glass of water. He rinsed his mouth and then drank, gratefully. And when he was alone again he noticed the myriad stars above him and the black scars of trees against the sky which hung so low his hand, he felt, could touch it.

He moved away from the wall and found his way back into the bungalow, and as he walked into the dining-room he heard Gower say from the sitting-room beyond, "Well, if I *am* finished, Dor, we'll pack up and go home."

She said, "You're finished all right, in Marapore. I suppose I ought to warn you though that if you go home to England you go alone."

A door banged shut.

MacKendrick stayed where he was and in a moment or two Gower came through the archway into the dining-room.

"Tom –"

"Yes?"

"I'm going now."

Gower accompanied him to the porch. As they shook hands he said, "Excuse my wife, won't you? She wasn't well. I forgot she had a head from this afternoon. Forgive us both, won't you?"

As MacKendrick took his hand Gower said, "Please come again."

He stayed on the verandah as MacKendrick walked off down the drive. Looking back over his shoulder MacKendrick could only be angry. It was too easy for him to see the likeness between Gower and himself. Both their skins bore the smell, the taint of defeat.

When, as a boy, driven to tears by Dwight, he had had time to lick his wounds, a cold and impotent fury saved him from despair. He felt it now, like a growth inside him, deep in his bowels and when confronted at Smith's Hotel by a man he did not know, a man who barred his way into Room Three, he struck out with better luck than judgment or design. The man, a tall, burly Indian, fell heavily against the door.

"Get out of the way, you goddam bastard," MacKendrick

shouted, and then the door opened, the bodyguard lurched to save himself falling backwards into the room and dropped on his knees between MacKendrick and Jimmy Smith. Behind Jimmy, seated on the new couch, was Harriet Haig, her hand raised and pressed against her white cheek.

"You must be Mr. MacKendrick. I see you're a man of action. Is this poor Jai you've reduced to such a shadow? Where is tactful Freddie? Freddie! Someone ought to look to Jai before he dies where he is. Now does this indicate the sack for him or promotion for you, Mr. MacKendrick? Believe me," and he stepped from the room and held out his hand, "Miss Haig has only just told me that Desai had the impertinence to turn you out of this room to make way for me. I shall now put him to the inconvenience of changing you back again just so that he'll learn you're not a man to be trifled with, as my poor Jai has learned. Where did you hit him?"

"I –"

"Never mind. Somewhere effective. Freddie!"

"Look –"

"Not a word, Mr. MacKendrick. Desai! Freddie!"

"Look, Maharajah, or whatever you are –"

"My name is Smith."

"Look, Mr. Smith. You've got Room Three. Let's leave it at that. I'll see your bodyguard is looked after. I'm sorry. I got mad without thinking."

MacKendrick turned away to find Desai poised behind him, hands wringing, terror brightening his eyes.

"Mr. MacKendrick –"

"Okay. Where do I sleep?"

"Mr. MacKendrick, this is all embarrassing you will understand."

"Where do I sleep? Cut out all the excuses. Just tell me where I sleep."

Swallowing, Mr. Desai turned on his heel and led the way to Room Twelve. He opened the door, switched on the light and waved MacKendrick in. "This room you will find comfortable. See, all is prepared. If you wish –"

"Okay. Now get out."

"Yes, Mr. MacKendrick. But, sir, there is one thing –"

"Get out."

He swung round threateningly and the manager stumbled out of the room. MacKendrick banged the door to and, trying to lock it, found no key. He stared at the keyhole and with a groan of shame and misery crossed to the chair by the mosquito-net shrouded bed and dropped into it. He let his head fall into his hands. His tongue was dry and there was a tight knot in his chest which suddenly resolved itself into a sob of weariness.

It was Miss Haig who, knocking and getting no answer, found him like that. She fumbled her slow way across the room until she stood in front of him. Behind her, Shafi closed the door on them.

"Mr. MacKendrick."

He shook his head.

"I have a message for you, Mr. MacKendrick."

He muttered, "The staff can deliver messages."

"The staff are afraid of you."

He looked up at her. She seemed huge, menacing. The rings shone malevolently on her curled fingers as she leaned her weight on her thick walking-sticks.

"What's the message?"

"Your office in Bombay rang and asked you to ring back."

"Thank you. I'll ring in the morning."

"May I sit down?"

He got to his feet. "I can't talk any more," he said.

"I want to talk about Tom and Dorothy Gower."

"There's nothing I can tell you you don't know."

"I think there is."

He blurted out, "There's nothing I can tell you or anybody. And if there was I wouldn't. You're all dried up and rotten, the whole lot of you. You're all dead and finished. You're not alive any more, any of you. If you were you wouldn't stay another

99

minute in this goddam funeral parlour. You wouldn't sit quiet while they wrap you up in shrouds. That's what they're doing. Gupta and Nair and Vidyasagar and the rest."

She seemed to shrink from him, but it was only a tired contraction of her body as she leaned more heavily on the sticks. Her shoulders sank wearily. Involuntarily, he moved from in front of the chair and put out a hand to help her into it. She sat for a moment with her eyes closed.

"Perhaps you're right," she said, and her voice was so low he heard the words only with difficulty; "but in our own way we're not sitting quiet. We're not so tired of the world we won't do our best to find a place in it again." She opened her eyes and looked at him. "Are we?" she asked him.

He turned away.

"In my case," she said, "it's a question of helping other people, like Tom and Jimmy. There wouldn't be much point in –" She stopped. MacKendrick had sunk on to the edge of the bed, drawing the mosquito net taut by his weight.

"If you're going to help someone you've got to know them," she went on. "I think I know Tom and I think I know Jimmy. I think I know where they're a danger to themselves. But you've got to know more than the person you're helping. There's an old saying, Mr. MacKendrick, Know Thine Enemy."

He glanced up at her and their eyes met.

She said, "Were you and Dorothy ever lovers?"

"No."

She nodded, as though accepting his denial. Then she said, "Have you been to their bungalow tonight?"

"Yes."

"Who asked you?"

"Tom."

"In what circumstances?"

"His wife phoned him at Sanderson's."

"I see."

"You don't. I know what you're getting at, but it wasn't like

100

that. I know you phoned her and I know you said something about me. I know why. In a way you're right. You guessed the name MacKendrick would mean something to her. But she didn't ask Tom to take me back. She left it to chance."

"To chance? Yes, that's very like Dorothy."

"What do you mean?"

"She gives the impression of leaving things to chance. Actually I believe she controls things and people purely by will. For instance, I'm fairly sure she's never once suggested to Tom that it's time they went home, but I think she's willed it fiercely. To the exclusion of all else."

"You're wrong."

"Am I?"

"She told him tonight that if he goes he goes alone. I overheard her say that, Miss Haig. So you're wrong. And she didn't say it for my benefit, she didn't even know I was there. She said, You're finished in Marapore all right but if you go home to England you go alone."

Miss Haig sat very still, so still, so silent, that he said harshly, "So perhaps it's Tom who wants to clear out. Perhaps that's what you ought to help him do."

"No. No."

"Why not? A whipped dog goes back to its own kennel."

"I think you know more about whipped dogs and their habits than Tom will ever know." Miss Haig's voice stung him. "You dare to come here and judge us? You dare to come here and judge a man like Tom? To you it's all a game and the losers whining for a bit of lost power and the right to lord it over a lot of blacks. All right then, there are whiners like that, don't worry about them, they'll find somewhere else and when they get there they'll still be all in one piece. But there'll be lots of people who won't be in one piece and one of them's Tom Gower. If Tom suggested going back to England he did it for Dorothy's sake. That's where he's a fool. That's where he's a danger to himself. And if Dorothy told him he'd go alone it's because – " she paused, as if to sharpen

101

the edge of her anger, "– it's because she's got another lover! And it's because you think or know she's got another lover that you're sitting there like a whipped dog yourself!"

He sprang up, his own cheeks, like hers, red with temper; but she gave him no chance to speak. She raised herself up, supporting herself on the arms of the chair. "D'you think I'm a fool? Do you think I couldn't see right away that you and Dorothy had had an affair? D'you think you didn't give yourself away completely? The name MacKendrick would mean something to her! Of course it would! The name of someone who'd had his fun with her and had come back to have more. When was it? In the war with Tom safely out of the way? You bored and sorry for yourself? And what happened this time? Bored and sorry for yourself in Bombay or Calcutta or wherever it was? Of course! What better than taking up again with such easy game, if only you could find her! Well, you found her all right. I'm glad you did. I'm only sorry you found her otherwise engaged. You might have induced her to run off with you this time and leave poor Tom alone. But you wouldn't do that, would you? You're not that sort. I know what you are. I know your sort, you have everything in life, so much of everything that you think there must be more. You think you've only to –"

Suddenly the breath seemed to leave her; she went ashen grey and sank back into the chair, her fingers curled, her mouth open, the lines of her face smoothed. He moved towards her, but her eyes did not follow him; they stared at a point beyond his shoulder. With the beginning of panic he took her left hand and chafed the wrist. Then her other hand moved and fumbled for his head. He kept quite still. It seemed as though she sought him with her hand, as though suddenly she were blind. It rested now on his head and her eyes moved round and met his own. Her mouth began twitching. He held his breath so that he could catch the words she whispered. "Forgive me," she said, "please forgive me." He could only nod. Memories stirred in him; memories of longing for a hand upon his head, gentle as hers was. She said again, "Forgive me." Then her brow puckered. Some of the colour came back to her cheeks, but he saw the tiny, close-packed beads of perspiration on her forehead. "I've got it wrong, haven't I? You're not like that. We were friends, weren't we? You're not like that at all. You're here for good, not evil."

He put her hand on the arm of the chair and straightened up. "I'll get you a glass of water," he said, and went over to the bedside table where glass and carafe stood. As he poured he heard her handbag clasp shut with a click. He returned and held the glass out to her. As she took it she put her hand to her mouth and swallowed something. Then she drank.

"Thank you. I'll be all right now." As he went back to the table with the empty glass she asked, "Why have I got it wrong?" He did not turn round. He faced the wall, standing there, with his hand still on the glass. "Why have I got it wrong?" she asked again.

"Because it wasn't me, Miss Haig. It was my brother."

"I see."

"How can you see? Of course you don't see."

"Where is he now?"

"He's dead. He was killed in the war."

"How did he meet her?"

"He was over here in '44. He met her in Calcutta."

"Was he killed in Burma then, or China?"

"No. In the Pacific. He went back to the States, first."

"Then why are *you* here?"

He looked round. Her eyes followed him as he walked the length of the room. "I don't know," he said; and then, with a sudden sense of release, "But I can go back now."

"What did you come for? Did he ask you to see her? Before he was killed, I mean?"

He laughed. "Dwight? No, he got engaged before he went to the Pacific. I didn't see him at all. The last time I saw him was in '43."

"Then how did you know about him and Dorothy?"

103

"I found letters."

"Oh."

"No. I wasn't prying, Miss Haig. Just doing a family duty. Just going through my brother's papers to make sure they were – worthy of him."

"You say that as though it were distasteful."

"Well, it was." He passed his hand through his tumbled hair. The room was wrong, quite wrong. This was not the room which laid the burden of secrecy upon him. In it he was nothing; in it he was minute, the walls infinitely far away, the ceiling impossibly high; their voices distorted. *Get it in tune*, he thought. *Get it in focus*. By his foot was the suitcase – way down on the remote floor. And in the suitcase were the letters. Steadying himself against the edge of the table he bent slowly and hooked the case by the handle. He knelt and undid the clasps, lifted the heavy leather top.

He crossed over to the bed and sat down, shuffling the letters in his hands, pieces of paper which no longer had the power to move him.

"Are those the letters?"

"Yes."

"From Dorothy to your brother?"

"All except one. That one's from Dwight to her, only it was never finished. It was the only letter he ever wrote her after he'd gone home and he didn't even bother to mail it. Look – it might interest you." He held it out.

As she unfolded it and began to read she heard him begin to tear up the other letters. One by one they dropped on to the floor in pieces at his feet. From the corners of her eyes she saw the white fragments of paper falling – saw the little spurt of flame as he flicked on his lighter and burned them carefully. She read Dwight's letter through without understanding it. Then, with the acrid smell of burning paper in her nostrils, she read it again.

Dear Dorothy,

    Sorry I never wrote you before. Maybe you'll wonder why I'm

writing now. Just to say I'm off somewhere in the Pacific. Say a prayer for me.

Honey, I guess we were a bit crazy all those plans we made for after the war. Seeing it now both of us see I guess you couldn't divorce as nice a guy as Tom. How is he, honey? Still crusading?! I'm glad you didn't burn your boats then and there, Dorothy. Sweetheart, please don't still be in love with . . .

Then there was a sentence crossed out. The letter became incoherent, as though the writer had suddenly lost interest.

. . . please don't be more in love with me than you can help, sweetheart, I've got myself engaged to . . .

again, another sentence crossed out.

I'm going to be honest with you honey and tell you that what you told me that time *would* make a difference. Back home I see just how much and I guess thinking it over you . . .

it ended abruptly. Down in the lower corner a telephone number had been scrawled, as though at that moment the phone had rung, and an appointment been made.

She gave the letter back to him and he touched the corner of it to the tiny flame of his lighter.

"Now you know about my brother, Miss Haig. He was a great man, I'm told. Big. Successful. He had a wonderful career mapped out and he ended a fully fledged colonel, keen fighter, tops with his men, least that's what he said. Maybe though he was shot in the back, I don't know. All I know is from as early as I remember I hated him. He was the family all bundled up and rolled into one and I was just something that happened along and got stuck with the MacKendrick name. I had it drummed into me right from the start that in the MacKendrick family Dwight was the one who was going to set the standards. Maybe I hated him because I knew I could never reach those standards, or maybe because whenever I did he'd thought up a set of new ones."

He rubbed the sole of his foot over the charred paper. "Dwight streamlined himself for success and cut his way through anything and anybody. But why talk about it? I know what you're thinking and you're right of course. It's sour grapes, isn't it? We'd all be like Dwight if we knew how, but because we don't we cook up a lot of hooey about truth and honour and decency and fairplay when all the time the only thing that adds up is our own goddam selfishness."

"Don't you think you might be misjudging Dwight?"

"Misjudge? How misjudge?"

"That letter —"

"It's burnt."

"I know. So are the others which you wouldn't let me see. Without seeing them Dwight's letter doesn't show in too bad a light, you know."

"Without seeing the others. You're right. But you'll never see the others, nobody will, so you'll only remember Dwight's letter. That's how it should be, Miss Haig. He wasn't the sort of person who ever let you see the other side of the argument. Let it be like that."

"And you're letting it be like that?"

"Why not? I thought I saw the other side. When I first read Dorothy's letters I was haunted by them. I'd never read real love letters before and it was worse because I knew Dwight wasn't worth a damn of any woman's time. It took her six months to realise he wasn't ever going to write her, six months to get to the point where all she could write was a couple of lines pleading for some word from him, pleading with him not to let her down. You saw what he was going to reply to that. You know the rest."

But she said, "No. It's the rest I don't know."

"There's nothing more to tell."

"You came to find Dorothy."

"I didn't find her."

"Why did you come to find her? Because you'd fallen in love with her?"

"I don't know. In a way, I suppose. In another way it was like coming to find myself. We'd both been hurt by Dwight. Or I thought we had. But there wasn't anything to find. She wasn't the Dorothy I knew at all. She was like –"

"Like what?"

"Like Dwight. Cold. Hard. Selfish."

"What did you say to her?"

He looked up, surprised. "Nothing."

"Didn't you even mention Dwight?"

"She asked if there was any relationship. She didn't know he was dead. I said nothing about what I knew."

"How did she take the news?"

"It – it didn't seem to affect her in any way."

"Tom knew they knew each other, didn't he? One gathers so from Dwight's letter."

"Yes, he knew. In fact he introduced them, it seems."

Miss Haig paused. "Then what do you suppose it was she told Dwight that he said made a difference after all?"

He got up. "I don't know. I used to wonder. Now I don't wonder, and I don't care. It seemed important once. I wanted to know. I felt it might have been that she couldn't have children."

"Yes. It could be that. I think that may be true."

He frowned, remembering. Inside his inner pocket was the photograph. He took out the envelope and slit the flap. For a few moments he stared at the girl's image. This was all he knew; the image. But now another image was forming over it and for the first time since he had held the photograph in his hands he realised with something of a shock how many other hands had held it: the photographer's, Dorothy's, Dwight's; and to whom had Dwight not shown it? How many perspiring hands in messes, on troopships, in army-camps had fumbled with it as Dwight handed it round? She had never been his. Even the image had never been his.

"Is that Dorothy's photograph?"

He passed it to her without answering. At first she did not

recognise Dorothy Gower. The photographer had caught a look of tenderness and a look of trust, and behind the look of trust one of preparedness, of expectancy of hurt. She gave it back to him and said, "You found that with the letters?"

"Yes. She had it taken in Calcutta for him to take back with him. She mentioned it in one of her letters."

He looked at it once more, then threw it carelessly on the table by his bed. He flinched, somehow, from burning it along with the letters. Later, perhaps, he would.

"What will you do now?" Miss Haig asked.

"Go back."

"When?"

"Tomorrow, or the next day. It makes no difference."

She looked down at her rings. "Then if I invite you to dinner tomorrow night you'd come?"

"Alone?"

"No. She might be there. And Tom."

"Then –"

"Are you afraid?" She gazed at him steadily.

"No," he said at last. "I'm not afraid. She means nothing to me now."

"It would be better to prove that to yourself." She grasped her sticks and for a moment or two neither of them spoke. Then she said, "Jimmy will be there too. Jimmy and Tom must meet."

"Is this some plan of yours for Tom?"

"Yes."

She smiled, sadly. "I know what you're thinking. You're thinking I shouldn't interfere with people and that I shouldn't try and make plans for them. But then if before you left the States someone had told you Dorothy would be better off without you, would you have taken any notice?"

He said, "No. I'd have had to come."

"That's your answer then." He helped her to get up, and helped her towards the door, but she stopped. He saw little muscles flickering in her cheeks. She said, "It's a pity we feel there's nothing to be learned from each other's mistakes, isn't it? But we all have to work in the dark." She paused, thinking: And we are all afraid of the dark.

8

In the morning Gower arose as soon as he heard the servants' voices in the courtyard. He thrust his feet into his slippers, moving cautiously so that he should not wake Dorothy, then, drawing on his creased khaki trousers, he tiptoed through the bathroom and out into the courtyard.

There were still stars to be seen, pale in the sky, and the courtyard was still shadowed, the trees surrounding it etched sharply along the wall which faced the east. Gower breathed in deeply, grateful for the cooler air which brought with it the bitter, nostalgic scent of burning cow-dung as the morning fires were lighted in Marapore. Beyond the wall he heard the soft groaning of ox-cart wheels, the bells like sharp needles of sound which pricked awake his night-drugged senses. Not that he had slept.

He turned to greet Abdul who came swiftly across the compound to see what his master could want at so early an hour; prepared, he brought with him an enamel jug of hot water.

"That's the ticket. I'm going out early, Abdul. Just get me a pot of tea and a biscuit. I'll take it on the verandah." He took the warm jug from Abdul and went back into the bathroom. Shaved and washed, he returned quietly to the bedroom. A freshly laundered bush-shirt and pair of trousers were spread out on his already stripped bed. In the adjacent bed Dorothy still slept. He dressed and filled his pockets with the odds and ends he had scattered last night on the table, but which Abdul had arranged neatly. Abdul was a good servant, the best he had ever had, and he had had him a long time, now. He felt a pang of conscience. If he himself were finished in India, what would become of Abdul? No – that was the wrong outlook, the outlook of the Burra Sahib believing in his own omnipotence; this possessiveness, this feudalism, this benevolent despotism which passed for racial understanding.

He turned to go, aware there was something missing. His watch, of course.

Without looking at Dorothy he walked quietly through the dining-room and sitting-room out on to the verandah where chair and table had been set ready with a pot of tea and a plate of biscuits waiting for him. There was fruit too, to give colour. Already the sun was warm. Abdul came with a pair of newly polished brown shoes and laced them on Gower's feet as he drank his tea. They spoke in Urdu.

"Sahib, where are you going?"

"To the house of Nair Sahib."

He watched the top of Abdul's head. The black hair was flecked with grey. He went on, "And after that to Ooni. In the evening I shall return." It was a simple, familiar programme. Yet today it was different. He said, "Tell Memsahib."

"Yes, Sahib." Abdul raised his head. "Sahib?"

"What?"

"Sahib, today I should come with you."

"Why?"

"On the road there could be bad men."

Gower smiled, touched. He said. "I've gone to Ooni many times without meeting bad men. You stay here and look after the bungalow." Abdul rose and went inside. When he returned he handed Gower the revolver and said, with a wide grin, *"Banduq."*

"But I've no ammunition." He laughed, quietly, and Abdul still grinning said, "Ammo is no matter." Gower took the revolver and Abdul went on, in English, a language he reserved for witticisms, "One look at this revolver, Sahib, and this Vidyasagar straight away think a race is in progress and run quick."

Five miles up the Ooni road was the hamlet of Marpur and on its outskirts Nair lived in the sort of poverty only the wealthy enjoy. His house stood on the top of an upward fold of the other-

110

wise flat earth, and the wall enclosing its barren compound observed the contours of the fold or, rather, had the contours imposed upon it; for where the earth dipped, so did the wall. There were few trees. Sun had stripped the house of its plaster, the shutters of paint. No attempt had been made to cultivate a garden.

As Gower drove the jeep through the open gateway a tethered goat started away in surprise, straining at its rope, then composed itself as suddenly as it had taken fright. Cows which Nair would let none drive away wandered aimlessly across the path. There was an isolated tree where the path curved round to meet the house and beneath it a man, naked, with long, matted hair, sat in an attitude of contemplation. A few flowers were scattered at his feet, and there were brass bowls which held offerings of goat's milk. Fifty yards away, a group of young boys stared at the Sadhu until called away by the women who moved restlessly to and fro between the outhouses. These were servants, the relations of servants, the friends of servants. Within Nair's compound was nomadic life.

He found Nair sitting cross-legged on a rush mat in a room otherwise unfurnished. Nair wore a white homespun dhoti which left the upper part of his body naked. By his side lay a closed book.

Nair had not spoken as Gower was ushered in by one of the servants, but he had smiled and returned Gower's *namaska*. Then, as Gower lowered himself to the floor and sat cross-legged like his host, Nair said, "On Sunday morning I always read Proust." He indicated the book and then passed it to Gower. It was *The Sweet Cheat Gone*. With a smile Gower returned it. "I've never yet read him."

"That is a pity, for then you could have explained the difficult passages. Perhaps if I were to learn French and read him in the original I should understand better. Tell me, is the Holy Man still there beneath the tree?"

"Yes."

"He has been there a week. I have been reading Marcel Proust for three years. Would it not be odd if the Sadhu stayed until I had finished?"

"I find it too incongruous to express an opinion."

"Ah, yes. Will you have refreshment?"

"No, thank you. Do you want me to resign my editorship of the *Gazette*?"

Nair did not drop his eyes in confusion, but slowly he let his gaze wander across to the blank wall on his left. He was silent for what seemed to Gower at least five minutes. At last he said, "My will is subject to your action. I have been considering the quality of will. Ideally we should desire nothing. Desiring nothing we take no action. Thus God can act in us. But if I desire nothing you must desire nothing also so that God may act through both of us. It is a matter for God." He turned his eyes back to Gower.

Gower said, "Or a matter for Gupta? For Gupta and his group of fanatics?"

"If it is, as you say, a matter for Gupta, then it is to him you should go. I speak theoretically."

"I speak practically, Mr. Nair. It is you who appoint editors. Gupta has no official position."

"Then let us not bring him into the discussion."

"Very well. We'll discuss other things. Did you like my editorial last week?"

"It was well written." Nair smiled. "Your prose is simpler than Mr. Proust's."

"Did you understand that when I used the words 'Let us embrace the fact of Pakistan' my meaning was not a political one?"

"Yes. But then neither of us is a politician."

"Meaning Gupta is and that consequently he saw only its political interpretation?"

"Could a political interpretation be found?"

"I imagine so."

"Then, if we do not like politics, we come back to the importance of silence. Only by silence can we avoid misinterpretation, for there are no words to interpret. I have thought deeply about the quality of will and the quality of words, written words and spoken words."

"Certain words were painted on the walls of the *Gazette* building last night."

"All Marapore knows this."

"There is also the question of Ooni."

"Yes."

"I'm going up there this morning. Steele phoned me last night to tell me the staff were on strike."

"Yes, this I know too."

"Do you know why?"

"I know only what you know, Mr. Gower, that they complain about having an estate manager for only three days of the week."

"In other words they complain about me."

"Or about Mr. Steele."

"It isn't clear what they'd say were I to give up the *Gazette* and concentrate all my time on Ooni."

"No, that is not clear."

"It's clear though that there's a pretty strong feeling I've out-lived my usefulness."

"You may be misinterpreting both words and actions."

"You can hardly misinterpret 'Go Home Gower'. It means my sort of person isn't needed in India any more."

"Mr. Gupta will say you can hardly misinterpret 'Let us embrace the fact of Pakistan'."

"That's as may be." Gower paused. "Mr. Nair, I realise you don't intend to commit yourself to any opinion about my possible resignation and I'm prepared to work that out for myself. But we're old friends now. I'd like you to tell me what I've done to make myself disliked so suddenly. It seems absurd that that single article can be the cause."

Nair smiled. "My friend, since I do not dislike you I am at a loss myself to explain it. I know no more than you, no less than you. There was the article. There is the fact of your delegation of duties at Ooni to Steele. They are our known quantities."

"There's one more known quantity. Gupta."

"He is a man. We do not know him consequently."

"He's R.S.S., isn't he?"

"I believe so."

"Then he believes in militant Hinduism."

"How do we know what he believes? Membership of a party tells us nothing of a man's beliefs. Perhaps it tells us a little only of his aspirations."

"Are *you* a member of the R.S.S.?"

"No, I am not a member."

"Have you given them money?"

"No, I have not given them money."

"Do you intend to?"

"To have an intention is to have a desire. If we desire God cannot act in us. Were I to give money to Mr. Gupta and his friends the money would come to them from God." Nair raised his hands, palms outwards, in a gesture of negation. "You see, Mr. Gower, how difficult such conversations are. Who can say with what impression you will go away?"

It was a dismissal. Gower rose to his feet and stood hesitantly above Nair who, bowing his head over hands held palm to palm, effectively brought the interview to an end.

Ahead of him on the grey-yellow ribbon of road lay Ooni. Here, the road, unmetalled, creamed with a rich layer of dust, cut through the dried fields of paddy on a high embankment which was lined on each side with trees whose knotted branches stretched upwards towards the merciless sky. On either side the plain lay flat, blued and hazed by heat like a mirage of the water for which the cracked earth groaned. But ahead, the ground began to rise, patched with scrub, in smooth folds; higher, rounder folds beyond them; and there within the heart of the gentle hills was home, was Ooni.

The jeep followed the curving road into the hills. A black goat, careless of life, dashed from the shelter of a mud hut across the road where shouting children played in the dust and waved as Gower passed them. He left the tiny village behind. From here to Ooni, five miles away, there was no further habitation. The hills grouped themselves in silence.

Within the shallow cup formed by the hills, the estate spread itself in squares of arable fields. After the rains the green of the slopes would be almost an English green; but the great heat of April and May had burned it with the same scorching hand that had left its mark on the plains. The road led through a gap in the hills and followed a course as though at a point half-way up to the rim, the ground sloping away to a flat bottom on the left, and upwards on the right. The manager's bungalow was built into the side of the hill and commanded a view of the whole valley. Scattered below the road were other buildings, offices, equipment sheds and lower down, where the fields spread out, the model village. Closer to the road, but off to the left, in comparative isolation, Steele lived alone; and Gower, stopping the jeep on the road by the steps which led up to the verandah of his own bungalow, saw Steele approaching.

Steele wore nothing but a pair of old khaki shorts, rolled well up on his thighs; a pair of army boots with grey regulation socks rolled over the tops; a floppy green jungle hat on his head. His skin was burned copper, and while he was not above medium height, his body and limbs were thick and sturdy. He carried himself easily, the hat pushed to the back of his head. If asked to describe Steele, Gower would have said he had an 'open' face.

They said good-morning to each other.

"Come and have a beer," Gower said.

"Fine."

"Then you can tell me what's up." Gower took the revolver from the small open compartment on the dashboard of the jeep and explained, a little wryly, why he carried it. They climbed the wooden steps to the verandah. Prabhu, Gower's factotum at

Ooni, greeted them and went to fetch bottles and glasses. The beer would be warm, for they had no refrigerator.

Steele sat back in the wicker chair and waited for Gower to ask questions. He knew, of old, that to launch into any sort of explanation was a waste of time before Gower had signified in some way—usually an opening wide of his pale blue eyes, which were set so deeply in the wrinkled, yellowed flesh – that his mind was not on other things. Quietly Steele took out and lit a cigarette while Gower settled himself, then rose and went inside, came back to the verandah without the gun.

A queer cuss, Steele thought, and grinned to himself because Gower had gone back again into the living-room, probably to put the gun away safely. No doubt about it, absent-minded wasn't the word for old Tom Gower.

The beer came and Prabhu poured two glasses as Gower returned, strapping on his wrist-watch, and settled himself at last in the other wicker chair. They raised glasses and drank; but Gower sipped where Steele swallowed.

The eyes were turned on him. It was the signal. Steele began, "First of all, would you ring Miss Haig?"

Gower, after a moment, nodded.

"Next, the strike."

"The which?"

"The strike."

"Yes, of course. How is it?"

"Over, as you might say."

"Over?"

"They're working tomorrow. It was only the office staff as I told you."

"They're *all* going back?"

"Yep." He smacked his lips. His glass empty he reached for another bottle. It was an unspoken agreement between them that they should not stand on ceremony with each other.

"Why are they going back?"

"I persuaded 'em it was what they ought to do."

"Persuaded?"

"I just talked to 'em."

Gower looked away. There was a darkness coming up behind the rim of the hills. For a moment he watched it, puzzled. Then he pointed. At first Steele saw nothing and then he noticed the changing colour of the distant sky. He said, "Dust storm. And rain tomorrow maybe. Here's hoping."

Without shifting his gaze Gower said, "How – persuade?"

"I threatened 'em."

"Not physically, I hope."

Steele looked thoughtful. "I know it's wrong," he said at last, "and anyway I didn't actually do it like that. At least –"

Gower stared at him now. Steele was, in a way, a promising boy. If he wasn't clear about his motives he ventilated his doubts by talking about them.

"I saw the leaders this morning," Steele went on. "The chief clerk's at the bottom of it, of course. And the whole thing's so bloody meaningless, I saw red, or anyway pink." He looked at Gower all the time as he talked. "After I'd talked to 'em I took Muttra Dass on one side and I could see he was bloody scared. I asked him what the hell and hadn't Gower Sahib always looked after him and all of 'em and of course he couldn't say a bloody thing. I'd 've liked to 've hit him I admit, but I'm not such a fool. Perhaps I made some sort of movement. I don't know. I *felt* like knocking his teeth back but I didn't. I didn't even look aggressive. I mean –"

"More than you could help?"

"You know what I mean. We were alone of course and I expect he thought he was in for a bashing. But I honestly didn't do a thing except *want* to bash him. Anyway it had the right effect."

"What happened? Try to remember exactly."

"I told Dass I knew damn well he was the ring-leader."

"He wasn't of course."

"Eh?"

"He was the leader at this end, I agree, and that's all that concerned you. Go on."

Steele looked puzzled, but he said, "Well, I told him that unless they went back tomorrow I'd make sure he was replaced and that if necessary we'd replace the whole lot of 'em. Babus are two a penny after all, and they'd got no proper grievance."

"They live on what would be starvation wages for us. But go on."

"I told him he wasn't going to try his bloody bolshie stuff up at Ooni. I told him his strike was half-baked and a lot of bloody nonsense. Then I told him to go and tell the others that if they went back on Monday nice and orderly we'd have a pukka durbar and they could all shoot their mouths off properly in the way laid down."

"And then?"

"By then –" Steele paused, and laughed. "By then he was shivering in his shoes and if he hadn't bunked I think I *would've* bashed him. But he skedaddled and after about twenty minutes he came back pretty smarmy and said the Sahib was a good man and Bless my old father and mother, my nieces, nephews and aunts and Pray God long life to Steele Sahib and Gower Sahib and they'd go back tomorrow."

"Where did this interview take place?"

"In the office."

"Were you alone?"

"Yes."

"I see."

"Well, what d'you think?"

"You should never take a man like that on one side without witnesses. I think you've been unwise."

Steele's mouth dropped open. He asked, "Why?"

"Send for Dass now."

Steele hesitated, then he got up and leaned over the balustrade, cupping his hands round his mouth to yell. He remained, then, both arms supporting his body on the balustrade, and Gower noticed the width and power of his shoulders. He stared at Steele's back.

He would be, undoubtedly, attractive to women.

"Steele," he said, and Steele faced him. "I want to talk to you."

"Yes, of course. What about?"

"About Dorothy."

After a moment or two Gower allowed his own glance to drop because he knew the boy wanted to look away himself but held it a point of honour not to do so first.

"Do sit down."

Steele did so and poured himself another beer. He cleared his throat and asked, "Is there anything wrong?"

"I think so. I thought perhaps you'd be able to throw light on it."

"Me?"

Gower looked at Steele's profile: deep forehead; short nose; firm chin; a fullness about the lips. "I've discovered she's not happy. And I have an unpleasant feeling it's the sort of unhappiness I ought to have noticed before. Can you think what might be the cause?"

"No, no, I honestly can't."

"Then you agree she's unhappy? You've noticed it yourself?" Gower waited, then continued, "I don't find it easy to talk about, Steele. So please don't brush it off as a sort of conversational gambit."

Steele was intently watching the foam-scum on the sides of his glass. He said, "It's not my business, but I don't think she cares for it much in Ooni."

"Or in Marapore?"

"I don't know."

"Or India?"

Steele stubbed out his cigarette. Gower noticed it was only half smoked.

"Or India?" he repeated.

"I honestly don't know. Frankly, we – well, we don't get on all that well. I thought you'd have noticed."

They watched each other.

"No. I haven't noticed, but then –" Gower's voice trailed off. He frowned and said suddenly, "You used to get on well."

"Oh, well – at first."

"At first you got on extremely well. I suppose that's natural in a place like this. New faces, new things to talk about. You came from the same part of England as Dorothy, didn't you?"

"Not exactly."

"You used to talk about it. That place where she went to school."

"I didn't live there. I only knew it quite well."

"You know what I'm getting at, don't you?"

Steele looked up sharply, as though caught out. He shook his head.

Gower smiled, faintly. "I'm trying to make you cast your mind back to when you first arrived."

"But why?"

"The conversations you had in those days must have been part and parcel of your first impressions."

"First impressions of what?"

"Of Dorothy and of myself. Of the two of us as man and wife." Steele flushed.

"What *was* your first impression?" Gower asked.

"I don't remember. I mean, everything seemed all right."

"It's important that I should know."

"I'd help if I could, but –"

"It's important that I should know, Steele." Gower heard the flat note of despair in his own voice and he heard again, like a warning, the words: *I hate you more than any man I know.* That was a statement, a simple, bare statement that needed no explanation, however much one found it impossible to believe. He had spent a sleepless night in not believing it. But there were also the words: *If you go home to England I ought to warn you you go home alone.* And that implied a wish on Dorothy's part to remain in India. An explanation of that seemed necessary. He could only think of one.

He kept his eyes on Steele. It was difficult to assess exactly another man's attractiveness to the opposite sex, but he knew of no other man remotely possible as a lover for his wife. And Steele was young. Gower said, "You don't have to put on a show, you know. I believe I'm a reasonably objective individual."

Steele said, "When I first came I saw you were fond of her."

"Fond, not in love?"

"They're the same, aren't they? I mean when you're married or something you don't fall over each other all the time."

"But you're not married."

Steele hesitated. "No. But I live with an Indian girl."

"Where?"

"In my bungalow."

"But –" Gower stopped. He had been about to say: But I never knew that. He said, instead, "Is she a local girl?"

"I'm not sure. I think so. My bearer brought her along one day – you know how it is – he did that sort of thing when he was my orderly in the war."

"How long –" Again he stopped himself. But Steele understood and replied, "Eighteen months. In fact almost ever since I came."

"I've never seen her when I've come round to you."

"She works in the kitchen." Steele got up and poured more beer for both of them. "If you object, of course, I'll put an end to it."

"Don't be absurd. Why should I object? It's rather expected, isn't it? And everyone must know by now." He smiled wanly. He recalled his own bachelor days, his firm refusal of such favours. He had been rather a prig about it, he supposed, a cold fish – as he had once overheard someone say. So long ago. Funny how a chance, almost forgotten remark returned, as though pertinent.

"Everyone except you," Steele said. "I thought once I ought to sort of get your unofficial sanction as you're the boss round here." He grinned. "But it seemed such a damn silly thing to ask about."

"Does Dorothy know?"

"Yes. I mean I think so. Women always guess."

"Do they?" Gower hesitated. "Is that why you're no longer so friendly?"

"Yes. Yes, I expect so."

But he had jumped too readily at the suggestion.

Gower leaned back in his chair and closed his eyes. He said, without opening them, "Mr. Dass is a long time answering that call of yours."

Steele yelled again.

"There's someone coming, but it's not Dass."

"No."

A pause; then Steele's voice – "Why do you say 'no' like that?"

"Because I don't expect Dass to come. I expect him to be on his way to see my friend Mr. Gupta, in Marapore. That's what I meant when I said Dass was only the ring-leader at this end." Opening his eyes he turned his head away from Steele as if to avoid further conversation. The man who came denied all knowledge of Dass's whereabouts. No, he had not seen Muttra Dass; not since Dass had gone back to report to Steele Sahib that the strike was over. "It is Sunday, Sahib. All now are taking rest."

Before Gower went in to phone Miss Haig he said to Steele, "I might not be in Ooni much longer. That could go for both of us. Shall you mind a great deal?"

The boy clearly did not understand. He said, "Of course I'd mind."

"What would you do?"

Steele smiled. "You're the boss," he said. Then the smile faded. He added, "I'd find something," and turned away, conscious that he had made Gower feel responsible for him.

Mrs. Mapleton removed the engagement ring from her finger

122

and passed it to MacKendrick. "How much d'you think it's worth?" she asked.

He held it between thumb and forefinger, twisting it round so that the small, single diamond flashed in the sunlight. Afraid to say what he thought, he muttered, "I have no idea, I'm afraid. This sort of thing's not in my line."

"I'd sell it if I could get fifty pounds for it."

"What's that in rupees?"

"Nearly seven hundred. Two hundred dollars to you."

"Is that all?"

"All? To me it's a lot." She held her hand out and he returned the ring to her. Putting it back on her finger she looked round her bedroom. "And it's all I've got left to pop. I suppose you wouldn't think of buying it from me? It's cheap at the price and diamonds are gilt-edged. You could sell it for twice that in Calcutta and have some fun on the profits."

"I wouldn't only pay fifty pounds if it's worth more. I couldn't make that sort of profit –"

"Don't be a bloody fool," she interrupted. "And don't look so uncomfortable. The embarrassment's all mine I can assure you, so let's forget it. I'll mix you a drink while you wait for Harriet to come back."

He followed her into the shabby little sitting-room, filled with old-fashioned mahogany furniture. The house boy was trying to look occupied.

"Bring drinks," she said. Then, as the servant disappeared, she lowered her voice. "Hussein's always trying to catch me out being immoral. He's a little bastard and why Harriet hasn't seen through him before now beats me. When bearers 've been with you more than five years they ought to be sacked or shot. Preferably shot. But he's been with her from the year dot. What do you want to see Harriet for, by the way?"

"Nothing special. If she's not back soon I'll have to go."

"Why'd you cut me last night at Sandy's?"

"I didn't cut you. I thought you were cutting me."

"I'm not such a fool. Men are scarce." This morning her only armour was her outspokenness. He admired her for it, almost. "You got pretty thick with Tom Gower, didn't you?" she asked.

"He seemed a nice guy."

"Did you go back to dinner with him?"

He nodded. She was waiting for a cigarette, so he gave her one. Blowing out smoke she asked, "And what did you think of that wife of his?"

"I guess I don't size people up that quick."

"You've sized me up though, haven't you?"

"No. I haven't."

"Then you're slower than I thought. I hear you created a rumpus at Smith's last night."

"Who told you? Miss Haig?"

"My dear man, it's all round the cantonment this morning. You ought to be more careful, you're not supposed to hit the bastards, you know. On the other hand, I like a man who'll have a go. Why *did* you have a go?"

"I was drunk."

"Was that all?" She seemed disappointed.

"And they'd changed my room without permission."

"Typical. They think they can do what they like to us already. They're in for a shock if you ask me. Someone told me this morning that Mountbatten's being pretty clever and all this business in Delhi is just window-dressing and we're not actually leaving India at all."

"That sounds phoney."

"Yes, doesn't it? Still, a phoney rumour's better than no rumour." She paused. "Look, about that ring –"

Outside there was the sound of a tonga. She stood up and said, "Blast!" He stood up, too, and they were close together. She put a hand on his arm. "Do something for me, will you? Come with me to the bazaar. There's an old Indian there who'll buy it from me. Come and help me force up the price. They take notice of a man."

When Miss Haig came in Cynthia had already gone to her room to put on a hat; she called out, "Don't let the tonga go." Hussein was sent to bring it back. Miss Haig did not seem at all surprised to see MacKendrick. She said, "How nice. I'm glad you came because I was going to ring you anyway. You don't have to go back to Bombay straight away, do you?"

"No. I just had to dictate a cable back home."

"When *are* you going?"

"Tomorrow?" He shrugged his shoulders.

"Then it's all right and you can come to dinner tonight?"

He smiled. "Yes, I can come to dinner. But it won't work, you know. You can't pair me off with her." She was about to speak but he said, "I came to ask you about that photograph. Did you take it last night by any chance?"

"No. You left it on the table."

"It wasn't there when I looked for it."

"When did you look for it?"

"After I'd dressed. I didn't remember it till then. I'd had a bad night."

"Did you ask the room boy?"

"I've got my own bearer. But he didn't know anything about it."

"Is he the sort you can trust?"

"I guess so. He's never stolen from me yet. And why take a photograph?"

"You'd better look again. Perhaps you didn't put it on the table after all. But I thought you did."

"I've looked all over."

"Then it's fallen on the floor and been cleared away by the sweeper." She smiled at him. She thought: He's different today, not exactly harder, but more resilient. "I shouldn't worry about the photograph. It's not important to you now, is it?"

"No, it's not important."

Cynthia came back. She said, "Mr. MacKendrick's coming out with me to the bazaar, Harriet. Anything you want?"

"Some cigarettes, I think. Yes, and call in at Hari Chand and tell him to send up half-a-dozen bottles of that nice South African wine we had at Christmas."

Cynthia stared. "Whatever for?"

"I'm giving a dinner party tonight."

"You never told me!"

"I only decided an hour ago."

"And what's the party in aid of?"

"The future."

"How nice and vague. And who's coming to it?"

"Oh, several people." Miss Haig turned her back. "The no-goods and the gone natives."

"Good God."

"And Jimmy Smith."

"I suppose that gives it tone." Cynthia swung round to Mac-Kendrick. "Have you been asked?" When he nodded she said to Miss Haig, "We can't cope with a crowd with only Hussein."

Miss Haig paused to consider this. "Yes, you're right. Mr. MacKendrick, since you're coming do you think that boy of yours could give a hand? It's frightfully pukka to have your own servant attending you at functions. I'd pay him," she added.

"Sure. He'll be here." She was making sure of him. Suddenly he felt trapped.

"If you're thinking of inviting Frank Milner," Cynthia said, "you'll have to change your mind."

"I've already invited him and he's coming."

Cynthia turned to MacKendrick. "I thought you said Frank Milner was expecting a guest at Smith's?"

"He is," Miss Haig interrupted, "and so he's bringing her too. Someone called Judith Anderson."

"All I hope is she's not quite coal-black. Come on, we'd better get going."

Later, as the tonga rattled over the level crossing into the native town MacKendrick remembered Gower's words. "Over there you'll see a light in the sky. Go towards it, into it, it

126

becomes a town with noise and people and smells. Beautiful and squalid."

He stared out at the narrow street of open shop-fronts, where the goods spilled out on to the roadside. Here, he and Mrs. Mapleton were aliens, not understood and not understanding. When the tonga stopped he helped her down and followed her across flagstones laid down like a tiny bridge across an open drain, into a trinket shop. A young boy, who looked consumptive, waylaid them inside. At a word from Cynthia he disappeared through a door at the back of the shop. They were alone. The bracelets, ear-rings, necklaces were garish. But when he picked one up and held it to the light he saw its individual beauty.

"Tourist stuff."

"But this necklace is great."

"For God's sake don't waste money on it."

A beggar woman, half-naked, her withered breasts flatly pendulous upon her brown, wrinkled stomach, whined from the street, her hand clutching the air as she gestured towards them. The boy returned and told them to go through to the back. The room they entered was dark and smelled of drains. At the tiny desk sat an old man with a stained turban slightly awry on his head. He did not rise. Cynthia came straight to the point.

"This ring. What's it worth?" She held it out and the old man took it in a hand which trembled as though with palsy. He stared at the quivering ring, which, in this light, had no radiance, seemed cheap, worthless. His voice was piercing. "It is worth not more than three hundred rupees."

"It's worth much more, you old fraud. What will you give me for it?"

"Two hundred rupees."

MacKendrick said, "You said three hundred."

"It is worth three hundred, but I do not want it, so I will give only two hundred."

MacKendrick smiled.

"All right, you don't want it. We don't want to sell it you.

127

We just want your valuation. We've been offered nine hundred rupees." He glanced at Cynthia, for approval; but her eyes were fixed on the ring.

"And who, young gentleman, would be fool enough to give nine hundred rupees for a ring worth five hundred at the very highest?"

"Ah! Five hundred?"

"At the highest. Five hundred for the ring. The stone, three hundred. The stone only I would want. For this, two hundred for it would be trouble to sell it again."

"Who would buy the ring as a ring?"

"This friend of yours? This one offering nine hundred? Or perhaps in Bombay?" The old man waggled his head from side to side.

"No one in Marapore?"

"There might be such a person."

"How much would that person pay?"

The Indian looked at the ring again for a long time.

"Four hundred, four-fifty rupees. Perhaps."

"Where can we find this person?"

"In two three days I might find him."

"If you take the ring now and sell to this person for four-fifty, how much will you pay us now?"

"Perhaps three hundred. Not more than three hundred."

"That's a high rate of profit."

"There is risk."

MacKendrick turned to Cynthia. He said, as a further gambit in the little transaction, "O.K., let's get out of here." But she moved closer to the desk and held out her left hand. "This wedding ring. How much for this and the other?"

MacKendrick said, "Mrs. Mapleton – you can't –"

"Shut up!" She was holding her hand stiffly. "I need money. Tell me your best price."

The old man smiled. "Dear lady. This ring, it is nothing."

"How much?"

"Twenty rupees. Three hundred rupees I will give for both rings. My final offer."

She let the hand drop. MacKendrick took the diamond ring from the shaking hand.

"Let's go."

She followed him out. He helped her into the tonga. With face averted she said, "Thanks for trying to beat him up. You did it well."

"Thanks. My one social grace, perhaps."

They sat together, without physical contact, and the tonga took them back to the cantonment, to Hari Chand's shop, which was a converted bungalow, and opened from nine until midday on Sunday mornings. There, while the tonga waited in the road beyond the overgrown garden, she bought cigarettes and ordered the wine. MacKendrick took out his wallet, but she said, almost angrily, "It's charged to Harriet."

When they came out the sunlight had gone. Looking up he saw that the sky was the colour of slate. The hot wind had died but suddenly it came fiercely alive again; an overwhelming force that whirled dust in stinging, angry clouds. "The shop, back to the shop!" she yelled, and together they ran back down the drive, half blinded. When they reached the door it had already been barred. The wind whipped round the bungalow and lashed their skin. There was a roaring above their heads as the trees tossed their branches in the storm. A violent gust shrieked down the drive and he caught her to him and covered her head against his chest with his jacket. He felt one side of his face pierced as if with a hundred hot needles.

The gale lasted for five minutes and then it whirled itself away from Marapore, leaving the dust floating like a mist. It lay on everything. It was in the mouth, the nostrils, beneath one's very clothes.

The tonga had gone.

Cynthia laughed. "I hope it bolted. I don't know about you, but I could use a drink right now. We can walk to the club from here." She was still avoiding his eyes. Her back was turned as she inspected her face in a small hand-bag mirror. They set off together. The wind had left the cantonment with an odd look of being out of drawing. When they reached the club she said, "Come with me, I know a quiet spot," and led the way into an anteroom where they could hear the buzz of voices from the adjacent lounge. When the bearer had taken their order she said, "You've still got the ring."

"Have I?"

"Yes, you put it in your pocket."

He made a pretence of looking.

"You can't have lost it."

"I hope not." He stood up. He knew his face gave him away. He felt through all his pockets again. Each time his hand closed on the ring he had to fight the instinct to give it back to her. He sat down, assuming a look of consternation which embarrassed them both. "I guess it fell out when we ran."

She half rose. "We'll have to go back and look." He put a hand on her arm.

"No, I was going to buy it from you anyway. That's why I dragged you out of the shop."

"Oh."

He counted out notes.

"But that's a thousand rupees."

"That's what I'm paying. That's what I judge it's worth." He put the money in her bag. Later, when drinks had restored their equilibrium, they both wondered whether he had purchased the right to sleep with her. They treated one another with a wary respect.

The girl pushed Milner away and said, "You're disgusting." She got off the bed and went into the bathroom.

Through half-shut eyes he watched her go. Then he looked at his own hairy wrist and at his watch which pointed to six-forty-five. He wanted to sleep now. But he wanted a drink even more.

He felt ashamed. He shouldn't have treated her like that. He leaned up on his elbow, staring at his gross nakedness, the paunch, the ginger hair on his chest arrowing down to his groin. He considered the act. At six they'd arrived at Smith's. It wasn't yet seven. At seven-fifteen they had to go out to dinner. Sod it. Sod it. Sod it.

He rose just as she came back into the bedroom, naked still. Chi-chi. Her skin was nearly coffee-colour. Café-au-bloody-lait. But her face was whiter. She'd made up already. The make-up on her face accentuated her nakedness, gave sensual meaning to the big, firm, satin-smooth breasts with their large brown nipples. She stared at him.

He said, "Well, girlie?"

"You're gross."

Chi-chi. That Welsh lilt to her voice. He stood up and quickly she turned her back and began to dress. He picked up his flask and drank from it deeply. Country-whisky. Rot-gut. Fire that warmed him.

She had her frock on now. Her natural beauty and dignity were gone. She looked what she was, an Anglo-Indian girl out for a white man. The dress was vulgar. If she put a white flower in her lustrous blue-black hair she'd look like an advertisement for some cheap lipstick.

She said, "You'd better get your clothes on."

"Judith . . ."

"Yes?" Her arms were raised, awkwardly, as she tried to fasten the buttons at the back of her frock. He moved over to her but she stood away from him. "Don't come near me like that."

He stopped in his tracks. "Don't be unkind, Judy. Sorry. Shouldn't have done what I did. You got me worked up."

"You're drunk. Drunk as a coot."

"Got reason. I got reason I tell you." He groped blindly for his underwear. When he had got his pants on he paused to get the better of the dizziness. She was watching him. "What reason?" she asked.

"They've bitched me at the depot."

"How?"

"They've put in a half-colonel over me. Over me."

"Who's 'they'?"

"G.H.-bloody-Q."

She shrugged and went to the mirror to comb her hair.

"You don't understand, Judy. He's a wog."

"Oh?"

"They've bitched me proper."

"I should worry."

He picked up his scattered uniform. When he was dressed he looked merely disreputable. He rolled down his sleeves. "I don' want to go to this bloody dinner."

"I do."

"We'd have fun back at my bungalow."

"We're going to the party." She looked at him coldly. "I like parties. I haven't been to a party in months." She screwed on plastic earrings shaped like stars, and thus adorned, she felt pre-pared, ready to face the world. And if the party was a success, she thought, she'd be able to cope with Frank. She had to cope with him. Frank might be the last chance.

There was sheet lightning. In its reflection the world was still and silent. There seemed to be no air to breathe. In Miss Haig's bungalow the ceiling fans had failed and she welcomed her guests with a growing despair at the probability of her party's failure. But when Hussein had mended the fuse there were cries of delight as the blades began once more to revolve and Jimmy, who had been the first guest to arrive, held up his glass and said, "Drinks on the house, Harriet, and send one to this magician of a bearer of yours."

"Good gracious no, he's a Muslim."

"So what? So is my chauffeur. He drinks like a fish. Come, bear me out, Mr. Gower – there's many a good Muslim who likes his tot."

"Quite so." Gower paused, then with a smile he added, "A man I knew in the war, for instance –"

Miss Haig smiled too, and turned away, leaving them together, isolated as two people at a party can be isolated. Later, she thought, much later, they'll have their talk, the way towards it paved by confidence in each other. It was important that Tom should not sense a pre-arrangement or interpret the suggestion of a job in Kalipur as charity. Jimmy had been briefed. She moved towards Dorothy, who sat on the arm of a sofa, not drinking, her hands folded on her lap. "My dear, I'm so glad you were able to come. As soon as Frank Milner gets here we'll go in to dinner." There was the briefest of answering smiles.

Taking MacKendrick's arm, Cynthia said, in a low voice, "I want to talk to you." He followed her out on to the verandah.

"Are you really going tomorrow?"

"Afraid so."

"Bombay?"

"Yes."

"You've booked your seat and everything, then?"

"Why, no."

"Oh, then you can't."

"It was easy enough to get a seat in Calcutta."

"You must have bribed somebody at the station."

He smiled. "It's all on the expense account."

"I see."

"What's on your mind?"

"I'm going to Bombay too."

"When?"

Ignoring the question she said, "A friend of mine's in Bombay and he's making enquiries about going to Kenya. We fixed up in Murree that we'd go together if it could be managed."

"When though?"

"I'll be quite frank," she said at last. "I badly needed that thousand chips you paid me for the ring. I owe Harriet for board and lodging here. I've a few debts to pay off. A ticket to Bombay's

133

going to leave me on the rocks again." Sensing his interruption she hurried on. "Confidentially, what I had in mind was asking you to loan me the cost of a ticket and directly I get there I can contact Ronnie – that's the man I mentioned who's going to Kenya – and pay you back."

"I'll gladly loan you the money."

She was silent. She came a little nearer him. In a still lower voice she said, "I thought perhaps we could go together. If you went to the station tomorrow night you might be able to book two reservations for the Wednesday train."

"I ought to head back quicker than that."

Her voice hardened a little. "I'd be grateful for the company," she said, making it sound purposely off-hand.

"Then come tomorrow."

"We'd get no reservation."

"Well, let's try."

"I can't do it tomorrow. I can't pack and make all the arrangements involved. You see – this time it's goodbye here for good."

"I've really got to go tomorrow."

She hesitated. "You're like all men. You hate to think you're being *made* to do something." She began to move off down the verandah.

"Hey, where are you going?"

"Only to my room."

He followed her. Turning the corner he saw that the verandah continued round the side of the house. A light shone from her room through open double doors.

"Aren't you nervous sleeping on the ground floor like this?" In the half-light she looked almost young.

"You get used to it. Of course we have a chowkidar."

"What's that?"

"A night-watchman. They sleep all the time themselves, but it's pretty safe because they pay all the local crooks a small fee every month to keep away. If they don't pay they have to keep awake. I tell you, India's fun if you've got a sense of humour."

He laughed and moved up to her.

"I can even leave my door unlocked," she added. "You'd better get back, while I powder my nose."

As she stepped past him she slightly lost her balance, and putting out his arm he found himself holding her. She made no movement away from him. He was flattered, in the way she meant him to be. He knew that to possess her would be for him at once an act of revenge and an act of surrender; revenge for what had been withheld, surrender to what he had tried to escape. An affair with Cynthia Mapleton would bear the hall-mark of his family: no risk, a sure thing. And, of course, he had paid for it already.

He said in a voice which shook a little, "Maybe we'd get a coupé on the train." And then the brashness of what he had said made him draw his arm away rather too quickly. For him, this sort of thing was only an act. He said, "I'll see you inside," and watched her as she nodded and passed into the room.

When he returned to the sitting-room, Milner and Judith Anderson were just arriving. He saw at once that Milner was drunk. The man seemed to have reached a point of saturation. But, unsteady on his feet, he walked in, leaving Judith on the threshold, and went to the table where drinks were set out.

MacKendrick looked at the girl. Easy to see what she is, he thought. But her air of uneasiness, the way she avoided looking at any of them, her incongruity, made him at once sorry for her. She stood in the doorway and when Miss Haig stumped up to her she put out her hand with a sudden gesture of defiance which was immediately confounded when she realised Miss Haig, dependent upon her sticks, had no hand immediately free to shake.

"Miss Anderson? I'm Harriet Haig. I see Frank's a little under the weather." The girl smiled, then giggled in grateful embarrassment. All the artificial poise she had had, when in front of the mirror at Smith's, had gone. Miss Haig whispered to her, "I'm so glad you were able to come. Come along and meet my other guests."

Led by Miss Haig, the girl moved awkwardly round the semi-circle of guests. Her dress was too short, the material too shiny; more obviously so in comparison with the dinner gowns Miss Haig and Dorothy Gower were wearing. The light in the room was bad and her skin showed dark and swarthy.

"This is Mr. Jimmy Smith. He's staying at your hotel, too."

They shook hands, wordlessly. Even Jimmy with his whimsical smile could not disguise his attitude towards her.

"And this is Mr. Gower."

Gower's eyes had the same look as Jimmy's. MacKendrick caught its meaning. Try as one would to ignore it, instinct said: This girl is a freak. Half-European, half-Asian, the only unity she has is a sexual one. Because of the colour of her skin one's mind immediately recalls an act of union.

Turning from the fireplace where Gower stood the girl came face to face with Dorothy.

"– and this is Mrs. Gower."

Judith was suddenly transformed. Her whole body seemed to tense up and then relax as though she had come through danger to safety, from enmity to friendliness.

"Dorothy!" she said. "Dorothy Robertson!"

She put out her hand eagerly. "Gracious, I haven't seen you in years." But as soon as Dorothy's hand closed over hers the sparkle went out of her eyes, as suddenly as it had come. She glanced swiftly down at their joined hands; then up again.

"Oh – have I made a mistake?"

"Apparently not. I was Dorothy Robertson before I was married."

"I'm Judith Anderson."

"Judith Anderson?"

The two were staring at each other.

"Judith Anderson? Oh yes. You lived not far away from my aunt's place in Calcutta before the war."

The girl made no reply, but when she moved round to MacKendrick he realised she hardly saw him. Automatically she took

136

his hand. Hers was quite cold. He pressed it, but she was oblivious of his gesture – only remembered it after she had passed him. As she moved her lips to say some trivial thing, she looked from the corner of her eyes at Dorothy Gower who had turned her back.

"Now we must get you a drink."

"No thank you. No, I never drink."

"A *nimbopani*, then?"

"Yes, please. A *nimbopani* would be very nice."

It was then that Cynthia Mapleton returned. She greeted Frank Milner. "Well, hello. I heard at the club this afternoon you'd been pipped at the post."

"So what, Cynth?"

"Is it true?"

"Yes, it's true."

"And is the new man really an Indian?"

"So G.H.-bloody-Q. says."

"Dear me. How dreary for you. Shall you go back to tea?"

"What's it to you?"

"Nothing at all if you want to know." She turned and found the girl at her elbow. "Oh, and is this your little friend?"

On that note they went in to dinner.

Suddenly there was the pain. Miss Haig sat quite still, her hostess's smile fixed on her face like, she thought irrelevantly, a rubber ring that was going to snap so that her cheeks, her jaw, her neck and arms would collapse about her body. Now the pain was going. She breathed in slowly on its outgoing tide, grateful for the return of warmth to her limbs. The lightning was frequent. Tomorrow it would rain. Or the next day. Or the day after. Sometimes, when she listened, she could hear far-off drums: incantations, for rain, for the deluge. The long, gleaming table, with its occupants, seemed now, as the pain subsided, already to be floating on dark, swirling waters, like an ark borne to safety.

"Don't you think so, Harriet?"

"Oh, yes, Jimmy. Yes, I do."

"You weren't listening."

"I was. Truly I was."

There was gentle laughter. "Then what did I say?"

She smiled. "You said what I'm sure was very wise and completely meaningless."

"How well you know me."

"I ought to. Tom, is that business settled at Ooni?"

"What's that?"

"The strike at Ooni. I heard there was some sort of strike."

"Yes, in a way it's settled. I think."

From the opposite end of the table Cynthia said, "I hear that young Mr. Steele has a way with him."

Twirling his empty glass on the polished table Gower asked, "What do you mean, a way with him?"

"I heard at the club he'd brought the strike to an end in time-honoured fashion."

"But what is time-honoured fashion?"

"My dear Tom, you don't expect me to repeat a rumour of that sort."

"I don't see why not."

"Oh well, but don't have me up for slander. There's just a rumour going round that your Mr. Steele resorted to violence to knock sense into them."

Gower leaned back, still twirling the glass. "I see."

"Well, don't look at me like that."

"You're not spreading this rumour, I hope."

"It's true then?"

"No." He looked down at the glass. "It's not true."

"Well, you know how these things get distorted. You can't track this sort of thing to its source." She turned to MacKendrick. "It's what we call a bazaar rumour. The Indians can't stop gossiping, they know *everything* we do, and what they don't know they make up. After all, you can't blame them, it's the only other way they have of amusing themselves." She eyed Judith Anderson who sat on MacKendrick's other side and had had, she felt, more than her fair share of his attention. She then turned to speak to Frank Milner, but before she could do so Gower had said, "What details are there of this Steele rumour?"

"Steele? Oh, that again. Tom dear, is it important?"

"I'm afraid it might be."

"Really? How exciting. Will he get into trouble?" Again she spoke to MacKendrick. "It's awfully dangerous to be *caught* bashing an Indian. Oh, but then you say he *didn't* beat this man up, Tom."

"There's a particular man, is there?"

"I don't know."

"What do you know?"

"Well, nothing. It was just people talking at the club. You know how the bearers bring in all the news from the bazaar. Someone pumping a bearer, I expect. There are people who do. And talking of bearers," she went on, glancing at MacKendrick and then across at the door, "where did you pick up this man of yours who's helping out – this what's his name?"

"Bholu. I picked him up in Bombay."

"He looks the shifty type to me. Every so often he stands over beyond the door there where he thinks he can't be seen and literally *peeps*."

Milner snorted, his eyes on the point where her V-necked dress exposed the beginnings of her flat breasts. "Who at? You, Cynth?"

"No. Not at me. Actually at you, Dorothy."

Dorothy sat, very much as her husband did, leaning back in her chair, twisting the stem of her wine-glass. She looked calmly at Cynthia and then at MacKendrick. She smiled. But she said nothing. When Milner nudged her she moved her arm away politely.

"He knows what's what, eh, Mrs. Gower?" And then, "Oh, sorry. Sorry." He winked at Judith, but Judith was studying Dorothy Gower. Bholu and Hussein brought in fruit plates and finger bowls.

"Tell me," said Jimmy Smith. "What is this Ooni?" He addressed the question to Dorothy.

"My husband will tell you."

Miss Haig pressed her lips together.

"Mr. Gower? This place called Ooni?"

"Yes – Ooni. I run an experimental agricultural station up there."

"Ah. Does it belong entirely to you?"

"No. Chap called Nair owns the land."

"I've heard of him. He's a rich man, I'm told."

"I suppose he is. He owns the little *Gazette* in Marapore too."

"*Does* he! A paper I greatly admire. Does he edit it himself?" Gower raised his eyebrows and licked his lips. "No, I do."

"Truly? Then you wrote that piece I read the other day. I should like to talk to you about that."

Miss Haig pressed Jimmy's foot with her own, and said, "But not at dinner, if you don't mind. Not all of us are interested in politics and such-like."

Jimmy grinned. "You should be. Mrs. Gower, if you and your husband ever thought of coming to Kalipur you must let me know. I believe your husband could help me a great deal."

For a moment it seemed as though she had not heard; then she turned, inclined her head a little. She said, "Oh? In what way?"

Again Miss Haig's foot pressed his. He lost the thread of conversation and ended lamely, "Oh, in – in lots of ways. You must persuade him, persuade him to come to Kalipur."

Cynthia laughed. "There might not be a Kalipur by the time the Government's finished dividing India up into little pieces."

There was a short silence. Suddenly Judith said, "Where's Kalipur?" and at once Jimmy chuckled. "Ah, where indeed is Kalipur? It is a small Indian State, Miss Anderson. Spiritually of course it might be anywhere. But only Mr. Gower – I think – will appreciate that." He smiled across at Gower whose eyes suddenly lit up with interest. "Kalipur," Jimmy went on, "is almost a state of mind. Politically it is unimportant – so far."

Mrs. Mapleton said, "What does that so far mean? Are you going to have a coup or whatever it is called and march into Marapore with flags flying and drums beating?"

"Would you like that, Mrs. Mapleton?"

"I shan't be here to mind or not."

"Where are you going? England?"

"Good God, no. Kenya."

"Why Kenya?"

Cynthia smiled at him grimly. "I have a taste for being waited on by – coloured servants." The unspoken word nigger hovered above them.

"I see. And when are you going, Mrs. Mapleton?"

"In a few days. Actually Mr. MacKendrick and I are going to Bombay together as soon as we can get reservations."

MacKendrick looked at her. She stared back, challenging him. He said, "I – I've been thinking about that. I really ought to leave tomorrow."

"Oh?"

Jimmy laughed and called over to him, "Let me take you as far as Delhi in my car and I'll wangle you on to a plane for Bombay."

"When are you going?"

"Tomorrow. Very early. I will start about half-past six in the morning." He paused, enjoying Mrs. Mapleton's anger and Mr. MacKendrick's embarrassment. "Don't bother to say now. Think it over. My young Shafi will tap at your door about half-past five. Unfortunately my bodyguard will not be available." He smiled broadly. "Our friend over there will explain. Now my poor Jai is back in Kalipur in disgrace. I didn't need him anyway. He was, like so many things, Mrs. Mapleton, only an affectation."

Judith, interested, said, "What happened? To your body-guard, I mean."

"This is something only Jai or Mr. MacKendrick can answer. Let us just say they had a difference of opinion. Short but sharp."

Cynthia saw the girl's eyes turned on MacKendrick with revived

141

interest. Spitefully, she said, "And what will *you* be doing when the British go home, Miss Anderson?"

The girl, sensibly, replied, "Nothing, Mrs. Mapleton. I live in Lahore."

But she had reckoned without Frank Milner. Throughout the meal he had been observing her with growing distaste. He had seen her interest in the American. Fuddled with drink and the day's frustration he said, "Thought you'd be trotting back to Brighton, Judy."

Cynthia laughed, too loudly. "Brighton!" she said. "Do you really come from Brighton?"

"Tha's right, Judy, isn't it? Told me you came from Brighton when I first met you."

"I adore Brighton," said Cynthia. "What part of Brighton did you live?"

Judith shrank back in her chair.

"Where's Brighton?" MacKendrick asked.

"Oh, in England," said Cynthia. Then, winking at the others she added, "On the west coast. Isn't it?"

Judith panicked. West coast. West coast. No, that was wrong. It was the South coast. It must be the South coast. The map. The Channel. Brighton. But she said, afraid to disagree, "Yes." At once she knew, from the way Mrs. Mapleton leaned back as though basking in sunshine, that she had irrevocably given herself away. It was so ludicrous. She felt near to tears. She had not meant to pretend. She had known, as soon as the evening began, that this sort of pretence was, in this company, a waste of time. She wished wildly that she had never pretended even to Frank Milner. But he had been drunk that first time; drunk as always; and she had not really expected to see him again. It was so unfair.

The interrogation was not ended.

"Whereabouts in Brighton did you live, Miss Anderson?"

"In – in Lewes Crescent."

"But I know it! I adore the Hove side. Far better than the Kemp Town side."

"Yes."

"Let me see. Lewes Crescent is just opposite the pier, isn't it?"

Judith stared at her tormenter. She fired her one shot. "There are two piers, Mrs. Mapleton. Which one do you mean?" But the shot found no mark, for even as she spoke she knew she was only giving herself away the more.

"Oh, I'd forgotten the two piers. Well – *I* don't know which one. Which one is it?"

"It's – it's ages since I was there. I – I hardly remember. I was only four."

Frank Milner laughed. "You told me you came out just before the war."

"No. I was only four."

"Did your parents live in Brighton always?" Cynthia smiled poisonously.

"No, Mrs. Mapleton. My father did, but mummy – mummy was Italian." Somehow one felt safer in the shield of the fantastic lie; for the lie had become part of life.

"Oh, then you speak Italian, I expect." Cynthia wished she did herself. That would have been funny.

"No. Mummy died when I was very young."

"In Brighton?"

"No. In Lahore."

"How old were you then?"

"Very young."

"And your father?"

"He's dead, too."

"How sad. In Lahore as well?"

"No, in –" She stopped abruptly. She looked round and for an instant her eyes met Dorothy's. Swiftly, as though compelled, she said, "– in – in Calcutta, I think."

"Think?"

"I don't know."

"Oh?"

143

"He died before we – oh, long ago. Please don't ask me any more questions."

"Why shouldn't I?"

"Please don't."

Miss Haig said, "Cynthia, I think you might –"

"Might what?"

"Change the subject. We all – we ought to go next door and have coffee anyway. There's some rather peculiar port for the gentlemen if they like to stay here for a while and talk." She gave Hussein a sign, and he came to her chair and, with Gower's assistance, she got to her feet.

"Thank you, Tom." She let her hand press his arm meaningly. In a voice he scarcely heard she said, "Jimmy wants to talk." Then, smiling, she led the way into the sitting-room. As soon as she sat down she realised, watching Cynthia, Dorothy and Judith Anderson, that none of her women guests had anything in common. But only Dorothy Gower seemed unperturbed by the uncomfortable silence. And yet, when Bholu brought in the tray of coffee Miss Haig noticed how whitely the knuckles showed on Dorothy's clenched hand, how rigid she remained for as long as Bholu was in the room.

MacKendrick lit another cigarette. Gower and the Maharajah had been talking for half-an-hour, and what they talked about was, to him, utterly incomprehensible. He looked across at Frank Milner. Milner was slumped in his chair, fallen at last, the scale weighted by the 'peculiar' port, into a drunken stupor. Bastard, he thought. Bastard. He'd helped to bait the Eurasian girl.

But why not a bastard? This morning he had told himself – "Right, be a bastard. Be a bastard like Dwight. You'll get fun that way." And he had gone to the office and telephoned Bombay. The cable from his father, read to him by the agent, was brief. Two words. 'Report Progress.' He had dictated a reply, and the agent had been impressed; impressed and flattered. "Bombay okay maximum representation possible present conditions stop advise consideration switch representation Calcutta to Johnson stop full report in writing three days stop currently investigating onspot requirements in field."

Putting the skids under the agent in Calcutta had seemed a simple way of proving to oneself what a bastard one could be. There was no difference, so far as he could see, in the efficiency of either agent. But his father would expect fault to be found somewhere. Fault had been found. It did not have to be explained. And tomorrow, when this man Shafi tapped on his door he would be ready with bags packed, and that would be the end of his escapade.

Why despise Milner? Why pity the girl?

The doors which led into the sitting-room were opened and Hussein came in. He looked ill at ease and when he saw Milner he stopped dead. MacKendrick asked, "What's wrong?"

Hussein indicated the sleeping Milner. "Sahib – Memsahib is going home." Miss Haig followed Hussein into the room. She said, "Oh, no, please don't all get up." She bit her lip and turned helplessly to MacKendrick. "May I have a word with you?"

He went back into the sitting-room with her. Only Dorothy Gower was there. He nodded, then moved so that his back was towards her. Miss Haig hesitated. Then she said, "I hate to ask you but could you see Miss Anderson back to her hotel? She wants to go home now, and Frank's in no fit state. She ought to have someone with her."

As she finished speaking Judith came out of Miss Haig's bedroom. He saw that she had been crying. Miss Haig came straight to the point. "I'm afraid Frank's passed out, my dear, but Mr. MacKendrick will take you back to Smith's."

She did not demur. She even looked grateful. She said, "Thanks. I hate it at night, alone. Especially these days." Her voice was very shaky. As she stood, close to him, he noticed that she was trembling. He said to the other two, "I'll say good-night, then."

145

"Oh, no." It was Judith who spoke. "Please don't let me spoil your evening. It's not far, and you can come straight back."

Miss Haig nodded. He stared at the back of Dorothy's head. She seemed unaware of his existence.

"Good-night, Miss Haig. Thank you for having me." Judith put out her hand and Miss Haig, supporting herself on one stick, took it. "I'm sorry, my dear. Oh, I'm sorry you feel you have to go."

Judith nodded. Then she said, "Good-night, Mrs. Gower."

Dorothy rose.

"Good-night, Miss Anderson."

But she was looking at MacKendrick.

Judith hesitated, as though about to say something more, but quite suddenly she turned away and MacKendrick followed her out on to the verandah, and down the steps. Together they walked down the drive. She said, "Do you mind walking?" He shook his head. "I'd like to. But it's tiring for you in this heat, isn't it?"

"I'm used to the heat."

For a few minutes they walked without speaking.

She said, as they arrived under a street-lamp, "Can I have a cigarette?"

"Surely." He fumbled in his pockets.

As she bent her head to light the cigarette from the match he held cupped, he said, "What went wrong?"

"Wrong?"

"Sure. You've been crying."

She started walking again, but he put out his hand and grasped her arm. With the pity he felt for her was a desire in him to hurt. She stopped, and made no movement to get out of his grip. The flesh of her arm was warm, soft. He put down his head and kissed her gently. When he straightened up she kept her head down. She muttered, "Why did you do that?"

"Because I wanted to." He put his arm round her protectively and they walked on thus, like lovers who have no room to go to.

146

"What did they do to you in there?"

"You know what they did."

"I don't."

"You saw it begin, at dinner."

"They started again?"

"She did. That Cynthia Mapleton. It was a horrible party."

"Why did she start again?"

"Because she hated me. She hated me because you talked to me."

"What've I got to do with it?"

"She likes you, doesn't she?"

"I wouldn't know."

"You're going to Bombay together."

"Like hell we are."

"She said you were."

"I'm hitching that ride to Delhi, tomorrow. And tomorrow won't be too soon."

He felt her stiffen in his arm.

He had to say, "You ought to've arrived sooner. Then maybe I'd 've stayed."

"You don't mean that. You're just being kind."

"All right. I'm just being kind."

He let his arm drop to his side, and walked with his hands in his pockets. He kept watching her profile. It was turned slightly towards him. But even this was pretence. They were both play-acting. He was sick of pretence, sick of the whole business of simulated attraction and counter-attraction; tired of the little moves one had to make to show one knew what added up, show one knew the score.

He said, "Why do you pretend like that?"

At once she was on her guard. "Pretend like what?"

"All that hooey about Brighton or wherever it was. All that hooey about your mother being Italian. You only make it bad for yourself. You only make people who don't know any better act the way Cynthia acted. Then you get hurt. You get sorry for yourself."

147

She made no reply. Yes, he told himself, I want to hurt you too. That way I'll feel better myself. He laughed. "Listen, Judith. Anyone can see you're a Eurasian. *Anyone.* All right, you ought to tell yourself, so what? I can still have a good time –"

Then she stopped and twisted round. She almost spat the words out. "Have a good time! That's funny. That's really funny!"

"What's so funny?"

"I'll tell you what's so funny. It's funny because it's funny to be treated like dirt. Everyone treats us like dirt. It's funny to be insulted by people like Cynthia Mapleton, and funny to be laughed at by people like Hussein. If they don't insult you or laugh at you it's because they want something from you, like Frank Milner. Oh, yes, it's funny all right. If you were an Anglo-Indian you'd laugh like hell all the time."

He matched her tone. "Maybe I would," he said, "and maybe I wouldn't. At least I wouldn't make a goddam fool of myself pretending to be what I'm not."

"No? No? Perhaps you'd be one of the lucky ones then."

"What d'you mean lucky ones?"

"Perhaps – perhaps you'd be like Dorothy Gower with a skin white enough to get away with it! Perhaps –"

She left him, but she had only gone a little way when he caught up with her. He took her by the shoulders. They were standing beneath another street-lamp.

"What did you say?"

"Leave me alone."

He tightened his grip. "Tell me what you said."

"Let me go. Oh, let me go, please."

"What did you say about Dorothy Gower?"

"You heard what I said."

"I didn't understand it."

"Don't you understand plain English?" She smiled, sarcastically, but beneath the bravado he sensed her fear. He suddenly let her go. "Tell me what you know about Dorothy Gower."

"Oh – we were friends, you know."

"I didn't know. When were you friends?"

"Oh, at school. We were best friends."

"You're a damned little liar, aren't you?"

She smacked him across the face, a stinging blow which caught him unawares. Angrily he seized her elbows. "You're a damned little liar. You weren't friends and you weren't at school together because she was at school in England."

Judith laughed. "We were at school in Assam."

"That's not what her husband said."

"It's not her husband I'm talking about. D'you think she'd let on to *him*?"

"Let on about what? What you getting at?"

"I'm not getting at anything. There's nothing to get at. Except the truth. And the truth's what I said, that we were at school in Assam and her mother had the same sort of complexion I've got. We've both of us lived in India all our lives. Does that satisfy you?"

He let her go.

"No. It's all lies. She didn't even recognise you tonight."

"It would have been too embarrassing for her, wouldn't it? I might have given her away by talking to her too much. So I had to be choked off. Oh, I didn't mind, didn't mind at all. In a way I'm rather sorry for her. Anyone can see what I am, but she must wake up every day wondering if she's going to be found out."

"I still think you're lying. If what you say's true her husband would know."

"Why should he? Her mother was dead before she got married, so was her father. She was living with an aunt in Calcutta, last I knew."

"How d'you know?"

"I was in Calcutta, too, only I wasn't allowed to know Dorothy by then. We had to meet on the sly because her aunt tried to hide the fact Dorothy was really like me. I can tell you all sorts of –"

"I don't want to hear." He stepped back. "I don't want to hear. Not from you anyway."

149

"I don't suppose she'd tell you herself." The girl's tone was mocking. When he made no comment she asked, "Well, are you going to see me back safely?" He turned in the direction of Smith's and they walked the rest of the way in silence. At the gateway she stopped. "There's no need to come further," she said, and without saying good-night, she left him.

When he was alone, he thought: She told Dwight. That's why he ran out on her.

He began to walk. He knew he could not go back to Miss Haig's. He recalled Dorothy, saying good-night to Judith, but watching him. He could not go back to Miss Haig's, and he knew he would not be going to Delhi in the morning. Not now. Not yet. He let his feet guide him. They led him from the darkness of the cantonment, past the offices of the *Marapore Gazette* where the words *Go Home Gower* had been crudely painted out. *Go Home Gower*. But England was not home to her. England was a lie. And she was afraid to go. Afraid of the lie. Afraid of it, but living it; having to live it.

He walked across the level crossing into the town. He saw nothing that registered on his mind, but he was grateful for the strident music which came from the shops, still open and bright and evil-smelling and vicious and pitiless. Sometimes faces were pushed close up to his own and hands grabbed at his clothes and there was laughter, bitter and merciless laughter and voices which derided and begged and scolded and threatened and pleaded so that it seemed a whole world to which he was forbidden entry revolved before him like a shining fairground wheel: and somewhere in the centre of the wheel was understanding and love. Somewhere in the street there was himself to be found. Was it there, beneath the gaunt breast of the beggar with twisted limbs and feverish eyes? Or there, smug and smooth like the folds of the white dhoti of the man cross-legged upon a wooden charpoy set under a tree; or there, in the eyes of the little naked boy who ran by his side and begged for dimes or food or offered women?

Or here, in the old woman whose saree was drawn quickly across her face so that he should not gaze upon her? Or here, or here, or here? Up there in the coloured lights strung in the peepul tree? There – stretched like the skin was – on the ribs of the pariah dog who muzzled offal? Did it sing in that haunting voice? Or laugh behind the red-stained teeth and lips of the youth who spat betel-juice in the gutter? Did it sound, then, once, as a tinny gong was struck? Or rise into the hot, parched air with the smell of incense?

MacKendrick stopped, dazedly, in the middle of the tumultuous road: a Brahmini bull, its eyes like liquid fire as it gazed at the open, brightly lit shop, barred his progress. Slowly it moved away. He looked at the shop. Naphtha lamps purred and beneath their light an old man squatted and slowly wrote what another man dictated. As though mesmerised the younger man gradually turned his head until his eyes met MacKendrick's.

It was Bholu.

For a few moments they looked at one another, and then MacKendrick turned back and went along the way he had come. It couldn't have been Bholu, he thought. Bholu is not here. The road back was strangely deserted. He passed along it like a man watched from windows, from behind doors. Not here – the voices shouted. Not now – the music sang.

The arc-lamp shone upon the gleaming metal of the railway lines; beyond them was darkness. He entered the darkness. Gradually the noise behind him died away. But there was another sound. It seemed to sing in his ears. He found himself walking away from it, only to walk into it. What was the sound? This new sound? The darkness of the cantonment was almost tangible; a barrier; a barrier like that which had separated him from Dorothy Gower when first he had seen her. When? Last night? Last week? Never? He found himself approaching the bungalow, and as he neared the gate, walking on the other side of the road, he heard the jeep engine in the distance and stepped quickly behind the trunk of a tree. When the jeep passed he saw that she was alone. The engined revved as she changed gear to turn into the drive. He listened until he heard the squeak of the hand-brake being drawn back. Then he walked to the gateway. He stood there for a long time. Once he lit a cigarette to give himself courage. But he had smoked it through and still he had not moved. He walked a little way down the drive. A light, from one of the rooms, shone out at the side of the house and he saw the huddled form of a man, bearing a lantern, walk along the verandah and settle in the shadows beneath the porch. The chowkidar.

MacKendrick retreated into the thick foliage bordering the drive. The old man was humming. But that was not the sound. Now, he knew what it was. The sound of night, of crickets, of stranger insects too, perhaps; the sounds of India when the sun has gone. Why had he not heard them before? Last night the sounds must have been there, singing and soaring through the night air, making the thick blackness alive with unseen movement. He gazed at the light in the bungalow. Did she hear them, too, these sounds? Sounds which penetrated even the thickest wall?

Suddenly the barrier collapsed. She was there, in the house – approachable, linked to him as though both had waited for a dream to end and reality to begin. The barrier collapsed and she was naked before him, so that her wounds, her scars were close enough to touch; to heal. All her pride and fear were there for his eyes to see, his heart to respond to.

And out of his own response would surely come hers?

There were footsteps turning in from the road, coming down the drive. As soon as Gower came opposite the spot where Mac-Kendrick was hidden, he stopped, and MacKendrick thought he had been seen. But Gower only paused to light a cigarette. His thin face was illuminated as he struck a match. Then the match went out, and after a moment MacKendrick could smell the fragrance of the tobacco. Gower stood where he was, as though thinking, as though making up his mind. Then he continued on to the bungalow. MacKendrick heard the chowkidar greet Gower and Gower's reply. Then silence.

When Gower walked into the bedroom he found Dorothy seated in front of the dressing-table, brushing her hair. Their eyes met in the mirror's reflection.

"I'm sorry to 've been so long."

She said nothing, but continued brushing her hair.

He said, "Look —"

Then he went over to her and stood behind her.

"The Maharajah's offered me a job."

He waited for her to speak.

"Aren't you interested?"

Suddenly he twisted away and began walking to his bed. But then he changed his mind. He returned to the dressing-table.

"We can't go on like this."

"Like what?" she asked.

"As we have this past two days."

He leaned on the edge of the dressing-table.

"Dor."

Still brushing her hair she stared at him.

"Yes?"

"This job in Kalipur. I think I've got to take it."

"Well?"

"I haven't said definitely. He's coming back from Delhi on Friday. That gives me almost a week to think it over. I've invited him to come up to Ooni while he's here. I think I'm going to say yes."

"Well?"

"Dor. Don't be like this. Please don't be like this."

He stopped in surprise. He had never pleaded before. No, more than that. He had never shown emotion to her before.

"Well?"

"Dor, I can't say about the job until I know something."

"What must you know?"

"Last night you said if I gave up here and went home you wouldn't come with me."

"Yes?"

153

"Can't you see? Before I make up my mind about Kalipur I've got to know what *you'd* do."

"What I'd do?"

"Would you come with me?"

She looked at the mirror. Slowly she put the brush down on the table top and folded her hands.

"Yes."

He took one of her hands, but she drew it away.

"What's wrong, Dor?"

"There's nothing wrong."

"Then why will you come to Kalipur but not to England?"

She dipped her fingers into a pot of cold cream and began spreading it over her face.

He said, "Won't you tell me? Is it – is it because –"

Her hand stopped moving and she looked at him again. He noticed how dull her eyes had become.

"Because what?"

"Because you – because you have a lover, a lover in India?"

She turned to the mirror, smiling slightly.

"Would it please you to think I had?"

"Then you have?"

"I don't want to talk. Please go to bed."

He straightened up.

"Is it Steele?"

"I thought you knew what arrangements Mr. Steele had."

As he watched her he thought: Jealousy, this is what it's like. Was it Steele? Or rather had it been Steele? Was she hoping it would be Steele again?

He cleared his throat. The idea of physical jealousy repelled him. He said, "Dor, if we go to Kalipur, might it be different?"

"Different? Different from what?"

"Different for us. Different for us, together. I don't want to know what's wrong here any more. If I'm responsible I'm sorry. That's all. Let's forget here. But might it be different in Kalipur?"

She said, "It might," but she had spoken to her own reflection.

Had there been an unsteadiness in her voice? Signifying what? Hope? Hopelessness?

But she would go with him. Tentatively he caressed her shoulder – once. He felt embarrassed. He had never been demonstrative. It only looked vulgar, now. But she would go with him. He crossed over to his wicker chair and began to take off his shoes.

Once he looked over at the dressing-table. She was still smoothing cream into her face; but, for the moment, she had stopped; one hand resting on her right cheek, just below the eye, where the skin showed darker.

Part Two

1

Next morning, Monday, there was no sign of rain. The sky was bland, the trees unruffled except by the sudden movement of crows, scared into flight by the sound of a klaxon horn on the road beneath their perch. The Cadillac retreated northwards, to Delhi.

As Gower finished his breakfast the telephone rang.

Dorothy lay still, staring through the white mosquito netting at the familiar shapes of the bedroom. Her husband came to the doorway. She did not turn her head.

"That was the hospital," he said. "I've got to go up there." He came to the bedside. "Dass has been hurt."

She closed her eyes and, immersed in the privacy of her own darkness, she was able to say, "How?"

"I don't know yet. He was admitted last night. Now we'll get to the bottom of Cynthia's rumour about – about Steele."

After the sound of the jeep had died away she opened her eyes.

On the wall a lizard basked in a streak of sunshine that speared in through the fan-light window in the opposite wall. In Calcutta she had watched a lizard; a lizard, so still, her own heart hardly beat. But her lover's hand had moved, slowly, caressingly, up and over the sweep of her breasts; moved until it, too, became still. When Dwight's hand had stopped moving it had become cold, so cold it seemed to burn into her bare flesh: and neither of them had spoken. What she had told him could, after all, only be received in silence.

Then, it had been afternoon. In silence they had lain together until the shadows lengthened across the room and, in the half-light, he had answered her by taking her swiftly, violently. Knowing it to be lust, a punishment, she had yet told herself: He loves me in spite of what I've told him. He loves me more.

The lizard moved.

Pulling up the net she slid out of bed and, as a precaution against scorpions, tapped her slippers on the floor before putting them on. She avoided looking into the mirror and went straight to the bathroom where Abdul had already filled the iron tub with tepid water. She bathed slowly, sometimes holding the pudgy yellow sponge high in the air, then squeezing it gradually until it was almost dry. Sometimes she sat perfectly still, one hand arrested in the act of soaping her shoulder, and looked up at the little window beneath the steeply sloping roof. There, outside, was the world. She let the water become quite cold.

When she was dressed she sat in front of the mirror of the dressing-table and closed her eyes so that she could concentrate – become aware of the existence of the day, its sound, its meaning. In this way she could allow the day to enter into her. She could absorb it, consider its aspect, sense its capacity. Once, when this ritual had been new to her, she had envied those who could leap into a new day, unarmed.

Knowing that Abdul had come into the room she opened her eyes and saw that he was standing just behind her. She saw that he hated her and despised her no less this morning than on all the previous mornings. The knowledge gave her a sense of security. Abdul held out a grimy envelope and when she raised her hand, without speaking, he thrust it into the curve of her fingers and thumb. He waited while she slit the envelope and read the note. She said, as she folded it again, "Who brought this?"

"*Chokra.*"

"Speak English."

"Young boy."

"Fetch him."

"He ran."

"Ran?"

"Ran away. Quick."

"Who was he?"

Abdul put his head on one side. "I do not know." She knew he lied. She said, "If he comes again –" Then she hesitated. She waved Abdul away and as soon as she was alone she re-read the childish note.

Dear Lady, I am poor man already in want of Rupees Five hundred for my far away family. It is you who can ever provide. Put secret Rupees Five hundred in hollow tree close by to twelve number milestone on road Ooni side. Don't wait. I shall be secret in watch. Don't fail. This very day provide Rupees Five Hundred before your husband is told. Act prompt. Failing this your husband will get letter. Don't tell Police. I shall be invisible. This day after tiffin bring Rupees Five hundred so that your husband is without information of your heart-close secret.

She got up from the stool, found her handbag and put the letter inside it. She walked through the dining-room, ignoring the breakfast Abdul had set out for her. On the verandah she settled down in one of the wicker lounge chairs. There she sat and began to consider, as she had on so many different occasions, exactly what she should do.

"To be quite truthful," said the little Hindu doctor to Gower as they crossed the bare patch of ground which separated the main building from the long, low hut which housed accident cases, "this business is rather absurd."

"Absurd? In what way?"

"Absurd because he won't say who caused the injuries."

"Who? They're those sort of injuries then?"

"Soon you'll see what I mean, Mr. Gower."

"Is he bad?"

"Not at all. He reported himself in, last night."

"Did he, by jove?"

They entered the hut. Passing through the tiny lobby, a screened-off portion where the ward-sister wrote up her records, they came into the ward itself. At the far end a screen hid Dass's bed, put there, the doctor explained, so that Mr. Gower might enjoy some privacy at the interview. Gower nodded and followed the doctor down the centre of the hut.

Dass lay, chest downwards, his left cheek resting on his folded arms. As soon as he saw Gower he jerked into a sitting position, and half rose; but not before Gower had had time to notice the strips of sticking plaster which were gummed across his back.

"Well, Dass? What's all this about?"

The doctor thrust Dass ungently back on to the bed. Dass's face was swollen, the eyes puffed. One cheek gleamed shiny and yellow where the deep grazing had been painted with iodine. On the whole, Gower thought, the first aid which had been given made the injuries look worse.

"What's all this? Who's done this to you?"

Dass, without warning, burst into tears. Gower nodded at the doctor, who waited, unsympathetic, impatient.

"I see what you mean about 'who'."

The doctor pulled Dass's hands away from his face and pointed to the marks. "A man's fist did that, that's fairly obvious. And –" he twisted Dass round, "– there are several not very severe lacerations on the shoulders. Someone laid into him with a bamboo stick. We removed a splinter." Suddenly he shook Dass roughly. "But the bloody fool won't say who. Or will you? Gower Sahib is here. If you won't tell us, tell Gower Sahib. Come along. Be a man. Now you can go back to Ooni, isn't it?"

Gower touched the doctor's arm. "Leave me alone with him." And as soon as he had said that he saw the evasiveness that flickered in the doctor's eyes. "Leave me alone with him," he repeated. "He might talk to me."

After a show of uncertainty the doctor nodded, shrugged his shoulders and went. Gower waited until he heard the sound of the doctor's voice as he spoke to the ward-sister. Some order was given about arranging for Dass's discharge.

He sat on the edge of the bed.

"Now. We're alone. Tell me who messed you up like this. And remember – whoever, *whoever* it was will pay suitably." He waited. Dass continued to weep, but silently now; and after another minute or so Gower judged the time was ripe to try again.

162

"You'd better get away from here and come back with me to Ooni."

Dass uncovered his battered face. "No, sir. I cannot stay in Ooni." His words sounded strangely sibilant; then Gower realised the clerk had lost several teeth.

"Why not? You can stay in your quarters there and be looked after. Better there than here. Much better."

The man looked frightened. He shook his head dumbly.

"Very well, then. Where do you propose you should stay?"

Dass lay back, as if to answer: Here.

"You can't stay in hospital. They won't have you. You're only an out-patient case. As I remember it your home is in Travancore. That's a long way."

At the mention of home Dass opened his mouth to speak. Gower waited. But the man said nothing. Gower asked, "Perhaps you have some kind friends in Marapore here?" He saw Dass's lips tremble. He knew his own forehead, like Dass's, was bathed in sweat. Which of them, he wondered, was the interrogator, and which the prisoner hypnotised under the arc-light? "No?" he went on. "No friends in Marapore? Not even Mr. Gupta or Vidyasagar?" Dass twisted his head away to one side.

Gower asked, "Why don't you make a charge?"

Dass seemed to be trying to press himself further into the bed and suddenly Gower wanted to strike him. At the same time he was shocked that this should be so. He stood up. The obscenity of violence; his skin crawled.

"I'll leave you to make what arrangements you wish, Dass. Your salary'll be paid until you notify me of your plans." He could not resist adding, "Though I suspect you're not in need of money as a consequence of your strike."

When he got outside into the blinding whiteness of sun and sky he heard the doctor calling, but he deliberately looked in the other direction and walked towards the jeep. There was something wrong, he felt, something wrong about the day and the way it pressed down on him; the way it muffled his intelligence

163

and his powers of deduction. It seemed to him as though he had only to lift a stone from the ground to find there the clue to what had happened to Dass. But he dare not lift the stone. He dare not lift the stone for he feared that the stone was the day which weighed upon him. To lift the stone might, perhaps, reveal nothing but himself.

As he pressed the starter he thought momentarily of going to see Gupta, whose house in the town he knew by sight. The engine fired and, for a few seconds, he listened to it, considering its power and its complexity. He would not, he knew, go to see Gupta; for Gupta would come to him. Gupta would lift the stone.

When he arrived at the *Gazette* office he found Gupta waiting. Gupta was, in fact, seated behind Gower's desk.

Gupta rose to his feet. "Good-morning, Mr. Gower."

Gower expected him to come round from behind the desk; expected an apology. When none came he said, abruptly, "Well, what can I do for you?"

"Please sit down, Mr. Gower."

"I beg your pardon?"

"Please draw up a chair."

"I'm afraid you have me at a disadvantage. I thought –"

"Please." Gupta extended a hand. With the other he picked up a little brass bell and rang it. Gower turned as Mr. Chatterji, his assistant editor, came in. Chatterji ignored him and spoke directly to Gupta.

"You rang?"

"Yes, we are not to be disturbed, you will understand."

"Very well."

Chatterji was turning to go. Gower said, "Just a moment, Chatterji."

"Yes, Mr. Gower?" The man was obviously ashamed.

"Hold on a moment. Look, Gupta. This is my office."

"That is so."

"I'm glad you agree."

164

"But it is also mine."

"Since when?"

Gupta spread his hands. "I think Mr. Chatterji need not remain with us."

"Very well." Gower nodded at Chatterji, who then went away with the air of a man who escapes unpleasantness against his better judgment.

"Also yours, Mr. Gupta? Since when?"

"Since this morning, you will understand."

"I trust I shall."

"Mr. Nair was not acquainting you of my appointment? No – well. My credentials so to speak." He passed over a letter, typewritten on *Gazette* note-paper.

Dear Mr. Gupta,

This will confirm your appointment as Director of my new company, now in formation, which will control my publishing interests. Also your appointment as Managing Editor of my weekly newspapers in Travanapatam and Marapore. Please take an early opportunity of discussing editorial policy with the editors of both these periodicals.

It was dated Monday, June 9th, and was signed by Nair. Gower handed it back.

"Yes, I understand. As from today."

"It was arranged early this morning. Mr. Nair was here. Please be seated. When we are better organised we must have two desks in this room." Gupta sat down.

"I don't think that will be necessary. Not as far as I'm concerned, anyway."

"As you wish. Of course, I shall not be here often."

"Frankly, Gupta, I wouldn't give a damn."

Gupta smiled. "Do you imply your resignation?"

"I imply nothing." So that he should not feel like a schoolboy on the carpet he crossed over to the window and sat down on the leather arm-chair beneath it. Immediately he knew he had made a mistake. The chair was low. Gupta looked down on him.

165

"Well, Mr. Gower. Let us proceed to our discussion of editorial policy."

"When I said I didn't imply resignation I meant that between you and me the point doesn't arise. It only arises between myself and Nair."

"I understand. Unfortunately, Mr. Nair has left Marapore for a short trip."

"Quite so."

"Then let us talk."

"I'm willing to listen while you talk."

"You are a – cautious – man, Mr. Gower."

The jibe went home, and Gupta saw that it had done so. He pressed his advantage. "Perhaps I should have said liberal-minded?" Gower made no comment. "But you see, Mr. Gower, liberal-mindedness and caution are qualities so easily misinterpreted."

"In what way?"

"Oh, many and various ways. On the one hand people will believe these qualities actually disguise more precise views. If they are believing this also they may believe the precise views to be opposed to theirs. On the other hand, people may interpret caution as lack of conviction, or even lack of courage. Oh please – I am only discursive."

"Discursive and cautious."

Gupta's smile disappeared. He tapped his finger on the desk. "I am by nature not a cautious man. I have precise views which are the views of an Indian National."

"Do you mean Hindu National?"

"They should be synonymous."

"Shall we come to the point? I gather you have policy changes to outline."

"Ah yes, indeed. There is a wish here in Marapore for a paper reflecting public opinion. There is little need for me to tell you that last week's *Gazette* hardly did that. I refer of course to your editorial on Pakistan and the Kalipur affair."

"Oh, is there a Kalipur affair?"

"There will be unless public opinion has a chance to express itself."

"And how do you propose it should?"

"I shall contribute a leader about Kalipur myself. This week. Here is a copy which perhaps you will read at your leisure and give me your opinion about."

Gower hardly looked at the sheets of paper. Gupta dropped them back on the desk. "I propose," he continued, "to make plans for an edition of the *Gazette* to be published also in Hindi as soon as convenient."

"A good idea."

"Eventually the English edition will become unnecessary."

"That is possible." Gower stood up.

"I'm glad you agree. There is one other thing –"

"Yes?"

"There is a rumour going round which concerns you, Mr. Gower."

"I can well believe it."

"I think we should try to clear it up, don't you?"

"It depends what it is."

"It is a very strong rumour. There is bad feeling in the town. So much so that the *Gazette* cannot ignore it. Some reference will have to be made to it, you will understand. Especially as we are anxious at this time that the British should remain popular. I think we should investigate the rumour and – scotch it? I think the expression is."

"And the rumour?"

"It is that your young Mr. Steele assaulted one of the estate clerks at Ooni. One Muttra Dass."

"Why should Steele assault Dass?"

"Why indeed?"

"Well?"

"Now we hear that Dass is in hospital and afraid to make a charge."

167

"He is in hospital. Certainly he's making no charge."

"You've seen him?"

"Yes."

"Then what is there to be done?"

"Nothing."

"To do nothing is dangerous. To do nothing will be as good as admitting young Mr. Steele assaulted him. Taking into account the mood of the people here –"

"What is the mood of the people? Really, Gupta, I'm trying very hard to understand you."

Gupta rose. They faced each other across the desk.

"Ooni, Mr. Gower, is never a popular place."

"Why? It does a lot of good."

"This Steele. They say he is living with a Hindu girl. Moreover that the Hindu girl was brought to him by a Muslim. He has a Muslim servant, I think?"

"Yes."

"Some say this Hindu girl was abducted."

"That can only make Steele unpopular, not Ooni. As an experimental station it does a great deal of good."

"That is a matter of opinion. Actually, Mr. Gower –"

"I don't intend to discuss Ooni with you. Ooni is entirely my province. What happens or doesn't happen at Ooni has nothing whatsoever to do with you, Gupta."

"This is not so!"

Gower saw, with surprise, that Gupta was losing his temper. Instinctively he felt they had reached the core of their contention. Instinctively he shrank from contact with it. But Gupta attacked. "This is not so. The things you are doing at Ooni concern us all very much indeed. To this place you bring our young peasants, you bring them and teach them methods they cannot hope to, hope to – emulate when they return to their villages –"

"You mean we teach them non-Hindu methods."

"Hinduism is a way of life not only a religion. And there are glorious traditions, Hindu traditions, from which our young

168

men and women in the flower of their youth should not be wooed."

"I see. Traditions of poverty and starvation. Traditions of wealth that can't exist without poverty and starvation."

"Rome, Mr. Gower, was not built in a day."

"Quite so. In India, Mr. Gupta, the day has been a long one."

"It is ended now for you, for the British."

"Yes."

There was a sense of shame, for both of them.

Gupta recovered first. He smiled. "I suspect you and I will not work well together."

"That's a foregone conclusion."

"Then what are we to do?"

"I shall do nothing. You expect me to resign. I presume you thought your appointment alone would make me. I presume you thought I'd stand on my dignity as an Englishman. I've no such dignity, Mr. Gupta. I'm afraid you'll have to sack me."

Gupta was nonplussed. Gower added, "Obviously you'll have to consult Mr. Nair first. One can never be sure of Mr. Nair's reactions, can one? I think you need to be sure."

"Aren't you afraid of being a laughing stock? Who has heard of an Englishman being sacked by an Indian?"

"Is there a fundamental principle involved?"

"A fundamental tradition."

"You're a great man for traditions. I'm not. I shan't fight you."

"Ah. Ah, then it must be true."

"True? What must be true?"

"That you have already made up your mind to leave Marapore, because you are going to Kalipur." He laughed, aloud. "My dear Mr. Gower, all are knowing you dined with the Maharajah last night. Two and two are easily put together. This morning they certainly make four. It is easy to say you will not fight to stay when you have already prepared your lines of retreat. You lose

169

nothing." Gupta was suddenly angry. "You English are fine at that. Very fine. In such a way you impose Pakistan on us! It is very spiteful!"

"We've no more to say to each other. Which of us stays in this room?"

"As I have no confidence in your editorial judgment, Mr. Gower, I shall certainly stay. I shall discuss these matters with Mr. Nair at an early opportunity. Meanwhile I shall determine the attitude of this week's *Gazette*."

"That's all I want to know."

Outside in the assistant editor's office, Gower spoke to Chatterji.

"Find out where Mr. Nair has gone and ring me through."

"Yes, Mr. Gower. Where will you be?"

"Either at Cannon Avenue or at Ooni. Try both."

"Rightio."

"The staff'll take instructions from Mr. Gupta." As he gave the order he recognised its futility. The staff were already taking orders from Gupta. He forced himself to nod pleasantly to Chatterji, but his exit was, for all its dignity, a retreat.

At the bungalow Abdul told him Dorothy was out. He did not know where.

"Tell her I've gone up to Ooni. If she wants to come up too, just ring and I'll send Prabhu down with the jeep."

Then he set off again knowing that the first thing he must do at Ooni was have things out with Steele.

2

MacKendrick walked back across the club lawn from the pool, and as he climbed the steps he came face to face with Cynthia Mapleton.

"But I thought you'd gone to Delhi."

"I decided not to."

"Indeed? I'd like to ask why but obviously it's none of my

170

business." She began to walk into the lounge but paused on the threshold. "Or is it?" she asked.

"If you're referring to the loan, that's okay." He put his hand in his inner pocket.

"For God's sake, not here. Are you having tiffin?"

"Not at the club."

"Nor am I. If you've got a tonga you might give me a lift to the bungalow."

"Sure."

They walked through the lounge to the front of the house. In the tonga he gave her a thousand rupees. "There, buy yourself a ticket, Cynthia."

"Thank you, Mr. MacKendrick."

"My name's Joe."

She laughed. He nearly added: I guess it's appropriate.

"All right, Joe. Thanks anyway. I'll be at the Taj in Bombay."

"When are you going?"

"I'm not sure. Towards the end of the week. When are you?"

"I can't say."

"You make a point of being mysterious, don't you?"

"Do I?"

"Last night you had to hare back to Bombay. Now it doesn't seem to matter one way or the other. What's up?"

"Nothing's up. I'm going to look round the countryside."

"What on earth for?"

"I'm supposed to be selling farm machinery. There's a limit to what you can do sitting at a desk in Bombay or Cal."

"And what are you going to look round in? A tonga?" She smiled, sarcastically.

"No. Maybe I can rent a car."

"All on expenses?"

"All on expenses. Where can I rent transport?"

"There's a place near the station. Ram Lal."

"Thanks."

"Give me a ride some time. Or are they all reserved for Miss Anderson?"

For a split second he was surprised. But almost immediately he realised that the conclusions to which she had come were obvious ones. He decided not to deny the implications.

"They might be," he said.

"How was she this morning?"

"I haven't seen her yet."

"I suppose you think I'm a bitch."

"We'll talk about that in Bombay."

"Fine. Ronnie'll enjoy it."

He looked at her, thinking: All right, I get it. Nothing doing once you're at the Taj.

The tonga stopped. He did not help her down. She looked up at him speculatively. "You're prickly this morning, Joe."

"Sorry."

"But you're not prickly when you apologise. Do I see you again?"

"I swim most mornings."

"And I'm at the club most mornings." She began to walk away, then came back. "Reminds me. Harriet was feeling guilty about not having paid you for your bearer last night and she thought you'd gone."

"Tell her to forget it."

"Why should she? Send him round this afternoon."

"I can't. He's gone off for the day to see relations."

"That's an old one. He probably won't come back. I hope you didn't pay him up to date."

"Actually I did."

"I suppose he said he wanted to take presents."

"That's what he said."

"Well – if he *does* come back, remember we owe him a tip. *He* won't forget, anyway."

MacKendrick grinned. "No, he remembered all right. I paid him overtime. He asked for it."

She put a hand on the tonga. She said, "I suppose the reason you and I never get anywhere is because whenever we meet we always talk about money. Let's have a drink some time and talk about something else for a change. What you've made your mind up about, for instance."

"We'll have the drink. But I don't get you."

"My dear Joe, it stands out a mile. You've lost that strained, anxious look. Judith Anderson's a very lucky girl." She frowned. "So am I, come to that. You've – you've been a brick." She walked through the gateway and didn't look back. MacKendrick told the driver to go to Ram Lal's.

Paying off the tonga he walked into the yard. Ram Lal seemed to run a filling-station, repair shop and automobile graveyard; and beneath his name on the red and white sign was the legend: Exporter and Importer. Agent. He walked into what appeared to be an office. A very fat man reclined there on a charpoy and at a desk sat a very thin man wearing an enormous solar topee.

"Mr. Ram Lal?"

The thin man said, "Yes, please?"

"Are you Mr. Lal?"

"I am dealing with all things."

"I believe you rent transport."

"This is so. You are requiring a lorry?"

"No. Not a lorry. Just a car. A car for myself."

The topee shook. "No cars."

"But I was told to come to you."

"Who by, please?"

"A friend."

"By what name?"

"Does it matter?"

"Please?"

"Mrs. Mapleton."

The topee swung round. For half a minute the two men argued. MacKendrick concentrated on trying to catch a single, comprehensible word. The topee twisted back again.

173

"Where do you wish to be driven?"

"No. Look, you don't understand. I want to drive myself. I want to hire a car for a few days. I'm staying at Smith's Hotel and my name is MacKendrick." He put his hand in his pocket.

The two conferred once more. Suddenly the thin man said, "Excuse me," got up and left the office. The fat man – who was, MacKendrick guessed, Ram Lal – stared up at him. Neither spoke. Neither smiled. Unable to bear the silence longer MacKendrick said, "This car now –"

"He is looking."

When the thin man returned MacKendrick knew he had been phoning Desai. His first words were, "It is expensive."

"First let's see the car."

He was led out to the yard and shown a dilapidated pre-war Ford model. He shook his head. "Couple of miles in that and I'd be riding the springs. If she has any springs."

"There is nothing more. It is a good car. Reliable." The topee nodded in emphasis and a bony hand patted the bonnet.

"What's that jeep?" He pointed up the yard. "A jeep's what I need on roads like these."

"This? This jeep? It is only for sale. But quite cheap."

"I'll hire it."

They argued for several minutes and then the thin man went back to the office, leaving MacKendrick to inspect the vehicle. He was determined to have it. He glanced round the yard. An old three-ton lorry, its coachwork painted grey, cast its shadow over the jeep. It was very hot. Tired of waiting he returned to the office himself. The fat man had gone, but the thin man, who now sat at his desk again, thrust forms at him.

"These are for signing."

"What are they?"

"Insurance. Indemnity. Many things. All are necessary."

"How much a day for the jeep?"

"Two hundred rupees."

He signed. When he had done so the thin man added casually, "Five hundred deposit. Payable in advance."

"A deposit usually is." He paid.

"Petrol extra."

"Okay. Fill 'er up."

"Please?"

"Fill up the tank. I'll collect it after tiffin. At this rate I need to see the bank. Can you tell me where there's a branch of the Imperial?"

"Just exactly opposite the station."

"Thanks."

He walked off to the station, but when he reached the bank it was shut. He found the post-office and cabled the agent in Bombay. "Arrange facilities five thousand rupees Imperial Marapore Urgent."

He felt he was burning his boats. The idea vaguely pleased him.

At half-past one he drank his first cup of after-lunch coffee. Opposite, the offices of the *Marapore Gazette* appeared to be closed for tiffin. With the coffee he smoked a cigarette. At one-forty-five a yellow-painted jeep drove by; Gower's jeep, driven by an Indian boy whom he did not recognise. Twenty minutes later, as he paid his bill downstairs, the jeep returned. He went quickly to the door and recognised Dorothy. She was driving alone.

He ran to the end of the line of shops, where the road turned right, past the station. Four hundred yards ahead was the junction of Victoria Avenue and the Ooni road. The Ooni road stretched straight and yellow. She had taken the Ooni Road. The dust from her jeep rose, billowing, in the distance.

He went into Ram Lal's yard and collected his own jeep. The metal of the bodywork burned like fire where the sun had shone down upon it. It was no longer partially shaded by the lorry, for the lorry had gone. The thin man watched him as he let the jeep roll slowly out of the yard. At the junction he changed his mind and drove round into the cantonment. On his left was the *maidan*,

175

wide and empty, guarded by the Laxminarayan College. When he reached the Gowers' bungalow Abdul came out on to the verandah.

"Hello, Abdul."

Prabhu came from the back of the house. MacKendrick looked from one to the other. "Is Mr. Gower in?"

"No, Sahib. He is at Ooni."

"And Mrs. Gower?"

"Also she is gone to Ooni."

"When'll they come back?"

"Tonight. Tomorrow." Abdul's head went to one side.

"How far is it?"

Abdul gave way to Prabhu, who came forward, smiling in a friendly way. "Thirty mile, Sahib. Sahib . . . ?"

"Yes?"

"Just now you are going to Ooni?"

"Yes. I think I will."

"If I come also this is okay?"

"Okay with me. But what about Gower Sahib?"

"Sir, just now I am bringing the jeep from Ooni for Mem-sahib. But Memsahib telling she not wanting me driving. Telling I can stay with Adbul. But, sir, much work Ooni side."

"Hop in, then. You can show me the way."

The boy grinned happily and spoke to Abdul, who continued to look glum. Before MacKendrick had started the engine Abdul had walked back inside the bungalow, as if washing his hands of the arrangements. Prabhu jumped in and sat at the back. MacKendrick turned round. "Come up front."

"*Thik hai*, Sahib." Prabhu scrambled over into the seat by MacKendrick's side.

"Name?"

"Prabhu."

"*Thik hai*." He pointed at himself. "MacKendrick."

"*Thik hai*, Sahib."

As he drove out of the garden on to the road MacKendrick

thought: Now I'm not being pushed around. I'm on my own. And I'm in control.

Light-heartedly he drove towards Ooni. It was ten to three. The jeep passed through a sleeping village; a village which gave an indelible impression of sleep, so hot was the sun, so exhausted the air. In the village tank a solitary boy swam and cheerily MacKendrick waved to him. The heat had entered his bones and he felt as though it were, for the first time, part of him. Now a group of trees gave shade, the road was dappled, and beyond the trees the ground curved upwards. A switch-back, toppling wall enclosed the barren compound of a shuttered house. He looked at the house, fascinated by its silence. Behind the house, as he looked back, he saw the grey-painted lorry he had seen earlier at Ram Lal's.

Prabhu grabbed his arm, then roared with laughter as, swerving, they avoided running down a pi-dog which yelped and whined, a thin, drawn-out complaint that faded on a note of enquiry. MacKendrick slowed, then stopped.

"Cigarette, Prabhu?"

They lighted up.

"Prabhu – what is Ooni like?"

"It is a good place."

"Good?"

"Very beautiful. See." He pointed to the hills.

"You like it there?"

"With Gower Sahib and Steele Sahib it is a good place."

"How long 've you worked there?"

"I am friend of Steele Sahib's orderly. I am coming to Ooni since more than a year. In war, sir, Steele Sahib was a very fine soldier."

"You were in the same outfit?"

"Sir?"

"Regiment?"

"Not in same battalion. But all men are hearing of Steele Sahib. Very brave soldier. Very fine soldier."

177

"And Gower Sahib?"

"Gower Sahib not a soldier, but also a very fine man. Very gentle man."

"And – Mrs. Gower? Memsahib?"

Prabhu looked away, drawing on his cigarette. He said, "She is a nice lady."

MacKendrick pressed the starter. Three miles nearer Ooni they came upon Bholu, walking back to Marapore.

Abruptly, MacKendrick was suspicious.

"What d'you mean, walk? Come on, Bholu, your day off's finished. Get in."

Bholu hung back. To Prabhu MacKendrick said, "What's he trying to say? You ask him."

Prabhu called across MacKendrick's shoulder, and then Bholu began to whine – like the pi-dog, MacKendrick thought. He became angry; angry that his own servant should show up so badly in front of one of Gower's. "What does he say?"

"Sir, he says you are giving him day off to see relations. Now he says it is only afternoon."

"Has he seen the relations?"

Prabhu asked the question of Bholu. Bholu answered at length. Prabhu, cutting him short, said, "He is saying still only that you are giving him day off and that only is it afternoon."

"Where are these goddam relations of yours?"

Bholu extended a thin arm. The direction was meaningless. It embraced the whole plain.

Out of patience, MacKendrick shouted, "Come on, get in! You can see your relations some other time." Unnecessarily Prabhu translated. Reluctantly Bholu climbed into the back, losing his balance as MacKendrick let in the clutch. Relations! Here? There wasn't a village in sight. For miles there seemed to be nothing but the dried-up paddy. But a few miles further on they came to a small dusty track, marked by a milestone, milestone twelve, and a very tall tree with an unusually large bole. A

178

hundred yards up the track MacKendrick noticed a cluster of huts. He slowed and twisted round to Bholu. "Is that where your relations are?"

Bholu sat hunched up.

"What are you looking scared for?"

But Bholu remained silent. MacKendrick shrugged his shoulders. "Okay, Bholu. You're not doing yourself any good, though."

At four o'clock the jeep passed round the spur of a hill and Ooni lay in front of them and below them. He stopped the jeep and stared down at the pattern of fields, the shapes of the gentle, sheltering hills, purple and blue behind the haze of the afternoon. The impact of its unexpected beauty was almost physical. Awareness of it seemed to tug at his arms as though inviting their embrace. He turned to say something to Prabhu, but the boy was obviously unmoved; puzzled, perhaps, at whatever signs he saw in MacKendrick's face that he was bewitched.

The road sloped downwards a little, and he coasted the jeep for a hundred yards or so; sometimes pressing the foot-brake as some variation of the formation of hill and tree and field caught his breath. There was a clarity about the air, a sense of freshness, despite the heat; a lack of familiar smell. He looked up, over his right shoulder, where the hill rose steeply above the road, thickly wooded. There against the dull, summer-green foliage, some bright-plumed bird darted and was gone.

This was the proper setting. Here, he would find her and face her with a courage Dwight had lacked.

3

But Gower did not have things out with Steele. Confronted by the younger man, seemingly tall, infinitely powerful above him as he climbed the wooden steps of the bungalow, he experienced a sharp twist of physical fear.

"Did you get my message?" Steele called.

"What message?"

"I phoned you at the *Gazette*."

"What time?"

"Early. Before you'd arrived."

"What was the message?"

Steele stood aside to make way for Gower as he came on to the verandah.

"Well, what message?"

"Everyone's cleared out, except your domestic staff and mine."

"What on earth are you talking about?" Gower stared at him open-mouthed. Steele, embarrassed, turned away and made a short, jerky movement of his arm. "What I said. Everyone's clearing out. Look, you can see the last of 'em trekking across to the railway."

Gower looked where Steele pointed. Away in the distance a line of men and women, their belongings on their heads, moved in slow motion across the fields towards the re-entrant on the far side of the valley which gave access to the plains beyond and the railway halt at Ooni.

"Do you mean – that we're alone here?"

"Yes."

"But what have you done about it?"

"What I could. I tried to stop 'em but it wasn't any use. The admin staff went first and after they'd gone the field workers got together and cleared out. They were already packed, too. I went down to the village to see 'em. They were just standing around all ready to go."

"But the headman?"

"He's stayed. But he won't come up here. I've tried."

"Tell him I want him."

"It's no good, I'm afraid."

Gower shouted, "What the hell d'you mean, no good? They can't go like this! They can't just walk out!"

"But they have. I told 'em they'd have to wait for you –"

"They're not soldiers, Steele! You can't order them about like soldiers! You're not in the army now, for God's sake. You're

180

supposed to be a civilian dealing diplomatically with civilians. Go and damn well get the headman here. You've bungled the whole thing, you bloody young fool!"

Steele went scarlet. He clenched his fists. Gower braced himself for the expected blow. But Steele turned and bounded down the steps two at a time. When he got to the road he walked along it with his hands cupped round his mouth calling for the headman.

It was fantastic. Gower shaded his eyes and watched the far-off line of retreating field workers. Steele's powerful voice echoed across the valley. The workers did not even look round, so far as Gower could make out. Fantastic. A dream. He found Prabhu standing in the doorway with a tray of beer.

"Yes. Yes. I'll come inside."

He expected the sound of his voice to allow him to enter the dream; but he still spoke and moved outside it. He felt that if only he could enter the dream, as Steele seemed to have done, then he would be able to think. The bungalow, constructed of wood, was suffocatingly hot. He sat down and let Prabhu pour beer. He took the glass and swallowed the bitter fluid, warm, brackish to his tongue. His pulse had quickened. They're driving me into a corner, he thought. On all sides there were enemies.

And Steele? Yes, always Steele; Steele in the background, messing his life up, smashing a way through the calm halls of reason and gentleness. Steele. Steele. Blundering. Thick-limbed. Aggressive. So damnably, smugly adolescent. Steele. Steele cuckolding him. Steele blinding him. Why should he believe Steele's innocence in the affair of Dass?

When Steele returned the headman came with him. Gower joined them on the verandah. The headman was middle-aged, with grizzled hair, but upright and dignified. He salaamed.

"What's happening on the estate?"

"Sahib –" the man raised a thin, sinewy arm towards the sky. "The rains have not come. All these people must return to their villages."

"Why?"

181

"Their families have trouble because of the famine."

"Famine? What famine? There isn't any famine!"

"Neither is there rain, Sahib. Without rain there will be famine."

"And what about the work here?"

"Sahib – these are not their own lands."

"They are well paid."

"Now it is rain we are wanting. Not money."

"And why are you still here?"

"Just now I am going. I stay to tell these things to the Sahib."

"And what about the money owing to these people?"

The man shook his head slowly, from side to side. "Sahib, *babu-log* all are gone, and on Friday all were paid. There is but two days' wages due. The Sahib will be making arrangements for this?" he ended, hopefully.

"I'm damned if I will."

"Then the matter is with God."

"Or perhaps the matter has been attended to."

"The Sahib talks in riddles."

"Let's stop talking in riddles then. Tell me what you're all afraid of."

"Sahib, they are afraid for their families at home. Soon the rains must come or many will die of starvation. These young people must provide for their families in this trouble."

"All this is nonsense. What are they afraid of?"

Steele interrupted. He said, "Would you rather I went?"

"That's up to you."

When Gower and the headman were alone he asked again, "Now, what are you all afraid of?"

The man looked troubled.

"As I have told the Sahib," he said at last.

"They were bribed to clear out, weren't they? Or warned to clear out? Which?"

The headman did not answer.

182

"All right. I've no more to say."

As Gower walked back inside the bungalow the telephone rang. It was Dorothy. She said, "I want the jeep."

"Are you coming to Ooni, then?"

"I might. But I want the jeep."

"Actually I don't advise you to come, Dor. I feel there might be trouble here." He was going to add: Everybody's cleared out. As though the decks are being cleared.

But it sounded nonsensical.

He said, "When d'you want it?"

"Immediately after lunch."

"I'll send Prabhu with it. You'll see he brings it back?"

"You'll be put to no inconvenience."

He moistened his lips. He thought of Dorothy in Steele's arms.

"Right. I'll send Prabhu." He put the telephone down. He had forgotten Kalipur, and the possibility of things being different in Kalipur. He had forgotten everything but Steele and Dorothy. And again Steele. And finally Dass, bruised and scarred. Was that the sort of man she wanted? A killer? Yes, Steele. Have things out with Steele.

When he looked round Steele was in the room. Against the open door his thick body was in silhouette, the details of his face obscured, for it was dark in the room with all the windows shuttered against the sun.

"Well," asked Steele. "What did the headman say?"

Gower stood motionless. He knew that Steele was waiting to be accused. But he wanted Steele to suffer; suffer in the way he himself was suffering; feel driven into a corner; feel those first, exploratory tentacles of fear.

He merely answered, "Nothing."

As Steele turned to go, Gower said softly, "By the way, I saw Muttra Dass this morning."

"Oh? Where?"

"In hospital at Marapore."

"Hospital?" Steele's voice was hoarse.

"Yes. He'd been struck in the face by somebody's fist and across the shoulders by a bamboo stick." He waited; then added, "He must have been held down."

Gower pursed his lips, remembering Steele's orderly; remembering the man's absurd, unquestioning loyalty.

Steele said, "And you think I did it."

"Why should I, Steele? You gave me your word."

"Did Dass say nothing?"

"Nothing. He's afraid, you see."

"Afraid of what?"

"Afraid to bring a charge."

Steele passed a hand over his mouth. Then thrust his hands into his pockets. "Do you think – do you think that chap Gupta might have something to do with it?"

"Why?"

"You said – you implied Gupta was Dass's boss in the strike business."

"Did I?"

"Well, didn't you?"

"We aren't talking about the strike business."

"No." Steele bunched his shoulders. "No. Well. That's that."

"Yes. That's that."

Steele went out. The sun spread its light across his shoulders and slowly he disappeared from view as he descended the steps.

The moment of accusation was past, and Gower was committed to the purgatory of his self-imposed silence. He went outside and sat on a chair on the verandah. The line of field workers was just disappearing behind the spur of the hill. To the right, Steele walked along the road until he came abreast of his own bungalow, on the lower slope. He went inside and then the valley was empty and silent and strangely peaceful.

Gower had an early lunch and sent Prabhu off with the jeep. When Prabhu had gone he walked down to the clerks' huts, but did not enter them. He did not wish to disturb the silence. He walked carefully, as though afraid that too hurried, too careless movement would cause waves of air to expand and disrupt the valley.

In the village there was no sign of life. Without inhabitants he saw it for what it was, a faintly ridiculous exhibit, a model which, for all its life-size proportions, remained a product of the drawing-board. There was a single street, and on both sides of it the little two-roomed huts, brick-built and mud-plastered, stood in dry uniformity of design and structure. The corrugated iron roofs sloped down to make with the pathway an arcade: a shelter from sun and rain alike for those who walked outside. At the far end of the street the arcade became two covered ways which converged on the village well.

He thought: Not homes, hostels. The smell of grains and spices and wood fires still hung in the shadows. Behind the houses, runnels had been built to conduct waste water down to little patches of cultivated soil where domestic vegetables grew in the darker, moister squares of sandy earth. Waste nothing, he had taught; and the neat rows of onions were a testimony to his thoughtfulness. Frayed ropes hung from posts where tethered goats had given milk into little brass bowls. He looked in at the doorway of one of the houses. The few sticks of furniture provided by the estate had been scrupulously left behind. But the sagging string nets of the charpoys were innocent of the bright shawls and thin blankets which had made them beds; only last night.

He left the deserted village and walked towards the large go-down – a corrugated roof supported by a framework of stout wooden poles – where grain was threshed and winnowed; where men's voices had called shrilly and women, bright rings in their noses, had helped their husbands and left their children to their wild, high-spirited games beneath the burning sun. They had come, bringing life with them. They had gone, and Ooni was asleep.

He went up the sloping pastures where he had experimented with grasses, where once he had made plans to raise cattle. He climbed back up the hill and caught a glimpse of Steele staring from the verandah of his bungalow across the shimmering fields. Gower struck off to his right. On the road he stopped, turned round and surveyed the place that once had given him pleasure.

Amateur. He narrowed his eyes. He did not even want to save it. Let it grow wild, he thought. Beneath the earth the vigorous jungle crouched. Let it come up. Let it take back what I've stolen. What have I ever done but scratch at the surface?

He returned to the bungalow and entered his bedroom. At Ooni Dorothy slept in a separate room. The shutters were closed, but a fan-light above the door at the back gave some light. He lay back on the bed and closed his eyes. Chatterji had never telephoned with Nair's address, he remembered. But he did not stir. He knew he ought to get in touch with Nair.

– and with the police.

Surprised, he opened his eyes. He got up and crossed to his bureau, unlocked it and looked for the revolver Abdul had forced on him the day before. It was there. He searched for ammunition. But as soon as he had found the little carton he put it away again.

Why the police?

He paused, listening. Then he closed the bureau and went outside. Steele was walking down to the village. From here, how easy it would be, he thought, to shoot him. He went back to the bedroom and looked for his binoculars. When he had found them he stood in the shadow of the doorway and twisted the little wheel to bring Steele into focus. He felt his heart beating.

Steele stood in the sunlight, one hand shading his eyes as though he were looking for something. Or was it someone? He could see every detail of the boy's face, which was serious and drawn. Gower moved his head and shoulders stiffly to keep Steele in view as he walked further into the village. For a minute he was invisible, then he re-appeared on his way to the go-down. Inside the go-down he sat, half hidden by a pile of straw. His bare arms were clasped round his knees, and then he let his fore-

186

head rest on his arms. Gower lowered the binoculars. Without them, Steele was indistinguishable.

Gower sat on his wicker chair and let inertia sink deeply into him. Let Steele sweat. Let someone else make the next move, he told himself. Steele, or Nair or Gupta, Dass – or Vidyasagar. What had Nair said? Something about desiring nothing, willing nothing, doing nothing; and thus, God could act.

He watched the wooded hills which lay between Ooni and Marapore. A man and his world, he had thought once, could not be separated. But what was his world? Had he a world at all? As he watched he received an impression of being watched himself, as though the woods were full of eyes. The thought forced him to consider what sort of a target he made. How was he sitting? What picture would he make to someone spying on him through a pair of binoculars, for instance? Was he sufficiently composed?

Then he realised he was sitting almost upright, with his hands folded neatly on his lap, outwardly calm, secretly wary. He frowned, trying to think why this particular attitude was so familiar to him, and why recognition of it in himself seemed to dig down to destroy the last feeble roots of what had been, he supposed, his complacency.

He had walked round the encircling hill to a point where the road cut round a spur and veered away to Ooni station. From here he was almost directly opposite his own bungalow and he both heard and saw the jeep as Dorothy drove in from Marapore. He began to retrace his steps, walking slowly, so that it was some half-hour later that he passed Steele's bungalow and saw another jeep appear on the crest of the road ahead.

He met MacKendrick at the foot of the bungalow steps and knew that Steele was walking up behind him to see who the visitor was. As they talked, MacKendrick kept looking over Gower's right shoulder at the approaching Steele.

"Hello, Tom. I've taken you at your word."

They shook hands.

187

"I hope it's not inconvenient my dropping in on you."

"Why should it be? Is this your own jeep?"

"No, I rented it." He was expecting Gower to say: But I thought you were going to Bombay. But Gower had forgotten. MacKendrick grinned. "I was going back today," he said, "but I decided to see something of the countryside around here and I wanted very much to see Ooni." He glanced round the valley. "I think it's great, Tom."

"Yes. Let me introduce you to John Steele. He's my assistant." They waited while Steele came the last few steps. "Steele, this is Mr. MacKendrick."

"Joe MacKendrick. I'm glad to know you."

Steele took MacKendrick's hand, smiled, then looked at Gower enquiringly. But Gower deliberately made no attempt to explain who MacKendrick was. He said, "I see you've got Prabhu with you."

"D'you mind, Tom? I wasn't sure I was doing right, but I called at your bungalow first and he seemed anxious to get back. So I gave him a lift."

Gower nodded, and then spoke to Prabhu in Hindustani. MacKendrick heard the word *Memsahib*. He could tell the boy was being taken to task. Prabhu was looking sheepishly from Gower to MacKendrick, and MacKendrick caught the look of confusion, almost of hurt, that crossed his face. Seeing it, he noticed that Gower's manner had changed. There was a touch of malice in it.

MacKendrick, indicating Bholu, said, "This is my own boy. I hope he won't be a nuisance."

"Prabhu'll look after him."

Bholu climbed out of the jeep. He looked quickly up at the bungalow and then around for the surest means of escape; but only Prabhu noticed. He pushed Bholu ahead of him up the rough pathway which climbed the hill to the rear of the bungalow.

"You'll have tea, now that you're here?"

"Thanks, Tom. That's a pretty warm drive from Marapore."

188

He stood aside and Gower began climbing the steps. Smiling at Steele, MacKendrick said, "You first"; but Steele hesitated. Gower turned round. "Come along then, Steele."

"Thanks, but I ought to do one or two things –"

"As you wish."

As Gower climbed the steps he heard their slightly embarrassed exchange of pleasantries. He climbed slowly. When he reached the verandah there was no sign of Dorothy. Turning, he watched MacKendrick ascend.

"Dor's somewhere around, but come along and sit down. Or would you rather clean up a bit first?"

"Thanks, I'd like to do that."

"Through here."

Gower led the way to the bathroom and left MacKendrick washing his hands in a blue-patterned china bowl. In his bedroom he took his two ebony-backed hairbrushes and tidied his thinning hair. There were sounds from Dorothy's room. Her door opened and he heard her going through the sitting-room. Why had she left Prabhu behind? He put the brushes down and passed his hands over his temples. A vein stood out, blue and jagged; he could see its regular throb. Where had she gone that she hadn't wanted Prabhu to know about? Had he maligned Steele? Was there someone else? Or not? *Or not?* She'd not had much time to go anywhere. Why had she come to Ooni? Had Steele arranged to meet her somewhere? Perhaps she'd come to Ooni to find out why he hadn't turned up. He saw that his hands were trembling. His determination to do nothing wavered. Get Steele here, he thought. Get Steele here and watch them together.

There was an intercommunicating telephone between the two bungalows. It was in the sitting-room. He opened the door quietly and listened; but all he could hear was MacKendrick's intermittent splashing. The sitting-room was empty. Then, through the open doorway, he saw Dorothy sitting on the verandah. She sat upright, her hands folded on her lap. He recognised the attitude. She always sat like that, he realised. Always.

He stood there in the dimly lighted room trying to analyse the nature and quality of his own state of mind when, earlier, he had sat as she was sitting now, so that, having pinned it down, he could consider it in relation to Dorothy. Why had he sat thus? Because he was afraid? What had been his fear? Fear of being watched? Fear of what lay in the air, invisibly ready to spring? Yes – this; and something else. There had been, still was – he felt fingers of it tugging inside him now – a formlessness, an almost negative despair which was at once part of him and outside him, suspending and sustaining him between two worlds as it were. Only there were never two worlds. There was one world and one world only. And in it one had one's place or had no place.

She turned her head and did not seem surprised to see him watching her. She said, "Who is that who came in with you?"

He walked to the verandah. "MacKendrick."

He saw a muscle twitch in her cheek. After a moment she replied, "I thought he'd gone."

"Gone? Gone where?" They were slipping back into their familiar pattern of conversation.

"To Bombay."

"Why?"

"He said last night he was going to Bombay."

"Last night?"

"At Harriet's party."

"No. He's here. I've asked him to tea." He passed his tongue over his tightened lower lip. "I think I'll get Steele over as well." He wanted her to ask what had happened in Ooni. He knew she would not. She turned her head away and he felt released from the little bondage of their civilised politeness.

He went to the telephone, and turned the handle which would ring Steele's bell.

"Steele? You'd better come over and have tea with us." There was a pause. He imagined Steele – not standing by his phone, in

190

the dimness of his own room – but crouched by the pile of straw. He felt no pity. Steele's mute sorrow – for he knew that was what had sent Steele out to the village alone – only sharpened his hatred. He hated Steele now for many things; not least because the boy was joined to him in exile in some odd way.

"Well, are you there, Steele?"

"Look, what are you doing about all this business?"

"What business?"

"About everyone — off." The boy's voice was hard.

"There's no need for you to use your army expressions to me, Steele."

Again the pause. "I'm sorry. But what are you doing about it?"

"Nothing. When I do it'll be my business."

"I don't like it."

"Oh?"

"Have your servants said anything?"

"No." He wanted to say: Have yours? But he restrained himself.

"I may be talking a lot of rot, but I think we ought to have a word with the D.S.P."

"I can't by any stretch of the imagination see what it's got to do with the police."

"Don't you think there might be some sort of – well, demonstration?"

"No. Do you?" Gower felt his heart beating again. Steele was right, of course. The place was wide open.

"Frankly, yes. The – the girl's urging me to take her away."

"Indeed? Then shall you be going?"

"Of course not."

"Then you'll come to tea." He waited for a second or two and then replaced the receiver. He paused with his hand still upon it. He ought to ring the D.S.P. He ought to find Nair. He ought to go to Marapore. He ought – in the face of threat, however vague, to property and life in Ooni – to ensure in some way the safety of those left behind. Instead, he joined Dorothy on the verandah and together they waited for their guests.

After tea Gower suggested to Steele that he should take MacKendrick round the estate. Dutifully they went. Steele, for once, was wearing a shirt, and Gower noticed, with disgust, that he sweated like a pig: the cloth which was stretched tightly across his back was drenched. He watched them go down the steps. Nothing had been said, at tea, about the desertion of Ooni, and MacKendrick had interpreted the unnatural silence as normal peacefulness. He had remarked upon it, and Gower had abruptly agreed before Steele could open his mouth. Now, of course, Steele would tell MacKendrick what had happened, and when MacKendrick came back the subject would be opened. Then Dorothy would know.

He looked sideways at her. She had not asked about it. But in a short while now she would know. He was suddenly filled with admiration for her. How long ago, he wondered, had she learned the lesson that words, that actions – being precipitous – were dangerous? – that through silence, through inaction, one was never uninformed, and better armed?

He turned on the wireless and European dance music drifted intimately upon the shadows; but grotesquely in the open where the sun still leaned its weight. As MacKendrick and Steele returned, the news came on. There had been an abortive attack on Jinnah at the Imperial Hotel in Delhi, where the All India Moslem League had held a conference.

Steele said, "Good Lord! The Imperial!" and his eyes lighted up with nostalgia. "Sounds as if they busted the place up nicely."

"Who are the Khaksars?" MacKendrick asked.

"Moslem fanatics."

"But Jinnah's the head of the Moslems."

Steele smiled. "So what? The Khaksars think he's let 'em down by not insisting on a corridor. Anyway, they're fanatics. Like the R.S.S. on the Hindu side. You don't take 'em into account."

MacKendrick shook his head. "I'd 've thought just now both Hindus and Moslems alike 'd 've kept their fanatics in place. They're liable to ball things up, aren't they?"

Steele shrugged his shoulders. MacKendrick turned to Gower, who was leaning back in his wicker chair, eyes half closed. "What do you think, Tom?"

Gower said nothing for a moment or two. Eventually, without moving his position, he replied, "Fanatic is only a word we use to describe people who hold run-of-the-mill convictions strongly enough to take action on them. The danger isn't fanaticism as such, or even conviction. The danger is action." He paused. His voice lowered; thinned out; so that MacKendrick inclined his head towards him. "In not disputing India's intention to rule herself we're avoiding the danger of taking action. We recognise we're in too great proximity to forces we don't begin to understand. I think if we're to blame for anything in the years we've ruled it's our failure to understand these forces even at the moment of departure. All we understand is that individual kindness isn't enough. But perhaps our strength lies in the fact that we don't understand what *is* enough. Perhaps we don't want to understand."

And then he smiled to himself; smiled at his own tone of voice, his dry and uninspired monotone; his platitudes. And at the lie. One could never kill the wish to understand; only disguise it, so far as one could disguise the existence of a caged beast.

"What's going on here, Tom?" MacKendrick asked, after a while.

"Is there anything going on here? I should have said not. It's very peaceful."

"John says all your staff and workers have walked out."

"That is so."

"But what does it mean?"

"That they have more urgent affairs elsewhere? Or is it perhaps a dress rehearsal for the great exodus we'll witness shortly?"

He seemed, MacKendrick noticed, to be talking to himself; lightly, almost sarcastically, as if he no longer cared.

"John wondered whether Gupta had anything to do with it."

"Ah." Gower opened his eyes fully, and looked across at Steele. "That's an idea I planted in his mind yesterday with reference to something else. It could be that there's a connection. But we shall never know, so it's useless to discuss the possibilities. There comes a moment, MacKendrick, when the European mind is forced to recognise its own limitations. I think we've reached that point. If we have, then we must content ourselves with admiring what promises to be a fantastically beautiful sunset." He paused. "I think it will rain tomorrow."

MacKendrick, looking at Steele, saw the queer look in Steele's eyes. The thought came to him that Gower had a touch of the sun. He was sure the same thought was in Steele's mind.

Gower said, "I usually go for a stroll just about now. Would you care to come?" He glanced at MacKendrick, and rose. "No –" and now that he was on his feet he returned to his normal insignificance of voice and stature. "No, you've had your stroll, with Steele. I'd forgotten. You'll stay to dinner?"

"May I?"

"Yes. I'll warn Prabhu. Steele?"

"No, I've got some letters to write. But thanks."

With the exception of Dorothy they were all standing. Gower half motioned Steele away. "Well, then –" he began, and Steele put out his hand to MacKendrick. "Goodbye."

"Goodbye, John. Thanks for showing me everything."

Steele murmured good-night to Dorothy, who nodded her head. Then he ran down the steps and after a moment or two Gower picked up a walking-stick from a little stand by the doorway. "I'll go out by the back and tell the kitchen," he said.

MacKendrick sat down. When Gower appeared, scrambling down the rough track by the side of the bungalow, he waved his stick, and MacKendrick raised his hand. They watched him strike off to the left, up towards the crest of the road in the direction of Marapore. Soon the sound of his stick on the stony surface faded. The sun had gone; but the sky was shot with layer after layer of gold, of yellow, of rose, fading to turquoise blue. The whole valley gave off from the surface of its earth the glowing colours of the dying day. The green of the trees was russet; in the distance the fields were purple.

Without looking at him she said, simply, "Why did you come?"

And he answered, "To talk of Dwight."

She sat perfectly still as he leaned forward a little, watching her intently. She did not move, but her look of composure changed to one of infinite sadness.

4

"But Dwight is dead," she said at last. He nodded. She went on, "I think I knew. I'm sorry. You were hurt because you saw it wasn't a shock."

He could only smile, encouragingly, but instead of saying more she turned in her chair and looked at him. It was as though they had never really looked properly at one another before. Then, quite suddenly, she said, "But that's not why you came. I suppose you came to find out whether what Judith Anderson told you was true."

Surprised, he put out his hand, and would have touched her arm.

She said, "Don't do that. We're being watched, you know."

Again he was startled. Looking round and seeing nobody, he said, "Who by?"

"Oh, in India you're never alone."

"That's not what you meant."

"No." She held one hand in the other, inspecting the palm. "Tom is somewhere."

"Where?"

She smiled. "In the woods on the hill there – no, don't turn round. He doesn't suspect you of anything. He's merely watching."

"You've seen him?"

"No."

"Then how do you know he's watching?"

"It doesn't matter. Forget it. But don't give him cause to suspect you. He couldn't cope with being suspicious of you as well as of John Steele."

With deliberate care he took out his cigarette case; an old trick, to gain time. He was unprepared for such revelations. He felt that the stage which he had set was no longer his. She shook her head at the offered case. He said, "I didn't know Tom was a jealous man. It's rather a surprise to me."

"I think it's a surprise to him."

"Then it's only recent."

"Quite recent."

"Since when?"

"Since I gave him cause."

"In what way?"

She turned her fingers in, over her palm, and pressed the nails with the thumb of her other hand. "He thought he might have to go back to England. I told him that if he did I wouldn't go with him." She watched the smoke drift away from his cigarette. "Being a conventional man he's arrived at the conclusion there's only one explanation of that, that I must have a lover here. And the only man he can think of is John Steele."

She leaned back now, and turned her head away from him. "And that has a humour all of its own, because apart from yourself and Judith Anderson, John Steele's the only person round here who knows I'm an Anglo-Indian."

"How – how does he know?"

She said, quite conversationally, "Oh, I was rather unlucky. He actually came from the part of England I pretended to have been at school in. Eventually he saw through me. I had to talk about it because Tom would keep bringing the subject up. I

196

suppose he thought it was nice for me to have someone to talk to about it. John saw through me, but he never said anything. He's despised me ever since. And I expect Tom thinks our unfriendliness is an act put on for his benefit."

"You're being very straightforward with me."

"I've no option, have I?"

She sounded tired. He cleared his throat. "You don't have to talk to me about it, if you'd rather not. I'll go if that's what you'd like. Do you want me to go?"

"Where would you go?"

"Where? Why – I'd –"

"You're like me, aren't you? You haven't anywhere to go."

He had been sitting forward. Now he felt himself forced back in his chair and at once he noticed something incongruous in her own attitude. He had supposed that, in leaning back as she was, she had been relaxed: but now he could see from the tautened sinews of her arms, understand through the muscular contraction of his own, that her whole body was tensed as if against a spasm of acute pain.

He said, "Why d'you say I'm like you? That I haven't any place to go?"

"Isn't it true?"

"It may be. In one sense it may be, but what makes you think so?"

"Miss Haig told me why you'd come to Marapore."

"How much – how much did she tell you?"

"Most of what you told her yourself, I imagine. About the letters. I drew my own conclusions. If you had had somewhere to go you'd never have come to Marapore."

"When did she tell you?"

"At the party after you'd taken Judith Anderson home. We were alone."

"She had no right – why should she tell you all that?"

"I know why."

"Why then?"

197

"To show she had me in her power."

"Why should she want that?"

"Don't you know?"

"Yes, I suppose I do. Something to hold over you if you messed things up for Tom, or threatened to."

"Roughly speaking, yes."

"What did you say?"

"Nothing. I was too relieved. I thought she'd cottoned on to *me* after what had happened when Judith Anderson came in. She hadn't though. She just thought I was being unkind to someone I ought to have remembered."

For a minute he smoked in silence. Then he said, "How did you know Judith Anderson told me about you?"

"She rang me this morning."

"Rang you!"

"Rang me to warn me. Her conscience pricked her, I suppose. We were very good friends once."

"I understand."

Already the short twilight had come.

"And knowing all this, you do nothing, Dorothy. You just come to Ooni as though nothing had happened." He paused. "Or were you running away?"

"From what? Where to? Where should I run? What's the difference between Marapore and Ooni from my point of view?" He saw that she had closed her eyes. "I suppose there was a time when I'd have thought coming to Ooni in such circumstances was running away. I suppose I'd have thought there was safety in doing so. But not any more. Especially now – because time's getting short –"

He put his hand on the arm of her chair and this time she did not stop him. She said, "You don't like that idea, do you? But it's true, and you know it's true. Just look at Ooni now and tell me if I'm not right. There are usually sounds of people and signs of people over there but tonight there isn't anything. If you don't see that it's because you don't want to. Miss Haig wouldn't see it, or if she saw it she wouldn't believe it because it would make nonsense of all the things she plans and does for the best all the time. What would be the good of making plans at Ooni tonight, Joe?"

He hardly noticed that she had used his first name. He was listening to her voice, hearing it as a voice crying over a deserted landscape, not filling it with sound, but echoing its emptiness.

"And I'm sorry, I'm sorry because you thought it was at Ooni you were going to find everything clicked and fitted into place. Right here on this verandah as soon as Tom went –"

He took his hand away from the arm of her chair. He leaned forward with bowed head, his elbows resting on his knees, his fingers locked together.

"But it'll be dark soon," she went on, "and Tom'll be back. What will you do? Sit down and have dinner with us? What will you find to say? Sooner or later you'll find there isn't anything. Nothing will have clicked or fitted into place. You'll want to say something but even before you've worked out the right words you'll know they'd be dangerous because words always are. Let other people talk. You'll learn all there is to learn, but you won't have given yourself away. You'll sit tight and wait to see what it's leading up to, wait to see all the pieces fit in. But they never do fit in. So you go on sitting tight and gradually you'll empty yourself completely. Then you'll be able to analyse exactly what you're doing and why and you'll see right back to the very beginning and you'll realise it isn't things outside you that have got to fit in but you yourself. Then you'll ask yourself, yes, but into what?"

The night had spread out its wings. He stood up as she finished speaking and said, "Not here. Not yet," and held out his hand to help her to her feet. She followed him down the wooden steps, without questioning where he was going or why she should go with him. For all that, he felt himself impelled by her.

For an instant they stood by the jeep, staring out across the

199

valley whose encircling hills bulged blackly against the paler, luminous sky. He helped her in and took his place by the wheel. He did not switch on the headlamps until they were abreast of Steele's bungalow, and then he drove steadily, saying no word. After a while she touched his arm and he pulled in to the side of the road and then, noticing the beginning of a track leading off up the hillside, he turned sharply into it. She had left the jeep and started up the track before he had switched off and turned the headlamps out. Her movement dislodged small pebbles which tumbled down the incline. He followed and found himself, after a moment or so, climbing steps like those at the bungalow, up to a verandah, a small hut, whose shape he could not clearly see, so closely had the jungle grown around it. But when she halted him and turned him round, he saw, through the branches of trees, lights in the distance, and realised they had come in a half-circle round the valley and were standing exactly opposite the farm buildings, the village, and the two bungalows at Ooni.

He heard her unclasp her handbag and then the faint rattle of a key, the creak of a wooden door. He stayed where he was, until, inside, she lighted a hurricane lantern and set it on a small bamboo table in the corner of the room. He went to the open door and when she turned to face him she said, "This is mine," but she was untouched, it seemed, by any kind of pride.

"What is it?"

"Just an old bungalow. There's a kitchen at the back, but this is the only room."

He saw the divan, covered in shabby cretonne. "Do you ever sleep here?"

"Sometimes."

"Is it safe for you alone?"

She unclasped her fingers from the handle of the lantern and stood, her arms limp, her head erect. "Nowhere is safe."

In one corner stood a battered, roll-top desk to which she went, sorting the keys on a ring which she kept in her handbag.

"Does Tom know of this place?"

"Yes, of course."

"Does he ever come here?"

"Sometimes." She found the right key and twisted it in the lock. She pushed the corrugated lid up.

"You like it here?"

"It exerts its own sort of tyranny, like all such places do."

"Such places –"

"Hideaways. Nurseries." She was selecting another key: with it she unlocked one of the tiny drawers which the opened lid had disclosed. "Anticipation or memory of them is better than the experience." From the drawer she took what looked to Mac-Kendrick like a photograph. She looked over at him, and then back at the photograph. She said, "It's your eyes that are different, of course. When I first saw you I wondered what it was that made you different from your brother. But everything else is there, in some degree or another." She moved, as though to give him the chance to join her. But he stayed where he was, just inside the doorway; and eventually she put Dwight's photograph back. She took out another, closed the drawer and walked over to the divan, sitting on one end where the lamp cast its light.

"I wonder if you can think who this is?" she asked gravely. He sat by her side and stared at the picture. It portrayed a young girl in her very early teens. There was no likeness at all to Dorothy, that he could see, but he said, "It's you, isn't it, when you were a child?"

"It isn't really."

Somehow she had been pleased.

"Who then?"

"My sister, or my half-sister more exactly."

"Is she older than you?"

"She's dead. But she was older."

"Where was this taken?"

"At her school in England." She smiled. "The one I pretend to have been to, but it was only her."

"What was her name?"

"Dorothy."

She turned her face to his. "I'm afraid my real name is rather theatrical. It's Amanda, but I used to shorten it to Daw. Then the Daw became D-o-r, or short for Dorothy. That was when she was sent home to school and left me behind in Assam with father and my mother."

"Your mother – but not hers?"

"Yes, mine. Not hers. My mother had the same sort of complexion Judith Anderson has. Perhaps a bit lighter. But anything to do with father's second marriage wasn't recognised by his family. He hadn't much money and he couldn't afford to send us home to school. He had a sister though. She paid for Dorothy, but she wouldn't pay for me."

"Where are your parents now?"

"They're both dead. They were killed in a motor-smash because father was driving and he was drunk. They'd just had a cable from Durban from this aunt who was bringing Dorothy back to India. Dorothy had been taken ashore with infantile paralysis and she died in hospital there."

"So – you were all alone?"

"Yes."

"What did you do?"

"Judith's father lent me the money to go to Bombay and meet my aunt. We hated each other right from the beginning but she had no alternative but to take me in. I don't think she would have if she hadn't been out of India for five years or more and lost touch with all her old friends out here. She took me straight down to Calcutta, where she'd never been before, and I had to pretend more than ever that I wasn't a half-caste. I remember –"

"What?"

"The first thing she said to me when I met her in Bombay was Thank God you're still white. As if she'd expected me to have gone dark while she was away." She smiled. "I had to pretend I'd been to Dorothy's school."

"But you didn't know anything about it."

"Oh, Dorothy wrote me. She wrote long letters and Judith helped me memorise them. All about what it looked like, what people did, what they said. She knew it might be useful to me." She looked at him. He saw that she was on the defensive. "We have to do things like that, you see. Even people who aren't half-castes are suspected of being if they can't prove they've been to what we all call 'home'."

"But suppose you'd met someone who'd actually been at the school?"

"Yes." She smoothed the surface of the photograph. "Yes, that's something that has had to be faced every day."

She waited, but he could find no words to express what he felt: pity; pity and something else. He thrust the other thought away.

She went on, "My aunt faced it too, of course. When she was annoyed with me she used to say 'Your luck'll run out one day. Don't think I'll stand by you'."

"But it was her idea about the –"

"Deception? Yes, but she only carried on the deception I'd played as a child. She couldn't admit she had a niece who had a touch of the tar-brush, could she? People might have thought she had as well." Again she smiled. "Or perhaps you don't appreciate how important these things are out here? Or how important they have been, I should say. I learned when I was seven."

She got up and walked out on to the verandah. When he joined her she said, "The tar-brush! How silly it sounds, doesn't it? You'd think it couldn't matter less. That it was all a joke anyway. My father and mother taught me it wasn't a joke. I only had to watch them together and hating each other. He hated her because being married to her made him an outcaste too. It dragged him down to her level. And she hated him because he couldn't pull her up to what he'd once been. D'you think he'd have got drunk like that if my sister's death hadn't been the end of the world to him? While she was alive he could always point at her, always say 'What she is, I am'."

"But you. There was still you."

"Me? And what was I except a daily reminder of what he'd become? Don't deceive yourself, Joe. Don't be taken in the way people like Tom are taken in. Underneath all the so-called trust and understanding between white and black, there's mistrust and dislike. We fight them and they fight us." She hesitated. "Us? But then I'm not 'us'. A union between black and white is an act of treachery. Each side hates to be reminded of it. From time to time they can forgive each other and call the battle off, forget it for a while. But they never forgive themselves their own treachery. They never forgive my sort of people –"

He felt for his cigarettes. He said, "You've never told Tom?"

"No."

"But you told Dwight."

"Yes, I told Dwight."

"Why?" He had intended the question to be gentle, but it was abrupt.

"Because I loved him. He asked me to divorce Tom and marry him after the war. I was prepared to do that. But only on the basis of Dwight knowing everything there was to know. Only on the basis of honesty. I needed honesty. I thought it meant life could begin at last. It couldn't have done if I'd gone on, saddled with a lie."

"Which means – you're not in love with Tom and never have been?"

"Yes, that's what it means."

"Why did you marry him?"

"Oh, my aunt made me. In its own way it was blackmail, but she dressed it up as doing her best for me. In her way she was like Harriet Haig in that. Doing her best for people so that she could feel secure herself. And then Tom wasn't the really pukka sort. But he was English, and it was a way of getting me off her hands. I expect she thought she'd done well for me and done well by me. I suppose she had. But the blackmail came in because she made it clear she'd have nothing to do with me unless I accepted him. I didn't have the courage to stand out against it. I knew well

204

enough what would happen to me if she cast me off and I was too afraid to face it then. I'd have no background and no prospects. I'd have become a somewhat paler edition of Judith Anderson." She let her voice die away so that the name Anderson was hardly articulated. She said, "May I have a cigarette?"

He gave her one. All her movements were slow, their slowness giving an impression of assurance; and yet it was, he knew, the calculated slowness of uncertainty; the slowness he knew so well himself. He felt, as she stood close to him, the warmth of her body and the rise and fall of her breathing. As the cigarette went to her mouth a faint glow fell on her cheeks. She said, "Poor Judith. She'd give her right arm to be in my shoes."

"If she were, I'd pity her."

"Would you? Does that mean you pity me?"

When he did not answer she turned her head, looking towards Ooni. She said, "You shouldn't be ashamed of that." And then, in a lower voice, "Pity's not to be despised."

He wanted to touch her, but there was an aloofness about her which rejected physical contact.

"Dorothy, may I ask you a question? You needn't answer it if you don't want to."

"Perhaps I shan't be able to."

"What makes you tell me all this?"

"You already knew."

"Not the details. I didn't know those. You could have denied the whole thing."

"Yes." She moved her head and settled against a post of the verandah roof. "I could have denied it."

"Then why didn't you?"

"Because time is getting short."

She drew on her cigarette again, then threw it out into the darkness. He thought: Like a falling star. Its spark was a fleeting light leaving no mark on the indifferent universe. Suddenly a picture conjured for him that night by Gupta returned like a dream: a green, shaded lawn, and across it – advancing, fluttering

205

parasols, the merging of colours, the white with the dark, the white with the deeper, exotic shades of wind-flecked silks; an outward blending of grace, of distant, musical laughter, stifled at last as the fraternisation ended and the Raj retreated. And now, in the end, the lawn deserted forever.

She was speaking again, across and above the dream. "Time's running out, so what point would there have been in denying it? She always said my luck would go, if you can call it luck. It hasn't gone, but it's changed. It doesn't matter what happens now. And Tom and I'll go to Kalipur. I can stay with him in Kalipur so long as he never knows about me. I think I can live with him in Kalipur and not mind. Exist, not live. I've lost that chance, or never had it. Which, I wonder? And Kalipur won't be like Marapore, or Calcutta, or Lahore. It won't be British India. That's all in the past, it's all going into the past. If I went to England I'd be going with it, taking it with me. I can't do that, not with Tom. Tom mustn't know."

She looked at him, as though startled by the move he made to come closer to her. He thought, at first, that she would go away, back into the room. Panic had not entered into her, but he felt she saw it like a familiar spirit by her side. Her hands were behind her, clasped, he guessed, round the supporting post; and the upper part of her body was bent towards him.

"There's something else, too, something to do with roots, feeling they're here, in India, wanting them, or pretending they're there. Sometimes I think I've dug fear into the ground and made my roots of that. Sometimes I think I have no roots at all. Then there are times when I look at India and know it's inside me as it was in my mother, and her mother, and her mother's mother. Failing a different sort of love, there's always that sort to be looked for and found."

"Have you found it?"

"No. We have that sort of love to give. When I come along the road to Ooni and see men and women working in the fields I feel that sort of love going out. And then I envy them because in

them that sort of love isn't rejected. It's fundamental. In us –"
she hesitated. "In us, it's always suspect."

She relaxed her grip on the post as though giving in at last to
whatever it was she had been fighting. She turned away and went
back into the room. He stood in the doorway and watched her put
the photograph of her half-sister back in the desk, and lock it,
cross to the lantern and turn it out. From the deep shadows he
heard her say, "There's nothing more to tell."

"And if Tom doesn't go to Kalipur?"

"He will. The Maharajah's offered him a job."

"Was that the reason for the party?"

"Yes. Harriet's reason."

"And he's accepted?"

"Not yet, but he will."

"But if he doesn't? What then?"

"He'd drift. Perhaps he'd drift around India."

"Would you go with him?"

"Yes."

"But not to England?"

"No, not to England." She paused. "You don't understand
that, do you?"

"Yes, Dorothy."

"I don't think so. You just think it's because I couldn't bear to
be found out and laughed at."

"No. I know it's not that. You'd face up to that if you could
go with someone you loved."

She did not answer, and he could only just distinguish the outline of her body. "If it were someone you loved there'd be no
question of being found out, because you'd have told him."

"Yes." She spoke hardly above a whisper.

"Dorothy – is it something more than just not loving Tom?"

"Yes."

"You hate him?"

"Yes. Like you hate Dwight."

"I don't know how myself. Tell me how."

She was waiting for him to move from the doorway.

"Don't ask me any more questions," she said, finally.

He said, "There's one I've got to ask. You must know there's one I've got to ask. Why else d'you think I'm – a man doesn't –"

He broke off, afraid of the unknown, afraid of himself, afraid of Dorothy; and appalled at his inability to seize one single, clear-cut desire out of the tumult of his different longings. He was at once close to her and yet so far away; borne with her in grey limbo, but powerless to reach for her hand and guide her to what, perhaps, was safety. They faced the same abyss: were separated by it.

He said, "You told me I hadn't any place to go. But I have, Dorothy. Lots of places, and I can go to any one. It's just a matter of choosing. I can go home, if I want, go back to the life I've learned to despise, or told myself I despise. I don't know which it is, but I can go back to it. I'm expected to go back. But I can drift too. D'you know how I'd do that? Perhaps I'd start in Bombay, or Calcutta, Singapore, Cape Town, Rome. I've enough money of my own to be able to choose my place, enough money to look for jobs and give up jobs and go on doing so until I don't want to any longer. And maybe you'll be doing the same, with Tom –"

Suddenly the pieces fitted into place.

He said, "You'll do that with Tom, even though you hate him. Although I can't ask – can't ask that you should care – care in any way for me –"

He knew there was nothing more he need say. He stood for a moment, quite still, and was glad she made no sign that she understood. Now that the way was clear, now that their hands could join above the abyss, it was better that each should remain on his own ground, with freedom of choice.

He turned away from the door and stood near the balustrade, but she did not immediately follow him. When she did it was with the steps of one not fully awake. She pulled the door to, and fumbled several times with the key. When at last she had turned the lock home, she replaced the key in her bag, still facing the door, and it was not until she stood at the head of the steps that she hesitated, and turned to wait for him.

Tentatively, he put his hand under her elbow, a token gesture of support. The intensity of the first darkness of night was going as the combined brilliance of the stars grew stronger. He could see her eyebrows were drawn slightly together as though she were unsure, not only of him, but of herself. He released her arm and she led the way down the steps and then, at the bottom, she waited for him again, turning just before he drew level, to walk not quite by his side down the rough track to the jeep.

As he leaned forward to turn on the ignition, he moved his head so that he could see her profile. She sat gravely staring ahead to where the headlamps splashed across the road. He let the jeep roll slowly down the incline and it was only as he swung the wheel round to head back to Ooni that they noticed the tongues of fire leaping upwards from where the model village lay.

5

When it grew dark, Gower scrambled down the hillside. Once, he paused, and looked back over his shoulder, listening for a repetition of the sounds, the little scatterings of stones and the low murmurings of a wind which unaccountably did not stir the leaves. He waited for a return of the inexplicable, now vanished coruscations, which a few moments before had pricked the shadows.

Gaining the road he walked with caution. Once more he stopped, turned swiftly, but saw nothing; and so continued on towards the bungalow. When he reached the foot of the steps he saw three people coming towards him. One of them was several paces in front of the other two, and Gower recognised Steele.

Steele called softly, "Is that you?"

"Yes." Gower put a hand on the wooden hand-rail. "Steele?"

Steele came close. He said, "I thought you'd gone off in the jeep."

"No, that was MacKendrick. Who's that behind you?"

"My bearer. And the girl."

"What are they doing?" He realised they both spoke in under-tones: like soldiers, he thought, soldiers on night patrol. Was Steele, too, aware of the enemy's approach?

Steele said, "I thought you'd gone. I just wanted to check up." His hands were pressed palms downward, almost in the small of his back. His shoulders were hunched. He jerked his head towards the other two. "They wouldn't stay behind."

"Are they the only staff you've got left?"

"Yes, afraid they are."

"Why didn't you tell me?"

"You didn't seem interested."

Steele moved one of his hands to his waist. It appeared to find support there, with the thumb tucked into a webbing belt. Attached to the belt was a revolver holster.

"Why've you got a gun?"

"Just a precaution."

"Against what?"

"I'm going to scout round the village in a moment."

"There's nothing in the village."

"You just been?"

"No. I've been up on the hill there. Why go to the village with a gun?"

Steele paused. "I might get a jackal."

"Don't be a damn fool."

"My bearer's coming with me. Can the girl stay here with your servants? She won't stay alone in the bungalow."

"Look here, Steele. What are you afraid of? Dacoits?"

"I don't know. Something up, though." He motioned with his thumb at the two silent figures who waited a short distance away. "They think so too."

Gower laughed.

"You're not going down to the village playing soldiers, Steele. If you've any definite reason to suspect there'll be a dacoit action,

I'll go now and ring the police *thana* at Ooni." He began climbing the steps, but Steele called after him, "No good. I've already tried. The line's been cut."

Gower stopped. "Cut?"

"Well, it's not working. I thought perhaps you'd found out too and had gone down to the station."

"I should have told you if I'd decided to do that." He hesitated. Would he have told Steele? Probably not. Steele had guessed as much. Gower blurted out, "When d'you find this out about the phone?"

"Just now. I thought I saw lights up on the hill. I tried to ring the *thana* to make sure in case you didn't get there in time."

"What sort of lights?"

"Electric torches."

"Dacoits don't carry electric torches."

"No. But there are people on the hill, I'm almost certain. And the girl's afraid of being abducted."

Gower cleared his throat. "You'd better come up. Tell those two to go round the back." He mounted the steps and as soon as he got into the sitting-room he went to the telephone. It was dead. "Is our intercom working?" he asked.

"I haven't tried."

Gower tested it.

"What's the use, Tom. There's nobody at my place."

It was the first time Steele had ever called him by his Christian name. Why did he now? Gower glanced at Steele, who stood in the doorway, massive, assured, enjoying it, exuding *camaraderie*; *enjoying it.* He was standing there, scenting danger, inviting Gower to share his pleasure.

Gower stared at the revolver, fascinated by it and by the boy's muscular hand clasped round the holster. A killer. It was dangerous to have him in the bungalow. A killer embraced destruction, wooed it; brought destruction close, his brain clear, his blood on fire.

Steele asked, "Where's Dorothy?"

"Oh. Is that why you came, then?"

"What d'you mean?"

How well he dissembled, Gower thought. How well he acted the role of protector. Gower was pleased that Dorothy was not here to see Steele like this, legs slightly apart, balanced, poised; the man you depend on: *the man you depend on in a tight spot.* But in reality, the man who brought the tight spot with him. Gower smiled, and said, "She went with MacKendrick."

"Where?"

"I've no idea. I imagine they're safe enough in the jeep." He went to the passage and called for Prabhu, gave him instructions about feeding Steele's people. When he came back Steele had gone out on to the verandah.

"I say, look over there," he called. Gower joined him. On the other side of the valley a light glowed faintly.

"What about it?"

"That light over there."

"Yes?"

"What is it, do you think?"

"Dorothy's hut, of course. She's showing it to MacKendrick, I expect. Don't start getting jumpy." He felt Steele's movement of mute protest. "I suppose, Steele, you want to dash over there in my jeep and bring them back under armed escort."

After considering this, Steele answered, "No, I don't think so. She has MacKendrick with her and they've got a jeep which means they're mobile. If anything starts over here they'll hear it more than likely."

"I see. What do you call that? An appreciation of the situation?"

"Yes. In the army we called it that." Suddenly he added, "Look here, I don't know why you've taken such a sudden dislike to me, but if you want to kick me out of Ooni, then for Christ's sake do so, or for Christ's sake accuse me of whatever it is you think I've done."

"Not a very original gambit, Steele. Haven't you grown out

212

of the straight, clean Englishman stuff yet?" He took out his cigarette case, but did not offer it. "I suppose the trouble is," he continued, "that your intelligence hasn't yet caught up with your essential ruthlessness."

Steele went back into the bungalow, without a word, and Gower thought: He's gone. At once the bungalow felt abandoned, at the mercy of whatever stalked it, whatever threatened it. He forced himself to sit in his chair. He stared at the sentinel of light in the dark hillside where Dorothy must be, and remembered how she and MacKendrick had sat here; had risen, and gone down to the jeep, and driven away. For what purpose? Why to the hut? Who *was* MacKendrick? And where was Steele?

He relaxed; Steele's footsteps were in the room, on the floor-boards of the verandah now, heavy, self-confident, reliable. Steele said, "That chap of MacKendrick's is missing."

"Who?"

"That chap of MacKendrick's."

Yes: there had been a man. Prabhu had taken him under his wing. "Missing?"

"Prabhu can't find him. He was here a quarter of an hour ago, he says."

"It's his look-out."

"Yes. Well, I'm going to the village, now." Steele unbuttoned his holster. "You got a gun yourself?"

"Yes, Steele. I've got a gun."

"Okay, I shan't be long."

"You'll stay here."

Steele was already at the top of the steps. The light from the room behind shone on him. Gower prepared himself for the expected sneer: What? Afraid to be left alone? He looked down so that Steele might more easily charge him with cowardice. But Steele came back, dutifully, and said nothing. The action shifted responsibility. It put Gower in charge. Steele fumbled in his pocket for a cigarette. Then he went into the room and turned off the light. At once the dark shapes of the valley were clearly etched.

Returning, Steele said, "Better visibility this way." He stood against the door-jamb, behind Gower's chair, drawing slowly, contentedly on his cigarette.

Together, they waited.

Bholu paused on the hillside and listened. He could hear the voices of Gower Sahib's cook, and of Prabhu: and now other voices, of Gower Sahib himself, and of the young Sahib. He crept forward until he could see, to his left, the vague bulks of their bodies. Bholu waited until they had gone and then he squatted within a screen of bushes and checked his belongings with possessive fingers: the sharp knife which glinted momentarily before he put it away again in its sheath and tucked it in the belt at his waist; the money MacKendrick Sahib had given him to bring his wages up to date; the money the woman had left in the hollow tree; the photograph of the woman which he had not meant to steal, but which he had hidden behind his back even as MacKendrick Sahib asked him where it was; all these, and a packet of cigarettes. He badly wanted to smoke, but that would have to wait until he had left the valley behind and could walk quickly to the railway halt at Ooni. By Wednesday he would be in Lahore. He smiled as he folded the five one hundred rupee notes and put them away.

He stood up, impatient to be off and to put this evil place behind him. Had it not been for his ill-luck in meeting Mac-Kendrick Sahib on the way back from the twelfth milestone he would already have been well forward on his journey. Such ill-luck, following such unhoped for good-luck; for he had prepared himself to find his letter to the *memsahib* ignored. The letter had been a shot in the dark. But the woman had paid, and now the lovers had gone. And Ooni was an evil place, a dangerous place. There was no time to return to Marapore and pay the letter-writer the agreed fee, the fee that would ensure his silence. But one had to take risks, and the fee for the letter itself had been outrageously high. In Lahore was temporary refuge.

When he got to the edge of the road he could see far off across

214

the valley the gleam of a single light, and he knew, from his careful scrutiny during the hours of daylight, that it was just about where the light was that the road turned sharply out of the hills and led to the railway. The light was a beacon, guiding him. He looked to his left where Gower Sahib's bungalow stood, and as he watched, the light in it was extinguished. He hesitated, for this seemed odd; then he turned to his right, walking softly on the edge of the hillside, just above the road, towards the other bungalow which was also in darkness. When he came opposite it he walked a few more paces and then ran across the road, skirting Steele's bungalow. The slope down to the fields was gentler, and the going was good. When he reached a clump of stunted trees he paused for breath, and to check up on the position of the light across the valley.

He thought, at first, that a wind had sprung up, but then quite suddenly he knew the wind was human voices raised in wild crying, and now there was a bright flare up on the part of the hill which separated Marapore from Ooni, and miraculously this single flame spawned other flames which swerved down the hill, as the invaders touched off brands from a petrol-soaked rag and careered, shouting, towards the village.

Momentarily, the power went out of his limbs, as fear claimed him. The night's evil was resolving itself before him in fire which performed strange, intricate measures as though devils danced. The fires were coming nearer to him, and crashing above the shouts were loud cymbals; down the village street, four hundred yards away, the procession came, and now he saw these fires were torches carried by men and realised too that the cymbals were petrol cans scattered along the street; along the street, down to the well: and now a great roar and a rushing of flame which threw into silhouette the group of plunderers making for the go-down.

Bholu lost his head. The obvious course for him to take was one leading straight across the fields where no buildings were, but a primitive instinct drew him to the protection of the hillside. He ran to Steele's bungalow and pressed himself against the wall, fearful of death, his hands fumbling for his knife.

And now so bright was the light from the fires he felt himself dangerously exposed and naked to it. He ran up on to the road and round to the far side of the bungalow. But there he saw, ahead, the large go-down splashed with fires and the enemy dashing up the slope towards him.

He turned and ran to a bush, but within its branches he knew his insecurity. He scrambled out again, but in his confusion he had misjudged both distance and direction, and all at once he faced the shouting men, less than ten yards away.

He threw up his hands and cried out and so was marked by them. He heard their gust of laughter and knew himself hunted. The laughter followed him, up to the road, along the road; swayed with him down the hill again, closer and closer: the laughter of boys, of youths, the high-pitched baiting of students who had discovered a clown. But Bholu could not distinguish its particular quality. To him it was the blood-thirsty yelling of thieves and murderers. The flames in the village warned him in his direction, and he turned, hopelessly, and stumbled back up the hill, to the road.

Steele said, "Here they come."

Gower touched his left arm. His right held the revolver. Behind them, in the dark room, the girl's cry was stifled by Prabhu. Gower said, "No, they're going back." For a moment it seemed he was right. Then, all at once, the running figures changed direction yet again, and came up the hill. Bholu's knife glinted as he waved his arms to steady himself on the last few feet on to the road. At the same time he recognised the bungalow. He shrieked, "Sahib! Sahib!" and shrieked again as he felt the sudden touch of a hand plucking his sleeve from behind.

Steele went to the head of the steps, raised the revolver and fired into the air. The sound of the shot slammed against the hills and the expanding echoes momentarily stunned the men as they gained the road. Steele shouted, "Get back! Get back or I'll fire into you!"

Reality seared through Bholu. As his pursuers gaped at Steele's half-seen figure, Bholu shrieked again, "Sahib! Sahib!" The shriek was incoherent, pitched as it was to frenzy. He stumbled across the road towards the steps.

Steele shouted again and fired once more into the air. Bholu flung up his arms in entreaty, unable to comprehend, supported only by his own innocence. He called again, "Sahib! Sahib!" and dashed up the steps, holding his right arm with the knife in his hand, upwards, upwards to infinite mercy.

But Steele saw none of this. He saw only the bright metal of the knife, heard only the harsh breathing and crying of a man who surged up the steep steps intent on glory. He called "Get back, get back!" but Bholu came on, and even as Steele stopped calling his finger was pressing the trigger.

Bholu's eyes widened with surprise as he twisted grotesquely, feeling his arms pinned to the stars. He seemed for an instant suspended in space and then he tumbled, backwards, downwards, over and over, clattering into oblivion.

Silently, dismayed, those who had laughingly pursued him to death turned and fled into the night.

The girl was whimpering. Afterwards, when Gower thought of this moment, that is what he remembered; the low whimpering of the girl, the reflection of the flames on Steele's face, and the wish again to be allowed to enter the dream.

Bholu lay spreadeagled, his face on the road, his feet on the bottom steps. Steele, cautiously descending, stepped over him, still holding the revolver ready in his hand. After crossing the road to search for hidden stragglers he returned to the foot of the steps where he was joined by his bearer. Together they hoisted Bholu and carried him up into the sitting-room where Steele shouted for Prabhu to put on the light. In its harshness the girl hid her face and moved into the shadows of the passage.

They lowered Bholu on to the floor, still face downwards. Steele straightened up. "The knife," he said, "the bastard had a knife. Go and get it." He was looking at the body, frowning. Prabhu edged closer.

"The knife, Prabhu," Steele repeated, as though to a child. "Go get the knife."

In the doorway Gower watched. He did not stand aside when Prabhu tried to get by. Together they stared at the body. Steele knelt down and said to his own bearer, "Let's turn the beggar over." The blood from the great wound in Bholu's chest stained the floor.

"This is Bholu, Sahib."

Steele looked up at Prabhu, who had spoken. "What's that?"

"This is Bholu. Servant of MacKendrick Sahib."

After a moment, Steele repeated, "Go get the knife." Then he turned towards the body again. Later, he stood up and rubbed the palms of his hands slowly. Gower had still not come into the room. Steele took out his handkerchief and wiped the perspiration from his face and neck. He said, "One of us 's got to go for the police. Will you or shall I?"

Gower stared dumbly. Police. The glare of the electric light had not ended the dream, then.

"I'd better get going," Steele said, and pushed the handkerchief back into his pocket and then Prabhu came in and put the knife on the table, under the light. Steele looked at it, fascinated. He said, "Why should MacKendrick's bearer carry that about?" He paused, glanced at Gower. "He was coming at me with it. I don't get it."

He went, but half-way down the steps he was called back by Gower. He protested. "We've got to get the police." He returned, reluctantly.

"That's my job," Gower replied.

They faced each other. "That's my job," he repeated. "We can't afford any more of your bungling." He held tightly on to the balustrade for support.

"All right."

"Is that all you can say?"

"What d'you expect me to say?"

"You'd better think up something. You'll have to say more than all right to the police."

A look of astonishment came into Steele's face.

"The police? What 've they got to do with what we're talking about?"

"The police have got everything to do with what we're talking about. We're talking about your bungling."

"But I tell you he was coming at me."

"You know what I mean by bungling, then."

"Christ! Anybody can call it bungling after it's over! Any fool can be wise after the event. Come to that it's as much your bungling as mine. If you'd let me go down to the village I'd 've fired over 'em as soon as they came down the hill. They'd 've run like rabbits." Steele wiped his mouth with the back of his hand. "And when they first came down the hill if you'd let me fire then as I wanted to –"

"You miss the point, Steele. The only reason you've killed a man tonight is because you had a gun."

"Fine bloody mess we might 've been in if I hadn't."

"I don't agree."

"But he was coming at me with his knife. Christ! You saw it yourself. You all saw it and you didn't stop me firing then because you were scared stiff the same as I was."

"We can't avoid fear, Steele. But we can avoid doing violence by not preparing for it. You were prepared for violence. You are an apostle of violence. Your whole personality is conditioned by it, and if I blame myself at all it isn't for having stopped you firing earlier but for having allowed you to stand here with a gun in your hand."

"You'd rather see us carved up."

"As it turns out we shouldn't have been carved up. Bholu was running to us away from them, not to stick his miserable knife into us."

"A pity you didn't tell me that when he rushed across the road yelling like a maniac."

"I didn't tell you then because I thought the same as you were thinking."

"Well then – "

Gower shouted, "There's no well then about it! There's only your damned gun and your damned ingrained desire to use it." He flicked the holster with his hand. "*That's* the main factor in tonight's little scene. That and you. Not Bholu. Not Bholu's knife. Not the fire. Not the people who caused the fire. But *this. This!*" He flicked it again, and then again, this time purposely missing the holster and hitting Steele on the belly, curling his fingers in as he did so, so that his hand was a half-fist. At once Steele raised his hands, and jerked his right shoulder back, displaying the quick reflex of the fighter, before restraining himself and standing back a pace, his arms lowered as suddenly as they had been raised.

Gower smiled. "Now you see what I mean. Everything I've said is the truth, but you'd as soon knock me down as listen to it. I'm going to the police now. Before they come just put yourself in their shoes and think what they'll see and what they'll find. Some quite extensive fires obviously caused by a gang of hooligans. Beyond that, only a dead man who wasn't a hooligan but a servant of one of the Sahibs. And you, of course, you and your gun."

As he went down the steps he saw the headlights, heard the engine of the returning jeep. He climbed into his own and waited while the other drew up. MacKendrick jumped out, came running. "What's going on, Tom?"

"Exactly what you see."

"We heard people firing."

"No. You only heard Steele firing. You'd better go up. Our telephone isn't working, so I've got to drive down to the police *thana.*"

MacKendrick pointed at the fires. "What about that? Do you have any fire-fighting equipment?"

"It was over in the go-down."

"Then what's to be done?"

"Nothing. Let it burn."

He drove away. MacKendrick went to Dorothy who stood by the jeep still watching the fire as she had when the shots shattered the valley and he had pulled in to the side of the road, uncertainly. She too had said, in answer to his question: Let it burn.

Steele met them on the verandah. "You two all right?" He was blocking the doorway.

"Yes, we're all right, but what's happening? What was the shooting?"

"You'd better come and look." He stood aside and let them go in first. MacKendrick turned away when he saw the blood. He had never seen a dead body before.

"I'm afraid it's your chap Bholu," Steele was saying. MacKendrick did not properly understand. The name Bholu registered but not in connection with the body. Fighting his nausea he said, "Is it? Is it?" and his own voice was very far away, as Steele's had been to him. He noticed that Dorothy looked down at Bholu as she had at the fire. Let it burn. Let it burn, she had said. Now – Let it lie there.

He began to say, without thinking, "Why is it B –" but stopped himself before ending the question and exposing his panic. Why is it Bholu? It couldn't be Bholu. He was responsible for Bholu. Bholu couldn't be dead.

Steele was explaining. MacKendrick caught the words – "I thought he was coming at me with the knife." He interrupted, "Knife? What knife?" Steele pointed. "But why'd he got a knife? What else 'd he got?"

"Want to look?" Steele asked. He both saw and despised MacKendrick's dismay. In it he found a balm to his own pride. To show his indifference he knelt by the body as if to examine the wound, but a thought had crossed his mind. Gower had said: Not a hooligan but a servant of one of the Sahibs. But there was the knife. That made him half a hooligan. And now he recalled

221

Bholu's shiftiness as, that afternoon, he had glowered in the back of MacKendrick's jeep, and been sent packing with Prabhu in charge of him. What kind of a man was this Bholu? He said, "It's queer, you know. Bloody queer. He may've been running away from those other bastards, but he wasn't up to any good out there on his own."

Bholu's jacket was open, so that the inner pocket was exposed, and when Steele touched it MacKendrick said, "You oughtn't to touch it. Not till the police get here."

Steele grinned up at him. "We've carted the perisher up the steps since I dropped him." Then he leaned over the body and thrust his hand into the inner pocket. The jacket had not been buttoned across – perhaps Bholu had loosened it in his exertions to escape – and because it had not been closed across his chest the blood from the wound had not penetrated to what lay inside, had left no mark except for a small stain on one edge of the photograph.

Even from where he stood, well away from Steele, MacKendrick recognised it. He took a step forward, alarmed and puzzled, and he could not help exclaiming aloud, causing Steele to look up and say, himself, "Yes, Good Lord –" Steele looked from the photograph to Dorothy and then back again. It didn't add up. But then he realised he also held some folded one hundred rupee notes in his other hand. And then, to him, it began to add up.

"Look, all this must be yours."

Dorothy came closer and he held the photograph and the money up for her inspection. "All this must be yours, mustn't it? The little tyke must 've pinched it and then skedaddled."

MacKendrick began, "But the photo –" and then checked himself and looked, ashamed, at Dorothy.

"Yes, the picture's an odd idea." Steele smiled at her. "Must 've taken a fancy to you."

"What is the money?"

"Eh?"

She repeated, "What is the money?"

222

"This. Look, this –"

"I can see it's that. How much is it?"

"Sorry. Here, you'd better –" his voice trailed off. "No, I'll count 'em for you." He did so. "There's five hundred rupees in hundreds and this other – wait a moment –"

"No, the five hundred –" She hesitated. "If any of it's mine, it'll be the five hundred. I drew that amount from the bank this morning."

"Well, this must be it, then."

"No. No, wait." She seemed half afraid to touch it. She said, "Let me check up in my room. I left it in my room." She paused. "I left it in my room in the drawer of my writing table." She said to MacKendrick, "Will you come with me and just look?" and she slightly emphasised the 'you', as though to exclude Steele.

"Surely."

In the room she crossed over to the table, but did not open the drawer. At a sign from her he shut the door and went to her side. Urgently she whispered, "I've got to get that stuff back." She opened her handbag and passed him a folded piece of paper. He read it through. *Dear Lady, I am poor man already in want of Rupees Five hundred. . . .*

"But –"

"It was *him*. Don't you see?"

Quite suddenly he did. He said, exploring the truth, "But Bholu couldn't write English."

She took the note from him impatiently. "It's written by a professional letter writer in the bazaar. You can tell from the script and the style."

"Yes." He stared at her. "And you left the money today?"

"Yes."

He knew this was no lie. Bholu had been walking back from the milestone when he had come upon him. "But how would he know about that place? Know about the tree, I mean."

"The letter writer would know."

"Yes. I guess so."

"You've got to help me to get it back from John. The money and the photograph."

"Why didn't you take it just then?"

"I had to think. I had to –"

He interrupted. "I'm sorry about the photograph. He must have picked it up from my room. It's the one you gave Dwight."

"I know all about the photograph. Harriet Haig told me. We've got to get it all back and we've got to get John to agree to say nothing. We've got to think what to say."

He took her arm. "Yes, but why? If you just say both the money and the photograph were stolen, what's wrong with that? Nobody'll know Bholu was blackmailing you about me –"

He broke off, checked by the look of complete incomprehension on her face. It drained his confidence in his own grasp of the situation. She turned and sat down on the stool which stood in front of the desk, her shoulders hunched up.

"What's wrong, Dor?" He spoke tenderly. Like this, she was desirable; like this, needing support, needing affection, guidance. She said, "I've got it wrong. I thought it was about *me*. I thought the letter was about me, but it wasn't, was it? Bholu couldn't have known about me. Unless someone told him. Another bearer, Hussein, Abdul. Abdul knows. I'm sure Abdul knows. I don't know. I don't know." She put her hands to her face and drew them down, over the skin. "I can't risk it not being about me. We've got to get it all back, make Steele say nothing to Tom. Or to the police."

"You're all worked up, Dor. You can't think straight."

She looked up at him, her eyes narrowing. "You don't understand. You'll never understand. You don't know India. You can't kill someone like that and not raise an outcry. There'll be an outcry and then someone'll say he was a thief and only got shot because he was running away. You'll say it, or John, or Tom, or me. But we don't know what'll happen then. We don't know who there is to get up and say he didn't steal it because I gave it to him to make him keep his mouth shut about what I am."

224

"Who is there to get up and say that? Dor, who is there possibly to get up and say that?"

"I don't know. I keep telling you I don't know. But I can't risk it. It might be anyone. The man who wrote the letter for Bholu, or someone who's known about me and just used Bholu. Anyone. Anyone in Marapore who knows about me."

Rapidly she drew him into the net of her own confusion. He cried, "Say I gave him the money. Say it was my money." But she shook her head. "You didn't claim it. John would know I'd got you to say that, then he'd wonder why. And what about the photograph?"

"He could have stolen that. Just that. Not the money."

He knew it was hopeless, and the burden of fault was being placed on him. He should have claimed ownership right away. But how could he have done? No, she was all wrong. She was in a panic. He began, "What does it matter about Steele smelling a rat. If we're going to coerce him, what does it matter?"

"We're not going to coerce him. Just get him to hand it over and say nothing."

He tried once more to escape into lucidity.

"You said it didn't matter, about you, because time was running out."

She stood up and said, coldly, "It's Tom. Tom mustn't know about me."

He had ceased, in his mind, to question her tenacious hold to this axiom, and he accepted it now as she did herself, as a fundamental belief to which one must hold as though to life itself. Tom must not know about her. Tom must not know what she is.

Returning to the passage they noticed the girl standing, far back, and at once Dorothy stopped. The two women watched each other warily, the length of the passage between them, and as Dorothy went on, into the sitting-room, she whispered to him, "You see? You see what I mean? It might be anyone."

Bholu had been covered with a blanket.

She said to Steele, "Yes, the money's mine and the photograph of course."

Steele was lighting a cigarette. "Good," he said. "Good. I'm glad of that."

"I want it all back, please."

Steele grinned. "Oh, you'll get it all back, all right."

"I mean I want it now. Before the police get here."

"Whatever for?"

Only MacKendrick saw the slight hesitation. "I don't want a lot of bother," she explained. "You know what the police are like. Besides, he's dead, so what good can it do to say he stole it?" She reached for the notes and the picture, but Steele put his hand over them. MacKendrick jerked himself into action. "Look, John – much better forget it. I don't want him branded as a thief. I'm responsible for him after all. I'm sure there's been a mistake." He glanced at Dorothy and was grateful for the smile she gave him. "Let Dorothy have it back," he went on, "and don't let's say anything. I mean, not even to Tom. I'd really appreciate that."

Steele's mouth had fallen open. Now he closed it, firmly. His face coloured. "The bastard stole it. We'll leave it there." He had become truculent. He shifted round a little and added, "Sorry, Dorothy, but I need this evidence."

"Why do you need it?"

"It's safer. I mean safer for me. Tom said when the police get here all they'll find are the fires started by a gang of hooligans and other than that only me and Bholu who wasn't a hooligan but – your bearer." He nodded at MacKendrick.

"Tom said that?"

"Yes. I need this evidence. It'll prove Bholu was skipping out and that'll explain why he got mixed up with the others."

MacKendrick said, "But you don't have to prove you killed him because you thought he was a – well, whatever the others were."

"I hope not. But this –" and he tapped the table, "this makes me feel better."

Dorothy had said nothing and now MacKendrick turned to

her, trying to catch her eye. But she was watching Steele. She was still standing by the table, one hand resting on its surface. The money and the picture lay in the middle. She said, "You know, John, I should have thought all this would make it worse for you."

"What do you mean?" He laughed, uneasily. "Hell, it couldn't be worse. I believe I'm suspected of beating a chap up and I know damn well I'm not the best-liked man around here. How could it be worse? It's this –" and he jabbed his finger at the things on the table, "– this that gives me as clean a sheet as I can get. I don't mean they're going to stick me in clink." He had turned to Mac-Kendrick. "We're all clear on the official score. It's the unofficial one that's the trouble, the things that get around and get you in bad." He spoke again to Dorothy. "It's this that gets me as far out of bad as I can go in the circumstances."

"No. It's this that gets you in worse than ever," she replied.

He shook his head, but they could see that his confidence was going. "No –"

"Don't you think so? Personally, John, I should have thought shooting a man who turns out to have stolen something from one of us would look very bad – on the unofficial score, I mean."

"I don't get you. Don't get you at all."

"I think you do. If we say Bholu was a thief, what is there to stop someone saying you found him stealing and shot him and pretended you'd shot him during all this other business?"

Steele stared at her, then looked swiftly round the room. "There's all these witnesses," he said.

"We're not talking about witnesses. Witnesses are official. We're talking about unofficial things. And anyway – these witnesses are our servants."

She waited again, but this time he made no answer.

After a while she put out her hand and picked up the money, and then the photograph. Steele watched them go. Once, he appealed mutely to MacKendrick for guidance and again Mac-Kendrick thought: She's wrong, she's got it wrong, it's Steele who's right. She had injected something tortuous into another thing that was perfectly straightforward, he felt. It was that air about her, that air of intrigue – as in Sanderson's bungalow the night of the party – that had wrapped itself round Steele's common sense; something that sprang from inside her and compelled you; something that was in her that she despised and did not despise; something that sent her off on the road to Ooni to leave money in a hollow tree –

She turned to go back into the bedroom, then paused, seeing the girl, still huddled at the end of the passage. Swiftly she turned back. "You'd better tell all these people what you've decided to do, and why. Then they won't give you away if they're questioned."

Steele nodded, and MacKendrick watched him call the servants together, heard him talking to them in halting Urdu. The words jerked round the room, and they nodded, vacantly, not taking it in, but fixing their loyalty on the young man with the gun at his waist, as though loyalty came first, understanding after.

Loyalty first; understanding after. MacKendrick looked at Dorothy. When Steele had finished she nodded, satisfied, then went down the passage, brushing past the girl who shrank as she passed, and went into her room, closing the door behind her.

Dorothy's victory rose up before him like a wave he could not breast and when Steele came over and said, in a low voice, "Have I done right?" he answered, "Yes," and in his mind all doubt had gone, drowned by the belief that you could not play with a man's safety and still look him in the eye, as he was doing now.

They went out to the verandah to wait for Gower and the police. The first fury of the fire had gone and the flames did their work in silence. Once, in the distance, an engine revved, and MacKendrick said, "That's the jeep. Tom's coming back." But the sound, far off as it was, receded yet farther until there was no sound at all.

Steele shook his head. "No," he said, "that wasn't a jeep. It was

228

a three-ton lorry. It was going back to Marapore." He blew out smoke. "That's how they got here, then."

Below, faintly illuminated by the dying fires, was his own jeep, and MacKendrick looked at it, wondering why there should be, in his mind, a connection between the jeep and the sound of a three-ton lorry. He wanted Dorothy to come out and join them and then, he believed, he would be able to think.

But she did not come out.

6

After their first joyous greeting of it, the people of Marapore had taken shelter from the rain. It fell now as though it would never stop, as though it had been falling since the beginning of time. Rivers of ochreous, muddy water covered the *khattcha* strips at the sides of the roads. People who lived beneath roofs of corrugated iron shouted, to make themselves heard, and in shouting found their spirits lifted. Even the black, turbulent clouds rolled and tumbled in the sky as if pleased to be released from the bondage of warm oceans, exploding their mirth in cracks of thunder, linking hands whose touch sent streaks of lightning to the earth like fireworks thrown in time of carnival.

Before midday the storm had passed; but the rain continued, driving its fertile rods into the gaping fields and down through parched leaves to waken the roots of trees; beating on hard tarmac, on sun-peeled walls, on stone, on gravel; prodigal of its bounty.

Steele watched it through the unglazed windows of the little waiting-room in the District Magistrate's office, whither Gower had brought him that morning without explanation, but with a hint of apology. *Chaprassies* sat in a row on the bench outside on the verandah, slightly to the left of the window. Sometimes he crossed from the window and passed the closed door, pausing, expectant of Gower's voice and the D.M.'s. Seated, he watched the Indian clerk, meticulous in movement, birdlike in watchfulness, smug in the prim world of files. A bell rang and from the verandah the first *chaprassie* on the bench came and went into the D.M.'s room. He returned, spoke to the clerk, who rose and indicated to Steele that he could go in now.

The room was large, alien to the world of rain outside, its single ceiling fan throwing the room's stillness into relief. Steele walked the wide space of the uncarpeted floor to the desk where Gower stood, with Foster, whose genial smile and outstretched hand Steele found forbidding, like the smile and handshake of a doctor.

"Well, Steele. Nice to see you again. How long since we met?"

"About a year, sir. You looked us up on the way through Ooni, one day."

"So I did."

But Steele knew Foster's memory needed no jogging. And he wished he could retract that 'sir'. It had irrevocably put him at a disadvantage. He sat, at Foster's direction, in a low, leather chair, took a cigarette, and tried to veil his uneasiness by smiling at Foster, display his independence by ignoring Gower whose wavering smile of newly-offered friendship he found as nauseating as incomprehensible.

Foster nodded towards the windows, drawing their attention to the downpour. He said, "It's a pity this didn't happen last night at Ooni, eh?" He pulled the corners of his mouth down. "Well, Steele. Let's hear what happened."

Steele braced himself and began to talk, noticed the way his voice seemed to bring Foster's face alive: the eyebrows flexing, the eyes deepening. It was the face of a man to whom the spoken word was everything and who formed his judgments on it, cared not how clearly those judgments were discerned in their formative processes by those who told their stories to him; relied, in fact, on their being discerned, so that a lie, if contemplated, might wither on the lips.

Steele had hardly begun when Foster waved his right hand in front of him. "No, Steele. I meant from the beginning." And when Steele looked blank, he added, "You know. All this obscure business about Muttra Dass."

Steele fought the instinct to look at Gower: fought, and won; began again, watching his story take root, grow branches of its own in Foster's mind, through the changing expressions on his face, the movements of his hands and head – which now was nodding, slowly at first, gathering momentum, spurred on in the end by grunts and then by the reiteration of the word 'yes'. Yes. Yes. Yes: until Steele felt his own words lagging behind Foster's understanding of the tale. He increased the speed at which he told his story, to the point where sentences, phrases, and the odd exclamatory remarks grew staccato, disjointed. When he had finished he did so with the relief of someone who knows he has achieved his object in spite of obstacles. He knew, at least, that Foster had believed him. He and Foster spoke the same language.

Foster's stream of 'yes's' ended abruptly. There was a second or two of complete silence and then a final, unexpected 'yes' forced itself out and Foster leaned back as though delivered of a painful knot in his throat. He smiled, Steele smiled himself and, off guard, looked at Gower. Gower was smiling too, and leaning forward in his chair, possessively, showing pride, as it were, in Steele's performance. You bloody bastard, he thought, so now you want the credit.

"This chap Bholu, now," Foster was saying. "You say he was MacKendrick's man. What's MacKendrick's opinion of his character?"

"He seemed attached to him," Steele replied cautiously.

"The knife *motif* is interesting. No reason why the fellow shouldn't carry a knife. Lots of 'em do. Pathan servants for instance. But of course this is rather different. No idea what Bholu was up to? Got frightened, I suppose, and thought he'd make a dash for it only to find he'd made a dash in the wrong direction?"

Steele nodded.

"The fellow hadn't stolen anything, had he? Didn't get mixed up in the *tamasha* while making a run for it?"

For a moment Steele hesitated. Foster was looking now at Gower, but turned again to Steele when Steele said, "No. He hadn't pinched anything. At least –" and he saw Foster's eyebrows quiver, "– I mean the police found some money on him but MacKendrick had given it to him. His salary, I think."

"That's right. He had fifty-odd rupees in his pocket. Pretty high pay – still." Foster half turned in his chair and watched the rain falling. He seemed to be thinking of something else, but suddenly he said, "Yes, Gower. I think you're right. I'll arrange for an inquest to be held tomorrow."

"Good. I'm sure it's the right answer." Gower straightened, as if now ready to go, but Steele said, "Inquest?" and the tone of his voice made them both look at him questioningly. "Is there going to be an inquest?"

"Pure formality, Steele. Mr. Gower thinks it'll be in your interests and I agree with him. All this Muttra Dass nonsense and the business about the girl you live with. Now this Bholu affair. Feeling is pretty high against you, y'know. Better clear the air and make it official that no blame attaches to you concerning his death. The Indians'll love it. Nothing like a *pukka tamasha* for them. They've great respect for courts and such like." Foster grinned. "You see, clearing you on the Bholu affair 'll have the effect of ending all the silly rumours about what you've done or haven't done at Ooni." He jerked his head towards the window. "Air's being cleared anyway. You know how tensed up people get when the monsoon's late."

Steele felt Gower's eye on him. He thought: The bastard's fixing me. He wants me to take all the bloodiness there is to take.

He said to Foster, "Supposing they turn up expecting a kill and don't get one. How does that clear the air for me?"

"My dear boy," Foster began, leaning over his desk. "My dear boy, take it from me, this won't be a case of John Steele on trial, it'll be what I said, a *tamasha*. If we don't lay on a *tamasha* then I see Mr. Gower's point."

"What point?"

"One he made before you came in, actually. That it's possible the population 'll turn round and say we're closing a blind eye to a killing because the man with the gun was British and the man with the bullet in his guts was Indian. It isn't *only* to clear things for you."

"A killing can't always be avoided in cases like Ooni. Damn it all, they fired the place."

Foster's lips tightened. He said, "The difficulty is, Steele, that it's pretty clear the demonstration at Ooni was a student's prank. Ruthless, yes, – but a student's prank. It can't be called a dacoit action by any stretch of the imagination. And it can't be called an act of outraged citizens –"

"Why outraged anyway, even if it could be called that?"

"Outraged at what *you* were supposed to 've done. But Ooni's thirty miles away, and outraged citizens don't go rushing off into the night to set fire to model villages. They have a deep sense of property. Students haven't. There's strong evidence my people have collected that a bunch of chaps from the Laxminarayan are the chaps we want – or rather the chaps responsible. We don't particularly want 'em."

He paused, to allow Steele to speak. When Steele kept silent Foster went on, "We even know how they got there. They stole a lorry from the compound of Gopi Nair's house at Marpur. It was one of Ram Lal's – and whether he's in with the Laxminarayan bunch or not, I don't know."

"What did Nair want with a three-ton lorry?"

"We don't know. He's away from the district. His head servant said it was for transporting bales of homespun cotton."

"I see, Sounds pretty silly."

"Perhaps. Perhaps not. The lorry's not the point. And short of arresting every student at the Laxminarayan we couldn't hope to get the right ones. And as a matter of fact everyone in Marapore's laughing like the proverbial drain this morning. People *do* laugh at the things students get up to. Any arresting of students at the Laxminarayan is going to stop them laughing and blow up

233

all kinds of damned nonsense. We don't want damned nonsense at this point."

"Then why the inquest? Isn't that –"

"No. Between you and me I don't suppose there's a soul who cares a fig for Bholu, but it might suit somebody's book to whip up feeling against you. We don't want that either. We want a quiet life, this last month or two, don't we?" He grinned. " Leave things as quiet as we can. Forlorn hope. But there's no reason why we shouldn't give them another example of the incorruptibility of British justice."

Foster had summed up, and now he, like Gower, moved in his chair to show that there was nothing more to discuss. But Steele settled himself back in his arm-chair. At any other time the things Foster had said would have persuaded him of the rightness of the decisions made. He would have seen them as appeals to reason and appeals to justice; appeals to the code long since adopted by himself. This morning the code did not work. One by one, he felt, his gods were falling, and he dimly knew, and sharply felt, that he, John Steele, was being exploited: to Foster's diplomacy, or to Gower's hatred – he did not know which. He said, "What about this Dass business? I'd like to be cleared on that score too."

"That'll die down. All be forgotten."

Steele reddened. "Not by me. If I'm suspected of something I like to be charged with it openly."

"Yes, Steele. We all do." Foster had stopped smiling.

"It's all over the place that I beat him up."

"Well –" and Foster's manner became judicial. "If you really had beaten him up he wouldn't have hesitated to say so. Chance of a lifetime for a red like Muttra Dass."

"Somebody beat him up. If it wasn't me, who was it?"

"Ah." Foster looked at Gower. "You said you had a theory about that, didn't you?"

Steele's mouth twisted. He said, "Yes. I'd like to hear that theory of yours."

Foster's eyebrows went up. He thought: Odd. They haven't discussed it. Why?

He nodded at Gower encouragingly. "All this is between these four walls, y'know."

"Theories are best not aired at all," Gower replied. He saw Steele grin. "However," he added. Then he leaned back, and watched a point on the wall behind Foster.

What was the price of silence? Perhaps it was Ooni, acrid, charred, under the leaden sky of morning. He said, "My theory is that Gupta was Muttra Dass's guide and mentor. Beyond a certain point, you know, the guide loses control. All Gupta wanted, I think, was to ridicule me, and see my life's work made light of. Yes. Yes, let's look at it like that. He had another disciple besides Dass. Young Vidyasagar. The purpose of the sports day incident was ridicule, the personal motive envy. But you can't inspire disciples with that sort of purpose or that sort of motive. You have to dress them up as something else and the logical result of that is that the motives of your disciples are fundamentally different from your own."

Suddenly Gower sat upright again, his elbows on the arms of the chair, his fingers clasped together, the thumbs splayed. "All Dass had to do," he said, "was organise a strike, which he did. But when he'd done it he was afraid and couldn't make out the sense of what he was doing. So he compromised with Steele and hurried back to Gupta for instructions. Gupta probably told him he was a damned fool and was prepared to let it go at that. In twenty-four hours I'd been insulted on the *maidan*, and had a strike at Ooni."

Foster nodded, and for a moment Gower was silent, searching in his mind for the right words. He began, "But – behind the scenes – yes, behind the scenes, is this Vidyasagar, whom I've seen at – seen at close quarters." He frowned, hunched his shoulders. Somewhere, now, in my mind, he thought, is the key, not only to what has been but what is to be.

"Vidyasagar," he said, "is the pupil who ends by being

235

stronger than the master – and remember that idea about a disciple and his motives being different. Vidyasagar isn't prepared to let Dass's defection go at that. With the help of his admirers he beats Dass up. Gupta would have no part in that, I'm positive, but he'd be the first to hit on the value of the evidence Vidyasagar had unwittingly arranged, and the first to sense its limitations. Sending Dass to hospital bears Gupta's stamp. It's the act of the intellect rather than the emotions. And bear in mind that by now Dass is thoroughly frightened and will do or say anything Gupta tells him."

"And what would that be?" Foster prompted.

"To – to do and say nothing. The limitations of the evidence. You see? Dass was sent to hospital to get fixed up. Like that he provides perfect evidence for the *rumour* that Steele used violence. And by not saying anything he strengthened the rumours – because while you or I know he'd have been the first to bleat if Steele really *had* beaten him, his silence is interpreted as fear of Steele and not for what it was, fear of Gupta and fear of Vidyasagar. It was important that the rumours should never become anything more than rumours. The longer they remain rumours, the more distorted they get. That way they do more damage."

Foster said, "As witness Ooni?"

Gower hesitated. "Yes. Ooni." He was back to Ooni. Back to darkness and groping. "I said that beyond a certain point you lose control." That was it. Go back to the starting point. Go back. "Gupta – Gupta's lost control now and perhaps he doesn't care, because he's got what he wanted – he's edged me out of the *Gazette*, you know."

The wall: *Go Home Gower*. But that was not Gupta. That was Vidyasagar.

"He's edged me out of the *Gazette*, but he butters up to Nair. I'd say he wouldn't in any event have a hand in burning Nair's property. Enough for him that with the feelings he and Dass and Vidyasagar touched off he put the fear of God into my people up there. You know how these things work, this strange fear of

236

gods and devils that's always at work under India's skin. They probably thought the place was doomed. Threatened at least."

"That would account for the desertion, but not for the fire-raising."

"Yes. The desertion. The desertion was all Gupta wanted. With Ooni like that he could convince Nair of its uselessness, or its incipient harm."

"Then, the burning. Vidyasagar?"

Yes. Was this the key? But then he remembered Vidyasagar's eyes, that day on the *maidan*. Was it through Vidyasagar's eyes he had first seen the flesh and the spirit yielding to corruption: his own flesh, his own spirit?

"Vidyasagar? Somehow I don't think so. You see – the moment Ooni's deserted the tragedy becomes a farce. And Vidyasagar's not cut out for farce. This whole business –" and he stopped, suddenly aware of the texture of Foster's skin, the reality of Foster's presence. "This whole business is a question of touching off a spark in someone else. Gupta in Dass, and Dass in Vidyasagar. Vidyasagar in – whom? His followers? Yes, his followers, his fellow-students would be ripe for farce, for out-pranking Vidyasagar. They probably came up to Ooni on a hooligan's picnic."

Foster laughed. "Well! As long as we end on a note of farce! The inquest rounds it off perfectly, eh?"

Gower smiled. But beneath the smile was the horror of the unknown. Foster said, "We have the *tamasha*, and everyone's perfectly satisfied." Gower, still smiling, nodded. But there was a ghost in the room, the ghost of someone who wasn't satisfied. Vidyasagar. There is the true fanatic, he told himself, the man who is untouched by the comedy he has himself created.

Was that the key?

In the waiting-room they put on their monsoon capes and exchanged farewells with Foster, who went to the verandah and waved to them as they climbed into the jeep, whose hood was weighed down with a pool of rainwater.

237

Gower drove towards the club. Regardless of the rain Steele was leaning away from him, so that his arm and shoulder were unsheltered. Gower wanted to speak, but Steele's silence was like a gag across his own mouth. One word, he thought, one word could save us.

At the club entrance Gower said, "I'll drop you here."

Steele nodded. Brusquely he said, "You're not coming in?"

"No. I'm going to see MacKendrick."

"He might be here."

"His jeep isn't. He'll be at Smith's." Gower, prolonging the conversation, offered friendship. "Probably just up. He didn't leave Ooni until two o'clock this morning, remember."

"Right. I'll wait here, then."

Steele went, leaving the proffered friendship still in Gower's hands. He shook out his cape and walked through to the bar. There was relief for him in the voices which greeted him, in the friendly hand that clapped his shoulder, in the words, "What's yours, John old boy?" He drew on his armour of toughness, planted his bulk squarely against the counter, and was unaware of the spectre of death he had brought with him as a man might bring a dog – a dog which he trusts to lie, patiently, at his heels.

The young boy whom Desai, on hearing of Bholu's death, had detailed to Room Twelve was still laying out the suit when MacKendrick returned from the bathroom. From a chair, Mac-Kendrick watched until he could bear it no longer. He told the boy to go.

Outside, Desai accused the boy of sloth, but rubbed his hands with satisfaction at the thought of the charge he could now make for personal service, a charge which would more than make up for the difference in cost between Room Three and Room Twelve; and, in any case, the Maharajah would return on Friday to stay for a day or two and, perhaps, pay his bill. As he stood in the porch, he heard, above the noise of the rain, the abusive

238

shouting of the Eurasian girl in Room Nine, as she scolded one of the boys. It was midday, which meant she had had no more than six hours' sleep, if that. He had himself seen her return at six that morning, in the truck from the M.T. School; the same truck in which she had driven away with Milner Sahib the evening before, after the quarrel in Room Nine which had set the entire staff grinning and exchanging lewd gestures. Desai frowned. He was on the point of going to the room to enquire discreetly, if maliciously, whether there was anything in the service which displeased her, when Gower arrived.

He called from the jeep. "Is Mr. MacKendrick in?"

"Yes, he is in his room." Desai watched with curiosity as Gower climbed from the jeep and came up on to the porch. It rather pleased him that so many notorious people should be, or have lately been, under his roof.

"Would you tell him I'm here?"

"He expects you, Mr. Gower?"

"No."

As Gower removed his cape Desai called for the boy and sent him with a cuff on his ear to deliver the message. He asked, "You are having lunch here, perhaps?"

"No thanks."

"On Tuesdays always we have a fine curry. Madrassi style."

"No, I'm going back to Ooni."

"Ah. Is there much wreckage?"

"No more than you'd expect."

"Are the miscreants apprehended to date?"

"Not to my knowledge. The police are dealing with it."

"Ah." Desai wagged his head from side to side, his eyes downcast. "Then all will be in order, doubtless." The boy returned to say the Sahib could go to MacKendrick Sahib's room.

"Which is it?"

"Show him! Show him!"

The boy grinned and led Gower to Room Twelve. Desai wished he could go too, for he had noticed the grim set of

239

Gower's face. He listened. The American Sahib's greeting was cordial enough, but the door closed before Gower replied.

"I'm sorry to butt in."

"My fault, Tom. I've only just got up. Sorry about the room. Just let me finish and we'll go into the lounge and have a drink."

"No. This suits my purpose."

MacKendrick paused, his right shoe held in his hand.

Gower went on, "You'd better finish dressing." Then, "I'll sit here if you don't mind." He sat down on the chair which faced the bed.

"Sure." MacKendrick bent to put on the shoe. "There's a pack of cigarettes on the table by your elbow."

"No, thank you."

He noticed that MacKendrick was having difficulty with the shoe-lace, either that or he was taking his time. Probably the latter. As well he might, Gower thought. As well he might.

At last MacKendrick straightened up. At once Gower said, "My wife tells me she might be going away with you." As he waited for MacKendrick's reply he told himself: The man's a coward. Look at him. I'd rather it'd been Steele. Much rather. "Well, MacKendrick?"

"Tom – I don't know what to say."

"So I see. Though obviously you must say something."

"But when did Dorothy – tell you?"

"Does it matter exactly when? Presumably you knew she was going to?"

MacKendrick stood up. He felt like crying out: No! She's trapping me! But immediately he felt ashamed. He turned away.

"I can't talk to your back, MacKendrick." He smiled with satisfaction at the deep flush which spread over the other man's face as he turned round again.

"When did she tell you?"

"This morning."

"But what were the circumstances?"

"Are you concerned with them?"

240

"No. No, I suppose I'm not."

"I don't mind telling you. We were on the verandah at Ooni. I said something about Ooni being effectively ended and mentioned Kalipur. The Maharajah offered me a job, by the way, but perhaps you knew that already. I mentioned Kalipur and Dorothy said that she doubted she'd be coming to Kalipur as she was probably making other arrangements with you. Those were the words she used."

MacKendrick nodded.

"It was a surprise to me, of course," Gower continued. "And as she refused to discuss the matter further I'm still rather at a loss. You see, I thought if she went away with anyone it would be with – Steele." He had difficulty in pronouncing Steele's name, and knew he had given himself away, displayed the emotion he tried to mask beneath urbanity. "I'd like to know what your plans are. I'd like to know precisely."

"I can't say."

"Can't or won't?"

"Hell, do we have to talk about it?"

"Why shouldn't we talk about it? It concerns us both. It certainly concerns me." He hesitated. "You've met her before, of course. You knew her before you came to Marapore."

"I suppose it must look like that to you."

"Naturally." He waited while MacKendrick took a cigarette from his pack with trembling fingers. He then went on: "It's odd the way one's mind is forced to work from time to time. I've been thinking about this carefully. The conclusion I came to is that you and Dorothy used to know each other and that you came back to Marapore to look for her and make some proposal about going away together. It was that first evening when you came to Cannon Avenue that she told me I'd have to go home alone, if I went home to England. And of course, you were with her for a time while I was phoning Steele." He motioned with his hand. "Stop me if I'm on the wrong track."

But MacKendrick couldn't stop him. There was an inevitability about Gower's story, a ring of absolute truth that made Mac-Kendrick want to shout, Yes! This is the truth. This is what happened.

"Thinking all this, MacKendrick, I'm forced to the conclusion that my wife has been unfaithful to me – with you – on some previous occasion, and that my suspicions that Steele was concerned at all with my wife are probably without foundation. What is so ludicrous of course is the fact that it's only over this past three days that I've suspected there was anybody at all. If I analyse that, I find that the beginnings of my suspicion coincide with your arrival."

MacKendrick lowered himself on to the bed. Gower leaned forward. "I've only got one more thing to say, MacKendrick. I can't expect to control my wife at this stage of things. Whatever I've done to make her life unbearable I obviously can't undo. I shan't attempt to hold her to what she finds untenable. She is absolutely free, to come and go as she pleases. But with you it's different. I have done nothing to hurt you and that gives me moral permission to control your comings and goings in so far as they affect my affairs. From this I hope you'll understand you're forbidden to come to Ooni, and you're forbidden to come to Cannon Avenue. I hope actually not to see you again, although I'll be forced to do so at the inquest on Bholu tomorrow about which you'll be hearing from the District Magistrate. I hope not to see you again because when I look at you I'm looking not only at my own stupidity but at my lamentable if human inclination to defend myself by doing violence." His voice wavered. He said, "I could, God help me, cheerfully murder you."

When he had gone MacKendrick found himself, not alone, but companioned by the fear of death. The fantasy had gone with the man who had created it. He was alone with the fear of death and when the first pangs of that fear had been borne and also gone their way, he was alone with the image of Dorothy.

He rose from the bed and walked out of the hotel. The rain had stopped and he was ten yards or so along the road, on his way to the station, before he remembered the jeep. Going back, unable to find it, he called out angrily, until Desai came out and calmed him down by pointing out where the jeep had been pushed, under cover of a lean-to shed at the back of the house. As he got into the driving seat, Dorothy was there again, in his mind, staring ahead at the road where the headlamps had lighted it. He drove, with her, and when he reached the station it seemed that she bowed her head suddenly in her hands and wept, crying out: No. No. For God's sake, don't desert me now!

He tried to push the vision away and, at the booking office, he asked for a single ticket for Bombay. "What train can I get?"

The clerk went away. And there she was again. She said, "The inquest. Inquest. Tomorrow. You can't go until after tomorrow."

Tomorrow was Wednesday. The clerk returned. "No bookings until Friday," he said, indifferently.

"When? What time?"

"Train leaves twenty-two hundred hours. Friday."

"Yes, give me a seat then."

"One seat?"

Her hand was on his arm. "No," he said, "I want two seats. Get me a coupé." And he passed a one hundred rupee note across the counter. Indifferently the clerk took the bribe. "Two seats. Coupé. Single journey Bombay. Wait a sec."

MacKendrick turned, half expecting to find her there, by his elbow. The clerk returned, with a book of reservation slips, and laboriously wrote up the details. The business done MacKendrick left the jeep outside the station and walked across to the post-office. He bought a letter card and wrote to Dorothy, leaning uncomfortably against the high desk, assailed by the smell of bodies, jabbed in the back by umbrellas, deafened by the shouting that passed between officials and customers.

Dear Dorothy,
    Tom has forbidden me Ooni and Cannon Avenue. I have just bought two tickets for the Friday night train to Bombay which leaves at ten o'clock in the evening. I've reserved a coupé. I . . .

He hesitated and stared at his handwriting, which was suddenly unfamiliar to him. But now it was as though she took his hand and guided his pen across the page, as though she whispered: Believe in me. Don't go on trying to believe in yourself.

He wrote:

... If you want to contact me I'll be at Smith's or leave messages where I can be reached. I hear there's to be an inquest on Bholu, and I guess you'll be there. But if we don't get a chance to speak just remember the arrangements are made, for Friday.

His writing was large: the card small. He had no room to sign his name, or send his love.

7

Next day, when Steele awoke, he put his hand out to touch the girl, but she had gone, leaving behind her the warm impression of her body. He let his hand rest in the little hollow made by her hip, and closed his eyes, drowsily content, half inclined to call her softly. But the stirring in his blood drove sleep away, and brought with it a faint, uneasy fluttering of his heart as his mind slowly adjusted itself to the reality of morning. Wednesday. There was the inquest to be faced. He contemplated this fact, was awed and challenged by its inevitability; finally accepted it and sat up, scratching his head, rubbing his unshaven chin with the palm of his hand. There was, from the next room, the subdued sound of voices, the chink of crockery. Routine: this is what saved a man from going downhill. He rose and walked, naked, to the bath enclosure on the rear verandah, where his bearer had erected a makeshift shower from old *ghi* tins.

The top of the enclosure reached no higher than his chest, and the morning air pricked his sweat-clogged body. The sun was coming up over the hills; golden clouds bunched their fists in the sky. Standing there, facing the sun, he breathed in slowly, deeply, dragging air down into his lungs. He exhaled quickly and repeated the process several times until he could feel the clear, sweet air cleansing his blood, impregnating his whole being. Here, like this, he wished he could stay.

Stepping into the empty canvas hip-bath beneath the home-made shower, he held his breath and pulled the string which sent cold water cascading on to his head, down his back, his chest, thinning out to rivulets down his legs. Then he soaped himself, filled the hip-bath with more cold water, and sat down in it with a grunt. He scooped the water into his hands, held them up and let it run down his arms. Taking the soap again he worked up a lather on his left arm. Gradually he ceased to move the bar of soap, extended the arm and observed its strength and shapeliness. As he twisted it round, the long muscles on his forearm braced up, ridging the skin. Then he let the arm drop, and stared straight in front of him, the pride he took in his own toughness gone, and, in its place, the memory of the thing Gower had said. You are an apostle of violence.

He dragged forward the last tin of cold water, raised it above his head, tilted it slowly and rinsed the soap away. Then he stood up, stepped out of the bath and wrapped a towel round his middle.

On one of the supporting poles of the roof a shaving mirror was fixed. While he shaved he watched the face reflected in it. The mirror was a relic of days in the Arakan, and his face was little changed since then; fuller perhaps; the lips less pinched, the yellow jaundiced look no longer staring from beneath the tan. When he had rinsed his face and cleaned his teeth he stood, looking over the enclosure at the hills; greener after yesterday's rain. The air was drying his body, and he stood there thinking of Bholu.

Bholu had had a knife and, because he had had a knife, he had shot him. Without the knife he would not have used the gun. Or would he? Steele frowned, trying to judge the affair of Bholu by the standards of his experience in the war. Surely it was the same? The compulsion of kill or be killed? Was to kill, in such circumstances, the act of an apostle of violence?

Impatiently he turned and, in doing so, became aware of his nakedness. He stopped short, in the act of returning to his bedroom. When, he wondered, had he ever faced a man who held a gun while he himself was unarmed? The answer came, after a while: never. He passed a hand over his mouth. To that extent, he knew, he had never had his courage tested. He went back into the bedroom and saw that a freshly laundered khaki shirt and pair of drill trousers were laid on the bed. The sight of the smart clothes emphasised that this day was unlike other days. Clean, snowy underwear, clean, undarned socks, his best shoes highly polished and gleaming with the beauty of old leather. He lit a cigarette and, with a sinking heart, clothed himself. Such clothes; one's first day at school.

When his bearer came in, Steele grinned, to hide his concern. "Help me with these, Mahmoud." And Mahmoud came and took his arm, rolled the sleeve up.

"Regulation three inches. That's it." Steele winked, then held out his other arm. As Mahmoud bent his head Steele noticed the strands of grey in the black, oily hair. How old was the little beggar anyway? Mahmoud smiled, stepped back a pace, then forward again, to adjust a button on the shirt.

"Okay for court martial, eh?"

But there was no humour in the situation.

He had breakfast on the verandah at the front of the bungalow, and when Mahmoud brought fried eggs, Steele attacked them automatically, the business of eating and eating well having long since become an action as uninhibited as breathing. He thought: Not many more breakfasts here, like this: for his days at Ooni were, he guessed, numbered. All right then. They were numbered. He'd look up Tim Allen in Assam. Join him perhaps in planting tea. Take Mahmoud of course and maybe the girl – or some other girl whose dark flesh beneath his would excite him as no white woman could any longer, for they lacked for him a subtlety, they lacked that elusive aphrodisiac scent. And wherever he went in India, would always be the heat, the blessed sun, the merging

246

of days that wasn't like time passing, or anything to do with time. Time was a glimpse of grey hairs on another man's head. But now behind these thoughts, always that other thought waiting to pounce. Before, you always had a gun.

He drank a last cup of coffee and lighted a cigarette. He was now almost eager to go and have done with it, eager to sit there at the inquest and give his evidence, simply and directly. When he had finished he called Mahmoud so that breakfast could be cleared. He looked at his watch. There was plenty of time; but time was what he did not want. He pulled on his soft hat and walked to Gower's bungalow. As he approached, Gower was coming out and they met on the road.

"I'm ready when you are," Steele said.

"The phone's on again," Gower replied. "I've just checked up with the D.M.'s office. It'll be you and me, Prabhu and Mahmoud. MacKendrick too, of course."

"What about the girl?"

"They don't want her."

"Nor Dorothy?"

"Nor Dorothy."

"When do we start?"

"Go now if you like. We can take it slowly. The road's pretty sticky."

"I'll winkle out Mahmoud."

Steele turned away and felt that Gower would have come with him, given half a chance. Bastard, he thought, a right bastard. Not because of the inquest. The inquest had suddenly assumed an unimportance. It would be a farce, as Foster had said. He could forgive Gower for the inquest; not for the other thing; undermining his pride, his confidence, questioning his courage.

He yelled for Mahmoud as he returned to the bungalow and Mahmoud presented himself, dressed in his best, like Steele; tropical khaki uniform, stripped of insignia. In the bedroom the girl was waiting. He went to her and kissed her lightly and then strode with Mahmoud up the road to where Gower's jeep was

247

parked. Once he looked back and saw that she had come out to watch him. He waved, briefly.

Prabhu was ready.

"Okay, you two, hop in the back." He waited for Gower and, when he came, asked, "You drive or shall I?"

"I think I will."

There was no sign of Dorothy. Steele turned to watch the verandah as the jeep began climbing the hill, but she did not appear. There was only the girl on the road, and now, as the jeep moved down the other side of the hill, the girl, the bungalows, the broad valley, all these were cut off. Gower spoke. "Just here is where they cut the telephone wire." Steele looked where Gower pointed, but there was no trace now of the cut; it was almost as though there had been no cut, no mob, no killing; like battles, with the earth growing new skin over its wounds.

Gower's voice: "Have you thought what you're going to do?"

"Do?"

"Yes, after this business."

"Not really."

Gower bit his lower lip. Then he said, "Did I tell you about Kalipur?"

"No."

"I'm getting a job there." He added, "Actually with the Maharajah."

"Sounds pretty high-flown to me. Personally I wouldn't put much faith in a job with one of those johnnies. Who knows what's going to happen to 'em?"

"This one'll be all right. He's pretty astute." Gower cleared his throat. Once he had thought of humility as part of his make-up, but now he had to force himself to speak, and force into his voice all the friendliness he could muster. He recognised how miserably he failed. "He's said he's going to be independent, but of course he must know he'll have to cede to India sooner or later. But whatever happens the job isn't affected. I made sure of that."

Steele kept silent. Gower began, "I thought –" and waited,

248

hoping Steele would ask him what he had thought so that it would be easier to tell him. But Steele merely faced him with a blank expression. "I thought you might like me to put in a word for you with him," he said at last, and at once felt himself go cold. He could not have put it more insultingly.

There was no going back along the road, no retreat to what had been, no possible means of making the boy trust him again or like him again. He drove on, mechanically, and when they entered Marapore at last, the clouds already gathering, grey and black and fringed with white, he had the feeling that the town was holding its breath. Ahead he saw a group of people gathered in front of the court-house. So few? He had, somehow, expected more, many more, for was this not the *tamasha*, the side-show? He drove into the parking space. MacKendrick's jeep was already there, and Gower drew up alongside it.

Afterwards, when letting himself look back to this day, he told himself MacKendrick's jeep was the deciding factor in what followed. The hood of MacKendrick's jeep was up, and just as the four of them began to walk away from it, across the parking space, Steele slightly in front, Gower stopped.

"We ought to put our hood up, too. It's going to rain."

Steele nodded, and told Mahmoud to give Prabhu a hand. The two bearers went back to the jeep and began unloosening the butterfly screws which secured the collapsed frame.

"Coming?" Steele asked.

"I'll help them out. You go in, Steele."

The cover had got caught up in the frame, and Gower, noticing it, told himself it was important he should help to free it, ensure it was not torn. The hood, the need to put the hood up, and now the imagined need to help the two men free the canvas were impressions he received, impressions thrown at him like a buoy, which, observed, was the first warning to him that he was in danger. He could not explain it and as he fumbled inexpertly with the frame and the canvas he knew no explanation existed. He saw Steele walking off, watched him from the corners of his

249

eyes, saw him pause to light a cigarette, and at once thought: No. Get on. Don't wait. For he and Steele had come to the end of whatever journey his own fear and suspicion had mapped out for them. Here, where the jeep was parked, was the end, and Steele, from this point, was on his own. He had to let Steele free.

And now Steele, flinging away his match, was walking to the door and Gower turned, quite openly, to watch him. There was about Steele an air of surrender, not in keeping with a man released. The broad shoulders had drooped, the back seemed to have narrowed. But quite suddenly the shoulders squared up and the head jerked to one side, and at the same moment Gower heard the sound which had brought Steele to an abrupt halt.

"Steele Sahib!"

The high-pitched voice called again. "Steele Sahib!"

Gower saw Steele twist round, his body uncertain, awkward, while the knot of people unravelled itself and left one solitary figure facing him.

Even from where Gower stood he recognised Vidyasagar, but before he could shout a warning to Steele, Vidyasagar had raised his revolver and pulled the trigger. The revolver was empty before Steele, jerked like a marionette with the impact of each successive shot, pitched forward on his face, with one arm clawed out at Vidyasagar's feet.

And as Gower began stumbling towards them, he was thinking: Steele went for him. He was reaching for the gun.

8

Steele was buried the following morning. Gower had tried to arrange for the funeral to take place the evening before, but there were endless formalities: the inquest on Bholu, the inquest on Steele and then, at the last moment, a change in plan for the funeral itself when it was discovered Steele had been a Catholic.

The tiny Catholic church in Marapore stood a little way off the Kalipur road. Its roof was made of corrugated iron and, as the service opened, the first rains of the day began to fall, so that nothing was heard above the drumming on the roof. When the time came to bear the coffin to the cemetery they had to wait until the shower ended so that those who had come to pay respect to the dead might follow.

They waited there in the church for the drumming to stop. With the exception of Gower and Foster, and a few officials from the cantonment, the mourners had seated themselves at the back of the church. As Gower went to the door he saw Miss Haig and Mrs. Mapleton. There was Milner, too, staring at the altar with beer-dazed eyes, MacKendrick next to him; Sanderson from the college, a few familiar faces, club friends of the man who was dead; unfamiliar faces, too. It surprised Gower for, in his life, Steele had kept himself so much to himself.

He walked behind the coffin, at the head of the silent, straggling procession. The rain had ended and the sun was already sucking the moisture up, blazing a vaporous trail of rising steam across the cemetery. He had expected to find Mahmoud waiting, but there was no sign of him, no sign of him anywhere among the overgrown graves, the stone crosses – some aslant with age – the occasional, spectral angel. Beyond the last grave, where a gate led out on to the Kalipur road he saw movement, but he could not detect its nature, seen, as it was, more as a shadow among the shadows cast by the trees.

The coffin was going now: down, down. And the rain was beginning again, thinning the mourners, spurring the last rites on until, quite suddenly, it was all over. He turned his collar up and half-way back to the church he came upon Miss Haig sheltering under a tree while Cynthia stood by, an umbrella held above them both.

Miss Haig said, "Did Dorothy not come?"

"No. She's at Ooni."

They were all three looking in different directions, afraid, it seemed, to let their expressions be seen. For a while nothing further was said. Gower was staring at the gate where the shadows were. Once, Miss Haig said, "I'll see you tomorrow, Tom, won't I?"

"Tomorrow?"

"It's the day Jimmy comes back."

"Yes, of course." He looked at her now. "I'll come down from Ooni for lunch. Not much point in him going up there to stay, now."

"He'd like to see it though. I'm sure he'd like that."

"We could drive up after tea. What time does he arrive?"

"About three, I think."

"You'll have dinner with us?" When she nodded he turned to Cynthia. "You too, of course."

"Afraid I can't." Her voice was too harsh, too loud.

"Oh, why?"

"I'm going."

"Where?"

"For good. A funeral is an appropriate ending." She gazed up at the sky. "It's stopped, Harriet. We'd better get a move on."

Gower said, "I'll give you a lift," but Cynthia snapped, "No need. We've got a tonga."

He watched them go. Harriet stopped as she neared the church, looked round, awkward upon her sticks, and nodded farewell. He did not acknowledge her gesture. He turned in the opposite direction and walked slowly towards the gate along the gravel path which glittered after the rain. From beyond the gate there was a murmuring of women's voices: and then, startling him, sudden shrieks of abuse and the sound of a stone flung against the bark of a tree.

He hurried along the path and when he came to the gate the women scattered and turned at a safe distance to call out, their thin arms stretched as though bidding heaven to judge their own innocence and the girl's sin. She was crouching by a tree, her saree spattered with mud, surrounded by stones; and she did not look up when Gower spoke to her.

Although he had never seen her properly – for she had kept away

252

from him, that night of the fire – he knew who she was, and knowing, he wanted to kneel by her side, comfort her, raise her up and bid her go unmolested to Steele's grave. The pitifully thin hands, the bowed head, the kneeling, shrouded figure, the bare calloused feet – all the poverty and wretchedness that was India, to these, surely, he could be tender? To these, surely, his heart would go out as for year after year he had bidden it go out?

He stood above her. He had only to bend down and touch her shoulder. He had only to do this simple, almost undemonstrative act, to prove his understanding and his compassion. But his arm was fixed rigidly by his side. Where there should have been compassion there was only distaste, and where there should have been understanding was only the desire to turn away.

He looked towards the gate and there, strewn on the ground with bruised stems and torn petals, were the remains of her bunch of flowers; and lying in the mud, a cheap, tawdry postcard with a picture in garish colours of the Virgin and Child; her offering to the alien grave, her charms against the spirits of evil.

He said, "Do you need money?" And when she did not reply, "You had better go now. While I am here they will not attack you." He watched her as she stirred. Still crouching, she began to gather up the flowers.

"Leave those. I will see that fresh ones are put where those were going."

Listlessly she obeyed, but standing, still did not face him.

He said, roughly, "Here. Here is money."

He hoped she would not take it. He thought: If she doesn't take it, then I'll be able to pity her. But he had forgotten the poverty. She turned to him and he held out the notes, his hand beginning to tremble because he could see her clearly now and see that she was not more than sixteen and already heavy with child. Knowledge of the child stunned him. The child was obscene, sprung from an act of lust and the urgency of the flesh's need. The child was not Steele's, nor was it the girl's. Rather it

253

seemed a growth, a canker, from which both would have turned in disgust, back to the inviolacy of their separate spirits.

"Here. Here."

She took the notes and at once turned and went quickly up the road, half running, half walking, away towards Kalipur. When she had gone two or three hundred yards she stopped and fumbled with her clothing, as though hiding the money. Then, without looking back, she hurried on.

Before he returned to Ooni, Gower went to the headquarters of the District Police, taking with him Foster's written permission to see Vidyasagar. He felt it his duty to see him. Kindness to Steele might have saved Bholu. Were Bholu alive, Vidyasagar would not be here, in prison. He had to wait ten minutes or so before being taken down to the cell where the boy was locked up, and as he paced up and down they brought Sanderson up. Sanderson cried out, "That boy! That poor boy down there!" He broke off and burst into tears. "It isn't true. It can't be true. They can't hang him. They can't!" He caught hold of Gower's arm. "You were there. It was a mistake, wasn't it? The gun went off by mistake, didn't it?"

"No, there wasn't any mistake. He shot him in cold blood, Sanderson. Six rounds."

"But he didn't try to run away. He let himself be taken!"

"Steele didn't try to run away either."

Sanderson dug his fingers into Gower's arm, and Gower saw the little lights of cruelty dancing in his eyes. "They've tortured him, you know. His face is dreadful."

"No, it was Mahmoud who did that."

They escorted Gower to the cell, but would not open it to let him go in. Vidyasagar turned his back and went to sit on his bed. He was carrying it off well, Gower thought. He had not yet grasped reality.

And now that they were together Gower knew the real reason why he had come. He wanted to see the boy cower. He wanted the boy to fall on his knees and cry and beg for mercy. And he wanted to beat his own hands on the bars, beat and beat until the skin was broken and the blood came and some of his own agony was released to enter into the boy. Hoarsely, he said, "I came to see if there's anything I can do for you."

It was as though Vidyasagar had not heard.

Gower went on, "It doesn't seem likely that you did what you did just on your own. I thought you might like to say who put you up to it."

And now Vidyasagar looked at him and the look in his eyes had not changed since that day on the *maidan*. There it was; there it had always been, waiting, unprofaned, this pure stream of hate; and Gower knew, then, that the act of killing Steele was Vidyasagar's alone. It had, now, a clarity, a completeness, which made it at once a beginning and an end. Vidyasagar shared it with no-one. Least of all, with him. He said, "They'll hang you, you know. None of your friends is going to stand by you. You've cut yourself off, cut yourself off from everything."

Vidyasagar smiled. His face bore the marks of Mahmoud's fists.

"You are wrong, Mr. Gower. It will be many days, many weeks, many months, before the trial takes place. By that time the British will not be here, and I will have justice."

And having spoken, he lay down on the bed and closed his eyes, excluding Gower from his dream of safety. Slowly Gower relaxed his grip from the bars and let himself be accompanied back upstairs. He drove to the bungalow in Cannon Avenue, and ate the lunch which Abdul served. In the sitting-room, afterwards, he found waiting for him an unopened copy of the latest edition of the *Marapore Gazette* and, attached to it, a slip with the editor's compliments. The leading article bore Gupta's signature, but it was prolix, meaningless. He searched through the pages for a report of the things which had happened at Ooni, but found none. Next week, perhaps? Then he knew that even next week the events at Ooni would be ignored. Ooni was beyond Gupta's grasp. The *Gazette* was blameless, feeble. Not a word in it had been dictated by passion. Gower, staring at its pages, realised that the *Gazette* had undergone no change at all. It was evidence of nothing but a man's ambition.

He rose and sought out Abdul, gave him instructions for the following day. The journey to Kalipur had begun. The arrangements made, he sat down and wrote out his resignation to Nair, and at three o'clock he set out for Ooni. The sun had gone in again before he reached Marpur and turned in through the gateway of Nair's still shuttered house. The tethered goat started away in fright. The Holy Man had long since gone. There was no answer to his knock on the wooden door; only the echo and a sudden gust of wind shaking the leaves of the banyan tree. He walked round the house and saw a woman draw her child into the shelter of a doorway to the servants' quarters. He raised his hand to her, but, for answer, she pulled the edge of her saree across her face and went inside. He called out, and a cow, cropping the poor grass, raised its head to watch him with soft, enquiring eyes.

He went back to the jeep and just before moving off he looked up suddenly at the house. But there was no one there.

Part Three

1

At midday on Friday the postman called at Smith's Hotel with a letter for MacKendrick and a telegram for Desai. MacKendrick was in the lounge when Desai walked in from the porch. He took the letter and ordered a John Collins. The letter was from Dorothy. She wrote:

Dear Joe,

Thank you for writing. You'll wonder why I said what I did to Tom without having really talked to you or agreed to anything. The explanation is simple. I told Tom what was in our minds because I knew he would take it up with you. It was the first definite thing he had had to go on. I knew he'd take it up with you and I knew that would give you the chance of denying everything and a chance of going away without seeing me again. In any case I wasn't certain that the things you said that night at Ooni really meant what I imagined them to mean.

You'll appreciate how careful I must be not to misunderstand a situation. Thank you for the details of the arrangements you have made for Friday. I'm sorry that I mistrusted you.

Dorothy.

His first reaction was one of relief, his second, one of confusion. He read the letter again, pacing across the lounge. She noted the arrangements he had made. She failed entirely to say whether she accepted them.

He looked round the walls of the lounge and knew that he was virtually a prisoner; forbidden by Gower to go to seek her out, forbidden by the loyalty Dorothy seemed to place upon him to leave the hotel in case she should need to find him. He walked from the lounge to his bedroom, fearful that a false move of his would leave him stranded with his own inadequacy once more. Not that, he thought; you've got to beat it this time. He sent a boy out for a new pack of cigarettes.

At four o'clock the telephone rang in Gower's study. Abdul, answering it, found his master at his side.

"All right, Abdul, go and see to the tea. It's news of our guest, I expect." Gower took the phone.

"Tom?" It was a woman's voice.

"Yes, is that you, Harriet?"

"Yes."

"Has Jimmy arrived, then?"

"No."

He thought her voice sounded strained. "What's happened?" he asked.

"I don't know, Tom."

"Perhaps he's held up in Delhi, then?"

She said, "Yes, possibly."

"Oh well, we'll hear tomorrow."

"I expect so," she said.

"Come over and have tea."

"No, I want you to come here. We're in rather a mess but you could say goodbye to Cynthia."

"Just a moment. I'll ask Dor."

He hesitated when he got to the bedroom. Inside there was no sound at all. Opening the door he found her, not on the bed as he had expected, but on a chair, upright and unrelaxed, as though the room were crowded, and she about to leave it.

"Harriet's asking whether we can go over to tea. It looks as if the Maharajah's been held up in Delhi." Speaking, he realised they had not spoken since the previous evening. "Shall I say yes?" He looked round the room. But there was no sign of packing.

"No. You go if you want to."

"I'll ask her here, then."

"As you wish."

He returned to the phone. "No, look. You come along here."

"Is it Dorothy who won't come? Why not come alone? We can talk more then."

All around him the place seemed to quieten and reveal its hope that he would go, and leave his wife unguarded. He said, "We'll call it off, then. Some other time, Harriet."

"No, Tom! Tom! Don't hang up – I'll come along right away. We ought to talk."

"What about?"

"I want to talk. I'm hanging up now, and coming right away." There was a click on the other end of the line. Slowly he replaced the receiver and stood quite still. Then he sat down at his desk and picked up Steele's Bible which Mahmoud had given him last night. Opening it he read again the formal inscription: To John, from Mother and Father, 23rd April, 1932. He stared at the words, trying to picture Steele's parents, now dead. He wondered that they had not inscribed it with any message of love.

He pushed the Bible away. Dorothy had not seen MacKendrick; of that he was certain. But she had received a letter from him and had replied to it. Beyond the exchange of letters – nothing; no word, no sign, *no indication of when*. He tried to ignore the possibility that she was leaving it to him to give that sign, leaving it to him to do some act, some insignificant act that would set in motion the wheels of her departure.

When Harriet arrived he saw at once that there was something wrong, but for the moment it seemed unimportant. The small gestures of offering tea took pride of place; were, to him, blessed for their absurdity and irrelevance. Dorothy did not appear and, sometimes, between the handing of a plate, the receiving of it back, he lost track of their talk and listened for her. At last he clattered down his cup and said, "It's no use, Harriet. Dor's going to leave me." He turned to her for support. Her face coloured up. A fearful joy had gripped her and before she could stop herself she had cried out, "Good riddance to her! Now you can begin to live!"

So astonished was he that for a moment he was unable to speak. She clutched the ends of the arms of the upright wooden chair in which she was sitting and felt the cold, metallic bite of the rings. For the first time since she had known him she was afraid of him.

"How can you say that?" He stood up.

"For your own good. For your own good, Tom." It seemed to her as though she pleaded with him, not for his sake but for hers. She tightened her grip on the chair.

"When – when is she going?" she asked.

"She doesn't say."

"Who with? With – with Mr. MacKendrick?"

He looked at her, surprised. "I suppose everyone knew except me," he managed to say.

"How could they know?" she began. And then the words she wanted to speak jumbled themselves in her brain. It was no good talking about Mr. MacKendrick, or about his brother. It was too confused, too far away, too hopeless to sort out now. To do so would separate her fear from her desire, and the two would then, she knew, stand opposed and crystal clear. Hang on to the wish, she prayed, cling to the desire. Let Dorothy go with this other man, no matter who he was, no matter what he was. Let them go, let them leave Tom. And bury the fear that this wish is evil.

"Kalipur."

She looked at him, startled. "What? What did you say?"

"Kalipur."

Her heart hammered against the vice of returning pain. Breathlessly she asked, "What about Kalipur?"

"I thought she was waiting for something I would do. But she's waiting to know about Kalipur."

"What difference will Kalipur make?"

"It might make all the difference."

"Kalipur's settled. She knows about Kalipur. Kalipur's all settled!"

"Is it, Harriet?"

"You know it is."

"Then why isn't he here?"

"That's nothing. He's been held up. It's not important whether he's here or not."

"What are you afraid of?"

"But I'm not afraid –"

"You're practically in tears."

"I'm so confused. Tom, Tom, you're making me so confused. Mixing up two totally different things."

"Is Jimmy unreliable?"

"No! Oh, no! You saw for yourself what –"

"You know him better. You brought him up. He's as good as your own child in that way."

"Yes. I brought him up."

"Where is he now?"

"In Delhi."

"Where was he staying?"

"I don't know."

She stared at him, unable to see him except as a blurred shape. She tried to shake her head but the pain was too unbearable.

He said, "We could ring Smith's. He booked a room there for the week-end. They might have heard."

"No!" she cried.

"Why not?"

"He isn't coming to Smith's."

"How do you know?"

"They – they had a telegram."

"When?"

"This morning."

"You've known since then?"

"No. I rang them – I rang them just before I rang you."

"What did the telegram say?"

"Just cancelling the room."

"And where was it handed in?"

"I don't know. In Delhi. It must have been in Delhi."

"Didn't you ask?"

"No. I –"

"You were afraid to ask?"

"No. No." She felt his hand take hers. "We'll ring the palace," he was saying. "They'll tell us where he is. Then we won't go on waiting for him unnecessarily." He was speaking very clearly, very quietly. "Then we'll all know what we have to do. Come. You ring him at the palace."

As he helped her to her feet the pain began to recede. She was praying that it would invade her whole body and drag her down into unconsciousness, drag her down into a deep sleep from which she would not wish to wake. But it receded. He led her into the study and helped her into the chair by his desk. "Let me do it alone," she breathed, but he shook his head and handed her the receiver. "Whatever you think, Tom, it's going to be all right. I tell you, it's going –" but she had to break off to speak to the operator. Gower stood over her, listening intently to her every word, every crackle that came faintly over the wire. When the exchange at the palace answered she asked to speak to the Maharani.

Gower put out a hand. "No. Ask for Jimmy."

She shook her head and, defeated, he went to the window. He heard her draw in her breath

"Boo? Is that you, Boo?"

Boo's childlike voice sounded so far away.

"Yes. Harriet? How are you, Harriet?"

"Very well, Boo. And you?"

"Oh, I am all right. How nice of you to ring. Where are you?"

"In Marapore. Boo, can you tell me when Jimmy's coming back from Delhi?"

"Jimmy? Oh, but he came back yesterday. And so bored. So distrait. Everything went wrong there."

"Is he coming to us?"

"No-o? Did he say he would?"

"He was coming for the week-end."

"Didn't he let you know he'd changed his plans?"

264

"No. No, we didn't know."

"He's a very naughty boy. But isn't it just like Jimmy?"

"But he did cancel his hotel."

"Oh, that would be Freddie. He's very meticulous."

"Freddie? Yes, yes of course, Freddie." She made a sound, half sob, half laugh, remembering Freddie, wondering irrelevantly what the funny story about Freddie had been. But Boo was speaking again.

"What, Boo? The line's bad."

"I said, did you want to speak to Jimmy?"

"Please. Oh yes, I think I must."

"I'll say goodbye then, Harriet. But don't ring off. And come soon to see us."

"Goodbye, Boo –" The line clicked. Once more she waited. She replied to voice after voice. At last she recognised Freddie, and asked for Jimmy.

He said, "Please, I do not think he can be disturbed."

"It's important. I must speak to him."

"I will see what I can do. Miss Haig, you said?"

"Miss Harriet Haig."

"Hold on."

And then, Jimmy. She trembled violently and hardly trusted herself to speak.

"Harriet! But what a surprise! Have you finally decided to come to Kalipur?"

"No. No. You were coming here, Jimmy. You were coming to Marapore!" She thought at first that they had been cut off, but then she heard his long, theatrical sigh.

"My dear, dear Harriet. Can you ever forgive me? I forgot all about it, really and truly."

"But you remembered to cancel Smith's Hotel!"

"Did I? Oh, that must have been Freddie. I didn't know he was so efficient. I must give him a rise." And the boyish laughter bubbled up over the phone. She looked up and caught Gower's eye. With a smile he went from the room. She cried, almost

265

angrily, "It's too bad of you, Jimmy. We were waiting for you here."

"But Delhi, Harriet. Delhi was awful." His voice gained in strength. Its assurance divided them. Yes, he had gone from her. The world of affairs, glimpsed once before, had carried him away. She listened without taking in what he said, but comprehending gradually that Delhi had turned his fine talk of freedom sour. She said, as he finished, "And what about Tom Gower?"

"Who?"

"Tom Gower. You must remember Tom Gower!" As she said it she remembered the door was open; realised she was overheard.

"Yes, of course I remember Tom. We'll have to have another talk some time when I know more how things are going. Do you think he'd like a job here?"

"But you've already talked to him about it."

"Are you cross with me, Harriet? You sound terribly cross."

"No. But what shall I tell Tom?"

"Oh, we must meet again by all means."

"But when?"

"I can't say, Harriet. Everything's topsy-turvy. I really can't be tied down to definite plans."   .

"No one's trying to tie you down."

"Harriet, dear –"

"Just tell me when you think it will be?"

"When what will be?"

"A meeting."

"Next month?"

"I see."

"All right? Next month it will be, Harriet, and we can talk to our heart's content. Just now there are all sorts of things to cope with."

"He wants that job, you know."

"Who? Oh, Tom Gower. Yes, tell him we'll plan that all out.

And, Harriet, do please ask everyone's forgiveness. I left Delhi much sooner than I expected and everything else has been driven out of my mind." He paused. "I wish I had you here to fall back on for advice. At the moment everything looks rather grim." But she knew he said it only for the sake of saying it. "Well, Harriet – a thousand thanks for ringing."

"Goodbye, Jimmy."

"Goodbye."

She replaced the receiver and looked at the instrument, expecting it to vanish. The call had never been made. There was no telephone on the desk. She had not spoken to Boo and she had not spoken to Jimmy. She was still living on the hope that her suspicions that the job had fallen through were groundless. In a moment – why, yes – right away! – Jimmy would bound into the room – Hello, hello – There, Harriet, take my hand – don't scold – father said I mustn't be unkind. So always there had been that secret knowledge of her love, her sorrow; that knowledge that turned his kindness into pity.

She heaved her unfeeling body out of the chair and felt blindly for her sticks. When she went through into the sitting-room she saw that Dorothy had come out of the bedroom and was standing, listening, in the dining-room, her eyes on her husband. Gower turned from watching Dorothy and spoke to Miss Haig. "I was right, wasn't I?"

She began, "In a month – he says he'll come over –"

"Yes."

"It will be all right, Tom."

"Will it?" He wavered. But then he knew. "When? This year? Next year? No – we cross off Kalipur. We cross off Jimmy, don't we?" He looked again at Dorothy who now walked back into her bedroom. He called out, "Dor! Dor!" and followed her.

She crossed the bedroom to her almirah, opened the door and pulled out a small suitcase. This she placed on the stool by her dressing-table. In a drawer she had placed a selection of clothes and personal possessions. They were all ready for packing. It

267

took her no time at all. The rapidity, the inevitability held him spellbound. When she closed the lid of the case he took a few steps into the room.

"Is it now, Dor?"

"Yes."

"Why? Why? Why?"

She put the case on the floor, sat down and began to tidy her hair. He approached the dressing-table. He said, "I thought you wouldn't go. With the Kalipur thing fallen through I thought you wouldn't go. I thought you were waiting, to make sure of what would happen to me. Make sure I'd be all right." A tick started up on his left cheek. His hands were so unsteady he had to clasp his left one round his right wrist. "If the Kalipur job had been all right, would you have stayed then? You said things might be different there. Would you've stayed? Dor! Dor! Why did you have to wait until we knew about Kalipur? You were waiting, weren't you? Why? Why?"

He could no longer bear the sight of her calmly brushing her hair. There was a look in her eyes, seen reflected in the mirror, which frightened him. So much hatred – surely now she would pity him? He went down on his knees and grabbed her arm so that she had to stop brushing. She looked down at him and he cried out, "Don't hate me, Dor! If you can't love me, don't hate me! I haven't anything left. I shan't know what to do or where to go. I can't be alone. Don't leave me alone! Don't keep me out any longer!" He raised his fists as though beating on a door, crying to be let in. "Don't keep me out any longer, Dor! Please don't lock me out." And then his cry died away and his hands fell, for he understood, quite suddenly, that they were each a reflection of the other.

She saw that he had understood, at last, and nodded.

"Yes," she said. "It's your turn now."

She called out for Abdul and with mechanical presence of mind he rose to his feet so that neither of them should be humiliated. When Abdul came, she told him to fetch a tonga and pointed to the case. The servant picked it up and carried it out. She opened her handbag and checked its contents.

He said, dully, "Where will he take you?"

"I have no idea."

"All your things, your other things, what about those?"

"I've taken what I want from here."

"Dor – tell me what I've done."

"You've done nothing."

"Then why are you punishing me?"

"You're mistaken. I'm not."

"Are you in love with him?"

"No. I'm not in love with him yet."

"You think you might be?"

"It's possible."

"But never with me."

"No. I could never be in love with you."

"Why, Dor?"

She paused. "Do you want to know?"

"Yes. Yes, I want to know."

"Very well, then. I could never be in love with you, because I find you physically repulsive."

It was several moments before he said, with a slight gesture of surrender, "Yes, I see." Then, without looking at her again, he left the bedroom and walked through the dining-room, through the sitting-room where Miss Haig still waited, and into his study. He shut the door and turned the key in the lock.

He had sat motionless for over two hours. It was nearly dark. Dorothy had gone, but Harriet was still there in the next room. Twice she had come to the door and knocked and automatically he had called out in answer. He knew why she was so restless and why she was afraid. Sometimes one of the servants was sent to walk past the window and look in, but it was getting too dark to see into the room, too dark as well to go on reading the same two words on the same page of the book he held.

Miss Haig was knocking again. He moved his cramped limbs and laid Steele's Bible carefully on the desk, still open at the page. He picked up a pencil and tore a sheet of paper from a memorandum pad. Then he wrote on the paper and placed it under a glass weight. He closed the Bible.

"Tom, are you all right?"

"Yes."

"Abdul is asking about dinner."

"I shan't want any. You'd better go, Harriet."

He waited for another quarter of an hour, waited for the scrape of wheels on the gravel drive, Harriet's tremulous good-night, and the wheels moving away again.

When these things had happened he went to the window and pulled the curtains across. Then he felt his way to the light switch. Flooded with light the room in which he had sat so long looked different, and he began to sweat. But to do the act in a dark room was cowardly. He walked away from the switch, withdrawing himself from temptation. Then he checked up on the time. Abdul would be in the compound, supervising the preparations for the evening meal. He went to the desk and opened the centre drawer.

Something was wrong. The revolver was not there. It was at Ooni. Abdul had given it to him to take to Ooni. He remembered now, remembered Abdul grinning. *Banduq, Sahib.* The emptiness of the drawer seemed to shriek at him, mockingly. Then he saw that it was not empty. There were a few papers, an old pocket dictionary, and – at the back – a large clasp knife with a smooth, bone handle.

Bholu had had a knife. He remembered how it had looked, alive itself with fire. He had been afraid of it, and Steele had been afraid. But, at the end, Steele had not been afraid. In his cell, Vidyasagar had shown no signs of fear. Gower stared at the knife. Of all lethal weapons, this was the most obscene. It seemed suddenly as though the knife had lain there always, waiting for him, waiting for this moment when he knew that there was only violence left, only destruction to embrace; waiting for him to break, revolted, under its challenge.

He must have cried out, involuntarily, for there came at once an urgent knocking on the door, and Abdul's voice shouting *Sahib! Sahib!* Gower raised his head, turning towards the door, and tried to call out to tell Abdul to go away, but no sound came, and the knocking began again, hammering an accompaniment to Abdul's repeated cry, *Sahib! Sahib!* Gower could tell that the man was weeping. The hammering became the pounding in his own blood, and when he heard Abdul shouting for help and crashing his body against the door to burst it open he knew that there was no time left.

Trembling violently he reached for the knife.

2

By five o'clock that evening MacKendrick could bear the suspense no longer. He had stayed all day in his room, starting up each time he heard someone moving outside. Once he had gone to the door and opened it because a girl had spoken, but it had only been Judith Anderson giving some order to Desai. She had glanced over her shoulder at him before running on high heels out to a waiting tonga.

At four-thirty they had brought afternoon tea on a tray. At five he had drunk his last cup and gone to find Desai.

"Look," he said, "I've got to turn in my jeep to the garage. I think I'll take my luggage up to the station and get rid of it." He saw Desai's eyes cloud over with doubt. "It's okay," he added, "I'll settle my bill now."

"Rightio." Desai pulled a long slip of paper out of his wallet. "You see, all is ready except for adding up."

As MacKendrick counted out notes Desai shrieked to the staff. Two bearers came running from the kitchen, hastily adjusting their turbans.

"Put the Huzoor's luggage in the jeep. Quick. Quick. The Huzoor is waiting." He bowed to MacKendrick as he took the money. "You will return for dinner?"

"I think so."

"Oh please. You must return for dinner. Already I have charged for it. And your room will remain at your convenience."

"Fine, that's fine, Mr. Desai." They parted to make way for the two boys who carried a suitcase each out on to the verandah. "I'll bring the jeep round. If anyone rings or calls for me, just say I've gone to the station with my luggage but will be back."

When he reached the station and walked to the luggage office behind two coolies who had fallen on his cases as though claiming some long-lost property of their own, he found that a train was just in from Delhi. The platform was crowded and it was impossible to distinguish between those passengers who had reached the end of the journey and those whose journey was just about to begin. Their luggage had lost identity, too, and was vociferously fought over. He watched the shouting men and women and tried to be amused, but the thought came to him that it needed only the passage of an undefined shadow amongst them to turn the farce into tragedy. Where in this scene, he wondered, was proof of the tenet that to Indians time did not exist? They were blistered now under its hot sun.

He had his baggage checked in and enquired about his train. There at the end of the platform, on a sideline, two carriages already waited. It was explained to him that these carriages would be shunted on to the train when it arrived in Marapore. Guided by an official he inspected them and found the coupé with his name misspelt on a card tucked into a special socket. MacKendrik. He nodded, smiling, to the official, and gave him a ten rupee note. At once the man shouted for a sweeper, unlocked the door and pushed the sweeper up to flay about him with his hand-broom.

"See. All is prepared for the Huzoor."

I could get in now, he thought. Here I could hide away. At the other end of the carriage was another coupé. He glanced up

272

at the card. "Mrs. Mapleton." At first he thought: Why have they got her name right and not mine? He looked at the official, who wagged his head roguishly. "A friend of mine," MacKendrick said, and the man replied, "The lady was asking."

"Asking about what?"

"Each day she was coming to ask when the Huzoor was going."

On the way back down the platform MacKendrick paused, recognising Frank Milner. Milner's drill uniform was starched until it shone. His Sam Browne looked as though it had been veneered with mahogany. His face was deeply flushed and for all his smart turn-out he was not at ease. In front of him stood a tall, ascetic-looking Indian, dressed like Milner, but with the insignia of a lieutenant-colonel on his shoulders. The colonel was nodding mechanically to whatever Milner was explaining. Once, he asked a question, and Milner's mouth opened and closed like that of a fish. They began to walk off, followed by one coolie bearing on his head the colonel's tin trunk, atop of which was a suitcase and a valise. One anna a head-load, MacKendrick thought, recalling the revulsion he had felt in Bombay when first seeing the price printed on metal discs which the coolies wore pinned to their chests. The colonel knew his rights.

MacKendrick waited until Milner and his new commanding officer disappeared. Over the angry tumult of voices came the indifferent call of the *char-wallah. Cha -e wall -e! Cha -e wall -e!'* Somewhere a bell rang and arms were stuck out of the windows waving the *char-wallah* towards them. A man at MacKendrick's side spat betel-juice in a bloody stream on to the platform. Bholu. Bholu. With sickness rising inside him he turned away and found his way out of the station.

When he got to the jeep, Dorothy was standing beside it.

He saw that she had no luggage. Disappointment and relief temporarily deprived him of speech. They gave each other no greeting, but they smiled, waiting for the other to speak first.

At last he said, "You're not coming then?"

"Yes, I'm coming."

"But where're your bags?"

"In the luggage office. I've just put it there." She looked at the jeep and at once he said, "I've got to turn it in to Ram Lal. Let's go round, shall we?"

If he could act, if he could move his limbs, touch familiar things, like the steering wheel, the gear lever, if he could draw them both into a simple, unimportant routine, there would, he felt, be salvation for them. Already he felt better and he drove round to Ram Lal's garage telling himself, "It's going to work out."

There was no sign of the fat man, but the thin man came out as they drove in and waved them imperiously to pull up in the place where the jeep had been when he had first seen it, alongside the lorry. The thin man joined them as they got out and Mac-Kendrick noticed that he was nervous, certainly irritable. He waved his hands and said, "We are closing. We are just now closing. Please, there is the bill to settle."

As MacKendrick passed through the narrow space between jeep and lorry his clothes caught on one of the hooks which secured the threaded ropes of the tarpaulin. Freeing himself, he followed the thin man across the park feeling he was moving away from identification of a piece which fitted into a puzzle. There would always now be a gap, and through the gap his understanding of something would filter away. Understanding of what, though? Of India perhaps. The vital piece of the puzzle might lie in the thin little man's heart, invisible even through the medium of his wary eyes, undetected beneath the camouflage of his cautious smile.

He paid his bill, not caring that he was outrageously cheated. The cheating was part of the camouflage concealing the secret. He smiled, and said goodbye, and held out his hand, half hoping that the gesture would strip the camouflage away, but the thin man shook his hand and looked him straight in the face. And all the look meant was – goodbye, goodbye.

274

Dorothy was waiting for him outside. Had he expected her to slip away? Yes, he had to admit that he had. The thread of their mutual belief in each other seemed so slender, their mutual trust so frail. Sense of its frailty welled up in him.

He looked at his watch.

She said, "How long have we got?"

And he replied, "Only a few hours."

He took her towards the Chinese restaurant, anxious now to see no more of Smith's, but when they reached the entrance and he paused, inviting her to go in, she said, "I'd prefer to go to the hotel."

"Okay. We'll go to Smith's."

Desai showed no surprise to see her, and MacKendrick thought she hesitated as if about to ask Desai a question. They went to sit in the lounge and MacKendrick ordered drinks, and discussed the menu for dinner, laughing too much at the quaint jokes the manager made as he hovered over them. The place was otherwise empty, and the shadows lengthened in the room, across the leather chairs with their faded patches, across the cretonne-covered ones, the old rocker which seemed doomed to stay forever leaning backwards in perpetual surprise.

And now, in the twilight, the picture above the fireplace flickered into motion, freezing its action when any human eye happened to look up at it: the out-thrust arms, the fierce eyes, the toy explosions of cannon, the wind-blown flags moving and stopping, moving and stopping, timidly reliving their greatness, gently whispering the praises of a glory now over, and gone forever into the past.

They were the only diners and Mr. Desai was determined to treat them royally. The entire dining-room staff stood around in comical attitudes of alertness, drilled by long experience of hard times to do their serving deftly in spite of the danger of treading on each other's feet. MacKendrick felt their eyes behind him, on either side of him. Was this how it would always be? Himself and

Dorothy cut off from the living, dining always in lonely rooms, in empty rooms, in rooms held together by nothing but hope and memory; was this, indeed, drifting? Was this the reality, the cold and unforgiving reality behind a dream of freedom? Get back! a voice cried. Get back! There's comfort in bondage.

It was as the meat course was whisked away and they had to face each other across the crumb-scattered cloth that the telephone in the glass cage behind them began to ring. At once she looked beyond his shoulder and he knew the sound of the bell was one she had expected. The ringing stopped as Desai lifted the receiver and all the bearers had paused, were watching the cage. He heard Desai's voice, and then his footsteps; looked round and up into his bent-down face, inclined his head to receive the whispered message.

"For you, Mr. MacKendrick. Miss Haig."

He rose and went to the cage.

When he came back Dorothy was no longer at the table. One of the bearers pointed to Room Twelve.

She twisted round from the looking-glass as he came in and shut the door.

"It's Tom," he said, and for an instant she remained with her hands still raised in the act of smoothing her hair. "It's Tom," he repeated. "He tried to commit suicide."

She went to the bed and sat on the edge. He thought she had not understood. He said, "With a clasp knife. He tried to slash his wrists."

"Tried?"

"Abdul got to him in time."

"Who was it who rang?"

"Miss Haig. She'd gone back there. She said she'd felt something was wrong." He walked across the room and found himself staring in the mirror. "He'd locked himself in his room. But Abdul broke in before he could – do it properly. She says he's lost some blood and has collapsed. They're waiting for the ambulance now."

In the mirror he could see her back. She was sitting very straight, waiting for him to make the next move. He knew that their future together was in his hands, that now, at the last, the decision was his. He muttered, "I thought Tom would be all right."

"Did you?"

"I thought he'd be all right on his own, Dor. Going to Kalipur and starting again."

"He wasn't going to Kalipur."

"Not going? Why?"

"The job fell through."

"When?"

"Just before I left."

He said, "Is that what you were waiting for?"

"What makes you think I was waiting for anything?"

"But you were waiting. I didn't even know whether you were coming or not."

"No."

"Why were you waiting?"

"I don't know."

"If the job hadn't fallen through you'd have gone with him, wouldn't you?"

"I don't know."

"You must know."

"No. I was waiting to know. Waiting to know what I'd do."

"You didn't trust me, Dor." Self-pity crept into his voice. He heard it and was ashamed. He thrust the shame away. Angrily he said, "You didn't trust me, did you?"

"No."

"You've never trusted me. You never trust anybody."

"No."

He turned from the mirror and went to the bed. She kept her face averted. He said, "Did you leave Tom wondering if you were coming away with me, too?"

"What else could I do but leave him to wonder?"

277

Because he could think of nothing in reply she turned, after a while, and looked up at him. She looked as she had looked that night at dinner when he had spoken of Dwight's death, totally unmoved.

She said, "You blame me, don't you, for what Tom has tried to do?"

He could not face her accusation. And he could not deny it. But he could not admit his cowardice, even to himself. He sat beside her and took her hand, but awkwardly, like an immature boy. He held the hand and stared at it. *There are ways of telling. Their hands are usually small-boned like Indians'*. Cynthia's mocking voice came from far off. And Miss Haig's; Miss Haig saying something about self-preservation.

"Well, you do blame me, don't you?"

"I don't know, Dor. I just don't know."

"You know all right. You blame me for what Tom has tried to do because you think I could have stopped him."

"Could you?"

"You think I could have stopped him by telling him what I am. You think that would have made him pity me and make him understand. You think that's the least I could have left him. You think he only tried to commit suicide because he couldn't understand at all what was wrong."

He had looked up in surprise and as she finished he said, "I didn't think that, but it's true. I didn't think it but you're thinking it."

He stood up, still holding her hands, pulling her forward so that her arms were stretched out. She was at his mercy. She was trying to pull her hands away but he tightened his grip, pressing his fingers deeply into her flesh. "That's what *you're* thinking, isn't it?" he repeated.

"Please let me go."

"You could have told him what you were long ago, couldn't you? You've deliberately not told him because all you wanted him to feel was how much you hated him. What happens now? You

278

can't go on hating somebody more and more year after year, can you?" Dwight's ghost taunted him. He cried, "What happens now? How long do you intend to hate me? That's what it's going to be, isn't it? Having your own back on me because of Dwight. Having your own back on Tom because you were forced to marry him. They're both the same. What happens when you've got nobody left to get your own back on? What happens when you've got nobody left to hate?"

She wrenched her hands away and shouted. "There'll be myself, won't there? *That's* what you want me to say! That there'll be myself!" She stood up and he was so close to her, so challenged by her anger and his sense of shame that he gripped her shoulders and pressed his mouth on to hers, not in physical passion but in a desperate attempt to show he was not afraid of her or of himself, to show that he could make a decision, take control, smash down opposition. But as he was about to push her away she suddenly arched her body, pressing her thighs against his, shooting her tongue up and into his mouth, pressing her hands into his back. For an instant his body responded and, with urgency, he lowered her on to the bed, to go through the preliminaries of an act of union, but as he did so, the urgency dissolved into the slow humiliation of impotence. He took her head between his hands and tried to recapture the moment of fever. But the fever had been in his mind, not in his blood. Now his mind had cleared. He was appalled by her indifference to what had happened to Tom. He was repelled by the physical hunger he had awakened in her.

He felt her body relax, and then go taut with scorn. They lay together until, acknowledging the futility of their inaction, he rose and straightened his disordered clothing. For a while she stayed on the bed, her back turned to him. He said, with the inspiration of stricken pride, "You were thinking of Dwight. That's why it wasn't any use. You'd always be thinking of Dwight. It'd never be me. It'd never be any use. Some way or another you'd always hold out on me. You'd never belong completely to me."

279

She moved off the bed and went to the mirror again. She began to straighten her hair. She said, "In one way I've always held out on Tom too, haven't I? There's always been part of me he hasn't knowingly possessed. That's the only reason I've been able to bear him coming near me. If he knew what I was I'd have nothing left to withhold."

He cried, "Always held out! Yes, but you were leaving him! There wasn't any need to hold out on him any more. You weren't ever going to see him again. . . ."

Her arms stopped moving. "Wasn't I?" she asked. "No. But as it turns out, I am. . . ."

Suddenly he could not bring himself to look at her. He heard her shut her handbag, knew she picked up her gloves. There were only a few more seconds to be got through. She stood by his side.

She said, "But don't think about that, Joe. Just keep on telling yourself I'd always have been thinking of Dwight or that I've always got to have someone to hate so that I don't hate myself. If that doesn't work then keep on telling yourself I can't be judged like an ordinary person by ordinary standards. Keep on reminding yourself that I'm a freak, like something in a sideshow."

When she closed the door and left him alone the formula was already beginning to work.

They lifted Gower from the bed on to the stretcher and carried him through the bungalow to the waiting ambulance. As they negotiated the steps Dorothy returned and stood aside to let them come down. If Gower saw her, he gave no indication that he had done so, and she herself hardly glanced at him. The doctor asked her quietly whether she wished to go in the ambulance with them. "He'll be all right. I've given him something to quieten him. It's the shock chiefly." But she shook her head and did not wait to see them off.

In the sitting-room she found Miss Haig, helped by Hussein

and Abdul, preparing to leave. For a few seconds she and Miss Haig looked at each other in silence. Then Miss Haig said, "Have you come back to Tom?"

She looked round the room, before she answered.

"I've come back here," she said at last. "And Tom will come back too, I suppose."

Miss Haig nodded, as though she understood. She said, "That note – on the table there – that is the note that he was going to leave." She thrust at it with one of her sticks, but Dorothy did not pick it up; instead she said, "What does it say?"

"It says – St. John, Chapter eleven, verse thirty-five."

"And what does it mean?"

Slowly Miss Haig moved away, supported by the two boys. At the doorway she turned and replied, "We don't know what it means."

And then she was gone.

3

MacKendrick walked through the cantonment towards the light reflected in the sky above the town. He reached the level-crossing and stood there, for a minute or so. But he did not cross the barrier to enter the bazaar. He turned aside and walked off in a new direction, the strident music dying away, a more familiar music drawing nearer. He walked towards this other music with its regular beat, its drum, its known pattern of trumpets. Ahead of him was an oblong building whose tall windows were brightly lighted, and he fancied he could see flags and streamers. There was no compound, no gate, no path. The flat, beaten earth was all the ground this place could call its own.

When he opened the door he found himself in a trap of curtains through which he pushed his way into the hall, where couples danced to the three-piece band on the stage at the farther end. In front of him, an enormously fat Anglo-Indian woman sat at a table on which were rolls of tickets and cardboard boxes containing money. In front of the table a poster swayed, loosely, from its mooring of drawing-pins.

Railway Institute

Gala Dance

Admission Rs.2.8

Bring your Friend

The woman was smiling at him, beating time with her foot, holding a ticket out with one hand, her other – palm uppermost – ready for his money.

He made a pretence of looking for it. He knew at once he could not stay here. As he fumbled in his pocket, he looked at the dancers and at the people who sat on the chairs which lined the walls. Most of them were looking at him, too, and once he caught a welcoming smile from a girl dressed in purple satin, a girl whose skin was as dark as Judith's, a girl who sat with her blousy mother and turned to her now, drawing her mother's attention to him. At once the mother put a smile on her face and turned to stare. He looked hurriedly away. There weren't many men. A lot of the girls were dancing together, not speaking, but swinging their heads against the swing of their bodies in a never-ending search of the hall. A couple of them veered towards the exit where he stood; they were twirling round on their high heels so that he had alternating glimpses of their faces. He noticed that one's skin was much lighter than her partner's, and she did not smile as the other one was smiling, as though she would show her contempt for the girl with whom she was dancing. Now they were off, swerving round the floor beneath the festival bunting, and at the far end of the hall he suddenly caught sight of Judith Anderson sitting out with Milner. Milner had come in mufti. She was leaning over towards him, explaining something with expansive gestures, and then she paused and straightened his tie, took his hand and turned to watch the dancers contentedly, possessively.

"Aren't you going to dance with anybody?"

The fat woman was still holding out the ticket.

"No. I'm sorry. I don't have any money."

Her mouth opened in surprise and disappointment. But quickly she recovered. "Oh, don't bother about that. You can pay me some other time. You'll have a lot of fun, here." She winked, and nodded.

"I'm sorry. I have to catch the train."

She struggled to her feet, but before she could grasp his arm he had moved the curtain aside and left the hall. The music stopped and as he stumbled away he heard the burst of clapping, was caught in the streak of light as the door opened and someone came out to call him back.

It was only nine o'clock, but he went straight to the station. Across the platform were the huddled forms of people asleep. In the luggage office he roused two coolies and pointed out his cases. There was another case close by. He tried not to believe that it was Dorothy's. He followed the coolies out on to the platform, along to the end, where the two carriages were. The door was locked and the two coolies unhelpful. He left them there and sought out the official he had spoken to before. But he had gone off duty, leaving in his place a man who was unwilling to produce the keys.

Once more he offered a bribe, and with a bad grace the official came with him and opened the compartment. Once inside, with his luggage, MacKendrick locked it again, and drew down the shutters. The lights were not working, and he sat in the dark and smoked.

At nine-thirty the train came in from Delhi and ten minutes later the carriages were shunted on. The station had come alive again. Once, someone knocked on the door and beat on the closed windows. He did not switch on the light. Lifting the shutter on the far side of the carriage he stared out of the window, watching the town. Its music rose up, blending with the cries and

283

the warnings of passengers afraid of being late, afraid of finding no standing room in the crowded third-class compartments. At ten minutes to ten he heard Cynthia Mapleton scolding Hussein: Cynthia leaving Marapore forever behind her; Marapore and India, and the unquiet ghost of Robbie.

He heard doors banging and the bell and the mournful call of the boy selling tea, and over it all the fierce music from the bazaar.

Now it was going. Oh, hold it, his heart cried, oh, enter it: dig deeply with the hands into it and raise out of it all the love and pity and compassion the music sings of. But now it is going. The light in the sky is going. The singing is fading. And the train is moving into the plain where night holds and the deep silence is broken only by the muffled drumming of the wheels and the distant cries of jackals.

THE END

Praise for the four volumes of *The Raj Quartet*:

"A major work, a glittering combination of brilliant craftsmanship, psychological perception and objective reporting."

ORVILLE PRESCOTT, *The New York Times*

"The strength, assurance and stamina displayed in *The Day of the Scorpion* are quite outstanding. [Scott is a] writer who has thoroughly mastered his material, and who can . . . work through a maze of fascinating detail without for a moment losing sight of distant and considerable objectives."

Times Literary Supplement

"Remarkable . . . Never has the theme—relations between Europeans and non-Europeans—been treated as brilliantly."

NAOMI BLIVEN, *New Yorker*

"Magnificent. . . . Scott throws us into India, wretched and beautiful. He makes us become his people, sometimes by grinding us down under their anguish. I cannot think of anything worth knowing about the raj that Scott hasn't told me. . . . His contribution to literature is permanent."

WEBSTER SCHOTT, *New York Times Book Review*

Phoenix Fiction titles from Chicago (2004)

Ivo Andrić: *The Bridge on the Drina*
Jurek Becker: *Bronstein's Children*
Arthur A. Cohen: *Acts of Theft, A Hero in His Time*
Jean Dutourd: *A Dog's Head*
Wayne Fields: *The Past Leads a Life of Its Own*
Bruce Jay Friedman: *A Mother's Kisses*
Jack Fuller: *Convergence, Fragments, The Best of Jackson Payne*
Randall Jarrell: *Pictures from an Institution*
Margaret Laurence: *A Bird in the House, The Diviners, The Fire-Dwellers,*
    A Jest of God, The Stone Angel
André Malraux: *The Conquerors, The Walnut Tree of Altenberg*
Dalene Matthee: *Fiela's Child*
Thomas McMahon: *Principles of American Nuclear Chemistry, McKay's Bees,*
    Loving Little Egypt
R. K. Narayan: *The Bachelor of Arts, The Dark Room, The English Teacher,*
    The Financial Expert, Mr. Sampath—The Printer of Malgudi, Swami and
    Friends, Waiting for Mahatma
Morris Philipson: *A Man in Charge, Secret Understandings, Somebody Else's*
    Life, The Wallpaper Fox
Anthony Powell: *A Dance to the Music of Time* (in four *Movements* with three
    novels in each volume); *The Fisher King*
Peter Schneider: *Couplings, The Wall Jumper*
Paul Scott: *The Raj Quartet* (in four volumes: *The Jewel in the Crown, The Day*
    of the Scorpion, The Tower of Silence, A Division of the Spoils), *Staying On,*
    Six Days in Marapore
Irwin Shaw: *Short Stories: Five Decades, The Young Lions*
George Steiner: *The Portage of San Cristóbal of A. H.*
Richard Stern: *A Father's Words, Golk*
Stephen Vizinczey: *An Innocent Millionaire, In Praise of Older Women*
Anthony Winkler: *The Painted Canoe*
Christa Wolf: Accident: *A Day's News*
Marguerite Yourcenar: *A Coin in Nine Hands, Fires, Two Lives and a Dream*